Ghetto Heaven

Ghetto Heaven

A novel by

Erick S. Gray

Q-Boro Books
WWW.QBOROBOOKS.COM

An Urban Entertainment Company

Published by Q-Boro Books

ISBN 0-9777335-3-X
First Printing November 2006

10 9 8 7 6 5 4 3 2

Cover Layout & Design – Candace K. Cottrell
Cover Model - Shenetta
Editors – Chandra Sparks-Taylor, Melissa Forbes, Candace K. Cottrell

Q-BORO BOOKS
Jamaica, Queens NY 11431
WWW.QBOROBOOKS.COM

-One-

Tedious, Toni Benjamin thought as she was sprawled out on stage butt naked, legs spread, on all fours staring at herself in the full-length wall mirror behind her. The men sitting on barstools and splintered wooden chairs gazed on at her rawness, some with dollars bills in their hands and eyes wide open with excitement.

This was her second shift dancing onstage at an underground strip club called the Bottom Dollar, located in Coney Island, Brooklyn, on Mermaid Avenue. It wasn't one of your upscale gentlemen's clubs like Goldfingers or Diamonds. No, in this grimy, low-key place, anything went—no restrictions. In here, a man could get his shit knobbed for the right price.

The dancers in this club didn't set many morals for themselves. Their only goal was to get money any way they could. In the Bottom Dollar, all a man had to do was flash a wad of bills, and he was able to bring some poor, unfortunate young female home for the night.

The club was mostly populated with Brooklyn natives—the young and the old, the thugs, roughnecks, and of course, the pimps. The girls ranged in age from fifteen to twenty-three, with their bodies and looks maturing faster than their minds.

Toni was still onstage and still naked, resting on her knees while the fellows just gazed with hard-ons and their sexual desires. Just beside her lay fifty crumpled dollar bills and her outfit—a black, sheer baby-doll negligee with a sequined lace hem, cut-out sides, and spaghetti straps, and white, knee-high boots. She sometimes took the boots off because she felt she could dance and move pretty damn good without them. When she first started dancing in knee-high boots, she tripped and busted her ass in front of her male audience. Since then she had gotten the hang of dancing in them, but she still sometimes preferred them off, just to be on the safe side.

The club was poorly lit with the same ol' poor regulars and the same ol' troubles. There had already been five shootings and one killing since its opening. The shootings were a result of rival gang fights, jealous boyfriends fighting because they didn't like seeing their girlfriends being fondled and molested, and envious females hating among one another. Tonight there were three gang members already packin', ready to pop some poor fool who was quick to start sumthin' up and run off at the mouth.

Toni continued to dance as the deejay, a thirty-year-old pervert, switched records, blasting "Fuck You Tonight" by the Notorious B.I.G. She swung herself around the pole in the middle of the stage. Perspiration trickled down her forehead as the hot lights above the stage gave her no break.

A man crumpled up a five-dollar bill, then flung it at her, hitting her softly against her breast. She picked up the five, smoothed it out, and softly said, "Thank you" to the gentleman, who had been tipping her big all night.

"Let me see that ass," he said, pulling out another five from his wallet.

She turned around, got down on her hands and knees with her back turned to him, and showed him what all these men came in there for—*pussy*.

She then took one hand and spread her ass cheeks wide open.

"That's what I'm talking about," the man excitedly shouted.

She heard cheers and compliments coming from the men who crowded around her as they continued to gaze and feel on her. Some squeezed her ass, others tried to cop a feel on her breasts, and some slid their nasty hands between her legs. They groped on her most lucrative possessions, but all she thought was that this was paying her bills. She brought home one hundred to two hundred dollars a night. On a really good night, maybe four or five hundred, but that was if she was doing VIP.

Soon she felt something that was far too familiar to her. One guy had taken the pleasure of sliding both his index finger and his middle finger into her, making it feel like a small penis had entered her. She turned around to see who it was, and it was a familiar face—a regular by the name of Pinch-Back. She didn't freak out, just let him go 'bout his business, which was finger popping her on stage in front of a small crowd.

"Damn, your pussy's mad wet," he proclaimed.

Pinch-Back was a small Brooklyn hustler with a temper like a high fever. He came around often, unable to control his hormones, fuckin' whichever bitch he could get his hands on in the club. But he knew his limitations with this one because Toni was the sister of a well-known hustler and the girlfriend of a bona fide killer and hustler who went by the name of Tec, aka Keith.

After her little segment on stage, Toni collected her things and her cash and walked off naked with her clothes in her hand. She was approached by a tall, slinky man who whispered in her ear, "How much for a VIP wit' you?"

"What you want?" she asked him.

"A blow."

"Fifty."

"Ayyite, cool," he said.

"Give me a minute."

She walked off to the ladies' room, where the females went to change outfits for the night. The ladies' room was as big as a small ghetto bedroom, and with five ladies all in there at once, it could get a little cramped.

Gina and Karen were inside smoking and chatting. Gina was topless in a red thong, and Karen was wearing a pair of tight blue jeans and a tight red T-shirt. They both glanced at Toni when she entered the room naked with her cash crumpled up in her hand. They weren't what Toni would call her really good friends. There had been a few incidents between Gina, Karen, and Toni.

Toni paid them no mind. She laid her cash on the floor near the corner and started to throw her outfit back on. She then neatly sorted each of the bills and placed them in a tiny handheld purse. She checked herself in the dingy, stained cracked glass that was hung up on the white, soiled bathroom wall, then headed back out into the club.

Wearing her knee-high boots, she looked five inches taller than she really was. Toni stood about five feet, six inches with a light brown complexion and long dark-brown curly braids with light brown highlights. Her light brown eyes, full lips, and well-toned body made her a very attractive woman and dancer.

She went up to the man who had asked her for a VIP earlier. Tonight she really needed the cash. Her rent was almost due.

"C'mon," she said to the man who was waiting in a corner.

He smiled and willingly followed her to wherever.

They came to a room where a burly, black male guarded the door. She smiled at him, and then a twenty was exchanged between the men. Toni and her client for the night were easily let into the room where sexual business was about to take place.

Inside, the man paid her the money for a quick blowjob. She got down on her knees, put on a Rough Rider condom, and started going to work on him. This would be her last VIP for the night. She was tired and was ready to go home.

Toni walked into her apartment around three-thirty in the morning. She was dead tired and just wanted to hit her bed and sleep 'til noon. Her mother was strung out in her own bedroom. Her mother's bedroom door was ajar, so Toni quickly glanced in at her. Her mother had been in the same clothes for the past three days. Her room reeked of old food, sex, and an unfamiliar odor. She was asleep with her legs hovering over the floor and her upper body sprawled out flat against her unmade bed. This year alone, Toni's mother had lost twenty-five pounds, and she was continuing to lose weight. She was a crack head, but also a diabetic.

Toni's mother, Angela Benjamin, wasn't always like this. Before Toni turned twelve, her mother was a career woman, studying to become a nurse practitioner. She was a loving mother to her children and tried to keep a good household while living in the projects. But that dream blew up in smoke, became nothing but a pipe dream, once she met and fell in love with a man named Derrick. He was poison to her from day one, and both of her children knew it. He gave off bad vibes whenever he was around Toni and her older brother, Thomas, who was known on the streets by the name Sheek. Day by day, Angela's life began to wither away once Derrick introduced her to street life. Soon he had her experimenting with heroin and crack.

Soon afterward, Toni's mother changed from being a caring mother and a good upstanding woman, to just another local crack head and one of Derrick's regulars on the streets. He used her, abused her, and used her apartment to run drugs out of, leaving Angela always stoned out and high, causing her life to do a 180-degree turn-around in the worst kind of way.

Derrick would constantly beat the shit out of Angela, leaving her with black eyes, bruised skin, and scars—emotional as well as physical. He would rape her, forcing himself on her whenever he felt like it, and he even sold her into prostitution, letting the fellows and some of his homies have a go at her.

This abuse went on for three years, until one day Toni's brother, Sheek, finally decided that enough was enough. He came home one night to find his mother lying in a corner, balled up in her own blood. Derrick had beaten her just inches from her life. She was naked, crying, and zoned out. Sheek and Toni had had enough of this shit. Derrick had turned their mother into the walking dead, constantly having her wanting to get her high on whatever drug Derrick brought home for her.

But Derrick was well known around the way, and Sheek's reputation was building rapidly around his peers and others. Many feared Sheek, with him running his own corners and crack spots with his number one man, Tec. They were ruthless together. Sheek and Tec's names were forever heard throughout Coney Island.

But Sheek and Tec's supreme team came to an end one day when Sheek put a nine-millimeter to Derrick's head and blew his fuckin' brains out in their mother's apartment. That would be the last day Derrick ever laid a hand on his mother. Sheek got twenty-five years to life for committing premeditated murder. But no matter what, it was already too late for Angela. She was now a full-blooded junkie. And her son spent the rest of his life in prison, Derrick having destroyed both a mother and a son's lives forever. Toni was left to fend for herself in this damn ruthless and cold world.

Toni slowly closed the door to her mother's bedroom then went into the bathroom where she brushed her teeth and scrubbed out the taste of condoms in her mouth. Even though she was used to the taste, it became a routine for her to brush every night. She then went into her bedroom, slipped off her clothing, and prepared for bed. She sat Indian style on her bed, counting up her earnings—$250. *Not bad,* she thought. Suddenly the phone rang.

She picked up.

"Hello."

"Yeah, Toni, I'll be over there in fifteen minutes," her boyfriend, Keith, a.k.a.Tec, told her, not bothering to ask first. But she was used to his just coming over whenever he felt like it, no matter what time it was, and getting him some ass. After all, he was her man.

It was going on four in the morning when she heard a knock at her apartment door. She didn't bother to ask who it was. She just unlocked the four or five locks on the door and let Keith in. He was wearing beige sweatpants, beige Timberlands, a white wife beater, and a thick, long gold chain draped down to his abs, with a TEC-9 for a pendant. Keith was brown skinned with black eyes and a medium build, but very muscular. He had dark black hair and sported the cornrow braided hairstyle that most of the youths rocked.

She headed back into her bedroom wearing a long sleeper white T-shirt that draped down to her knees, leaving Keith to close and lock the door behind him. He followed her, closing her bedroom door afterward.

She plopped back down on her bed, lying on her stomach, and flipping through the new issue of the *Source* magazine.

"Thomas asked about you in the letter he wrote me," she mentioned to him as Keith was getting undressed, ready to take care of business. He was tipsy and had just come from hanging out with the fellas all night. He would get riled up, getting hot and bothered, then all he could think about was some pussy from Toni.

"Word? What he had to say?" he asked, climbing onto the bed in his blue boxers and pressing himself against Toni while she continued to read through her magazine.

"He was just asking how come you don't come to check him."

He felt up her thigh, reaching between her legs. She made it easier by spreading her thighs.

Keith just wanted a quickie. He wasn't down for all that foreplay shit. He was only about getting his and that's it. If a bitch couldn't reach hers before he reached his, then it was too fuckin' bad for her. She shoulda tried harder. And he never ate pussy. It wasn't his thing. He felt it made a niggah soft to go down on a bitch. To him, it was like a fuckin' curse to a niggah to eat pussy. It was forbidden in his book of rules.

Toni turned herself over, lying on her back with Keith hovering over her and resting on his hands. She parted her legs, and he pulled down his boxers, quickly inserting himself into her, causing Toni to let out a quick gasp. She would lie there and just let him get his because she wasn't feeling it tonight. She thought about her brother while Keith panted and thrust himself into her uncouthly, like he was really trying to control and hurt something.

Five minutes later it was over. It finished as quickly as it had started. Keith pulled out, exploding onto her stomach, then rolled over on his back, leaving her to clean up the mess.

Toni went into the bathroom to wash up. Afterward, she climbed back into bed next to her boyfriend, who was already in la-la land and sound asleep.

This was Toni's life—her world. She knew nothing but stripping, dancing, pleasing her man, and Coney Island. Her boundaries didn't go beyond Flatbush to East New York. All she ever knew was the hood, the ghetto, and sex. She would always limit herself to certain things. But she felt that her main purpose in life was taking care of her sickly, drug-addicted mother. She felt it was her obligation to do so.

But it was hard to help those who wouldn't first help themselves.

-Two-

"Happy Birthday, Mathew," his mother congratulated, holding a cup filled with sparkling wine and dressed in a very expensive flowing halter dress with swirls of bronze glitter. She was as sexy as they come—brown skinned with long, sensuous, jet-black hair; stunning long legs; hazel contacts; and more curves to her shape than the letter S. She was Mrs. Pamela Rhonda Peters, a very, very wealthy woman.

It was her son's twenty-fifth birthday, and he was celebrating with family, friends, and a few business associates at his parents' 11.4-acre, traditional, shingle-style residence in East Hampton, Long Island.

A total of forty-five guests had arrived to celebrate this joyous occasion of the Peters' only child.

"A remarkable young man," they all said of him. A graduate of Harvard University who majored in political science and was soon to receive his MBA, Mathew was following in his father's successful footsteps.

Mr. Peters was the proud owner and CEO of a multimillion-dollar garment business called Emari

Couture. Emari was named after Mr. Peters' late mother. The company specialized in designing women and children's fashions, women's lingerie, and other naughty necessities. Mr. Peters was also in the franchise business. He owned a fleet of Pizza Huts and Burger Kings nationwide. He was a hotshot entrepreneur and a very successful attorney who worked his way up the ladder into having a partnership in Barton, Peters, and Binary, one of New York's top law firms.

"Happy birthday, baby," Mathew's loving and very beautiful girlfriend, Tina, said, following her statement with a sweet kiss on the cheek. Tina was dressed to kill in a bright red corset mini-dress, with the matching five-hundred-dollar Coach bag. And just like his mother, Tina was twice as beautiful, with long, silky black hair; flawless skin; long, shapely legs; light brown eyes; and a body some women would kill for. Sometimes, in her spare time, she posed for ads with Calvin Klein.

Mathew stood there next to Tina while the guests chatted and laughed with one another. There was a live band playing for the crowd, and five to six servants pranced through the room holding silver platters of finger sandwiches, glasses of wine and champagne, and raspberry and espresso truffles.

Mathew was also dressed to kill that night. He stood six feet tall and looked stunning in a gray Armani suit and Gucci shoes. He looked like money—very handsome, with curly black hair, smooth skin, beautiful black eyes, and a thin mustache just growing in. He was a natural pretty boy. There was not one pimple, scar, or mark on him from head to toe, like he'd been on reserve and carefully pampered every night for the past twenty-five years. But he almost was, because he was born with a silver spoon in his mouth. He'd been indulged with the best of the best since he was young, attending the best schools in the country, having the best tutors, living in swanky homes, and having everything handed to him from the day he was born.

His father, Perry Peters, was said to have a net worth of more than seven hundred million dollars, and still counting.

"How does it feel to be a quarter of a century old?" Tina asked.

"Feels the same as if I was twenty-one," Mathew replied.

"Would you care for a glass, young Mathew?" one of the servants, dressed in a black suit with white gloves, asked.

"No, thank you," he told him.

"Mathew dear, please come here," his mother called. "I would like for you to meet Mr. Parker, head of the grievance committee at our Oakdale Country Club."

They shook hands, and he asked, "So, Mathew, thinking of joining our prestigious club this summer?"

"I've been thinking about it, Mr. Parker."

"We would love for you to become a new member. It would be great to have you join, having a third generation in. Your parents have been loyal members since 1985," he informed.

"I'll give it a thought," he said. But he really had no interest in joining that old, tired club with the same old, tired activities and events. This was his twenty-fifth birthday, and he was spending it with most of his parents' friends and some of the club members. The only one in attendance at his parents' home who was even remotely close to his age, was his girlfriend, and she was two years older at twenty-seven. The rest of the crowd was thirty-five and over—snobbish assholes.

The only friends he had, if you could call them

friends, were the children of parents who were friends or business partners with his parents. And yet, the majority of them were as uppity, stuck-up, and arrogant as their parents.

Mathew, being bored and tired, retreated to the outside heated granite pool, and stood there alone peering up at the stars. It was a nice spring night—the weather not too cold or too hot—with the temperature at a comfortable seventy-five degrees. He could still hear the band performing from inside and the chatter of his mother's guests, supposedly celebrating his birthday. But it didn't feel like his birthday. The party felt like another dull event that his parents threw from time to time. It would be rude of him to leave so early, especially from a party in his honor. He wouldn't hear the end of it from his mother, who would go ranting on about how he embarrassed her in front of all of the guests who came to celebrate his birthday and how he would be dishonoring the family's name by being so unsociable.

But Mathew didn't care for all the things his parents, especially his mother, cared for. All his life he felt sheltered, living under his father's name and reputation. Whatever he wanted, he received in the blink of an eye. He was treated with respect whenever he attended social events that were being held in his father's honor. He was admired and adored by all the ladies. Even though he was handsome and charming, it was hard to tell if people were just out there for his money and not for his character. He was a really nice guy.

He'd been together faithfully with Tina for two years, and there was even talk about engagement and marriage. Tina was the daughter of a well-known surgeon who treated many wealthy clients and was well respected. They met through their parents, who were elated that they became a couple. Mrs. Peters felt that Tina was the right woman for her son. She came from a very good background, her father was also a member of the Oakdale Country Club, and she was also a graduate of Harvard, studying to become a doctor like her father.

After spending a few minutes alone outside, glancing up at the stars and catching a little solitude, Tina came searching for him.

"There you are, baby." She greeted him with a kiss to his cheek. "Why are you all alone out here?"

"Just catching a little bit of fresh air," he said.

"Well, your mother's looking for you. There are a few more guests inside that she would love for you to meet."

Great, more guests, he thought.

"It's a marvelous night tonight," Tina said.

Mathew embraced her. Nestling against each other, they both simultaneously glanced up at the stars.

"I love you, Mathew," she proclaimed, feeling the comfort of being in his arms on this lovely night.

But Mathew continued to peer up at the stars, wishing for this birthday to somehow be different. He needed some kind of change or a vacation from his folks, who he felt were driving him crazy.

"There you are, Mathew. I've been looking all over for you. I want you to meet Dr. Lacrosse," his mother said, still holding a glass of wine as she trotted across the manicured grass toward Mathew and Tina. "Come inside, Mathew. It's not polite to have your guests waiting. We're about to wish you a happy birthday."

"Yes, Mother," he answered.

He reluctantly followed her inside, pitying his twenty-fifth birthday. The cars, the money, and the twenty-five shares his father had given to him as a birthday gift couldn't make this day any less vivid for him.

It was like he was trapped inside a box. No matter where he turned, everything was still the same. His twenty-fifth birthday—twenty-five years and his life had not changed since the day he was born.

Money, money, money. Fuck money, he thought.

-Three-

Coney Island was a borough within a borough, the last stop on the F train coming from Queens, and home to probably one of the oldest and most famous amusement parks ever built—Coney Island, Astroland Park, and the New York Aquarium located right next door. Then there are the dirty beaches, the boardwalk, and the famous hotdogs from Nathan's. It is also famous for the roller coaster called the Cyclone. Thousands and thousands of tourists travel to the beaches, swim in the sea, ride the rides, and eat the hotdogs.

But Coney Island has definitely changed over the years. The streets are now mostly drug infested and filled with crime and prostitution from Ocean Parkway down to Neptune Avenue until Seagate, an isolated, fenced-off community populated with old wooden homes and mostly white Jewish America. But east from that, there are the housing communities and projects that stretch all the way down Neptune, Mermaid, and Surf avenues.

There are the Gravesend projects across the street

from Kaiser Park, and then there is Surfside Gardens, over by West 37th Street, and the Unity Towers between Surf and Mermaid. Then there's the Coney Island Housing buildings and O'Dweyer Garden west down Surf Avenue.

For many African-Americans, this part of New York was where they called home, where the streets were generally populated with more than twenty different gangs claiming different territories and buildings. This was where a hooker would happily bless you with a fuck and suck for forty-five dollars, where a crack head sold his or her mother's valuables for a three-minute high, and where the wrong stares and a sharp tongue could get you killed instantly—gunned down in a matter of minutes. It was poverty for some and strictly lavish living to others.

Toni, a resident living in the Gravesend Housing Projects, was about to take a trip to the Greyhound Port Authority in Manhattan. She would catch a bus from there and take the five- or six-hour bus ride upstate to visit her brother, who was being detained in Auburn, a maximum security prison located in Auburn, New York.

On the bus, after reading the hot book, *Streets of New York Volume One,* she read one of her brother's letters that was sent to her three weeks ago regarding his new transformation. He wrote that he was having fewer fights with other inmates, and he hooked up with a few Muslim brothers in his unit. One in particular was named Muhammad, and he was a former drug dealer from Coney Island who had been in jail since he was seventeen. Now he was thirty-one and had devoted his life completely to Allah.

She folded his letter neatly in half, then placed it

back into her jean pocket. It'd been two months since she had come to visit him, and for her, it'd been two months too long. She'd always talked to Thomas over the phone, constantly accepting every one of his collect calls, totaling her bill to almost two hundred dollars in one month. Now, she discarded a few of his collect calls. All of a sudden it was getting too expensive to have a twenty-minute chat with her brother. She loved him, but she had her bills.

Toni reached the prison a little past three in the afternoon, stepping off the bus with about twenty other females all coming up to visit boyfriends, husbands, fathers, baby daddies, brothers, and uncles. They were all in a single line, waiting to go through security searches. She locked her valuables and other contraband, like her bag of weed and a small razor she carried for protection, into a small locker.

Around four o'clock, she was in the huge visitors' room, sitting at a wooden table, waiting for her brother. The room was filled with people, about a hundred or so inmates with family and friends. There were correction officers posted all around the room standing strong and observing for any unusual activity.

Toni noticed her brother coming out of a narrow entrance with about three other inmates who were being escorted by a single C.O. Swathed in a gray prison jumpsuit and sporting box braids, Sheek looked around the room for his baby sister. She smiled, stood, and waved for him. He returned her smile with a broad smile himself and walked over to her designated table.

"How you doing, sis?" he asked, giving her a long hug and kiss.

"Fine. How about you?"

"I'm good."

He took his seat opposite from her, with his back facing toward the main C.O. near the entrance. It was mandatory for all inmates to sit in that fashion, visitors facing toward the main entrance and the inmates with their backs turned away from it.

"You got my letter?" he asked.

"Yeah, I got it with me right now. So how's this Muhammad? You trust him?"

"The brother's right. I ain't gotta flip on him or nuthin' like that, sis. Niggahs know my status up in here," he boasted. "I'm living."

"Damn, you're getting big," she said, stunned by his growth these past few months.

"Yeah, trying to get my swell goin' on, you hear?"

Thomas was five feet, eight inches tall, 175 pounds. Despite his size, he was very strong and quick and ruthless with his hands. When he was twelve, he started training to be eligible to box in the Golden Gloves, but that dream faded when he gradually traded his life in for the streets and the love for fast money. His seething attitude made him well respected.

"So, how's Ma doin'?" he asked.

Not being able to lie to him about their mother, she answered, "She's getting worse, Thomas. Every night . . ." She paused, choking up, feeling tears building up in her eyes. "I hate him so much, Thomas . . . what he did to her. I hope his soul fuckin' burns in hell."

There was silence between the two, then Thomas asked, "Do you regret that I blew his head off?"

"I hate seeing you up in here . . . this place, it's fucked up. You don't belong here, Thomas. You don't."

"Don't worry about me, sis. I'm living."

"But not like this."

"I did what I had to do. He wasn't going to keep disrespecting our mother like that. I'll do it again if I got to. Look," he said, taking her hand into his, "what's done is done. Ain't no changing that. I'm accepting my fate, so you gotta stop worrying 'bout me. You cool?"

She nodded, but it still pained her to see her brother doing hard time for killing some asshole who deserved it in the first place. *This system isn't fair,* she thought. Life wasn't fair. She had to strip and perform sexual acts just to keep her shit in order and pay her bills on time.

Sometimes she wondered if suicide was the only way out.

In Kaiser Park, five men were involved in a dice game, with three hundred dollars up for grabs. Tec rolled the dice against the cracked concrete and crapped out, rolling a one, two, and three. He cursed, then handed a C-note over to Willow, who had already won five hundred dollars and was blabbing at the mouth about his winnings.

They stood on shabby park benches, passing around two Ls between the five men. The group was decorated in lavish gold chains, rings, Timberlands, designer gear, and some were packing heat in the waistbands of their jeans. They intimidated some of the passersby in the park with their vulgar language and demeanor.

Tec took a whiff from one of the two Ls being passed around.

Soon all five men took notice of a bright red, two-door '97 Mercedes Benz 600SL, with chrome rims and the system blasting, cruising down Neptune Avenue. All five men were very aware of the driver of the car. He went by the name Chills, and Tec and his crew knew he was nobody to fuck wit'—for now, anyway.

Chills had almost all of Coney Island on lock down, running operations on almost every street corner, project building, and bodega in the hood. He was a man with clout and power. Chills was not a small guy either. He was a chubby niggah, standing at six feet, two inches, 245 pounds, rockin' a goatee and a thick black beard.

Tec's eyes stayed beaded on the 600SL as it headed east down Neptune. He was thinking that should be him, having the clout, the money, and the respect. But ever since his boy Sheek got locked up, all that had changed for him.

Little Boy Ronny pulled him to the side away from the dice game and said in his ear, "Yo, word has it that Chills is trying to move in over by 33rd and Bay View," he informed.

"What? That's our shit."

"Yeah, but he already got a few small-time niggahs working business for him."

Unhappy about the news he had just heard, Tec started to think. Chills already had the whole east side of Coney Island, and now his greedy ass wanted to move in on Tec's home territory, Gravesend projects. He knew that if Chills took that over, there wouldn't be nuthin' left, probably just nickel-and-dime hustles, and he wasn't about that. He was barely clocking dollars now 'cause of that greedy muthafucka.

-Four-

Mathew enjoyed the stunning view of the river and Central Park from the twenty-third floor of his luxury Manhattan condominium filled with several rooms fit for a prince, including a formal living and dining room, an eat-in kitchen, four spacious bedrooms, and one-and-a-half luxurious bathrooms.

It was three days after his twenty-fifth birthday, and he was glad to be back home in his Manhattan apartment with Tina. They were both having an elegant meal on the terrace. Spending three days in Long Island with his mother was more than enough for him. They dined on shrimp and salad, a little meal cooked up by his maid who came by four days a week to cook and clean.

Tina sat courteously on her seat in a V-neck silk-and-lace gown. She sipped on a glass of Cristal, enjoying the good life. Mathew, sitting opposite her, peered out into the beautiful city night-lights, deep in his own thoughts.

"Let's go out tonight, Tina," he suggested.

"Out . . . out where?"

"A club, maybe."

"Mathew, it's almost a two-hour drive to the Oakdale Country Club," she said, taking another sip from her drink. "Besides, it's getting late, soon to be time for bed."

"I'm not suggesting the country club. Let's go to a Manhattan nightclub. I want to dance, mingle, have some fun."

"Are you crazy, Mathew? They're the worst," she barked.

"How would you know? You've never been to one before."

"I've heard stories," she countered. "Besides, what would your mother think of us touring these vulgar city clubs at such an untimely hour?"

"My mother? Tina, she's miles away in Long Island. She doesn't have to know," he said, rising out of his seat.

"Well, I will, and it's disrespectful to her, as well as it is to me for you to suggest such an uncouth idea."

He sighed and walked off into the apartment. Tina wiped the corners of her mouth with her napkin, then followed him inside, where she found him sitting on one of his plush leather couches listening to one of his Curtis Mayfield and the Impressions CDs. He was a huge fan of ol' skool. Tina approached him, taking a seat on his lap and wrapping her arms around him.

"I love you, Mathew. I just don't want to see you getting hurt trying to venture out here in the city wanting to have a good time. You know how these people living in this city can be. You see it on television every day."

He looked up at her, but didn't say a word. He wanted to, but he knew Tina could get really stubborn when it came to discussing certain issues. It was to the point where she had to have her way, or have the last word—no ifs, ands, or buts about it.

Mathew placed his hand on her thigh, feeling the soft and sleek texture of her skin. He then slowly moved his hand, but was stopped with a quick slap to the back of it. "Stop it," she said.

"Why?"

"Because, we're not ready," she said.

"We?"

"Yes, *we.* I want our wedding day to be memorable, so keep it in your pants 'til then," she chided.

He'd been putting up with this for two years now. Twenty-five years old, and he was still a virgin. He had never experienced a woman fully. It was always just kisses and touches. Frustrated, he removed Tina from his lap and headed into the master bedroom where he was about to retire for the night. But when he got to the bedroom door, Tina said to him, "Mathew, I hope you have something proper to wear to next week's formal charity banquet."

"I didn't know that I was attending," he responded.

"Yes, Mathew. I can't be seen attending these events unescorted. How would that look for us as a couple? People would talk."

So let 'em, he said to himself.

"It starts at seven, so I would like to be there before six. So inform the driver two hours ahead of time. It will be very improper for us to be late."

He closed the door, stripped off his evening attire, and climbed into bed. His head was screaming for him to escape this madness—screaming for a change.

-Five-

It'd been a week since Toni's visit to her brother upstate. She wanted to tell her mother that Thomas was doing OK, but when she arrived home, her mother was nowhere to be found. She hadn't heard from her in four days. Worried, Toni tried calling the cops, but they told her that they couldn't do anything for her except file a missing person's report. They already knew about her mother and her junkie habit. Why waste time searching for a useless addict who probably didn't want to be found in the first place? Let her go off somewhere and enjoy her drugs, then maybe they could pick up her body later.

The past four days had been hell for her. She couldn't help but worry. She went out searching for her mother on her own, but came up dry. She went around asking the local dealers, but they knew nothing. Then she asked some of the neighborhood junkies. All they cared about was bumming some cash off her so they could score their next hit. She also asked some of the local residents. They just glared at her, looking at her and saying to themselves, *Why waste your time?* Frustrated, Toni gave up hope and tried to accept the worst.

One night she received an anonymous phone call around two in the morning. The caller gave her information on her mother's whereabouts. Toni was informed that her mother was on the boardwalk over by West 12th Street.

Toni hung up and called her friend Vinita who had access to a car. She lived on the floor above Toni. Vinita, obviously disturbed by the late-night call, shouted over the line, "Who is it?"

"I need a favor, Vinita," Toni asked.

"What is it now, Toni? It's two in the morning."

"I need a lift . . . it's my mother," she explained.

"Toni . . . "

"Please. I'll owe you."

"You better," Vinita said.

Within the next fifteen minutes, Toni and Vinita drove down to West 12th Street where the caller said she would find her mother. Vinita made a right. Straight ahead there was a dead end where they came to the Riegelmann boardwalk, an old dilapidated wooden structure that was plagued with overnight garbage; rats swarming everywhere, nibbling on the bits of food left on the ground by the amusement park goers; and some homeless taking refuge under the boardwalk.

Vinita came to a stop, leaving the car running. Toni stepped out.

"Hurry up, Toni," she said, feeling uncomfortable being there so late at night.

Toni headed up the ramp, stepping onto the boardwalk. She glanced to her left, then to her right.

"Ma," she called out, but there was no answer in return. She went with her instincts and headed toward her right. There was a homeless man, aloof far off in the dark corner, covered in rags and staring up at her as she passed by. He was mumbling something to himself, jiggling a cup filled with change at two in the morning, still begging.

She walked a few steps down the boardwalk with concern, and at the same time feeling anger toward her mother.

"Ma," she called out again.

Then she heard laughing from up ahead. She proceeded with caution, peering carefully. She spotted her mother sitting on a bench with some male stranger, facing the sea.

"Ma," she exclaimed, catching both of their attention.

Her mother looked up, sighing. "What, girl?" she said, snarling.

"You know what time it is?" Toni asked, then glared over at her male friend. He was dressed in a tattered blue Georgetown sweatshirt and worn blue jeans. He obviously looked the part of a junkie. Her mother, dressed in dirty black spandex shorts, white Reeboks caked with dirt and mud, and her soiled blouse unbuttoned, with her hair in disarray, glared back at her daughter.

"Girl, go home," she said, turning her attention from her daughter back over to her male friend.

"No, it's late. You got me out here worrying about you."

"Worrying . . . Child, I'm a gotdamn grown woman. I'm your damn mamma."

"Ma . . . please," she exclaimed. "Look at you. You look terrible. Let's just go home."

Toni tried grabbing her by her arm, but her mother jerked away, resisting.

"Let us play, young love," the man said, smiling, showing the four or five teeth still capped in his mouth.

She just ignored him, still trying to force her mother to come home with her. But her mother still argued, becoming more stubborn with every passing minute. Her mother crossed her legs, sitting still on the bench, looking up at the stars, and said to her daughter, "Me and Baron are going to sit here and watch the stars rise."

"You mean sun," Toni corrected.

"Sun, stars, who gives a fuck? They're still in the sky."

Toni just stood there, hovering over her tenacious mother and growing angrier.

"I'm not leaving here without you, Ma."

"Why you so stubborn, child? Didn't I raise you better than this?"

"Look at you. You're a fuckin' junkie. It's been four days, and you haven't come home, didn't even care to have me tell you how Thomas is doing. All you care about is this shit," she barked, picking up a few multicolored crack vials from off the wooden boardwalk, then tossing every last one of them at her mother, having a few hit her across her face.

She then heard a horn blowing from a distance, knowing that it was Vinita calling out for her.

"We gotta go," Toni said, grabbing hold of her mother again, this time with stronger force, and yanking her ass off the bench. She tumbled down to the floor, landing on her side.

"Girl, you gone crazy?" her mother hollered.

"No, you have. C'mon," she said, dragging her across the boardwalk by her blouse.

Her mother started yelling and carrying on as Toni struggled to carry her to the car. The drugs in her mother's system made her weak and decrepit, making her feel like it was the Incredible Hulk forcing her to the car, instead of her daughter.

Determined, Toni didn't let go of her raving mother until she was almost to the car, where Vinita was still sounding the horn.

"Bitch, how fuckin' dare you?" her mother cursed.

"No. Now you either get in this fuckin' car with me, or I swear I'll hate you and will have nothing to do with you from this day on," she threatened. But in her case, it was more of a bluff. She loved her mother too much for her to just abandon her so suddenly. She sometimes felt partly responsible for her mother's downfall, feeling that she could have prevented it from ever happening.

Seeing the seriousness in her daughter's eyes, Angela stopped her resistance and got into the car.

"Damn, it's about time," Vinita said, putting the car in reverse.

"Sorry about that, Vinita. I'll definitely make it up to you," Toni apologized.

"Shit, you better. Damn, your moms stinks. Ohmygod!"

As soon as they entered their apartment, Toni started stripping her mother down, ridding her of her filthy clothes, and started preparing a nice, warm bath for her. She became more disgusted when two vials of crack fell onto the bathroom floor. She looked down at the drugs and started to shed tears because of her mother's habit. She encouraged her drowsy mother into the tub and slowly bathed and washed every nook and cranny. Ten minutes into bathing her mother, she heard a knock at the door. Looking at the time, and seeing it was going on three-thirty, she knew it was Keith.

"Who is it?" she asked, as if she didn't already know.

"Girl, open the fuckin' door. Who else gonna be knockin' on this door fo' in the morning?"

She unlocked the door, and there he was, standing in a pair of baggy, sagging black Polo jeans, a black T-shirt, a fitted blue baseball cap, and as usual, a pair of beige Timberlands.

"Keith, I'm sorry, but it's late, and my mother—"

"What? C'mon, I ain't here for your mother. You know what I'm here for," he said, pushing up on her and placing his hand on her breast, squeezing abruptly.

"C'mon, Keith, not tonight," she said, pulling back from him. But he was not hearing that tonight. He was horny, and he wasn't trying to hear no for an answer.

He stepped into the apartment, taking off his T-shirt and baring his chest. His upper body was swathed with tattoos. Toni didn't argue with him. She knew it was useless.

He followed her to the bathroom where her mother was still soaking in the tub, half asleep and totally fucked up. Toni helped her out of the tub, wrapping her in a towel and drying her off, while Keith watched from the bathroom door, smiling.

"Your moms still got a little tight body for a junkie," he joked as they passed by him and headed toward the bedroom.

"Fuck you, Keith," Toni blurted at him.

"Soon," he mumbled.

She soothed her mother, putting her in her pajamas and watching her fall asleep while Keith sat in the living room watching TV.

A few minutes later, Toni came from out of the bedroom and joined Keith in the living room, sitting next to him and trying to cuddle. But he wasn't all for that. He looked at her and said, "Yo, let me get that blowjob."

She peered at him, then without saying anything, she got down on her knees with her face between his legs, unfastened his jeans, stroked his penis, and softly went down on him, causing him to drop the remote and grab a fistful of her hair.

Three days later, Vinita ended up giving Toni a ride to the Bottom Dollar, where she was about to start her ten o'clock shift. Vinita, feeling disgusted that Toni even worked there, was constantly trying to talk her friend out of dancing in the tasteless club. Vinita was in her second year at Brooklyn College, majoring in business and communications. Someday she hoped to work in TV broadcasting and succeed in a career of journalism.

"Toni, why do you still come here?" Vinita asked.

"I need the money," she replied.

"So why don't you go out and get a real job?" Vinita asked.

"What . . . like a nine to five?"

"It's starting something. You're selling yourself out here, dancing at this shit hole every night. This place is nothing but trouble."

"I bring home close to two hundred dollars a night working here," Toni said, trying to defend herself.

"Doing what? You think I don't know what's going on in there, Toni? I hear things, things about you."

"So what? Let 'em talk. They don't have my troubles."

"There you go again, always using your troubles as an excuse. You got bills, your mother's sick, your brother's locked up, so let you suck a dick and take care of everything. You're better than that."

"What am I supposed to do, Vinita? Go to school like

you, work at some hot-shot job like you? I'm not you, Vinita."

"Toni, I hear that new department store in Kings Plaza Mall is hiring. Why don't you apply for a job there?" Vinita suggested.

Toni sighed, sucking her teeth. "And how much are they paying?" she asked.

"Seven dollars and twenty-five cents an hour."

"That's OK." Toni shrugged off the suggestion.

"You're selling yourself short," Vinita said, peering hard at Toni.

"Vinita, you live your life, and let me live mine," Toni said, getting ready to step out of the car.

"Toni, wait," Vinita blurted out. "I'm sorry. I don't mean to put you down. It's just that you're my girl. I'm just looking out for your best interest. Look, come with me next week to this banquet a friend of mine is having."

"What kind of banquet?" Toni asked, with one foot on the pavement and the other still inside the car.

"Just a formal thing. It's in Manhattan."

"Formal? Vinita, I have nuthin' formal to wear," Toni said.

"I'm sure you have something. Rummage through your closet, go shopping, do something."

"I don't know, Vinita."

"Toni, you owe me. I don't want to go by myself."

Toni thought on it for a few seconds, then dragged out, "OK, I'll go."

"Cool, I'll pick you up around six."

Toni stepped out of the car while Vinita drove off down Mermaid headed to wherever. Toni headed toward the club entrance, a dilapidated place that looked intimidating and dangerous, with a black steel door, the windows painted black, graffiti scrawled all over the building, and the sounds of the bass of thundering music coming from inside.

Toni banged vigorously on the door. It was difficult for others to hear from inside, especially the bouncers who paid more attention to the luscious nude girls, than doing their job at the door, which was collecting a ten-dollar cover charge from the customers and the dancers. No one was excluded from the fee—even the club's best and most provocative dancers had to pay.

Finally, a slim black male answered the door.

"What's up, Toni?" he greeted, letting her in.

"What's up, Shame?"

Inside was loud, with the sounds of Mobb Deep's "Survival of the Fittest" blasting through the subwoofers of about eight speakers in the club. The Bottom Dollar was packed with people, filled with honeys making money, people drinking Hennessy and cognac, and niggahs lusting on the strippers.

Toni strutted through the crowd, dressed in tight blue Levi's jeans, a small white T-shirt, a pair of white-and-blue Nikes, and her braids pulled back into a ponytail. She carried a small Coach bag over her shoulder.

"Aww, my niggahs, my girl Toni's in the muthafuckin' house. The freak of C.I. is here," the deejay announced from his small boxed-in booth as he played records.

She didn't acknowledge him or his offensive shout-out. She just headed straight toward the bathroom to change.

In the bathroom, there were three ladies also changing, almost causing it to be a little too cramped. Toni dropped her bag off to the corner, unbuttoned her jeans, and decided to start changing in the cramped corner.

"Yo, this niggah had the nerve to try to stick his fingers up my ass," one of the girls in the changing room said. She was already in her outfit for the night: a red lace thong, red knee-high boots, and a tight, scanty white T-shirt, stopping just short of her breasts and tied in a knot behind her back.

"Niggahs is wilding tonight. This muthafucka wanted to pour beer down my pussy and then lick it up," another girl mentioned.

"Word."

"I'm sayin', I ain't stop him or nuthin'. He did dat shit, then he tipped me twenty muthafuckin' dollars. I got my pussy eaten out, then got paid for it," she hollered, slapping the other girl five.

The language inside was beyond vulgar.

It took Toni fifteen minutes to apply her makeup and change into her outfit, which was a long, sheer, exquisite white robe draping down to her shins and exposing a blue lace thong trimmed with white flowers. She was topless, displaying her perky brown breasts and dark circular nipples, and she wore a pair of open-toe sandals with three-inch heels.

As soon as she stepped out of the changing room, she felt someone grabbing her ass. She turned around, and a chubby guy just smiled at her, raising his drink. She sent a quick smile, then proceeded to the bar, where she ordered her usual—a glass of Hennessy mixed with a little Coke, no ice.

There was already a girl on stage, nude to the fullest, legs open and sticking a glass Heineken bottle into her pussy, pleasing the wide-eyed fellows. She wasn't the prettiest stripper, so she had to go to the extreme just to make her money, no matter how disgusting it looked.

Five minutes at the bar, and Toni already had a male coming to her asking if she did VIP. She smiled, told him her set price, and he agreed. Not even an hour up in the place, and she was already doing her first VIP for the night, which for damn sure wouldn't be her last. She was hot shit. She led the fellow to the secluded room. As usual, money was exchanged and later everyone was happy.

Meanwhile, during that same night in a different part of Brooklyn—Bedford Stuyvesant to be specific—Tec was chilling at the bar with his crew, Pinch-Back, Little Boy Ronny, and Lamont. Tec was drinking one of his usual cognacs, while the rest of the fellas were chilling out by his side gazing at some of the honeys who populated this low-key, but hood popular club called the Atlanta Spa. It was this huge looking warehouse that some locals from around the way decided to lease out and throw a party in every weekend when spring and summer came around. It had been abandoned for months, and it used to be a furniture store, but now it was a well-known hot spot for people who ranged in ages from seventeen to twenty-five. Inside it was nothing but one grand wooden dance floor, made to hold two hundred plus people, with a fifty-foot bar, employing three bartenders.

Tec, dressed in black Carhartt jeans, a Lakers jersey, and a pair of black-and-white Air Force Ones was rocking his fitted Yankees cap to the back. A long, thick gold chain with a majestic pendant, gave off that gangsta vibe to some of the club goers who gave him a second, maybe third glance, intimidating some.

The deejay spun off his umpteenth vinyl for the night, filling the vulgar atmosphere of mostly gangstas, thugs, hoochies, some killers, chicken heads, and wannabes, who bounced to Jay Z's single "Brooklyn's Finest," causing the crowd to go berserk.

But Tec kept his composure, and so did his niggahs, who still remained by the bar, cupping their drinks, bobbing their heads to the thunderous bass and gazing at almost every big butt cutie who passed. Some of the ladies were feeling 'em. They gawked at the men while walking by with their home girls to wherever, fond of the thuggish vibes the men were giving off.

"Damn, shortie got a phat ass," Pinch-Back proclaimed. His eyes were transfixed on her rear 'til it was no longer in his view.

Little Boy Ronny laughed. He also stared at the same time.

Soon, two ladies dressed in tight leather miniskirts, approached Tec and his crew, chuckling and staring over at all four of them. Pinch-Back and Lamont took notice, and they started cheesing.

"How y'all doing?" one of the girls asked, who was ayyite lookin', but not your average pretty girl. She had a bloated nose, a weave, and big bug eyes, but her body was tight—real fuckin' tight. And Pinch-Back definitely took notice as he gazed at her from head to toe.

"What's up?" Lamont said.

"Why y'all not dancing?" the second girl asked. She was a little bit prettier than her friend, slimmer in the waist, more petite, with brown eyes.

Tec still remained aloof from the conversation with the two young girls who looked to be no older than nineteen. But his buddies wasted no time, as Pinch-Back placed his arm around one of them and led her to where the party was. Lamont was the next to take charge. He took the petite one, following his friend. Little Boy Ronny stayed at the bar with Tec, and he ordered himself another drink.

"Yo, you ayyite, Tec?" Little Boy Ronny asked, looking at his friend who was hunched over the bar with his drink still in his hand, and staring up at the playoff game playing on the TV that was mounted over the bar.

"I'm cool, dog," he said to Little Boy Ronny.

A few females took a liking to Tec, but he just played the anti-social role for the night, having a few hoochies intrigued by his mysterious demeanor. Little Boy Ronny, who was only five feet, six inches tall and 145 pounds, was the smallest out of the bunch. He wanted to get his party on. He ordered himself another drink, rum mixed with just a little Coca-Cola, and tried to kick game to the female who was standing right next to him.

"What's up, love? You look good," he complimented, diverting all of his attention from Tec over to her. He gawked at her real hard from head to toe, admiring her little nighttime club outfit—tight black jeans, heels, and a little mini tight-fitted black T-shirt decorated in rhinestones that spelled out "Brooklyn Native" across her chest. Her hair was in two long exotic pigtails, falling down to her breasts. She was more than cute—actually stunning.

She didn't respond to him at first. She just stood there next to her friend, who was also fine. They were both chatting and sipping on their drinks.

"I'm sayin' tho', a brotha gives you a compliment and y'all can't holla back?" Little Boy Ronny said, up close and personal.

The one with the pigtails just looked over at him and sucked her teeth real hard, followed by the words, "Please, niggah."

"Oh, it's like that?" Little Boy Ronny said, getting kinda annoyed that this bitch was lookin' real stuck-up.

"Ain't it past your bedtime, little boy?" her friend responded, giggling at her smart remark.

"What?" Little Boy Ronny exclaimed. "Y'all bitches don't fuckin' know me."

"Please. Why bother?" the pigtail friend proclaimed.

"Yo, y'all bitches really need to shut da fuck up right now," Tec shouted, staring over at them, not appreciating how they were really disrespecting his man.

One of them sighed, rolling her eyes, peering over at Tec as if to say, *Who're you?* Tec not once averted his eyes from the both of them. He glared at both ladies like a bull seeing red.

"Fuck them faggots, Gina," one of them said.

"What?" Tec chided, moving in closer.

"Yo, my man, chill the fuck out," a man interrupted, stepping between Tec and the two ladies, hovering over everybody at six feet, five inches.

"What? Who you, duke?" Tec asked.

"Yo, that's my girl," he announced.

"I don't care if that's your fuckin' mother. She ain't gonna be playing my boy out like that."

"Yeah, whatever, dog, just back the fuck off," he stated in an unfriendly tone, thinking he was intimidating someone because of his height.

And this is how it started, either by an unfriendly stare or an unkind word to the wrong person.

Tec sized up the guy, who did not know that he was concealing a .45 in the waistband of his jeans, tucked deep near his crotch. But duke, who was thinking that he was playing the guy in front of his girl, didn't know his situation, being from Pennsylvania and only spending the weekend in Brooklyn. He didn't know that he was beefing with the wrong guy.

The club was big, so a lot of heads didn't take notice on the little intense situation that was taking place by the bar. The bass almost drowned out the sound of anyone's voice if you didn't speak loud enough.

"What, you steppin' to a niggah?" Tec said, his hand inches away from the gat.

Little Boy Ronny stood by Tec's side, ready to aid him in any kind of conflict. He may have been small, but he was just as lethal as any one of his homies.

"You don't know me, dog," the towering man warned, trying to put fear in his voice. But he now saw something wasn't right as Pinch-Back and Lamont came from the dance floor, sweating and standing closely behind Tec—ready to have his back.

Outnumbered four to one, no matter how tall he was, the guy knew his chances were slim. He knew that if he didn't play his cards right, he was about to become embarrassed and get fucked up in front of his woman.

"What, you ain't talkin' dat shit no more, huh, niggah?" Tec said, finally pulling up his Lakers jersey and flashing the .45 he had concealed.

He could see it in the man's eyes—the fear—fuckin' scared to death. Tec gave him a wicked smirk, loving the intimidation, the terror the guy was giving off. Pigtails also looked frightened, along with her friend. They both stood there speechless and wide-eyed. The crowd still didn't realize what was going on just a few feet from them, or else there would have been panic and uproar just from the sight of someone flashing a gun.

Not knowing what to do or say, the man just stood there frightened, as his woman came to his side, grabbing his arm and saying to him, "Jimmy, c'mon, let's go."

"Yeah, do that, pussy muthafucka," Tec proclaimed, still eyeing him down while the guy's woman hurriedly walked him away from everything. Not one of the three bothered to turn around.

Tec and the rest just started laughing.

"Stupid fuckin' bitches," Little Boy Ronny shouted. "You almost got your boyfriend shot up in this mutha."

Having a gun in Brooklyn was as common as people in white suburban America having a job, a home, kids, and a dog—you would feel out of place if you didn't have one out of the four in suburbia. In Brooklyn, it was said that one out of every three teens owned a firearm. And as overcrowded as Brooklyn was, causing beef with someone, especially on a hot summer day, could be the wrong thing to do—probably the worst.

As the night progressed, Tec still stayed seated at the bar. He had already forgotten about the little incident with homeboy a few hours back. He focused on the semi-finals, the Knicks versus Chicago, and with the return of Michael Jordan, the Knicks' chances of winning looked very bleak.

Tec was a huge basketball fan, following all the teams and their players, but he was a Chicago fan, cheering for the Bulls to go all the way again this year. Last year he won a grand betting for the Bulls.

His crew was all dancing up on a bitch somewhere in the midst of the dance floor, including Little Boy Ronny, who cared nothing about that rude rejection he received earlier. Now he was grinding against some big-boned, redboned girl who he was trying to fuck before the night was over.

The deejay played some Tupac mixed with a little R&B.

Tec cursed Rodman as he missed the open shot.

By 2:00 A.M., the club was almost filled to capacity. It was so tight inside you could pickpocket a niggah and scratch his nuts at the same time. In the midst of watching his game, Tec noticed an unfamiliar face clocking him hard from the other side of the bar. Not being intimidated by the stare, he peered back with a scowl like he had just sucked on a lemon.

Yo, who this fool staring at? Tec asked himself.

They both played the staring game as the man sipped on a glass filled to the top with Cristal. He was accompanied by two beautiful women who clung to him like he was the million dollar playboy himself, Hugh Hefner.

Little Boy Ronny came over to Tec, grinning over at his boy, happy 'cause he had just bagged this big bone's number, and he knew within a week, he'd be fuckin' her.

"What up, dog?" Little Boy Ronny asked.

"Yo, who this muthafucka over there clockin' a niggah like he know me?" Tec asked, his face still scowled up and showing no fear, no matter who it was.

"Yo, that's that niggah Cory-D, Chills' right hand man," Little Boy Ronny informed.

Without saying anything, Tec removed himself from the swivel barstool and headed over in Cory-D's direction, with his number one boy following him.

"Niggah, you fuckin' know me?" Tec asked loudly, eyeing Cory-D down in front of his bitches.

Cory-D turned around to him slowly, peering at him as he stood just inches from his face.

"Ladies, pardon me for a sec," Cory-D said kindly.

Both ladies passed briskly by Tec and Little Boy Ronny.

"Y'all fellows want a drink?" he asked. "It's on me."

"Fuck that drink," Tec cursed.

Cory-D was your upscale, gangsta pretty boy, with smooth brown skin, brown eyes, and sleek hair. He stood six feet, one inch; was dressed in cream khakis and an ironed white collared shirt; and he sported a diamond earring in his left ear and a 1.2 carat pinky ring on his right hand.

"Yo, you ain't got to be so harsh, niggah," Cory-D returned, tightening his face and showing that he was a little insulted by Tec's rejection of the drink.

He took his drink from off the bar, taking a quick sip of it, with Tec and Little Boy Ronny still standing in front of him. He then placed the drink back on the bar and said, "When a man offers you a drink, you take that drink."

"Tell your boy Chills to stay the fuck away from Gravesend. That's my shit. My niggahs are running shit around there," Tec rudely interrupted.

Keeping his serene composure, Cory-D stood there, then he uttered, "Gravesend" and chuckled. "You and your crew supposed to be running a six-to-eight-block radius of drugs, and y'all call that an operation? C'mon, dog, be for real. You must be Tec, I assume. I've been hearing quite some stories about you and your incarcerated friend Sheek. Y'all two were quite the dynamic duo back in the day."

"Listen—"

"No, muthafucka, you listen," Cory-D quickly and cruelly interrupted. "My partner Chills is a generous man. He's willing to cut you with ten percent of the business if you and your men come to terms with him. And let me give you a word of advice: My partner hates to be rejected."

"Me, come to work for him? For ten percent?" Tec retorted to this generous offer with a sinister grin.

"Ten percent, Tec, sounds like a lot of money, huh," Little Boy Ronny said.

"And let me tell you, Chills is offering you this little proposal instead of taking over your shit, outta respect that you used to be running with Sheek. He feels you'll add good value to his team."

Tec gawked at him, staying silent. He was either insulted, or he was thrilled—not. Tec didn't like the idea of sharing, and he liked the idea of having to answer to someone other than himself even less. It was all about greed, mixed with a little pride. Greed, because he felt that he should be the kingpin of Coney Island, not a fledgling underdog for someone who was holding a position he felt should have been his in the first place.

Who was Chills? He wasn't a cold-blooded killer like Tec and his boys. He had weak-minded niggahs to do his shit for him. That niggah didn't know Brooklyn—Coney Island—like him. Chills didn't know how to run the streets. He wasn't born and raised on the streets. He didn't have to tolerate the violence, the drugs, an abusive father, and the jealousy—all of the bullshit that Brooklyn streets had to offer since Tec was the age of seven. Unlike Tec, Chills was from out of town. He came up from North Carolina years ago and started hanging with his older cousin who ran with a few niggahs from the hood. A few years after that Chills came up big on his own by running his own organization.

Nah, it wasn't happening. Tec wasn't becoming an errand boy for some country cornbread-and-collard-green-eating hillbilly wannabe crack slinger, who wasn't even born and raised in this fuckin' borough.

Tec looked over at Cory-D and said, "You know what I think of your fuckin' offer?" He then spit a glob of spit onto Cory-D's expensive black Italian shoes. "Fuck your offer, and you can tell Chills to go fuck himself."

Staring down at the clump of spit on his shoe, then looking up at Tec as he still stood with fire in his eyes, Cory-D, trying not to get upset, calmly said to him, "Niggah, you've just signed your death certificate."

"What? Niggah, is that a threat?" Tec barked, reaching for his .45.

Suddenly two large men dressed in black turtleneck sweaters and black slacks came over to Cory-D's aid, grilling Tec and Little Boy Ronny with much intensity in their eyes.

"Look, little niggah, be easy. You don't want this shit to end up on the eleven o'clock news now," Cory-D said. "Too much death between niggahs on the block already."

Tec remained quiet, and so did Little Boy Ronny, but his eyes didn't divert from Cory-D's attention for a minute. He tapped Little Boy Ronny on his arm, signaling for them to leave.

"Stay the fuck away from Gravesend projects." Tec repeated his warning again, stepping back and getting ready to depart.

"Being hardheaded and stupid leads an already ignorant niggah to an early grave," Cory-D joked with his so-called boys/protection at the bar as they all returned their attention to the bar.

Riled up, and hating to be threatened, Tec felt that it was time for him and his crew to bounce. He told Little Boy Ronny to gather up Pinch-Back and Lamont and meet him outside by the car.

"Yo, you shoulda popped that niggah, Tec," Pinch-Back cried out to him, riding in the backseat of the black Ford Explorer. "That niggah must be outta his fuckin' mind. Yo, I tell you, if Sheek was out . . . "

"Fuck Sheek," Tec bellowed from the front passenger seat. "I'm running shit, not Sheek. Y'all niggahs don't forget that."

Everyone in the jeep was silent.

Tec felt like he'd been an underdog for far too long in a world that should have been his to rule long ago.

Yeah, him and Sheek were partners a while ago, but it always felt like he was the sidekick, the under boss. Tec was envious the majority of the time because his incarcerated partner still received more props and respect than he ever would. But now he felt that it was time for that to change, time for him to definitely make it happen, time for him to regain his manhood and bring that fear into the game.

Yeah, fuck Sheek. Sheek got twenty-five to life. Sheek ain't controlling shit no more. Sheek is the old and Tec shall become the new. Yeah, fuck Sheek.

-Six-

Riding in his twelve-passenger cream Lincoln limousine, on his way to some dreary charity banquet in midtown Manhattan, Mathew stared helplessly out the window while sitting next to his fiancée. He was dressed in a black-and-white tuxedo, sulking in his seat like an eight-year-old boy refusing to attend church with his mother.

"What's the matter, my sweet?" Tina asked, dressed in an eloquent, red, stretch matte jersey gown. Her hair was in a French roll, and she wore a 2.10-carat diamond-and-platinum necklace and diamond earrings. She looked a little too expensive. Overdoing it, Mathew might say.

"Daydreaming," Mathew responded, not once turning his attention over to her as he spoke and still gazing out the limo window.

"Well, snap out of it. We'll be there soon. And relax. You'll have fun. Trust me," she assured.

Define fun, he thought, cracking a small smile.

The limo pulled in front of the Plaza, a grand hotel

located on Fifth Avenue, across the street from Central Park. As the limo came to a stop, there were already two trendy doormen waiting out front for their arrival.

The limo door was opened, and the first to step out was Mathew, followed by Tina, who just loved to make a striking entrance.

Lined up and down the glamorous Fifth Avenue were different limousines of different colors, makes, and styles. The night was warm and humid—not a cloud in the sky. The atmosphere was filled with the rich, the famous, and the snobbish—men and women of all colors, races, and nationalities dressed their best in their custom-designed formalwear and high-priced jewelry. Short kisses to the cheek were exchanged as a greeting. It looked more like the Grammy Awards than some charity banquet.

Mathew and Tina walked side by side, hand in hand toward the Plaza entrance. Tina was smiling and greeting guests and companions. Mathew was also smiling, but just for show. He was just along for the ride.

It was only six-thirty, and the banquet did not begin until seven, so for the next half-hour, Mathew endured the useless chitchat and conversations to which he had no real interest in joining.

"Tina, darling, how is everything?" asked an elderly white woman who looked to be in her sixties and favored the famous Elizabeth Taylor.

"Why, fine, Mrs. Dunston."

They gave each other a quick kiss on the cheek.

"Have I introduced you to my fiancé, Mathew?"

"No, I haven't met this ravishing young man yet," she said, extending her arm to him.

"How're you doing, ma'am? Nice to meet you," Mathew greeted, shaking her hand.

Tina looked at him oddly, like he had just committed a terrible sin or crime. Mrs. Dunston just smiled at him.

"Oh, my, he is definitely a catch."

"Yes, he is. His father is Perry Peters," Tina informed, smiling broadly at Mrs. Dunston, who was dressed in a lavender silk charmeuse camisole with a deep V-neck and lace trim and wide-leg black pants.

"Perry Peters, huh? Quite an attractive and wealthy man. I see where he gets his looks from."

"Thank you," Tina uttered.

More guests started to pour into the lobby of the Plaza, as chitchat and richness filled the air. Everyone was dressed in their best formalwear. Some were a bit overdressed. It was a thousand dollars a plate at this banquet, where proceeds would be donated to the Young Inner City Youth Foundation, an organization that helped young city children and teens growing up without parents or parental guidance. The banquet was something that was thrown every year in the most extravagant hotel, something for the rich to think of as giving back. It made it easy to donate and not participate.

After the banquet there was a little ball for dancing and mingling, where a live band performed, and the guests got to mellow out.

Tina had a little quarrel with Mathew while the guests started to head into the Palm Court.

"What is wrong with you, Mathew?" Tina chided.

Baffled, Mathew shrugged and asked, "What did I do wrong?"

"It was embarrassing. I know your mother taught you better manners on how to greet a woman formally."

"Excuse me?"

"When a lady offers you her hand, you raise it and

gently kiss the back of it. Do you know how embarrassed I felt by you shaking her hand like it was some kind of business deal? Mrs. Dunston comes from family of great royalty. Her aunt is a duchess."

"Well, I'm sorry."

"For a man who's worth seven hundred million dollars, you sometimes act like you do not have two nickels to rub together. Now follow me, for I hate to be the last to enter after everyone else. It's impolite," Tina scolded, walking arm in arm with Mathew into the exquisite Palm Court.

"I thought I left my mother in Long Island," Mathew mumbled.

"What was that?" Tina inquired.

"Nothing."

The Palm Court was filled with discussion and laughter as invited guests took their seats next to eloquently set tables that were draped with white cloths. Small lamps sat in the center of the table—forks, napkins, and spoons were set and a bottle of champagne was placed on every table. A colossal crystal chandelier was suspended above the guests, and up ahead, there was a podium with a single microphone.

Tina and Mathew entered the room, taking a seat up above, close by the podium. Tina remained standing, waiting for Mathew to pull out her chair for her, allowing her to have a seat. He did and Tina smiled. "Thank you, my love," she said.

Two other women were seated at the table with Mathew and Tina. Both ladies were in their early forties and were very close friends of Tina. Tina seemed to gravitate toward older women, finding women her own age to be immature.

The room was filled, and every seat was taken. All the

men were sitting with correct posture. None of them were slouching in their seats, and none of them had their elbows resting on the table.

The ladies also sat correctly, legs crossed over each other, dresses and posh gowns draped down and sweeping the clean parquet floors, shoulders straight, eyes forward, and voices soft, just as they were taught in charm school.

The speaker came forward, a silver-haired, blue-eyed man dressed in a blue blazer, slacks, and a casual shirt. He uttered a quick joke, causing titters from his audience. He welcomed everyone and spoke for a total of fifteen minutes. After his speech, the meal was served.

The charity banquet had officially begun.

Toni and Vinita pulled up in front of the Plaza as Toni gazed out the passenger window.

"Damn, girl, we at the Plaza," Toni said.

"Yes, Toni. You need some culture in your life. It's time for a change, time for once to get the hell out of Brooklyn and away from that tired-ass club."

"We can't afford this shit," Toni said, staring at Vinita.

"Don't worry. A friend of mine invited me," she mentioned, pulling down the sun visor and checking her makeup in the mirror.

"A friend. Who do you know that works up in here?"

"Toni, it's cool. Trust me."

Toni sighed, feeling a little—no, very—uncomfortable.

Ten minutes after they'd found parking, which was nearly impossible in New York, the two ladies walked up to the entrance. They were an hour late, but just in time for the ball that was about to start.

Vinita strolled down the sidewalk dressed in a lovely black sheath dress, her jet-black hair long and falling off her shoulders, and a thin gold chain with a small cross set just above her breasts. She was looking marvelous, and she was trying hard to fit in with the crowd with which she was about to mingle.

But Toni looked the opposite. Toni, who was still very attractive, sported the wrong attire for the banquet. Her outfit would have the young women and men snickering at her, making her feel unwelcome, and the older gents and ladies would treat her no differently.

Toni had on a burgundy leather wrap skirt and a black sleeveless mock turtleneck with a pair of burgundy ankle leather boots.

Vinita tried to talk to her about her outfit, but Toni replied that this was all she could put together. Her closet wasn't filled with the basic casual and formal things that Vinita wore every day. Vinita's attire was more casual and formal—Wall Street, downtown Manhattan, while Toni's attire was more for the hookers from Hunts Point.

"You coulda lent me one of your outfits," Toni said.

And Vinita countered by telling her, "Girl, you know you're a size or two larger than me."

Which was a lie. Both women were about the same height, Vinita being a bit taller by two, maybe three inches. Both almost weighed the same and both had the same build. But Vinita was just cheap with loaning her wardrobe out to other people. She liked to keep her closet trendy.

They entered the Plaza, and Toni was astounded by its beauty and massive size.

"Damn, Vinita, we gonna get kicked outta this place," Toni said, peering around the lobby.

"Toni, stop worrying. Everything's gonna be fine. Trust me," Vinita assured.

"Excuse me, can I help you two ladies?" the manager of the hotel asked, gazing at them as if they didn't belong.

He was a clean-shaven white man with a receding hairline, dressed sharp in a gray three-piece suit.

"Yes, we've been invited to attend a charity banquet. My name is Vinita, and this is my friend Toni."

"Ladies, you do know that this is a formal function," the manager proclaimed, once again gazing over at Toni in her wrap skirt and boots.

"Yes, and I do apologize for the way my friend is dressed," Vinita said modestly.

Embarrassed, Toni just stood there, wishing for them to just leave.

"And may I ask, do you have an invitation or know the name of the party who invited you?"

"Yes, I do have an invitation. And my party's name is Richards. She's a dear good friend of mine," Vinita informed.

The manager left, asking them to stay in the main lobby 'til he got everything straightened out. He retreated to the ballroom.

"See, girl, I told you we shoulda just left. Now you about to get us in trouble."

"Toni, just relax. I told you that I was invited."

Ten minutes later, the manager came back down informing the girls that the charity banquet was almost at an end, but the ball was about to start, and Mrs. Richards did confirm Vinita's invite.

Delighted, Vinita flashed a smile.

* * *

As the banquet came to an end—with an hour and a half of speeches, congratulations, giving thanks, dedications, and tedious jokes—the crowd began to trickle out of the Palm Court and upstairs into the ballroom/banquet room, where a live band was set up.

Mathew and Tina mingled in with the crowd as the band filled the atmosphere with light classical hits and some light jazz—easy listening music for the Republican crowd. A few couples started to slow dance, while other folks refused to chat about anything but business.

"Mathew let's dance," Tina said, escorting him over to the middle of the ballroom.

She placed his hands around her waist, down to the small of her back as she placed her arms over his shoulders, and the couple slowly swayed to the music. Tina rested her head against his chest as Mathew softly caressed her in his arms. Together, slowly dancing in each other's arms, they looked like the perfect couple, happy as they could ever be. And the other folks took notice as they peered over at Mathew and Tina, smiling. They were two wealthy, healthy, and intellectual human beings. In the crowd's eyes, they looked like the perfect couple. It looked like the world belonged to them.

Vinita and Toni hurriedly walked into the ballroom. Toni was still nervous; her stomach had been doing flips all night, and she felt like a dozen butterflies had just hatched in her belly. But Vinita was more than confident. She gazed into the room, feeling that this was more of her type of crowd—the rich, the respectable, the educated, and the well known.

With a broad smile, Vinita walked into the banquet room casually, striding across the floor feeling like she belonged. But Toni was dazzled by the silk walls, the massive chandeliers hanging from above, the murals, and the people—the very rich-looking people dressed in very rich and expensive clothing. She suddenly became intimidated by such prosperity. She looked around everywhere and wished she were home. She wondered why Vinita had brought her to such a place, knowing she would be very much out of place.

Vinita was strolling around the room looking for her inviter, Mrs. Richards. She smiled at everyone, feeling that she was fitting in. She took a drink—a glass of champagne—from the silver platter that one of the uniformed servants walked around carrying.

"Good day," an elegantly dressed man uttered to her.

Vinita smiled and replied, "Good day to you too, sir."

"Vinita, darling, you've made it," one of the hosts of the banquet greeted. Mrs. Richards, a middle-aged white woman, was dressed in a long, beautiful winter-white silky dress with a string of pearls around her neck. She held a glass of red wine. She was standing with a group of females and one male, who were engaged in a conversation.

"Everyone, this is Vinita. She's one of the volunteers down at the center we're helping to raise money for," Mrs. Richards informed everyone.

Everyone greeted her with respect, as the male raised his glass of Dom Perignon and welcomed her to the affair.

"I thought you were bringing a friend," Mrs. Richards said, glancing around the room.

Vinita, too, looked around for Toni. "I did," she said.

"Well, where is she?"

"I have no idea. I must have left her at the door."

Toni was still standing alone, nervous and unintroduced as she slowly strolled into the room. She asked one of the well-dressed male servants for a drink. He looked at her, flashing a smile. He knew she looked out of place. He gazed at her from head to toe, admiring her leather wrap skirt and her boots.

"Miss, are you sure you're at the right party?" he asked.

"Yes. I'm here wit' a friend," she told him.

He smiled and said to her, "Have fun."

Toni walked around the room in search of Vinita. Some of the guests peered and frowned at her as they noticed her.

"What does she have on?" a woman asked, gazing at her, knowing that she didn't belong.

"My God, who invited her?"

"Seems like they'll let anybody in this place."

Toni gulped down her drink in seconds while she still stood alone.

"My, who is that dismal-looking woman?" Mrs. Richards asked, staring over at Toni leaning against the wall.

"Huh," Vinita murmured.

"I wonder who invited her," Mrs. Richards inquired. "Vinita, she's not a friend of yours, is she?"

Stunned, Vinita blurted out a no.

"Maybe she's lost," the male gentleman said.

"My God, she looks like one of those prostitutes on 42nd Street," another lady uttered.

Vinita shook her head as she backed into a corner, not wanting Toni to notice her and come over blowing up her spot. *Maybe it was a mistake bringing her,* Vinita thought. Besides, she hadn't wanted to come anyway.

Mathew and Tina still danced to the band's enchanting sounds. Tina felt like she was in another world. This was her world, her man, and she expected him to play by her rules.

Tina lifted her head from Mathew's chest, noticing the female standing aloof in the corner. She peered over at her, then said to Mathew, "My God, what is that?"

Mathew turned his head in Toni's direction, seeing her standing alone, feeling out of place and rejected by her supposed best friend who'd invited her to the banquet. She'd been there for more than thirty minutes, and not yet had anyone tried to introduce themselves to her or ask her who she was. No one showed any signs of human companionship. Nah, they just mocked her and whispered vulgar things, inquiring the worst about her.

"Maybe somebody should check to see if she's lost," Mathew said.

"She's not lost. She's just here for the free food, probably trying to steal and interrupt our perfectly put-together occasion," Tina protested.

"Tina, you don't know that."

"Please, Mathew, look at her. Someone needs to call security."

"I thought that this was a charity banquet to help raise money for the unfortunate," Mathew stated, breaking away from Tina.

"It is. So I don't see why these people just don't stay uptown. It should be like heaven for them in the ghetto. Don't they receive enough benefits from the government? For Christ's sake, Mathew, we give 'em just enough to be happy. And besides, look at her, dressed like some two-dollar hooker."

Mathew just gawked at Tina—his supposed love. Then he glanced over at Toni, still standing alone, still being ridiculed, and mocked, already being judged, no one knowing her character.

It was hurting her inside, the stares, the mockery, and the scowls. All she wanted to do was go home. She searched the room for Vinita, who happened to have disappeared from her sight in the past forty-five minutes.

"Care for another hors d' oeuvres?" the male servant asked, towering over Toni and carrying a silver platter.

Toni nodded, taking one off the platter. "Thank you," she said.

But the servant didn't leave. He looked at her, smiling generously. He was a handsome fellow, nice fade, smooth goatee, thick eyebrows, and broad shoulders. He leaned in toward her and whispered in her ear, "Look, my shift ends at midnight, so I was hoping that me and you could hook up later."

Toni looked at him, confused. "Excuse me?" she exclaimed.

"You know, probably hook a brotha up. I know you 'bout ready to get outta here soon, being around these tight asses. Cheeks so tight, they can make diamonds out of coal."

Toni laughed. It was the first laugh she had all night.

"Nah, I'm cool," she politely told him. She didn't take insult to his proposition. After all, it wasn't like she didn't get down for hers.

"Ayyite, don't mind these folks tho'. The closest they came to being poor was riding past Harlem."

She chuckled, amused by his silly antics. *He's stupid,* she said to herself.

Across the room, away from Toni's sight, Vinita was thrilled to be engaged in a delightful conversation with Mrs. Richards and her opulent circle of friends. Vinita sipped on expensive white wine, dined on truffles, and forgot all about Toni.

She was happy—happy to be fitting in with the elite

crowd, a crowd of people she felt she somehow related to, even though she didn't come from a wealthy background.

Born in Brooklyn, raised in Coney Island, and presently living in the Gravesend housing projects off Neptune Avenue, Vinita felt that the life she was living, residing in the slums of Brooklyn, was never meant for her. Since she was young, she always felt or tried to believe that maybe she was switched during her birth—her real parents were rich and wealthy with a house on a hill, a swimming pool, etc. She hated her real parents. Her mother was a waitress at a local diner on Cropsey and Canal. She'd been a waitress for more than twelve years. Her father was a city bus driver, which he'd done for twenty years. Her older sister, Nancy, was a mother to three children, unmarried, and living in a two-bedroom apartment in Queens, under Section 8, having the government support her. Nah, that wasn't meant to be Vinita's real life. She wasn't meant to live like that, with the family only having access to one vehicle, and with her having to deal with the drugs and the poverty that engulfed her home and her neighborhood every day. She was meant to live the good life, like the people at the banquet she was attending. This was how life should be—at least for her.

An hour had already passed, and still feeling not wanted, Toni attempted to leave alone. She was lost in her own private thoughts while the banquet still continued with her presence. She didn't seem to be a threat, so the guests carried on with their event, excluding the one unwanted outcast.

Tina was constantly gazing over at Toni. She was disturbed by her being there, feeling she was disrespecting her and every other decent citizen in the place. Chatting with a group of acquaintances, with everyone holding a glass, Tina ranted, "Somebody needs to do something about her. She's unwelcome."

"I certainly agree, Tina," a middle-aged black woman sided.

"Tina, she's not causing any harm to anyone," Mathew spoke in Toni's defense.

"Yes she is, Mathew, by coming to this banquet uninvited."

"How do you know she's not invited?" Mathew asked.

"For God's sake . . . look at her, Mathew, coming here dressed in that vulgar attire. Who would invite her to such a formal function like this? Who would even dare want to be associated with such . . . with such . . . an unscrupulous person anyway?"

"I thought this was a charity banquet for the unfortunate, the poor, the inner city, and yet we stand here and criticize—"

"Mathew, stop trying to justify the woman," Tina cut him off. "It's obvious that I'll have to be the *woman* of this event and see to it that she gets dismissed."

Tina hurried off in Toni's direction as Toni still stood there—alone. Toni's eyes were transfixed on Tina as she approached her with her luxurious gown flowing behind her.

"Excuse me," Tina said, catching Toni's attention.

"Yes?"

"Do you have an invite to be here?" Tina asked in a dreadful manner.

"Yes, but I came wit' a friend," Toni replied.

"Wit' a friend," Tina mimicked her, chuckling.

"Yes, but I lost her on the way in," Toni coyly said.

"You do know that this party is invites only. I've been watching you for the past hour, and it seems that no one has greeted you. So whatever it is you came to steal, you can forget about it. Now I would appreciate it if you leave here before I call security and have you arrested and thrown out."

Shocked and embarrassed, Toni's gaze darted around the room, staring at all the eyes glued to her. People looked on, and no one said a word as Tina humiliated her in front of hundreds of guests.

What bothered Toni more than the woman's words was when she spotted Vinita standing across the room, gazing over at her, not coming to her aid and not identifying her. Vinita stood there, peering over at her like she was some stranger.

Toni didn't call out her name, but she felt her eyes tearing up. "I'm sorry," she demurely apologized.

"Please leave," Tina repeated sternly.

Toni began to walk backward away from Tina. She bumped into one of the servants, toppling over him and causing him to spill his tray of drinks onto the floor, shattering glass and spilling wine and champagne,

"Dear God," a woman spoke. "Clumsy."

Toni scurried out of the room, not looking behind her, embarrassed and feeling disrespected.

Tina returned to Mathew and her companions, saying, "It had to be done."

Mathew glared at her, shaking his head in disbelief. "I need to get some fresh air," he said, leaving the scene with Tina gazing angrily at him.

Toni rushed to the elevator with tears in her eyes, feeling that Vinita had humiliated and betrayed her. *How she just gonna leave me out to dry like that?* The elevator wasn't coming to the floor fast enough for her.

Mathew, feeling that Tina was completely out of line, needed a break—both from Tina and the dull event. He strolled off into the hallway, still hearing sounds from that dreaded banquet as he waited for the elevator.

Toni dashed through the hotel lobby as her eyes filled with tears. She needed to get away. She wanted to go home.

Toni made her way to the glass lobby doors, flying through and collapsing onto the concrete steps in front of the hotel. She sat on her butt and wept. She didn't care what Tina had to say. It was just that she felt played and disrespected by her own friend, the one who had invited her in the first place, even when she didn't want to attend.

Toni sat there alone consoling herself. No one bothered to disturb the grieving woman. They just glanced at her and went on their way.

"Do you need a Kleenex?" Mathew asked, standing over her, feeling sorry for her.

"No," Toni answered, not bothering to look up at him.

There was sudden silence between the two as Mathew still stood over her and glanced up and down Fifth Avenue. He was at a loss for words. He felt bad for the poor woman.

"I'm sorry for what happened in there. Tina can be harsh with words sometimes," Mathew said, taking a seat next to her.

Toni didn't respond. She just continued to sit there, sulking. The truth was, she wasn't upset with Tina. She was upset with her best friend, Vinita, who'd abandoned her and started mingling with guests while Toni stood there alone and out of place. She was the one who'd brought her there. That shit was really impolite.

"Are you just going to sit here all night?" Mathew asked.

"I just want to go home," Toni finally said.

He gazed into her young, stunning face. *She's cute,* he thought.

"Do you need for me to call you a cab? I'll be happy to," Mathew offered.

"No. I can make my own way back home."

"Well, let me make up for Tina's rudeness and buy you a drink. You are over twenty-one, right?" he playfully asked.

Toni cracked a slight smile across her teary face and answered, "Yes."

She gazed back at Mathew and thought he was really attractive—dressed really nice too. But she knew that she wasn't his type and vice versa. She wiped away her tears with the tip of her fingers, then stood. Mathew did the same, rising to his feet.

"Might I add, you do look nice, and you're a very beautiful young woman?" He tried to cheer her up and meant every word of his compliment. "By the way, my name is Mathew," he introduced, extending his hand to her. There was something about her that he liked, that he was captivated by. *Maybe because she's different,* he thought.

Toni just looked at him, thinking he must be crazy, or worse, he probably thought that she was just another ho, and he was willing to pay a healthy fee for her services. Though it was true, that she did sell herself sexually for cash, she wasn't fond of the jobs she performed, but the rent and the bills had to be paid. And with her moms out of commission, someone had to step up and make due, make ends meet at her home.

"Look, I have to—"

"Mathew," Tina called out, standing at the top of the steps, her face scowled up.

Startling them both, Toni and Mathew looked up at

Tina. Her arms were folded across her chest, and she looked like the queen of all bitches.

"Tina," Mathew meekly responded.

"What in God's name do you think you're doing, standing out here chattering with that street trash?"

She walked down a few steps, looked fiercely over at Toni, and insultingly said, "Excuse me, but didn't I throw you out? My fiancé is not one of your tricks." Her eyes were cold as she stared at Toni.

"I'm sorry," Toni bleakly apologized as she darted down the steps to the street.

Mathew gazed on in sorrow. *She's a sweet girl,* he thought.

"Mathew, how dare you insult me like that, coming out here, holding a conversation with the likes of her? We've got people waiting for us upstairs. You have embarrassed me by rushing out like some fool, and then I find you out here with her. Now come on, Mathew, we have people waiting. We'll deal with this matter later," Tina spoke, heading back into the Plaza with Mathew following her.

He wished he could have chatted with Toni for a bit longer. She seemed like an interesting girl to get to know. The only ladies Mathew had been around were the ones who acted and talked like his mother and Tina. He was raised to marry high standards—a woman with a Ph.D., or nothing less than a master's degree; a woman with a healthy and wealthy background; a woman raised with both parents still married and living under the same roof; a woman who knew how to hold a fork and a knife and who could carry on a civilized conversation in the midst of a well-educated crowd.

-Seven-

There was the war on drugs, but who were the people at war with? The government? The Colombians? The street dealers or the kingpins? The C.I.A? Or, were they at war with themselves? In the seventies, it was heroin. In the eighties, it was crack/crack cocaine. In the nineties, when Tec was in his prime, it was marijuana/weed, cocaine, ecstasy, etc.

So many men, so many women, and so many companies became millionaires, even billionaires because of the drug trade. It was a profitable business—at a high risk. A low-key neighborhood dealer could make up to two, three hundred dollars a day standing on a street corner hustling, making ten times more than he would working in McDonald's or Burger King. It was a glamorous business, especially if you were growing up used to having nothing—not a dime to your name.

Tec at twenty-four years old was still running the streets like he was fifteen. His father was dead, shot ten years ago in a dice game gone bad, and his mother had been in and out of rehab since he was seven. His older brother was serving a fifteen-year bid upstate, charged with twenty counts of assault, armed robbery, attempted murder, and extortion. He copped a deal with the D.A. and received a reduced sentence.

He had no other family, no other relatives. It had just been him, growing up in Brooklyn, learning the streets, taking in negativity from so many folks all his life. It was easy for him to believe that since no one gave a fuck about him, there was no reason for him to give a fuck about himself or others, especially when no one had ever given him a chance.

His only family was his homies out there on the streets, hustling along with him day by day. His real family was fucked up and dysfunctional, with a father who drank every night, gambled, and beat the shit out of his young son for doing nothing more than breathing the same air. Seeing his older brother murder and assault someone at the age of eight, and his mother cradling and loving her drugs more than she did him, Tec felt unwanted and abandoned. There was no supporting hand or kind words—just hate, anger, and more hate. So Tec just took that same hate and anger coming from his household and distributed it out onto the streets, becoming a bully and punishing those around him—getting involved in incriminating situations. Why? Because he was born and raised around negativity. So now he had to bring that negativity.

On this night Tec was sitting in the front passenger seat of a burgundy Mazda 929 with dark tinted windows, cruising around Coney Island with his crew, Pinch-Back and Little Boy Ronny. Of course he was looking for nothing but trouble. It was in his blood.

Tec and his crew were cruising down Surf Avenue at around eleven at night, stereo blasting hot 97.1 FM, seats reclined, marijuana smoke filling the air on a warm spring night in June. It'd been a week since Tec's little run-in with Cory-D, but he didn't think twice about it. If that niggah was gonna bring it, he better come off strong, 'cause Tec was ready to kill for his.

The burgundy 929 headed west, profiling at thirty-five miles per hour as niggahs were checking out the neighborhood, seeing what was new and who was who. The ride was quiet as they all listened to some Tupac. Little Boy Ronny sat behind Pinch-Back, who was driving, and Tec rode shotgun with his window half rolled down. He just kept quiet. His mind was focusing on something, but he was not saying what.

They drove down 37th Street, riding parallel with Sea-gate, then turned right on Neptune, heading toward his buildings, Gravesend. In Brooklyn, especially in the spring and summer months, no one went to bed early, so eleven at night was like three in the afternoon.

They passed a few guys rolling dice in front of a bodega, then down a few more blocks they came upon three local females, who were walking and laughing and being very loud. Tec stared at one he used to fuck wit'. Her name was Giggles. But he didn't shout her out. He just kept his eyes fixed on her for a few moments while the 929 cruised by very slowly.

"Yo, ain't that Giggles?" Little Boy Ronny asked.

"Yeah, so what?" Tec responded offhandedly.

"I'm sayin'. You still fuckin' that bitch?"

But Little Boy Ronny received no answer, just eerie silence. The car turned down Bay View, driving past Kaiser Park, then around by the sea, where Pinch-Back parked the car across the street from the buildings. Tec stepped out and took a quick piss a few feet from the car. He returned just as the weed was passed to him.

The three men just hung around, got high, and drank Hennessy and E&J for the next hour or so.

By one in the morning, the ignition was started back up, and the 929 was on the move again. They navigated through the back streets, then proceeded back down Neptune.

"Yo, hit up Mermaid," Tec told Pinch-Back.

He did, driving west. A few blocks down, a couple of fellows were just hanging around, drinking, and some still were peddling off what was left of their drugs to the late-night creeps, who slept three, maybe four, hours a day.

Mermaid Avenue was somewhat quiet that night. Just a few Brooklyn heads were out, and the traffic was slow with only two or three cars passing by every few minutes. The only stores open were the twenty-four-hour bodegas that served their customers through a small, one-inch-thick, revolving square glass window, with the rest of the place caged off by iron gates.

Pinch-Back drove down Mermaid, doing speeds only up to twenty miles per hour. He pulled the vehicle to the curb where three men were passing the nightly hours away by gambling and chilling on the corner. All three men took notice of the 929 and became quiet.

"Yo, what up, Napo?" Tec greeted dryly as he stepped out of the car.

"Oh, what up, Tec?" Napo greeted nervously, a little startled by his presence.

The other two men standing next to Napo remained quiet, trying to mind their own business. Tec walked up to Napo, giving him dap and gazed into his eyes.

"Yo, you got my money?" Tec asked.

Napo nodded, reaching into his pocket. His baggy jeans were sagging just a little off his ass. He was wearing a wife-beater and a pair of old Jordans, with his hair in a frazzled state. He stood six feet, one inch and was a slender fellow.

He handed Tec a wad of crumpled bills—some tens, some fives, and some twenties. Tec took the money and started counting. Pinch-Back and Little Boy Ronny remained seated in the car, watching.

Napo stood nervously as he watched Tec count up his loot from the day. The other two who were standing on the corner took a few steps backward as one leaned against a payphone and the other stranger stood with his hands in his pockets.

"Yo, you're a few C-notes short," Tec proclaimed.

"I'm sayin' tho', Tec, shit's been a little slow these past few days," Napo stated uneasily.

"What? Niggah, no excuses. You're short," Tec repeated himself.

Napo shrugged as he indicated that he had no idea why he came up short or where the rest of Tec's money went. He continued to stand there in front of Tec looking stupid.

"Yo, you're short," Tec again angrily repeated. "What, I'm supposed to let this shit pass?"

"Tec man, I don't know. Business ain't picking up. Look, man, I'll make it up to you."

As swiftly as a cat, Tec reached for his .45 and pointed it at Napo's head. The other two men were in complete shock. One just bolted off, scared for his life. He ran across the street and became a blur. The other stranger stood by the payphone, frozen, scared to shit.

"Empty your fuckin' pockets," Tec shouted.

"What? C'mon, Tec, ain't no need for this—"

"Niggah, I said empty your fuckin' pockets," Tec shouted again.

Napo slowly complied with Tec's request, reaching

into his pockets and pulling out whatever contents he had in them. In his right pocket he pulled out nothing but change and a pack of cigarettes. But in his left pocket, Napo pulled out another wad of bills, clasping the cash in the palm of his hand.

Little Boy Ronny rushed out from the backseat of the car, aiming a silver .45 at the other man's head. The young stranger stared at Little Boy Ronny wide-eyed, looking like he was about to piss on himself.

"Yo, man, what's this about?" the frightened stranger asked with his arms and hands spread widely apart from his torso.

"Niggah, you holding out on me?" Tec asked angrily, staring directly at Napo.

"Nah, Tec, it ain't even nuthin' like that. C'mon, man, you know I ain't gonna do you wrong like that. You looked out for me," Napo pleaded and begged.

But Tec knew the deal. He knew about Napo playing both sides of the game, flipping chips for him and Chills at the same time. He knew something was up when Napo was constantly coming up short with his money for the past three weeks—two-faced muthafucka. And he was cutting him some slack since he used to fuck with his sister, but now this niggah was becoming a nuisance, and that could become a danger to his business.

On the verge of shooting and killing this niggah, Tec cocked back his .45 as Napo panicked and screamed, "C'mon, Tec, don't do this shit. Yo, I'll get you your money."

"Yo, Tec, hurry this shit up," Pinch-Back yelled from the driver's seat of the car, distracting Tec for a brief second, one second too long. Napo unexpectedly tossed the wad of bills into Tec's face, then darted off faster than lightning could strike.

Tec raced after Napo, licking off five shots, aiming directly at his head and back, but all five shots missed. Napo was too swift, racing down the block and disappearing into the dark, pumped with adrenaline.

"Yo, I'm gonna kill that niggah," Tec exclaimed.

He rushed back to where Little Boy Ronny still had the young frightened stranger at gunpoint by the payphone, with his eyes wide with panic, trembling.

"Niggah, run your shit," Tec said, aiming his weapon at the man's head.

But the scared young man just looked at him, not understanding or probably just too scared to comprehend. He stared at Tec, then over at Little Boy Ronny, as both men aimed their weapons point blank at some part of his anatomy.

"Niggah, you fuckin' deaf? I said run your shit, take that shit off," Tec angrily repeated himself, snatching a gold chain from around the man's neck.

The guy, shaking like he was in some kind of earthquake, slowly started to take off every piece of his jewelry—from the rings, to his bracelets and even his studded diamond earrings. He tossed everything to the ground, then stood there, peering over at Tec.

"Niggah, you ain't done yet? I said take all that shit off," Tec shouted.

The guy just stood there looking confused—lost.

"Strip, niggah," Tec shouted.

"Yo, Tec, c'mon, man, if you gonna shoot this niggah, then shoot him," Pinch-Back said, being aware that the five-O might be coming around soon, probably alerted by the five shots that were just fired. Although it was rare that a neighbor would call the cops, because hearing gunfire was like hearing fireworks on the Fourth of July—people got used to it.

The shivering man slowly started to take off his clothing, starting from his denim jacket, all the way down to his socks, leaving him standing in his boxers. Tec loved it. He loved to see the fear in a man's eyes once he had a nine-millimeter pointed at him. Niggahs were quick to follow orders when staring down a barrel of a chrome single-action caliber .45 ACP with a four-inch barrel.

"Niggah, the boxers too," Tec stated, smirking.

"Yo, you gonna leave this niggah ass out?" Little Boy Ronny asked, chuckling.

"Yup."

The man was in tears as he dropped his boxers, standing ass out and alone at one in the morning, naked from head to toe and covering his most prized possession.

Tec laughed and uttered, "Fuckin' bitch-ass niggah, it ain't that cold out."

It'd been five minutes, and five minutes too long, Pinch-Back thought. Little Boy Ronny scooped up the man's clothes, dashing back into the car. Tec stared at the frightened and humiliated poor soul and warned, "Niggah, if I catch you back around here again, I'm gonna gun you down. And tell that faggot-ass Napo he better leave town, 'cause I'm gonna kill that son of a bitch when I see his ass again." And then he quickly hopped back into the passenger seat as the car screeched off.

All three men started laughing at the expense of that poor soul they left naked on Mermaid Avenue.

"See how scared that niggah looked," Little Boy Ronny said.

"That's how we gotta start doing niggahs. If we ain't killing 'em, then we is stripping them niggahs down," Tec said. "You know how embarrassed a man is when he ain't got no clothes on? You strip a niggah of everything, and there goes his muthafuckin' dignity, his muthafuckin' pride, his self-respect. We gotta let these fools know we about to strike. I'm coming off hard on these niggahs. Fuck Chills. I'm about to let niggahs know who is running these streets."

"You about to go to war wit' that niggah?" Little Boy Ronny asked.

"Niggah, we been at war."

-Eight-

"C'mon Toni, I can't touch that raw?" the middle-aged man asked. He stood there in a red house robe and a pair of flip-flops with a cigar hanging from his lips. His name was Lewis, and he was willing to pay Toni three hundred for the night for her services.

"Sorry, Lewis. No glove, no love," Toni proclaimed the old saying.

It was eleven, soon to be midnight, and Toni found herself in Lewis' midtown apartment, ready to satisfy this man's needs. He had been trying to get a private VIP session with her for months. But Toni didn't do business outside of the club. It was for her own safety. But tonight, she was making an exception. Her rent was a week overdue and her phone was on the verge of being cut off. And the three hundred that Lewis was paying her would surely cover her rent since she was only two hundred dollars short.

Toni stood in the center of his bedroom wearing tight blue jeans that accentuated her hips and curvaceous, sexy figure, a small white T-shirt, and a pair of

Reeboks. Lewis came out of the bathroom wearing nothing underneath his house robe. He was ready to get down to business. Lewis was not an attractive man. He had a thick black mustache, big ears, a few razor bumps, and dark circles around his eyes. But he did have money, and he was willing to pay any fine, healthy woman for a night of pleasure. He had been eyeing Toni since he had seen her dance at the Bottom Dollar four months ago. He wanted her alone for a night over at his apartment. After being rejected by her many times, he was exuberant that this day that he had predicted had finally come.

"You not gonna get undressed?" Lewis asked, walking over toward the bed.

"Give me a minute," Toni said.

"I've got all night, baby," Lewis said, removing a CD from a case and placing it in the CD drive of the stereo system located next to his bed. He pressed play, and the sounds of Keith Sweat's CD, *I'll Give All My Love to You,* played throughout the bedroom.

"Dance for me, like you be dancing in the club," Lewis suggested, smiling while lying back against the headboard with one leg propped up on the bed.

"Where's my three hundred first?" Toni asked.

He reached into his robe pocket and pulled out three crisp one hundred dollar bills. He placed them on the nightstand.

Getting her nerves together, Toni took a deep breath and started to slowly strip. She tried to put herself in the mood for a man that she was not at all attracted to. She took off her T-shirt first, tossing it to the floor. In her bra, she then seductively started unbuckling her pants and moving to the rhythm of the Keith Sweat song.

"How old are you, anyway?" Lewis asked, interrupting her.

"Why does it matter to you? You still gonna fuck me, right?"

"Yeah, I just thought I'd ask," he said, chuckling.

Within minutes, Toni was in nothing but her bra and panties. Her skin was sleek and smooth—flawless. She touched herself from head to toe, caressing her breasts, reaching down to her stomach, then sticking her hands into her panties, massaging her vagina lightly for her host as she gazed up at the ceiling.

"Yeah, I like that," he excitedly uttered out.

Pervert, Toni thought.

She turned her back to him, squeezing her ass, and then parting her thighs by bending her knees. Lewis was very much turned on, as his hard-on came into full view from out of his robe while he stared at her wide-eyed.

"Get naked for me, baby," he said, panting while stroking his penis.

Following his instructions, Toni unfastened her bra from the front, exposing her petite, animated breasts. Her circular chocolate nipples were erect from touching herself lustfully. Then she slowly removed her panties by leaning forward and pulling them down nice and slow, letting them fall to the floor before stepping out of them. She stood in front of Lewis ass naked, with her beautiful brown skin shimmering in front of his eyes.

"You ready for this?" Lewis asked as he removed himself from off the bed, untying his robe and dropping it to the floor. He stood naked with his belly protruding about six inches. He had a hairy chest and flabby arms.

Keeping herself from gagging, Toni smiled and thought about the three hundred dollars, her rent, and supporting herself. *This is the only way,* she thought. She glanced down at his hairy, fat penis, which was about five inches hard, and prepared herself for the worst.

He walked up to her, cupping his hand around one of her breasts and covering it whole, then kissing and licking on her nipples with his wet tongue, and squeezing her ass with the other available hand. He then scooped her up into his arms, all 125 pounds of her, and placed her back down on her feet. For the next five minutes his hands were all over her, exploring every detail of her body, sliding between her thighs, kissing on her breasts, rubbing on her butt, and scratching her pubic hair. Toni closed her eyes as she reluctantly let Lewis molest her sexy body for the three hundred dollars.

They went over to the bed where Lewis took a seat and pushed Toni down on her knees, motioning that she give him a blowjob. She complied, gripping his erect penis, fondling it lightly for a few seconds, then unwillingly placing his erection into her mouth, bobbing her head up and down, hoping he'd come quickly.

Lewis let out a pleasurable moan, grasping a handful of her braids and leaning against one arm that he propped on the bed.

"Oh, shit, oh, shit . . . damn," he groaned.

Toni, stroking and sucking, stroking and sucking, gave him the works by also tickling his nuts. The Keith Sweat CD continued to play softly in her ear. She had been down on her knees for about five minutes.

"Okay, you can stop," he told her.

Toni stood as Lewis, with the broadest smile across his face, peered at her with high regard. "Damn, you give some great fuckin' head," he complimented.

"C'mon, Lewis, let's get this over with," Toni said to him.

"Ah, no rushes, baby. We got all night, don't we?"

"Whatever. How you wanna do this?" she asked, looking annoyed.

"Whichever way pleases you the most."

Toni climbed on the bed, lying on her back, parting her legs and waiting for him to enter her.

"Yo, do I gotta use this condom? I wanna feel that pussy raw. I ain't got nuthin'. You can trust me."

"I don't fuck without condoms," Toni sternly repeated herself.

"I'll give you another hundred," he offered.

"No! It's not happening. C'mon, Lewis, I don't have all night."

Lewis sighed, ripped open the condom, and rolled it back on his small penis. Toni didn't know what the infatuation was with him wanting to fuck her raw, but she knew, no matter how much money he offered, she still was not fucking him or any one of her tricks without it. It was like the one moral she had left for herself. The only man who had been screwing her without one was Keith, and she was still suspicious about having him going raw up in her sometimes.

What the fuck was she thinking when she let this niggah climb on top of her with his 265-pound heavy ass? His sweaty, fat belly was pressed against her as he tried to ease his penis quickly into her, not even causing her to let out a gasp of satisfaction. He started to thrust and pump, wheezing like some kid with asthma. Her legs were spread widely apart because of his gut.

"Damn, you got some good pussy," Lewis proclaimed while stroking it.

Toni just lay there, not responding to his comment. Yeah, she knew her shit was good. Many niggahs had already told her about her stuff. It was how she was paying her bills—marketing her pussy. Too bad she couldn't sell it over the Internet.

Toni continued to lay on her back while Lewis fucked her. She had to catch herself from yawning a few times, afraid it might hurt his feelings. But why should she care? She caught herself listening more to the CD than paying attention to the sex.

"Doggy style," he announced.

"You're coming, right?" she asked.

"Yeah, baby, I'm almost there," he said, sweating something seriously, with perspiration all over his face

She turned herself over on her knees, gripping the headboard of the bed with both hands. She felt him quickly stuff his dick into her, pumping hard, but it wasn't really doing anything for her.

They rattled the bed, with him moving tremendously, hitting it from the back, her ass slapping against his nuts, pushing air in and out of her pussy. He gripped her slim waist as he shouted out, "I'm gonna come, I'm gonna come."

And then within seconds after announcing it, he let it off into her, shuddering, shouting out, "Oooh, God. Damn . . . aaaaaahhh, that shit felt so good. Oh, I needed that shit." Afterward he pulled out and collapsed on his back beside Toni, breathless, relieved, and sweating hard.

Toni, feeling that something wasn't right, glanced down at his penis and noticed that the condom wasn't strapped on. While he lay there feeling like he was the shit, she frightfully asked, "What happened to the condom?"

"Oh, I pulled that shit off a while ago," he said, smirking up at her.

"What? Are you stupid? Muthafucka, are you crazy? Are you crazy?" she hysterically screamed, jumping off the bed in a panic and seeing the condom on the floor next to the bed.

"Don't stress it, baby. That shit wasn't doing it for me. I had to feel that pussy raw sooner or later. Besides, I ain't got any diseases."

"What? Lewis, I can't believe you did that shit. Oh my God, oh my God, oh my God," she raved, clutching her chest.

"What the fuck you getting so worried for? It was good, wasn't it? And it ain't like you didn't know."

Toni wandered around the room, collecting her things and saying to Lewis, "Never again, never again."

"C'mon, Toni, you're tripping over some stupid shit. I told you I wanted to feel it . . . ."

"Lewis, never again," she repeated, still hysterical.

She had her jeans on and her sneakers were in her hands. Lewis was still naked on the bed, watching her scurry around his bedroom acting a fool.

"It was good, though, right, bitch?" he stated.

"Fuck you, you nasty fat-ass bastard," she rebuked, throwing on her T-shirt.

"Now you're getting ahead of yourself," he angrily said to her, being very sensitive about his weight.

"You ain't nuthin' but a fat, ignorant asshole. I told you I don't fuck without protection. Why did you go there? That ain't right, Lewis," she said, feeling herself getting emotional.

She went to the nightstand to collect her money, but Lewis jumped in front of her. "What do you think you're doing?" he asked.

"Collecting my fee."

"No, you're not. You insult me and expect for me to pay you? Get the fuck out of my apartment, stupid bitch."

"No, you owe that to me."

"I don't owe you shit. Now bounce."

"Lewis, that ain't right. I want my money," she demanded.

"Get the fuck outta my apartment," he said, shoving her and causing her to fall to the floor, landing on her side. Then he reached into the drawer of his nightstand and pulled out a .22, aiming it at her. "Now, I'm not gonna repeat myself again. I said get the fuck outta my apartment." He scowled, looking like he meant business.

Toni gazed up at him, her face frightened, staring up at the .22 in horror. A few tears started to trickle down her cheeks as she slowly picked herself up and continued to collect the rest of her things with Lewis still pointing the gun at her.

She wanted to say something, but hesitated. She wanted to yell threatening comments to him, warn him to watch his back next time he came to the club, how she'd have a few niggahs waiting for him—waiting to kill him. But she kept quiet. She didn't know why, but she kept quiet, crying to herself, and being out of three hundred dollars that she was owed.

Lewis kept the gun in his hand 'til she was out the door and out of his sight. Then he slammed the door on her, cursing, "Stupid, dumb bitch. Pussy's better when it's free."

Toni burst out in more tears as she hurried out of the building, running up the block as fast as she could, nearly tripping and falling on her ass. Then she stopped on the corner and took a seat against a cold, brick wall. She continued to sob into her hands. What was she to do? She was out three hundred dollars for her rent, and what was worse, Lewis had totally violated her. The more she thought about his nasty semen swimming around in her, the more she wanted to throw up. Becoming pregnant was one of her worst fears, especially becoming pregnant by some john. And another fear was catching an STD. She didn't know what the fuck this niggah was carrying, even though he assured her that he didn't have any diseases. But the more she thought about it, the harder she sobbed.

Mathew relaxed in the backseat of his limo, cruising around midtown, coming from another senseless dinner with Tina, who loved to dine in the most distinguished restaurants around Manhattan, the country, and the world. It was the thing she loved to do. Just last month, they both flew out to London so that she could dine at L'Odeon, tasting the restaurant's exciting dishes.

He was thrilled that Tina decided to spend the night in her own luxurious penthouse apartment, located on the west side of Manhattan. Now he could relax and have his driver, Damien, drive him around the city without Tina's bickering.

He listened to his Marvin Gaye CD over the limousine's plush stereo system, collecting his thoughts. Tina didn't like listening to soul music, R&B—or worse, rap. She preferred the classical masterpieces, operas, string orchestras—that easy-listening crap. She said that anything else was tasteless and vulgar. And the only time Mathew could enjoy listening to the music he liked was when she was not around.

It was a warm night, so Mathew had the windows rolled down fully, taking in the picturesque sights of the city's nightlife. He was stretched out in the backseat and peered out the window, riding down Park Avenue.

"Do you want me to swing back around the block?"

Damien asked. He had been driving Mathew around Manhattan for the past hour or so.

"No, Damien, you can continue to head downtown," Mathew said to him.

They had become quite good friends and bonded as good companions. Damien had been Mathew's driver for a little over two years. Mathew referred to his driver as Damien, unlike Tina, who still continued to call him, "Driver." "Driver, pull over. Driver, stop here. Driver, run in and get me a cup of cappuccino. Driver, you're driving too fast. Slow down before you get me killed," she would say. Even though Damien was sick of her uppity, bitchy attitude and just wanted to toss her out the door sometimes, he showed her respect due to the fact that she was still Mathew's fiancée.

They came past Bryant Park, where Mathew noticed something. He called to Damien, telling him to stop the car and back up. Damien, without question, put the car in reverse and backed up a few feet. Mathew peered out the window, recognizing Toni, and seeing her seated against the concrete sidewalk all alone, seeming upset about something. It'd been a week since he tried to introduce himself to her. Now it was like fate or something, seeing her again for the second time, but also catching her in the same predicament that he had left her—upset, crying, and alone.

He stepped out of the limo, walking toward her slowly.

"Hello, once again," he said, standing over her while she had her head slumped over her knees. "Are you OK? Do you need some assistance?"

Toni, wiping her eyes, looked up and replied, "Just go away."

"You don't remember me. We met a week ago at the

Plaza, and you were crying then too." He paused, then asked again, "Are you sure you're OK?"

Toni didn't answer him. She just closed her eyes and continued to sob. Mathew just stood there, and once again felt sorry for her. He crouched down in front of her, and asked, "Excuse me, but can I be of some assistance?"

Toni slowly shook her head.

"Well, can I know your name?" he humbly asked.

"Toni," she coyly responded.

"Well, Toni, my name is Mathew, and I don't mean to be a nuisance to you—"

"Well, don't be," she interrupted.

"Look, let me give you a ride home. That's my limo over there," he mentioned, pointing at the white limousine parked just a few yards away. "It's the best I can do, and I apologize for Tina's behavior the other night. She was totally out of line."

Toni dried away the last of her tears, took a deep breath, then harshly said, "Look, what do you want from me? Do I look that pathetic to you?"

"No, no, I don't mean to be insulting. It's just, this is New York City, and things can happen late at night, especially to a beautiful young woman like yourself. I just don't want to see you get hurt."

"You don't even know me," she chided, "and besides, I've already done had worst things happen, and a rich jerk like you ain't gonna stop them from happening again."

"Let me just take you home safely. It's my way of apologizing for the way Tina mistreated you."

"I'm no charity case. I can take care of myself," Toni said, rising from off the concrete, with Mathew doing the same, standing straight up.

"I never said that you were," he said kindly, giving her a smile.

Toni thought it over, from Manhattan to Brooklyn by train was an awful long ride, especially with it being so late at night. And it didn't make her situation better by her only having four dollars to her name. She had already been robbed twice taking the subway home so late at night. The first time, two males jumped on her, snatched her purse and jewelry, and copped themselves a cheap feel in the process. And the second time, some unknown assailant held her up at gunpoint, forcing her to give up her $150 she had just made that night.

But then again, she didn't know this guy. He could be some rich serial rapist/killer, preying on young, upset, and vulnerable women, dumping their lifeless bodies in the East River. She weighed her options while she stared into Mathew's eyes, taking in his handsome and charming face. *He looks innocent enough,* she thought. *What harm can come about?*

She let out an agonizing sigh, then meekly said to him, "OK."

"I'm as harmful as a bee is to honey," he joked.

She let out a little laugh. She was slowly emerging from her sour mood. She collected her belongings from off the ground and followed Mathew to the limo.

Damien jumped out from the driver's seat, rushing to get the door for Mathew, but Mathew waved his hand, signaling for him to stay in place. He had the door. He opened the passenger door for Toni, displaying his gentlemanly manners and allowed her to step inside. Then he went in right behind her.

Toni was overwhelmed by the lavish interior—the plush leather seats, the legroom, the mini bar, the television, and the quality sound system playing Marvin

Gaye. Her gaze darted everywhere inside as she took a seat, touching the smooth leather. She'd never been in a limo before.

"Damien, drive us to . . . excuse me, but you've never mentioned your destination," he uttered.

"Coney Island," Toni blurted, thinking he might get scared and rethink giving her that ride.

"Coney Island, Brooklyn, it is," he told his driver.

Without any questions at all, Damien was en route to Coney Island, heading toward the Battery Tunnel, located in downtown Manhattan.

They went for eight minutes without saying a word to each other. Mathew placed in another Marvin Gaye CD and continued to sit quietly. Toni wasn't a big Marvin Gaye fanatic. She had heard a few of his songs, but collected none of his albums because she wasn't familiar with a lot of his songs. But Mathew loved listening to Marvin Gaye classics, such as "What's Going On" and "Let's Get It On."

"I'm not for sale," Toni suddenly uttered.

"Excuse me?" Mathew said.

"Whatever you're thinking, I'm not for sale," she repeated. But she said it to see his response. She wanted to see how nice of a guy he really was if she made it clear that she wasn't selling herself for sex, which was a boldfaced lie. With the money he was probably banking, she could probably ease a few hundred out of him, maybe in the range of five hundred to eight hundred dollars. But she wanted to catch on to his game. If she rejected him early, then maybe he'd show his true colors.

"I'm sorry, but pricing you for a night of sex was the furthest thing from my mind," Mathew responded.

"Then why are you being so nice to me? What's the catch?"

"There is no catch. I just saw you sitting alone and thought to be a gentleman and see if you were in need of some assistance, and besides, I owe it to you."

"You don't owe me shit. There are over a million ladies in this city, and you happen to come across me again, seeing me from God knows how far a distance. What, you got 20/20 vision? You got some kinda X-ray vision?" Toni reproached.

Mathew did nothing but chuckle, finding her amusing in some sort of way. "Let's just say, I have very good vision."

"Well, I'm gonna say again, I'm not for sale," she repeated.

Mathew giggled again, then said, "I hope you're not. I don't want any incidents with my fiancée."

They came to Battery Tunnel, where traffic was kinda heavy, causing twenty-minute delays and giving them extra time to associate with each other. Mathew continued to enjoy listening to his Marvin Gaye collection, while Toni just peered out of a limo window.

"So how long has she been your fiancée?" Toni asked.

"Two years now, but technically, she's really not my fiancée," he informed Toni.

Looking baffled, Toni uttered, "What is that supposed to mean?"

"I never proposed to her," he answered.

"So how did she become your fiancée if you never proposed?"

"I guess she figured we're going to get married someday, so she just went on to introducing me to folks as her fiancé, and I just went along with it."

"Y'all rich people are so damn weird. Why be engaged to a woman if you never asked her to marry you in the first place?"

"Well, my mother likes her. They get along really well, and she's like kin to my family. We're very much compatible."

"Your mother likes her," Toni sarcastically replied.

"Tina has some good qualities about her."

What, being a bitch? Toni said to herself. She wanted to get personal, but felt that it wasn't her business, and it wasn't her place to. So she left the issue alone.

"Do you mind if I ask you a question?" Mathew asked.

"Like what kind of question?"

"Why were you sitting alone and crying in the middle of Manhattan, when you live out in Brooklyn? Is there something I can help you with?"

"I mind you asking," Toni rebuked. "And like I told you before, I can take care of myself. What, you think just because you're giving me a ride home, that you can just pry into my private life?"

"No, no, it's nothing like that. Just thought I could help out."

"What is up wit' you with all this helping? What are you, the Red Cross?"

Mathew smiled, admiring her wittiness.

"I learned how to take care of myself a long time ago," Toni continued. "Growing up in Brooklyn and in my hood, sometimes all you have is yourself. But what would you know about that? You're probably so rich, you get people to wipe your ass."

"That's funny," Mathew commented.

"A rich boy like you probably wouldn't last five minutes in my part of town. The brothas would take to you something serious."

"You act like rich folks don't have problems too," Mathew said, still flashing her a friendly smile.

"Problems? What kind of problems do rich people

like you have? What, y'all can't figure out how many millions to invest into that new account, or a dreadful stock crashing? Y'all rich folks ain't seen problems 'til you have lived in a ghetto for quite some time, then you got you some problems," Toni proclaimed with some serious attitude.

"Yeah, just last week, my father lost two million dollars on a bad stock," Mathew said, smirking.

Toni sucked her teeth. She couldn't believe what she had just heard.

"Mr. Mathew, we're coming into Brooklyn now," Damien announced from his seat.

"Thank you, Damien," Mathew said pleasantly, he then asked Toni for her exact address.

All types of questions arose in Toni's head as she wondered how much he was really worth. She came up with a ballpark figure of about sixty, maybe seventy million. And why was he so interested in meeting or helping her out? He could have just easily driven by and didn't have to say shit. Maybe it was his way of giving back to the poor—the community—helping a little poor Negro girl out, then his conscience would be clear of being so filthy rich. Maybe it was his way of personally giving to charity, but despite what she thought, her mind still ran suspicious of him. He seemed innocent and cool, but today, you never knew with these crazies.

They talked during the rest of the ride. Mathew was delighted by her conversation. They disagreed on certain things, yet he found it so easy to talk to her—not like constantly being ridiculed and bickered at by his fiancée, who did most of the chatting while all he did was sit, yawn, and listen. Everything had to be her way, or it was no way at all.

He liked Toni. She was different. She lived in a world he'd never been to, nor knew anything about. He grew up living off *The Wall Street Journal* and *The New York Times,* attending social events and functions at private country clubs, yachting and receiving stockholders shares for Christmas gifts.

He saw Toni as being a sweet and intriguing woman.

The limo pulled up in front of Toni's building on Bay View Avenue. A few spectators outside took notice, curious to see who was inside.

"So, this is your place of residence," Mathew said, peeking out. "Interesting."

"Yeah. It can be a shit hole most of the time, but it's home for me."

There was a brief pause of silence.

"Well, thanks for the ride," Toni said, getting up from her plush leather seat, crouching, and heading for the door.

But Mathew took a hold of her forearm, surprising her. She glared over at him, thinking this was when he became a jerk. But surprisingly, he passed her a wad of hundred dollar bills—one thousand dollars to be exact.

"Here, take this," he insisted. "Maybe it will help take some burden off you."

"No, I can't," she rejected. Her mother, back in her loving and caring motherly days, always preached to her that a woman never received anything for free. Something, no matter how little the gift, always came with a cost sooner or later, especially if it was something given to you by a man. And she had always abided by those rules—never taking anything for free—so in return, she learned to give herself.

But she knew Mathew wouldn't allow it—giving herself for the one thousand dollars. He seemed to be a man with respect and dignity for himself. He insisted that she take the money, with no obligations at all. But Toni was too stubborn to accept free money, so she pushed it back into his hand, saying she couldn't accept it and explained to him why.

They disputed his offer for a few minutes, until Mathew came up with an idea. "Look, my personal maid is going to be out for a week or two, so why don't you work it off then?" he suggested.

"Your maid?" she inquired.

"Yes. If you won't take it for free, then you can work it off in a week or two."

Feeling reluctant, Toni peered long and hard at him. She definitely needed the money, being out three hundred dollars that was rightfully hers in the first place. But with this one thousand dollars, she could pay this and next month's rent, her phone bill, and still probably have a little left over to spend.

"I don't even know where you live," she said.

He reached into his pocket and pulled out a card with his telephone number and the address to his luxurious Manhattan apartment. "So, do we have a deal?"

She kept quiet for a few seconds, then nodded, agreeing to it.

"Good, then. I'll expect to see you next week Monday, say around eleven or twelve," he said, still giving off a warm smile.

She then stepped out of the limo, placing the card into her jean pocket and proceeding toward her building, with the limo still parked out front, not yet budging from its spot.

"I see you got yourself some rich trick," a tired-looking woman proclaimed, sitting on the bottom of the building steps with a friend.

"She got herself some platinum dick," the other joined in.

Toni sucked her teeth, ignoring their nasty comments, and walked past them. She glanced back, finally seeing the limo pull off. *Why did I say yes?* she asked herself, regretting agreeing to his terms. *Shoulda just taken the money in the first place. Fuck what Moms used to preach. Look at her now—a fuckin' junkie.*

She walked into the apartment to find it dark and empty—and, of course, her mother was not home. She had left the place untidy, and the carpet needed a serious vacuuming, but Toni was too tired to even attempt to clean. She just felt like passing out on the floor and not waking up 'til morning. Unfortunately for her, the phone rang, and she already knew who it was. Who else would call her at one in the morning? Why she picked up, she didn't even know, but no one other than Keith answered and announced that he would be over there in another half hour. She was too tired to tell him no. *Let him come and get his fuck on,* she thought. Why not? She'd already been fucked twice tonight, so she might as well make it official and have it happen a third time. He didn't care if she just lay there, as long as his dick was riding up in her.

-Nine-

Vinita stared at herself in the long dresser mirror, clad in a sexy red stretch lace slip, thinking about her date with Myron. She had met Myron two months ago at her college. He was a senior, majoring in computer science and drove around in a red BMW. His father was a proprietor of a few clothing stores located on Fulton Street, Fordham Road, and one in Queens on Jamaica Avenue. His son was one of the best dressed in his college, getting clothes for free, or receiving a phat discount.

Vinita hooked up with Myron, and because of him, she established a nice little job working at the Fulton Street store in downtown Brooklyn, snatching up a manager's position and raking in a nice little paycheck every week.

Myron really liked her. He talked to his father about her whenever he got the chance. He bought her things, took her places, and treated her quite well, yet, he had never met her parents. And this was the first time that he was coming to pick her up from her home—in front of the building anyway. Vinita had been to his exquisite Brooklyn brownstone apartment numerous times.

Her private phone line rang, and she picked up. It was Myron telling her that he was waiting downstairs in the car for her. She told him that she'd be down in another ten minutes.

Dressed in her lovely white lace top, a green herringbone skirt, and a pair of satin slingbacks with rhinestone trim, she stepped out of her bedroom, locking the door behind her, and headed out.

Her father, as he did every night, was passed out on the couch, fast asleep, missing the fourth quarter of the NBA finals— the Chicago Bulls versus the Utah Jazz. Her mother was working another late-night shift down at the diner.

Without waking her father, she walked out the door and proceeded downstairs. As she walked out the front door of the lobby, three young teenagers peered over at her, and one shouted out, "Vinita, when me and you gonna hook up? Damn, you is fine."

His partners laughed at his smart comment, as Vinita, which she did every night, ignored their vulgar verbal attacks and headed out. She walked briskly toward the car, hopping in and giving Myron a quick kiss on the lips to greet him.

Tonight he was taking her to some exclusive club in Manhattan—for members only. He and his father had been a member for more than five years. He was dressed nicely in pressed khakis, a silk shirt, and impressive shoes. He gripped the steering wheel of his ride with one hand, lay back in his seat, and turned up the volume to 98.7 KISS FM with the remote in the other hand. His fade was nicely trimmed and cut.

"What time do we have to be there?" Vinita asked.

"No rush," Myron said.

Myron pulled off. As he did, he slyly placed his hand on her thigh, hoping that that night would be the night. It'd been two months, which was too long for him.

But Vinita wasn't in any rush. She was no virgin, but she wasn't in any hurry to have sex. The last time she had sex was almost eight months ago, and it was with her supervisor, late at night, in his parked car behind the department store where they both worked. It happened once, and to this day, she still didn't know why she really fucked him. Maybe it was a power trip for her.

Her last boyfriend was in high school, some kid named Lenny, the pretty boy type. It lasted for eighteen months, and then she broke it off with him. After that, she never saw any man good enough to give her what she wanted out of life. One, he had to have stability and be financially supportive. Two, he had to be emotionally supportive, cute, and articulate. And three, he had to be able to bring her out of the ghetto, the projects, which meant he had to have his own place, his own home. If she wasn't able to do it for herself, then she needed to have a man to fall back on. She was tired of living with her poor and no-future-having family. She needed out, and if it meant marrying a rich man, then so be it.

Vinita didn't mind Myron's hand being on her thigh. So far, he was a good pick. He had a bright future ahead of him. He had money, good investments, and his father was an entrepreneur. And he had his own place

After their night out, Vinita found herself back at his place, with it going on three in the morning. She really wanted to spend the night with him, not rushing to return to that same ol' drag of an apartment she called home. She loved Myron's place, a two-bedroom brownstone located by Ocean Parkway.

She loved being around his handsome father. He always spoke the right words to her and forever complimented her on how beautiful and remarkable she was, and he was always telling his son not to let *this one* go. Myron would just blush and take quick sips of his drink.

At his home, Myron fixed her another drink, bringing it back into the living room and handing it to her. She sat on his stylish Italian leather couch, glancing over at a dozen pictures that hung on the wall.

He pointed to a picture of himself, a picture she'd never seen since she'd been coming there. He explained that that was him when he was a kid—covered in mud and dirt, standing next to a BMX dirt bike on his tenth birthday.

Vinita chuckled at the picture and said he was cute.

He then placed his hand on her shoulder, massaging it gently, while peering into her eyes. She gazed back, speechless, as Myron then removed the drink he recently gave to her from her hand, placing it on the glass coffee table beside them.

"I've wanted you for so long," Myron gently said as he embraced her in his thin arms.

Vinita's heart started to beat rapidly, and she could smell his minty fresh breath. It had been eight months, and for her, eight months too long, since she had felt the hard sensation of flesh inside her. But she wasn't in any rush—at least she thought so. Yet the slightest touch of him grazing against her skin made her panties moist.

He kissed her softly on her lips, then followed up with another kiss, and so on and so on, until their lips finally locked. Vinita finally gave in after two months and relinquished herself to her sexual desires. She panted heavily, excited as Myron picked her up and carried her off into the bedroom, for a night he had waited for for so long.

She knew Myron was her soon-to-be husband. He would rescue her from the streets of the concrete jungle that she had called home for so long. Like Prince Charming, he would take care of her for the rest of her life. She belonged to Myron that night. He was her rescuer.

-Ten-

Toni must have spent two hours looking for Mathew's apartment as she hopped from train to train, then traveled from bus to bus in search of his place. It was Monday afternoon, a glorious day, with blue skies and temperatures reaching ninety-five, as Toni, in some white shorts and a T-shirt drenched with sweat from the humidity and heat, wandered around Manhattan asking for directions to the address on the card she was given.

Many didn't have a clue. Some pointed her in the wrong direction, causing her to divert back and follow up different directions again. Twenty-one years, and she still didn't have a clue on how to travel around the streets of Manhattan, constantly residing and traveling back and forth in Brooklyn.

Finally, after being lost for forty-five minutes, she was on the right track. A city cabdriver gave her perfect directions, told her that her destination was about ten to fifteen blocks north—between Fifth and Madison avenues. He would've driven her for a fee of seventeen dollars, but she rejected his offer.

At twenty past one, she found herself standing in front of this high-rise building, nervous and having second thoughts. *Quite a wealthy-looking area,* Toni said to herself. There was a doorman standing by revolving lobby doors, a few Town Cars parked out front, and one lady coming out of the building, walking a tiny dog.

She took a deep breath and proceeded forward. As the doorman peered over at her, he stopped her and asked her who she was there to see. He told her that she had to be announced. She showed him Mathew's card, and he reluctantly looked at her, as if she was lying about him inviting her over.

"He knows you're coming?" he asked, seriously doubting her.

"Yes. I have an appointment to see him today," she informed the doorman.

The doorman made the call to Mathew's luxurious twenty-third-floor apartment and announced that he had a visitor out front, a young, intriguing female.

"Yes, let her up," he told the doorman.

"Will do, sir," the kiss-ass doorman replied.

Toni was let through. She waited for the elevator, gazing around the building that looked so fancy and so rich—not anything like the projects.

The elevator door finally opened, and she stepped in. Being the only one inside, she pressed twenty-three and waited. On the twenty-third floor, Toni was greeted with red expensive wall-to-wall carpeting, oil paintings hanging in the hallway, and quiet and serenity. She searched for his door.

Bingo. She found it.

She didn't even get to ring the bell. Mathew unexpectedly opened the door before she got the chance.

"So, I see you decided to show up. Thought you might back out, have second thoughts."

"No. I always keep my word," Toni told him.

"That's good to hear."

She stepped into his apartment, becoming overwhelmed by the structure and the beauty of his penthouse suite.

"Oh my God," she mumbled to herself, staring around the place. It was much more than what she expected.

"Would you like a tour of the place?" Mathew kindly asked.

Toni shrugged, flabbergasted.

He mentioned that his suite had several rooms, including the formal living and dining rooms, the eat-in kitchen, four spacious bedrooms, and one-and-a-half luxurious baths. He then took her out to the terrace that was overlooking the city and Central Park. Toni couldn't describe how she felt. She had never seen the city from so high up before. Her steady view of Manhattan was from the bottom looking way up. Now she was high up looking way down—weird. Toni stood out on the terrace, gazing over the city for a few minutes. Mathew stood next to her, smiling. Then they both stepped back inside.

"So, now that I've showed you everything, you think you can handle the place?"

"Yes," she answered. She had cleaned much worse off places than his apartment. Her apartment alone looked like it had been in World War II and back. *His apartment,* she thought, *isn't much to deal with in the first place.* It was pretty much already tidy, except for a few dishes in the sink, his unmade bed, and the bathrooms. Maybe the mirrors needed cleaning and the Jacuzzi and tub needed scrubbing, but other than that, everything was okay.

"Miranda usually starts the day off in the main bathroom," Mathew explained.

"Not a problem."

Then Toni started laughing.

"What's so funny?" Mathew asked.

"Nah, it just feels like I'm in some sort of sitcom, that's all. You know, me coming here to work for you. A girl coming from out of the ghetto, you being filthy rich and all. It's like something straight off NBC."

Mathew started to laugh along with her, then he said, "Hey, you never know. Write it up and send it in to producers. They may make it a weekly series."

"Yeah, whatever."

"Well, I have to go," Mathew uttered.

"Go? Go where? You gonna leave me here, alone, in your apartment for God knows how long? How do you know that I won't just rip you off and take everything you own?"

"Because I trust you won't."

"Trust? You don't even know me."

"But the fact that you've already brought it up proves that you won't. If you didn't say anything, then I might become suspicious. But you seem to be a trustworthy individual, and you said you're a woman of your word. So I know you'll do really good with the place."

"You are so weird," she said. "When will you be back?"

"Sometime tonight. I have to catch a plane to Baltimore."

"What if your girlfriend walks in?"

"She won't."

"Why not?"

"Because she's shopping in Paris."

Toni sighed. Shopping in Paris, how typical. New York, or anything else American made was probably too low class for her.

"If you have a problem with anything, here's my cell phone number."

Mathew got a call from downstairs from his driver, informing him that the limo was parked out front. He rushed out the door, leaving Toni alone.

Her gaze darted around the place, and she sighed heavily, feeling a bit uncomfortable being in this man's penthouse suite, alone. It gave her some kind of eerie feeling. Her whole apartment could probably fit into one of his bedrooms alone.

But keeping a promise, she retrieved the cleaning materials from a hallway closet and began cleaning, starting with the bathroom.

Within two hours, she was done. Nothing much for her. The bathroom was spotless and his bed neatly made. She mopped the kitchen floor, washed the three or four dishes in the sink, and tidied up the living room.

She became bored.

She went back out onto the terrace and peered over the city for about twenty minutes. Then she took a seat on one of his plush couches in one of the many rooms and relaxed for a moment. She was scared of doing anything else—touching equipment, turning on switches, even opening the front door and walking out of the building, fearing she might get locked out, or not let back in. So she rested her head against the couch and slowly dozed off, taking a three-hour nap.

At five-thirty she awakened from napping like a baby. His couch was more comfortable than her bed. She stretched and yawned, still finding herself in his apartment, thinking maybe it was a dream.

She became incredibly hungry, not having eaten since early morning. She searched through his fridge, but found nothing familiar to her. His fridge was three times bigger than hers, but carried nothing useful for her to munch on—mostly celery sticks, caviar, a few bottles of champagne, brown eggs, frozen liver, etc. It had none of the good stuff she was used to eating, like steak, chicken, a pitcher of Kool-Aid, Twinkies, Devil Dogs, or her favorite, spaghetti or lasagna. She would cook, could cook, and did it very well. But he had nothing to cook.

Hungry and going out of her damn mind, she thought about take-out, but didn't know any numbers to call that might deliver around there. And she thought about just leaving his apartment and going home. Why not? Her job was already done, and done to perfection.

By evening, she felt that it was time for her to leave. She needed something to eat before she passed out. It was about to become dark, and she thought it would be best for her to leave while there was still a little daylight outside, so she would be able to find her way back home. She wrote Mathew a little note, leaving her number, and placed it by the fridge, then she double-checked everything in his elegant apartment and slowly shut the door behind her.

On the way out, she told the doorman good night as she exited through the revolving doors. The doorman kept his eyes fixated on her, admiring her little petite figure and still curious about her visit.

-Eleven-

Four police squad cars drove hastily south down Still-well Avenue. There had been a shooting, possibly a homicide. It was seven in the evening, and the streets were still filled with bystanders, traffic, and pedestrians. The police raced to the scene of the shooting, West 15th Street and Neptune Avenue, over by the Luna Park houses.

There was already a crowd gathered around the taped-off crime scene. Nosy neighbors gazed on, asking what had happened. Flashing red and blue lights from about a dozen law enforcement vehicles drew people's attention.

The victim was twenty-year-old Hasheem Menderson, shot twice in his back. They found three vials of crack/rock stashed on him. Detectives didn't have any witnesses, and most likely this homicide would go down as drug-related and probably unsolved.

This had been the third shooting this week, two of them, fatal. People would talk about the shootings, but there would be no information given to the police. The body was covered, the area dusted and checked, and shell casings were examined.

The two middle-aged white detectives who were on the case probably wouldn't lift a fuckin' finger to solve it. All they probably thought of the man laying dead ahead of them was that some young hoodlum, drug-selling niggah had caught an unlucky break by receiving two bullets in his back. They probably thought he deserved it in the first place. No telling how long this kid's rap sheet could've been.

Across the street, gazing over at the crime scene, were Tec, Little Boy Ronny, and Wallace. They knew what went down, and they knew exactly how it went down. Wallace put the young niggah to rest in the first place. He just walked up to Hasheem, and bang, without warning he put two slugs into his back.

Hasheem was once a loyal solider to Sheek and Tec, but he had turned sides, hustling off vials for Chills, which was disrespectful to Tec. He knew the game. He knew the rules. You just don't leave camp like that. Nah, it didn't work that way. It wasn't that easy. So that 187 had to be done to give the message to any other niggah who was also stupid enough to leave camp and go work for Chills.

Tec was taking no prisoners in the street war between him and Chills. It was conquer everything or don't conquer at all.

All three young men stood, peering across the street for a few minutes, none of them having any remorse for the poor boy. He chose his own destiny.

Hours later, all three men entered the Bottom Dollar, where they paid no charge. Drinks were always on the house, and a few ladies flocked to them like they were silver and gold.

Tec ordered himself a Corona, while Little Boy

Ronny and Wallace went over to the stage to tip half-naked females dollar bills and to pull on their G-strings. The place was not that crowded—it was still a little too early on this Thursday night.

Tec knew about his woman Toni working up in there, doing her thing, getting that money. He didn't care. To him, it was just business for her—business was business, as long as nothing got too personal with any of her customers.

He fucked her for free anyway.

The owner of the club, Malice, personally went out of his way to greet Tec and his crew. Malice was not a small guy at six feet, four inches and 245 pounds, but he was mostly fat. He had tattoos on both arms, slanted eyes, and a bald head.

He knew Tec from way back, before Tec's older brother got locked up. Malice and Tec's brother used to roam real tight back in the day.

"Tec, what up?" Malice greeted, dressed in a blue silk shirt and gray slacks, rockin' a thick gold chain, diamond stud earrings, and a diamond pinky ring.

They gave each other dap, as quick stares were exchanged.

"Toni up in here tonight?" Tec asked.

"Nah, partner. She ain't been here in two days," Malice informed.

"You know where she at right now?" Tec asked

"I thought she was your woman," Malice said, becoming not too pleased with the inquiry.

"But she works for you."

"Niggah, I can't keep account for all my bitches," Malice said to him.

Tec hadn't seen Toni in three days. He'd been to her apartment twice, but she wasn't there and her mother wouldn't know if her daughter was dead or alive. He wanted to find out what was up with her and why she hadn't been around lately.

"Yo, if she comes by, you tell her to give me a call," he told Malice.

"Not a problem."

"Malice," a young employee of his interrupted, "you got some ho throwing up by the deejay," he informed.

"I already done told these bitches, if they can't hold their fuckin' liquor, don't be drinking up my shit. Excuse me, Tec, let me go handle this."

Tec sat slouching in his seat, peering over at the strippers cupping titties, fingering pussy, and trying to hustle for that dollar. He took a sip of his beer while looking around the club. He hadn't been there in a minute—probably weeks. Unlike his boys, Tec didn't hunt for pussy. Pussy just seemed to attract this niggah. The more he strayed away from bitches, the more they loved to come his way, as if he threw off some captivating vibe. He was a good-looking guy—well built too.

"Hey, handsome," a young stripper uttered, walking up to him, taking a seat, and placing her hand on his thigh. "Why you sittin' over here, looking so lonely wit' your cute self?"

Tec peered at her. She was in a red thong, a skimpy white T-shirt, and some red pumps. Her voluptuous, brown-skinned figure was drawing much attention from the other men in the club.

"I'm ayyite," Tec replied.

"You can be ayyite by letting me give you a lap dance," she said, smiling while squeezing on his thigh.

"Nah, boo, I'm cool," he calmly told her.

"Well, how 'bout that drink?" she asked.

"How 'bout it?" he countered.

"I'm sayin' tho', you can't buy a sista a drink? I know your pockets are good for it."

"What you know 'bout my pockets?" he asked.

She looked at him as her smile began to fade. Then she let go of his thigh. They both gazed at each other, Tec giving her a simple look.

"Look, boo, I don't pay for pussy, and I don't buy bitches drinks, so you're just wasting your time dealing wit' me," he proclaimed.

She flashed him a weak smile, removing herself from her seat. "It's cool, luv. You have a nice day," she kindly told him.

Tec didn't give her a second look.

Seconds after she left him, she was approached by another guy who was gripping a handful of money and grabbing at her arm, indicating that he was very interested in her company.

Wallace and Little Boy Ronny were having a good time—tipping strippers and fondling them on and off stage. Wallace disappeared with a young ho, maybe to get a VIP or private lap dance done somewhere secluded.

They spent close to three hours up in the Bottom Dollar, finger popping shorties and all. Tec was just there, waiting for Toni, to see if she'd come in anytime soon. He knew Malice probably wouldn't relay the message he'd given about Toni, so he decided to stick around to see if she'd show up. But she was a no-show.

Around two o'clock, Tec was ready to bounce. Wallace was drunk and acting a fool around a few bitches, and he wasn't ready to leave yet. But Little Boy Ronny was ready to bounce along with Tec. The club was now packed with niggahs ready to see and tip themselves some pussy.

Leaving Wallace behind, Tec and Little Boy Ronny exited the club, giving those close to them daps and closed fist pounds.

By two-thirty, Tec was knocking on Toni's apartment door, with Little Boy Ronny right beside him. After about five minutes of knocking, Toni finally answered the door in her huge white sleeper T-shirt with a multi-colored scarf tied around her head.

"Bitch, you ain't hear me knocking?" Tec chided.

"I was sleeping, Keith," Toni said to him, staring at him with drowsy eyes.

Tec barged his way past her, with Little Boy Ronny following him. Toni, frustrated, closed the door behind them.

"Where were you these past few days?" Tec asked. "I'm sayin', you being ghost and all."

"I got a second job," she answered.

"What the fuck you doin' with a second job? Ain't you working at the club?"

"And . . . it ain't like you're giving me any money," she countered.

"Where this job at? You hustling at some other club?"

"No, Keith, it's a cleaning job."

"What? You a fuckin' housemaid now?"

"I'm doing someone a favor," she told him.

"Bitch, this shit ain't personal, right?"

"Keith, it's just a cleaning job. Damn, I need the extra money."

"Why you ain't tell me about it?"

"Do I have to tell you when I take a piss too?" she snapped.

"Bitch, don't get smart. I'm just trying to look out for your ass, that's all. I promised Sheek that. What the fuck I'm gonna tell him when your ass gets killed out there over some bullshit, you wanna be creeping around late at night."

"I can hold my own," she said.

"Yeah, whatever."

Little Boy Ronny was just chilling, sprawled out on her couch listening to everything. His eyes were kinda fixated on Toni, admiring her little physique, her nice leg structure hidden under her huge, long T-shirt. On the down low, he had a little crush on her—nah, to keep it real, he just wanted to fuck her, and he was willing to pay for it too. But Toni had this thing where she wouldn't fuck any of Tec or Sheek's friends or homies. It was a personal thing with her.

"Toni, come here," Tec called out as she stood distant from him across the room.

"What, Keith? It's almost three in the morning," she told him.

"So, what does that got to do wit' anything? Come here. I wanna tell you something."

Toni sighed, knowing damn well what Keith wanted to tell her, or more like what he wanted to do to her. She walked up to him and he quickly pulled her by her T-shirt, embracing her, then placing his arms around her and sliding his hands down her back onto her buttocks. He then pulled up her T-shirt with both of his hands, exposing her raw behind to Little Boy Ronny as he smiled, seeing that she didn't have on any panties.

"Keith," Toni uttered, trying to bring her T-shirt back down.

"What? It ain't like he never saw you dance nude before," he proclaimed

"That's not the point," she barked.

He started to fondle her in front of his man's eyes, squeezing her ass, cupping her breasts, and pulling up her huge T-shirt again. Feeling uncomfortable about getting intimate with Keith while Little Boy Ronny was sitting behind them watching, she whispered to Keith, saying to him, "Can you please tell him to leave?"

Tec looked at her, then whispered in her ear, "You're

my bitch, right? What you do down at the club is business, nothing personal. I'm not tripping over it. It's business. And this house cleaning shit, it's business too, right? Nothing personal, Toni. Don't forget that shit. You're my bitch. Remember that. I don't care if you fuck niggahs just to pay your rent. I ain't trippin' over that shit, as long as niggahs is bagging it up, right?"

It was kinda sick how Tec saw it.

Toni just nodded, agreeing to his sadistic terms. Tec looked over at Little Boy Ronny, and said, "Yo, Ronny, bounce for a minute. Let me handle home."

Little Boy Ronny raised up from off the couch, gave Tec dap, and told him he'd be back down at the Bottom Dollar with Wallace.

Not a minute after Little Boy Ronny walked out, Tec had her ass naked, down on her knees, sucking his dick.

By three-thirty, he was thrusting himself into her on the living room floor. Toni was gasping with her legs spread and her nails massaging his back. As he was fucking her, he heard his pager going off, vibrating against the glass coffee table and distracting his attention from the pussy for a second. Not wanting to stop, he continued. But then his pager went off a second time. Toni paid it no mind. She continued to lay on her back with Tec still mounted on her.

"What the fuck?" he angrily uttered.

He pulled out, dripping, climbing off Toni to go use her phone in the kitchen. He made the call standing there naked. Toni gazed at him.

Tec heard the phone ring about three times before someone picked up.

"Yo, who paging me?" he asked.

"Tec, son, it's Ronny. Yo, they shot that niggah Wallace," Little Boy Ronny dreadfully informed Tec.

"What?"

"Shot that niggah in his head just a while ago."

"Yo, I'll be down there in a minute," he told Little Boy Ronny just before hanging up.

He walked back into the living room where Toni was still waiting for him, waiting to continue. But he had no more interest in pussy. One of his niggahs just got shot. He put on his jeans and got dressed as Toni, looking baffled, asked him what had happened. He didn't say a word to her, but just continued collecting his shit. Toni lifted herself off the floor and fixated her eyes on Tec scurrying around her apartment.

"Keith, you leaving?" she asked.

"Mind your business, Toni," he rebuked. He didn't address her anymore. He reached for his .45, concealing it in the waistband of his jeans, and walked out of her apartment. Toni didn't have a clue as to what was going on, or what had just gone down.

-Twelve-

East Hampton, Long Island, was home to so many upperclass folks—celebrities, doctors, lawyers, entrepreneurs, and so on—where many of their homes came with two- or three-car garages, manicured lawns, spacious living, and almost every backyard was inhabited by a swimming pool.

Miles away from the city, urban Brooklyn, and blue-collared folks, the people who resided in East Hampton got to enjoy the luxuries of being wealthy, where they tended to their gardens and relaxed in heated pools, Jacuzzis, or spas. They walked their precious puppies or dogs down serene blocks, where in almost every driveway, there was a Mercedes or Lexus parked. And in almost every household, there was a servant or maid tending to the occupants.

Mathew sat quietly around the dinner table with his mother, who sat at the head of the table, and Tina, who sat opposite from him. The ladies were dressed in their casual evening wear, enjoying the dinner that the servant had cooked up. Mr. Peters was away on business—

as usual. Mrs. Peters didn't mind. She had grown quite used to not having her husband home or around the majority of the time.

"Mathew, my dear, why are you so quiet?" his mother asked, sitting as a lady should be seated at the dinner table.

"Everything's okay, Mother," Mathew responded without once glancing toward her.

"Maybe he's nervous about the wedding," Tina uttered.

"Oh, the wedding. So when is the date?"

"I want a June wedding," Tina stated.

"Yes, Tina, an early June wedding is always so nice. A spring wedding is just so exuberant and passionate," Mrs. Peters said.

"But then I was also thinking about a winter wedding, maybe two weeks before Christmas. And I like the idea of getting married just around Christmas, then bringing in the New Year as man and wife. Mrs. Tina Peters . . . doesn't that sound so wonderful, Mathew darling?"

"It's great, Tina," Mathew dragged out.

"My son is so lucky to have such a creative and beautiful fiancée. You will make a great addition to this family, Tina," Mrs. Peters praised.

"Why thank you, Mrs. Peters. You are like a mother to me, and your son, Mathew, is the best thing in my world right now. I love your son with all of my heart. I'm so proud to become part of such an exalted family."

"After the wedding, are there any plans of giving your father and I any grandchildren soon, Mathew?" his mother asked.

A little stunned, Mathew turned toward his mother—speechless.

"We'd talked it over, Mrs. Peters, and we've both discussed that having children right after the wedding would not be the best idea. It might take up too much of our time. I have my modeling and school, and Mathew has the family business to run. I might want to adopt someday," Tina informed her.

"Adopt? No, child, adopting a strange child is so wrong. You don't have a clue about the child you're bringing into your home—their nasty habits or their background. I want this family tree to remain pure, remain with our genes and our genes only. Tina, if you must wait, then wait a few years, but don't adopt. Adoption is everything that's wrong with this country today—too many nice folks bringing strange children into their homes, not knowing anything about them."

Mathew was appalled by Tina and his mother. He loved children, and he wanted them someday. He stared over at Tina, thinking *bullshit*. The only reason Tina didn't want any children was because she didn't want to ruin her wonderful figure by getting pregnant and giving birth. And he felt that she didn't like kids anyway. And they never discussed having children. He was ready for a child in his life, but Tina had already made the decision that they were not going to have any.

And his mother, putting down adoption. *How dare she?* he thought. Sometimes he wondered if he'd been adopted his damn self because the majority of the time, he really felt like he didn't belong. He was so much different from his family and their views on certain things.

The servant, or as the Peterses liked to call her, the "help," came in with a tray of truffles, setting them down, and clearing away the dirty dishes from the Peterses' sight. She didn't make eye contact with any of the folks dining at the table. She knew her place in this home—being only the help. There was no Florence and the Jeffersons, or what Alice was to the Bradys, or how the Drummonds from *Diff'rent Strokes* treated their maid. Here in this home in East Hampton, that's all this hired employee was to them, their maid and their help. There was no friendship, no friendly chitchat, and no loving environment. If she was late, they'd dock her pay. If she fucked up, they'd dock her pay. If she didn't come to work or perform her duties as they saw fit, they'd fire her.

Yamane, their help, slowly and carefully cleared off the dining room table, while all three still remain seated.

"Can I get you anything else, Mrs. Peters?" Yamane asked.

"No, Yamane, that will be all. You can go now and attend to your business," she told her.

"How 'bout you, ma'am? Will there be anything else for you?" Yamane asked Tina.

"No. If I need anything from you, I will call for you and tell you. Now you can leave," Tina said to her in a rude, snobbish way.

Mathew looked at her. He was not too pleased by the way Tina talked to people sometimes, especially the ones she felt were inferior to her. Mathew folded his napkin, laying it neatly on the table.

"Mother, I'm excusing myself," Mathew said, rising from out of his chair.

"You don't want dessert?" his mother asked.

"No, I'm quite all right for now."

He headed out of the grand dining room, with Tina and his mother peering at him as he exited. As soon as Mathew left the room, Tina said to Mrs. Peters, "Mathew has asked me to move in with him," which was a lie. He had never even brought up such a silly idea.

"Before the wedding, Tina?" Mrs. Peters asked. She was not all that thrilled about her son living with his fiancée before marriage, but she loved Tina so much and thought she was best for her son and the family, that she'd let anything slide—even overlook certain things.

"Be careful with my son, Tina," Mrs. Peters added. "He's a very kindhearted young man. And I know you two will make such a great married couple, like his father and I. We've set up something special for the two of you after the wedding."

Tina smiled. She was in deep with Mathew's mother, and she knew that she had Mathew wrapped around her finger. She loved Mathew, but she loved the possibility of becoming part of his seven-hundred-million-dollar inheritance even more. She was already coming from money, her father being a popular doctor and all, but what her fiancé was a part of, it was too tempting for her not to be a part of too.

Mathew was back in his Manhattan apartment. He flipped through his collection of CDs, browsing for just the right one. He picked out the Curtis Mayfield and the Impressions CD, placing it in his high-quality sound, elite stereo system, and letting Mayfield's melodious words pour out through his entire apartment.

Tina had decided to stay out in Long Island, keeping his mother company. They both planned to have brunch at the country club later in the afternoon. He had had enough of the both of them the day before. Sometimes they looked like they were actually mother and daughter—biologically. To him, it was a little too scary.

Like a clown, he danced and sang the words to the Curtis Mayfield CD, enjoying his solitude. In nothing but his silk boxers, a pair of house slippers, and shirtless, he pranced around his gigantic penthouse suite, trying to dance ol' skool. He tried to do a spin, but fell on his ass, laughing.

A few minutes later, Mathew's solitude was interrupted by the buzzer. It was the doorman downstairs announcing that Ms. Toni Benjamin was there to see him again. He told him to let her up, then he dashed into his bedroom and donned his exquisite red silk robe, trying to cover up his indecency.

A few minutes later, he heard the bell ring. He went over to answer it, smiling as he opened the door. Toni quickly passed by him with an armful of groceries. She hurried past him toward the kitchen, trying not to drop the four bags she was carrying. She quickly placed the groceries on the counter, catching her breath and thanking Mathew for opening the door so quickly. It would've been a terrible mess if she had dropped all the bags onto the floor.

She'd been working for him for the past two weeks, getting more and more comfortable around him and his place. They'd become somewhat good friends, and Mathew was enthralled by her level of work and perfection. She was almost better than his hired maid, Miranda.

Toni loved working for him. To her it felt nice to be around change for a while, seeing something different other than Brooklyn, the projects, her boyfriend, and dancing at the Bottom Dollar. When she was in his penthouse, she felt somewhat at peace, a bit happy. He was a good employer. Mathew always told her that there was nothing hands-off in his place. She was allowed to use whatever piece of equipment she caught an interest to. She rested in his bed, used the kitchen, and even sat and settled down in his Jacuzzi.

She was doing a wonderful job cleaning and taking care of his place. So good, that he was thinking about bringing her on full-time.

"What's all the food for?" Mathew asked.

"I'm going to cook," she replied.

"You cook?"

"Like a five-star chef."

Toni was tired of spending money on a cheap meal whenever she was on her way to his place. Or starving herself to death, then rushing home to stop in at a diner where she could catch a meal before heading back home. What Mathew had in his fridge didn't gratify her appetite. It looked like *rich food,* something Jenny Craig might give to her clientele. She wasn't on any diet, so why eat like it?

Mathew, surprised, walked over to the kitchen where Toni was removing items from the bags and placing them onto the counter.

"How long have you been cooking?"

"I don't know, since I was seven . . . eight. My mother and grandmother showed me how. We have great recipes passed down from generation to generation," she happily informed him. "My grandmother, before she passed—"

"I'm sorry to hear about that," Mathew expressed.

"It's okay. She's been dead for about twelve years now. But she was one of the best cooks, or shall I say chefs, in New York City. She even prepared a meal for the president one time."

"I'm amazed."

"Yeah, I picked up cooking from her," Toni continued, still removing items from bags. "She used to bring me into the kitchen when I was about five, and she would start me off on little things, like peeling potatoes or scrambling eggs. By the age of seven or so, she would have me helping her season food, baking chicken, preparing collard greens, all sorts of stuff. She told me that cooking, it was more of an art than a job. In order for one to become a great cook, they had to enjoy what they were doing. It had to come from the heart. We would sit around the table, and she would tell me stories about her coming up in the old days, how she used to prepare the chicken from scratch, by killing it then skinning it. She would tell me what some recipes meant to her and the family when they were coming up."

"Your grandmother sounds like a wonderful person," Mathew proclaimed, leaning against the kitchen counter, staring at Toni.

"Yeah, she was. Once we were all one big, happy family," Toni sadly said.

"What happened?" he asked.

Toni looked at him, then said, "Look, there's a lot of work to be done. I don't have time for reminiscing with you about the good ol' days. I have housework and then I want to cook this meal."

"I'm curious, is all this for one or two?" Mathew asked, referring to all the grocery items she had spread across the counter.

Toni smiled. "It's for the both of us, silly. I like to cook for others. It brings me joy to see when others admire my home-cooked meals. I like to see 'em lick their fingers and continue fattening their stomachs because they can't get enough of my sweet potato pie or my macaroni salad or my fish."

Mathew continued to peer at her with such admiration. *She is something else,* he thought. With so much spunk and charisma, he wondered if there was more to her, and he was curious as to why she didn't take professional classes at some school to become a five-star chef, and maybe someday establish her own line of classy bistros.

"Excuse me," Toni said, gently shoving Mathew to the side. "If I'm going to cook, then I'm gonna need all of my kitchen space. You're in my way."

Mathew chuckled. "Pardon me," he said, stepping out of her way.

Three and a half hours later, Toni had a superb meal cooked up. She had steamed fish, collard greens, macaroni salad, baked chicken, and white rice. For dessert, she had a sweet potato pie warming in the oven.

Mathew was overwhelmed by all the food she had spread out. Having a meal like this was new to him; he was used to what his mother's servants cooked up—a little sushi, crab salad, shellfish, liver, truffles, and sipping on fine wine. He never acquired that soul food appetite that so many African-Americans grew up on.

Toni fixed him a decent plate filled with everything. Not being skeptical in trying it, he dug into her steamed fish and macaroni salad first. He was gripped by the taste, the seasoning. It was definitely something new for him. He loved it.

Toni smiled as he continued eating.

She then fixed herself a plate, feeling that she deserved a pat on the back for another job well done.

Mathew had seconds, and a little bit of thirds. Then he took a taste of her sweet potato pie and nearly caught an orgasm. He tore into her pie like it was the end of the world. He gave her thumbs up for her cooking. Toni was thrilled.

By five that afternoon, Mathew had a full belly and had enjoyed his first experience with soul food.

She fed him well.

They both relaxed in the formal living room and let their meal digest as Mathew pressed power to his home entertainment center, turning the channel to CNN.

"Are you kidding me? CNN? Who watches that channel anyway?"

"I do," Mathew admitted, "well sometimes."

"Turn to BET or something," Toni suggested.

"BET?"

"Yeah, Black Entertainment Television. You are black, right?" Toni uttered.

"I know about BET," Mathew said. "I'm not that sheltered from urban life."

"You could have fooled me."

"What do you mean by that?"

"Look at you, living in this fortress you call an apartment, with money to burn and lavish cars to drive around. Have you ever been broke or poor in your life?"

"Actually, there once was a slump for two years in our sales department, and we had a slow year on Wall Street last year."

Toni sighed. "I don't believe this."

"What about you?" Mathew asked. "You're so curious about my life. I want to know more about yours."

"There's nothing to tell. I'm a poor girl who comes from a poor place."

"And how poor of a place?"

"So poor that the roaches receive food stamps too," Toni joked.

Mathew chuckled. "Tell me about your mother. You hardly speak about her much."

"Because I choose not to," Toni sarcastically replied.

"Do the two of y'all get along?"

"Look, can we change the subject?" Toni chided, because Mathew was now getting a little too personal for her.

"OK, I'm sorry if I offended you."

"Apology accepted."

Changing the subject, Mathew asked her about her current occupation. She strayed away from that question, too, so he asked her for another piece of sweet potato pie.

They continued to talk through the evening, and Mathew strayed away from her private life. They both found each other funny, the both of them having a good sense of humor. And as a favor, Mathew switched the channel to BET, where they watched music videos, and to Toni's surprise, he was up on some of the hip-hop and rap videos.

"What you know about Busta Rhymes?" Toni asked.

"A lot more than you thought I did," Mathew replied.

Toni smiled and saw that he was more than just some uppity, tight-dicked rich boy with a wad of cash and a classy home. There was something about him that was appealing to her.

Losing track of time, the clock read nine-thirty. Toni found herself dozing off while watching television and talking to Mathew.

"I gotta go," she said to him, trying to rise up.

"Toni, it's late. Why don't you spend the night?"

"Please. I'm sure your fiancée will not approve of me spending the night in your classical home."

"She's in Long Island. And besides, this is my place, not hers."

"Whatever."

"Look, it's getting late, and I'll feel much better if you stay here for the night and leave in the morning."

Toni looked over at him, rethinking her decision. It would be nice, just for once, to stay the night somewhere nice, not worrying about Keith calling for a booty call in the wee hours of the morning, etc.

How does he talk me into these things? she said to herself. "OK, which guest bedroom?"

"Just pick one," he said.

"Why are you so nice to me?" she asked curiously.

"What, is it a crime to be nice?"

"No, but I'm not used to getting the royal treatment from men, especially black men. It just feels weird to me, that's all."

"Maybe you need to start dating different types of men."

"What is that supposed to mean?"

"Toni, you're a beautiful woman, and if any man can't find it in his heart to love and respect you, then it should be a crime. You're gifted. Take advantage of that, and don't let anyone take advantage of you."

"What are you, William Shakespeare?" she asked while smiling.

Keith, never in his life, told her that she was beautiful. He never really took her places, except to ride the Cyclone at the amusement park. Her self-esteem wasn't as high as it should be, between performing vulgar acts at the Bottom Dollar, Keith, her junkie mother, her supposed-to-be best friend Vinita, and the ghetto, just trying to live a regular life was a burden on her. Seeing so many wrongs and so many people disrespecting her, maybe that was the cause of the things she did.

It was peculiar for her to wake up in a strange but comfortable bed. She hadn't slept this well in months.

It stunned her for a minute to be in a different room, but then she remembered where she was. She stepped out of bed, trotted into his bathroom, washed her face, and then prepared to leave.

Mathew was still asleep. It was only seven-fifteen. Not wanting to wake him, she left him a note saying she would return to work in another three days. Then she collected her things and softly made her way out of his place.

It was nine-thirty in the morning, and as Toni was just coming in, Vinita was just exiting the building. This was their first run-in since that little fucked-up incident at the Plaza a few weeks back.

They stared at each other. Vinita was headed for work, and Toni was headed inside to do nothing but rest up in her apartment until she left for work at the Bottom Dollar. Toni was no longer upset. What had happened had already been forgotten.

"Hey, Vinita," she greeted casually.

"I'm late for work," Vinita said back.

"It's cool."

Vinita, who was rushing out, stopped and turned around. "Look, I'm sorry about what happened at that party," Vinita said. "I didn't have a clue that they would react to you so rudely. My bad about that."

"I'm not even sweating that issue. It's already forgotten," Toni told her.

"So, we're still cool, right?"

"Yeah, we're cool," Toni assured. She had better things on her mind.

Then they both parted. Vinita went her way, and Toni went hers. Before entering her apartment, Toni checked the mail downstairs and saw that she had another letter from her brother. It had been a while since he'd written to her. She wondered what he had to say.

She took the pissy staircase up four flights to her apartment. The building was quiet. The only folks up were the ones who were still heading to work. Most of the drug dealers, loud mouths, and troublemakers were still asleep.

Toni stepped into her apartment, and surprisingly saw her mother at home for once. She stepped out of her bedroom, wearing a house robe with nothing on underneath.

"Ma, we got another letter," she happily told her mother, who didn't seem to be too excited.

"Is he still in Rikers?" her mother asked.

Toni gave her moms an irritated look. "They transferred him upstate two years ago," she once again informed her mother as to her son's whereabouts.

"Oh, I forgot," she spat back.

For several moments Toni just peered at her mother, who hopelessly roamed around the apartment. She went to look out the window, then she glanced into the fridge, then she took a seat at the kitchen table. During all this roaming around, she still looked indecent, with her robe fully opened, exposing the somewhat decent body that she still had left throughout all the years of her drug use.

"Toni, you got ten dollars I can borrow? I'll pay you back. Promise," she said.

"No, Ma, I'm broke right now."

"I thought you had a job."

"Yeah, well, the bills and rent come first."

"You cooking breakfast?"

"Cook it your damn self," Toni spat back, heading toward her room.

Her mother scratched the inside of her robe, reaching for an itch by the side of her breast. She used to be a beautiful woman—used to be. Now she was slowly withering away, not caring about herself or her children, but instead belonging fully to her drug use. All the men around the way used to try to holler at Ms. Angela Benjamin—she was the shit. With an hourglass shape, long black hair, thick thighs, a plump booty, and firm breasts, she had a career going for herself. Before Derrick, her dead boyfriend, many men proposed to her, many men respected her, and many men would go out of their way for her. Now those same men who respected her back in the day were the same ones who treated her like shit and didn't give a fuck about her. Some men shook their heads, not believing what she had become. Some even tried to get her help. And many took full advantage of her drug addiction. Prying open her thick thighs and getting something they'd lusted over for years—a little piece of Angela—fucking her six ways from Sunday.

And after all the years of her drug use, prostitution, and a shitty life, it was hard to believe that she still had a little figure that some heads still admired. It wasn't like it used to be, but it was sumthin' sumthin'. She had lost a little weight, but not to an extreme where she was looking like that string-bean girl from *Popeye.*

But her beauty was definitely fading quickly. She had a gap in her mouth, which she could blame on a young hustler who knocked her front tooth out by punching her and beating up on her after she had tried to steal a few vials from him. Despite her fading looks, it was a fact that some young hustlers out there were trading drugs for sex from Ms. Angela Benjamin. That's why it appalled Toni when she went past her mother's room and saw a young, teenage drug dealer lying across her mother's bed with his pants off and a hard-on rising in the air.

She turned to look at her mother, who was now coming down the hall. It was shameful that she had to perform sexual favors in order for her to maintain this household and pay the bills, but it was even more shameful that her mother was doing the same in order to maintain her drug habit.

Toni retreated to her room with her brother's letter still in her hand. She was planning to stay locked in her room 'til she left for work down at the Bottom Dollar later that night.

She tore open her brother's letter. He asked when she was next coming to see him. He explained that things had been a little wild since she last came to visit him. They'd been locking down inmates for weeks, doing searches, and a few violent fights had broken out. He also told her that he was a little low on cash and asked if she could deposit a little money into his commissary.

Luckily for her brother, she was a little up on the cash, thanks to Mathew. And she planned to put three hundred dollars into his commissary the following week, when she visited him again. He also asked how their ma was doing, and he mentioned that he had called collect a few times, but no one was home to accept any of the charges.

After reading his letter, Toni folded it back up and placed it with all of his other letters in a shoebox that was placed under her bed. Then she took out three hundred of the six hundred dollars she had left, and put that in a separate box, stashing it above a shelf in her closet. Unfortunately for her, she had to hide money from her thieving, drug-addicted mother in places where she knew her mother wouldn't bother to look. She couldn't leave money out and around the house, not even a dollar or a quarter, or it would be picked up very quickly. After settling into her bedroom, she took a little nap, dozing off for about an hour.

By six, Toni emerged from her bedroom to once again find her mother, along with that young, teenage hustler, gone from the apartment. She went into the kitchen to fix herself something to eat, then afterward she got herself ready to go make some money at the Bottom Dollar.

It was ten-forty when Toni walked through the doors of the Bottom Dollar, paying the tip in and finding that the club was already filled with lusting young men. In a jean skirt, a blue T-shirt, and rocking a pair of Air Force Ones, Toni still turned heads as she strolled past the bar and the stage and headed toward the changing area. As always, the wide-eyed young men couldn't wait 'til she got on the stage to do her thang.

"Yo, Toni, Malice wants to see you downstairs in his office," a young male told her.

"For what?" she asked.

"Don't know. That niggah don't tell me shit."

Without any more information, Toni headed for Malice's office, which was located down in the basement. It was more like a storage room than an office, bedecked with gray brick walls and no carpeting. The only furniture was a fold-out chair, a fold-out table, a tattered La-Z-Boy chair, and a torn beige couch.

She walked inside. The door was already open, and she saw Malice sitting on the couch, chatting with some new stripper. Soon as he saw her, he told the new girl to leave and invited Toni to sit down.

Malice took a seat in the La-Z-Boy behind the fold-out table, and Toni took a seat in the fold-out chair, sitting directly in front of him. Toni had only been down there twice, both in the process of doing a VIP, where she fucked two young men on the torn couch.

"Toni, where you been for these past few days?" Malice asked, reclining in his fucked-up chair like he was some kind of New York kingpin.

"Why you care?"

"You got your boyfriend coming in here searching for you. Tec brings trouble, and I don't need any kind of trouble from anyone right now, especially from that lunatic boyfriend of yours."

"So, you gonna fire me?"

"No, I can't do that. You bring this place lots of money. Some niggahs come just to see you, and they spend money."

"Malice, I'm not getting your point," Toni said.

"Look, you be here when I want you to be here. I can't be having you disappearing for days and having you get Tec all riled up, then having him coming in here searching for you, wanting to blame me for your disappearance. You're one of my favorites, Toni. You're like the cream of the crop. You make good business here, and it's been peaceful these past few months. I would like for it to stay that way. Violence brings the cops around, and the cops will bring attention to me. Having too much attention on my place will have the city shutting it down. So, Toni, please, no more worries."

"Yeah, I understand," Toni said.

"Good, now go up there and hustle that pussy off for that money."

The truth be told, Malice feared Tec, even though he was tight with his older brother. Malice and Tec had never really been that close. They just showed each other respect because of Tec's older brother, Lonny.

As Toni made her way onto the stage to do her thing—make her money and turn the horny, sex-craving, dollar-waving niggahs on—she couldn't help but think about Mathew. *He's mad cool,* she kept saying to herself.

She had him all wrong, thinking one thing about him, and then he turned out to be the opposite of her thoughts. She was starting to like being around him. He had a wonderful sense of humor, he was charming and good-looking, he treated her with respect, and he was rich. But to her, that didn't matter, because she was not about his pockets. That had been the furthest thing from her mind ever since they'd met.

She could now see herself being with a guy like Mathew. Too bad he was engaged to a bitchy fiancée.

-Thirteen-

Vinita woke up between Myron's arms. She had spent the night over his place more than once. The night before was good to the both of them. He got his, and she definitely got hers. She was naked under his sheets. She turned herself around and took a look at Myron while he was still asleep.

It'd been a while since she felt this good, not just because of the sex, but because of Myron. He seemed to be the one for her, having it all going for himself. And it also felt good to be spending the night somewhere else other than in her gloomy, drug-infested building and her cramped room. Myron's place had space. His apartment wasn't cramped with wall-to-wall stuff, like her parents' place. It seemed like her parents didn't like to throw anything away, saving items that they came across and stacking them somewhere in the corner, then forgetting about them later.

Vinita always told herself that when she got her own place, it would be nothing like her parents'. It was always going to be tidy and clean, and there wouldn't be five or six kids running around making a mess of things. If she had kids, she only planned to have one. One child was all she needed.

Vinita climbed out of bed, throwing on a robe and leaving Myron still asleep. She stepped into his bathroom, turned on the water to the sink, and splashed her face.

"Don't fuck this up, Vinita," she told herself while staring into the mirror. "Myron's a good guy. He has money and his own place. And you love him, but not for all the wrong reasons."

She continued to stare at herself, with the water still running. Early in the morning and she was still a fine creature. Her beauty was natural.

She tied her robe and stepped back into the bedroom. She saw that Myron had awakened.

"Good morning," Myron greeted.

Vinita smiled and returned a good morning.

Myron got out of bed. He was also naked. He walked up to Vinita, wrapping his arms around her and whispering in her ear, "Was last night good for you too?"

"Better," she replied with a delightful smile.

They hugged and kissed on each other for several moments, causing Myron to become aroused again. But Vinita didn't want to spoil him. He had enough pleasures last night, so she gently pushed him away, telling him that she had to leave soon.

"So soon?" he said.

"I have things to do today," she explained.

"Well, I'll give you a ride back," he offered.

Vinita didn't say a word, just nodded and started to get dressed.

Back at her place, she was surprised to see her sister, Nancy, there with her three kids, ten-year-old Marvin, seven-year-old Danielle, and the youngest, five-year-old

Terrance. Everyone was home, and she didn't like that. She walked into the apartment. Her two nephews and her only niece came running up to her, shouting, "Auntie Vinita," and she gave them all a big hug.

The baddest one was Terrance. He never liked to listen. He just went about doing things on his own. He had a temper and always threw a fit when an adult tried to punish him.

"Hey, sis," Nancy greeted, smiling.

"I didn't know that you were coming over," Vinita said to her.

"Yeah, well, I have another job interview this afternoon, and Mama promised that she'd watch the kids for me," her sister explained.

"All day?" Vinita uttered, sounding disappointed.

"I'm not gonna take all day. I should be back around five or six."

"Where's this job?"

"It's in Manhattan."

Vinita looked at her sister. This was her seventh job interview this month, and she still didn't have employment yet. This was her older sister, who was supposed to set an example for the younger one, and have her life straight. But instead, she was twenty-nine, unemployed, on Section 8, and raising three kids alone, without any of her two babies' daddies around—what a role model for her children.

"You wearing that?" Vinita asked.

"Yeah, why, what's wrong wit' it?"

Nancy had on a long beige cotton skirt, a white blouse, some ugly-looking witch shoes, and her hair was pulled back in a ponytail.

"I thought you might want to go to an interview looking more formal, that's all."

"Well, this is the best I can put together."

No wonder she's still unemployed, Vinita said to herself. "What is the job?"

"It's a secretary position at some insurance company," Nancy told her.

"I didn't know you could type."

"I'm not that good, but I'm learning. I took some classes at the center last year."

"Nancy, hurry now, before you're late," their mother shouted, coming out of the kitchen wiping her hands.

"You sure you're going to be OK with them? They can be a handful now and then," Nancy asked once again.

"Nonsense, Nancy, these are my grandbabies. I'll be able to take care of 'em. You go ahead and get that job, and start bringing home a decent paycheck."

Nancy gave her children hugs, then grabbed her purse and rushed out the door. Vinita was still standing there and couldn't believe that her niece and nephews were going to be there all day. If she had known that, then she wouldn't have left Myron's place so early. But he was getting antsy again, and last night was enough. She didn't want to spoil the man. She had given him a little taste of it, and that was enough—for now.

Walking toward her bedroom, leaving her mother about to feed the kids, she heard her niece call out, "Auntie Vinita, can I chill wit' you today?"

"I'm busy," she answered.

"But you're always too busy," Danielle said.

"Next time. Promise."

Vinita then went into her private bedroom and locked the door behind her. She loved her sister's kids, but she didn't have the patience for them. She might spend ten to fifteen minutes with them, and that was it. She would play the good auntie for such a short amount of time, then leave them and go ahead with her business.

She stayed in her bedroom, listening to the radio and reading the latest Terry McMillan novel. She heard the children outside her door, laughing and running around the place. Then she started to think about her sister who Vinita tried so hard not to become—a struggling mother with three kids, on welfare, no husband, never been married, relying on the government for money. And worse, being almost thirty with no stable job or career going for herself.

Where did she go wrong? Vinita wondered.

But Vinita had a plan. She would not take a voyage down the road her sister had taken. She was already in school, and she already had a good-paying job managing a clothing store, and she had a good, stable, supportive, and financially sound man in her life. She could not go wrong. She would not let herself go wrong.

-Fourteen-

At a quarter to ten, four men in a black SUV loaded up semi-automatic weapons, loading rounds into chambers and cocking back .357s and .45s. One of the passengers was Tec. He was leading this team of bandits to do a stick-up. They planned to run up in one of Chills' illegal establishments and send him a quick message.

It'd been four days since Wallace was killed, shot twice—once in his head and once in his chest. They said that it was one of Chills' shooters. They caught Wallace standing on the corner down the block from the Bottom Dollar with some chick. One niggah crept up on him, and without warning, shot him cold-blooded in front of the bitch.

Now it was payback. Niggahs had to respond to that. If not, then niggahs was gonna be looking soft. But with Tec, he wasn't having it. With his reputation, niggahs from C.I. knew what to expect.

Tec rode shotgun, with a loaded, single-action caliber .22 resting on his lap, and a double-barreled shotgun lying in the back on the floor. Little Boy Ronny was concealing a .45 ACP. Pinch-Back, sitting behind the driver, was armed with a double-action .357, and the driver, Lamont, was also packin' a .45. It was a ride-or-die night.

The plan was to knock off one of Chills' stash houses located in the Luna Park houses—an apartment on the fifth floor more specifically. It was tight and risky, but at the moment, Tec didn't give a fuck.

"So, how we gonna do this?" Little Boy Ronny asked. "That niggah got that shit tight. Them doors is locked down. They would even give the police a hard time to bust that shit open."

"We gonna do this. I got it set up," Tec replied.

Chills had watchers all around the place. He even had a few niggahs on the rooftop and niggahs roaming around looking out for any suspicious activity, or the five-O. The apartment door was made of steel, bolted with five or six strong locks. It would take a niggah operating from inside a good one to two minutes to open the door.

Inside, there were about five to six heads running shop, and all of them were armed and dangerous. There was a small camera set up outside the door. It was nearly impossible to hit up this place. Niggahs had to be crazy to hit up that spot, but Tec was crazy enough to attempt it.

The SUV stopped two blocks from its destination. The driver, wearing a blue jogging suit trimmed with white stripes, stepped out of the car and placed the double-barreled shotgun into a large black duffel bag. He walked off, looking like he had just come from the gym.

The car then pulled off with Pinch-Back driving. The one area where Chills fucked up was that he had some of these ol' skool niggahs who used to run with Sheek and 'em, watching out. And Tec knew that these niggahs weren't reliable. They were gonna slip up, and all he had to do was wait.

The remaining three sat in the car, watching the territory and keeping an eye on the key players. They were gonna play it out. Tec knew that his crew would not be able to just barge in and terrorize the place. Nah, they probably would be dead before they even hit the floor. But he knew that around eleven someone would have to deliver the cash from the street to the apartment, or they'd probably have to re-up their hustlers soon. So he'd catch them then, when there was movement and not everyone was keeping watch at once.

At around 10:35, they noticed some activity. A guy on a black motorcycle rolled up. He stepped off carrying a brown book bag. He didn't look too threatening. He was light-skinned and slim, an easy target to take down.

"Yo, let's roll," Tec ordered.

The SUV pulled off, trying not to catch any attention and scare off niggahs and shit. Little Boy Ronny was hunched down in the backseat, attempting to hide himself from the outside onlookers. Already Chills' lookouts were fuckin' up. They were so distracted by duke rolling up on the bike, that they didn't notice two men quickly getting out of the SUV and going around to the back of the building.

The light-skinned niggah was making a dropoff, and Tec already knew it. Their plan was to catch them while the drop was being made, with the steel doors already opened. Catch them off guard. The light-skinned niggah stepped into the elevator, not knowing that he was being watched and followed. He was careless. He wasn't even packing.

He reached the fifth floor and didn't pay attention

to the second elevator also stopping at that same floor just a short time after his. Light-skinned guy walked down the corridor. Straight ahead of him was the man wearing the blue jogging suit, carrying a black duffle bag and jingling keys like he was on his way to his apartment. Duke just glanced at him, thinking he was nothing but a harmless tenant coming from the gym. And down on the other end of the corridor stood Tec and Little Boy Ronny with their gats already out, cocked back, and ready for action. To Tec, this was too easy. Niggahs was slipping, and it was gonna cost them big time.

The guy making the drop knocked on the door twice. Someone inside the apartment slid back a peephole, identifying the outsider. The man in the jogging suit stood two doors down, pretending to enter his apartment as he still jingled his keys and waited. But then he squatted down and slowly unzipped the bag, gripping the shotgun, ready to make his move.

Tec and Little Boy Ronny peered from around the corridor, observing everything, their gats facing down toward the ground. This stick-up had to be swift—no fuckups. One fuckup, and it was over. Tec watched, then he aimed his gun around the corner, pointing it at the light-skinned man's head. Tec's shot had to be accurate. He had to take him down with the first fired shot, then Lamont in the jogging suit would rush toward the door, providing the element of surprise. It was risky, but it could be pulled off.

The light-skinned man didn't even take two steps before Tec and Little Boy Ronny rushed out, firing and striking their target by the door, causing him to drop suddenly. Then Lamont rushed to the door with the shotgun in his hand. The guy in the doorway stared wide-eyed when he saw Lamont with the shotgun, aiming it directly at him. Then boom, a shot was fired, hitting duke and pushing his wig violently back a few feet. He was dead before he hit the floor. All three men rushed into the apartment, catching two more niggahs off guard as they tried to reach for automatic weapons, but were quickly gunned down.

They scattered around the apartment, shouting. With four already dead, they heard another person in the bedroom. Little Boy Ronny was already on it. He rushed into the bedroom to find one lone assailant trying to escape out the window, but there was no fire escape, so it would've been a very long drop for him, as they were five stories up.

Little Boy Ronny grabbed him by his shirt, pulling him back in. Once he hit the floor, Little Boy Ronny started kicking him and hitting him with the butt of the gun. The man pleaded and begged for him to stop, but it didn't do him any good. Tec and Lamont entered the bedroom, demanding him to tell them where the stash was hidden. He didn't play tough guy. He sang like a bird, telling them that the drugs were in the kitchen, in a cupboard. And then he told them that the money was under a loose floorboard in the next bedroom. They quickly took everything, stuffing all the shit into the duffle bag and leaving the one survivor stripped naked, bloody, and ashamed.

They quickly took the stairway down, avoiding the elevators, with their weapons still in their hands. They knew niggahs from the street would be coming up soon, and they planned not to be there when they arrived.

Neighbors had heard the shots and the ruckus going on, but they planned to mind their own business and not get involved. They didn't even open their doors anymore, trying not to witness anything or anyone—

fearing for their safety and their lives. They knew that this tragic event was going to happen sooner or later, thinking that maybe the police might have raided them first, and if not, then some rival gang. They tried their best to avoid that apartment whenever they could.

Tec, Little Boy Ronny, and Lamont quickly made it to the vehicle, with Pinch-Back still behind the wheel. The duffle bag was tossed in, and their ride screeched off, bus'ing a quick U-turn and leaving them idiots behind looking dumbfounded. It'd happened so quickly that the rest of them niggahs were left looking stupid. They'd raided one of Chills' stash houses and gotten away with their lives. Chills was soon gonna become a very pissed off and upset man.

Tec and his boys ran off with fifty-three thousand dollars in cash, two kilos of cocaine, and a few red tops, leaving behind four dead, and embarrassing Chills by hitting one of his supposed-to-be well-secured stash houses.

But retaliation would be soon to come.

Two days had passed since their major stickup. Tec split the money with his niggahs, a little over thirteen thousand dollars each, and sold the stolen drugs to the street, making his pockets a little richer. Being cautious, he and his niggahs stayed low for a minute, not hanging out in the streets gambling and smoking. He know Chills was gonna send a team of shooters out in search for them, so he shacked up with local bitches, and stayed indoors. Too many people knew about Toni's spot, so he knew it wasn't safe to hide out there.

Word out on the street was that Chills had put a twenty-five-thousand-dollar contract on Tec's life. That niggah became furious over one of his stash houses being hit, and he punished his niggahs for being so careless and stupid.

Tec wanted a war, and he was about to get a war. These Coney Island streets were soon about to become a battlefield filled with blood, retaliation, and greed.

A week after their little stickup, Tec and his niggahs decided to go out and have a little fun. He wasn't stressing that contract Chills had put out on him. Tec didn't fear anyone. He may be cautious, but he wasn't easily intimidated. He wasn't gonna let some down south faggot intimidate him into not getting his money on. He was about to bring it to Chills, let him know that these were his streets, his turf, his clientele, his ghetto heaven, and he wasn't backing down. He had a crew of niggahs ready to back him. It would soon be kill or be killed.

Tec, drinking his cognac as usual, stood by the bar with his peeps, Little Boy Ronny and Pinch-Back, checking out the scene as they partied at Wiggles, an urban nightclub located in downtown Brooklyn, over by Fulton Street.

They were celebrating. Each of them had a wad of cash on them—ballin', buying drinks, and catching eyes from a few ladies. They were young, but they were fine. Little Boy Ronny pulled out a wad of hundreds and told the bartender to bring him a bottle of Moet. He was about to get himself toasted. Tec, sitting on a barstool, smoked a cigarette and relaxed. He was catching a lot of stares and smiles from females, with his diamond pendant shimmering off his chest. The place was a bit crowded, mixed with different types of people. Even some Indians were up in the place dancing to the urban music as the deejay spun off Nas' "It Ain't Hard to Tell."

From the corner of his eye, Tec kept noticing this female clockin' him—hard too. She would smile and remain talking to her lady friend who was standing right beside her. They both had drinks in their hands, and they both were very attractive—really fuckin' fine.

The one who had her attention on Tec was wearing winter white wide-legged pants that hugged her sensuous hips and thighs, a blue silk blouse, and a pair of leather T-strap pumps. Her long, black hair fell down her back. She didn't look like she was black—more mixed.

It looked like she had her eyes fixated on Tec, following his every movement and throwing off welcoming vibes. A bit intrigued by her, he tapped Little Boy Ronny on his shoulder and pointed out the bitch. He said, "Yo, this bitch been clockin' me for a minute now."

Little Boy Ronny peered over at her, trying to get a better look, as she was somewhat distant from them. She took another sip from her drink and continued to keep her eyes directly on Tec.

"Oh, shit, dog, yo, you know who that bitch is?" Little Boy Ronny rhetorically asked with a little excitement in his voice.

"Nah, you tell me," Tec replied.

"That's muthafuckin' Chills' bitch standing right over there, dog. That's that bitch, Lana," Little Boy Ronny informed his boy.

"Say word?"

"Fuckin' yeah, yo."

"Then why she clockin' me hard?"

"I don't know. But I heard that that niggah is in love wit' that bitch, Tec. He supposed to have the pussy locked down and shit. She is fuckin' fine too. Yo, you gonna holla?"

Tec kept silent, staring over at Lana as she stared back, holding her drink and still standing next to her friend. How was it that Little Boy Ronny knew all about her, but he didn't know who the fuck she was? Tec wondered. But that's why Little Boy Ronny was his boy, because he knew shit. He knew people, and he kept Tec updated and shit.

"I heard that bitch got some good-ass pussy, too, dog. You should go and try and taste some of that," Little Boy Ronny added.

Lana was black, mixed with Indian and some Cuban. People sometimes said that she looked like Pocahontas. Her smooth brown skin and that long, black Indian hair fell off her back. With her seductive bedroom eyes, full lips, and plus-size figure, every man wanted her. But niggahs stayed away, knowing who was claiming her, who she belonged to. And if a niggah valued his life, then he would stay away from her. She definitely was Chills' number one bitch, and he loved her. But she loved Chills for all the wrong reasons.

Tec decided to make his move. He placed his drink on the counter and walked up to her. He wasn't nervous, just curious. As he strolled up to her, she gave him the most pleasant smile and waited for his arrival.

"You know me, boo?" he asked, standing directly in front of her.

"No, but I've heard about you," she responded.

"Good things, I hope."

She let out a slight titter. "Interesting things," she returned.

"So what's your name?" he asked.

"Lana," she answered.

"Lana, Lana, Lana. Let me ask you sumthin'," Tec said, not once diverting his gaze from hers. "Why is a fine muthafuckin' bitch like you fuckin' wit' some Alabama, greasy, fried-chicken-eating, cornball niggah like Chills?"

"So, you heard of me?" she mentioned.

"Recently."

"So, why did you ask for my name?"

"I wanted to see if you were honest."

"Did I pass your little test?"

"You doin' ayyite so far."

The attraction was there, as Lana loved everything about the man—his style, his approach, his demeanor, and even his wardrobe and badass street attitude. She loved thugs. She loved being around bad men—dangerous men—and Tec turned her on, turned her on so much that she was willing to fuck him that night, not giving a fuck that she was with Chills.

"What the fuck is that chubby muthafucka doing for you? I know he ain't fuckin' you right. A niggah like that can't be."

"How you know he ain't fuckin' me right?" Lana asked.

"Please, that niggah and his fat-ass gut? He probably can't even see his dick, much less get it up. Now a bitch like you need a niggah like me in your life."

"How you figure?" Lana asked, toying with him.

"Bitch, you've been clockin' me all fuckin' night. Now is not the time to be playin' fuckin' games. I got a big dick and a strong muthafuckin' back, and if you 'bout it, 'bout it, then let's roll."

"It's like that? You gotta be so fuckin' harsh?" Lana asked, knowing damn well that she was ready and willing. Plus Tec was right; Chills hadn't been fuckin' her right lately. All Chills was good for was his rep and his expanding cash flow, which Lana took advantage of, going on five-thousand-dollar shopping sprees and living a lavish lifestyle. She could see herself being with a man like Tec, physically and mentally, just by his tone, and the way he was would make her panties damp—if she had any on.

"See, let me inform you on sumthin', boo. Your man is already a dead man. I'm giving you that edge by telling you so you can come and hook up wit' me. I'll show you how it's really done."

"You think you can do me better?" she asked.

"I know I can," he confidently said to her.

She peered at him for a few seconds, really liking what she was hearing and seeing. In truth, she was getting tired of Chills. She needed something new, and Tec would be just that something new she was looking for.

She left the club with him, ready to get her groove on.

Tec was loving it, as she was eating his shit up. She was very attractive, but he wasn't stressing her looks. He was more attracted to her being so close to Chills. He wanted to fuck her for just that reason, to make the beef between the two of them very personal, by running up in his bitch and fuckin' her right. And he wanted the whole hood to know about it, have them talk about how he was fuckin' Chills' bitch. Tec wanted to hit Chills below the belt and strike him where it would hurt.

They headed toward the exit. Little Boy Ronny and Pinch-Back peeped them and nodded as Tec walked out with one of the finest bitches in the club, and in Brooklyn—Lana.

They drove back to C.I., where he took her to his crib, an apartment he had over on 37th and Bay View. As soon as they entered his place, she was all over him, stripping him, molesting him, kissing him all over. They retreated downstairs to his bedroom, where clothes came off, and skin and flesh rubbed together, causing friction.

The first position he put her ass in was doggy style, having her hands clasped against the pinewood dresser with her legs and cheeks spread, ramming himself into her from the back and clutching on to her soft, perky breasts.

Lana was loving every minute of it. She called out his name while staring at herself in the dresser mirror. For the first ten minutes, he worked that ass doggy style. And then he threw her onto the single mattress he had laid across the hardwood floor. He began working it in the missionary position, then he had her begging to climb on top and ride him, which she got to do. She rode him with her hands placed flat against his chest, pussy bouncing up and down on his rock-hard dick.

Then after it was all said and done, Lana passed out beside him, feeling exultant and ready for round two.

"I fucked you good," Tec stated.

"Yes, you did," she replied happily.

"Don't I keep my promises?"

"Yes . . . you . . . do," she again replied happily, smiling pleasantly.

Tec looked over at her as she lay on her side, her back facing him. He was loving this shit, already having proven that she was a ho who liked to fuck hood-rich niggahs. He thought that now there was so much that he could do with her, knowing that she was already on his dick. Soon, she'd be saying, "Chills? Chills who?"

-Fifteen-

It was going on eight, and Mathew and Tina had just come home from spending the evening out with his mother and father at the Oakdale Country Club. The apartment was immaculate. Toni was doing such a wonderful job. He thought about her for a minute, smiling, as he always did. His regular maid, or servant, or whatever people liked to call her, was coming back to work in another three days. He didn't know what to do. He wanted to keep Toni around, but he didn't want Miranda, his regular, to be out of a job. There was no need to have two women cleaning his apartment. He didn't make that much of a mess. So he thought about it and decided that he would make his decision on whom to keep the following morning.

As they entered the apartment, Tina entered first. She uttered, "I need a shower."

Mathew closed and locked the door. He needed a little rest, considering he'd been up since six in the morning and had to deal with his mother's complex attitude and emotions and Tina's bitchiness.

Mathew plopped down on his king-size bed, peering up at the ceiling. He heard Tina in the bathroom running water and getting undressed.

Oh, what a day, he thought, resting on his bed and collecting his thoughts. Damn, he sometimes felt his life sucked, even though he was filthy rich. And he also couldn't help but feel his hormones raging fast, feeling like he was a dog in heat. He was sprawled across the bed, thinking to himself, as he heard Tina taking a shower. When the water stopped, he sat back up and peered into the bathroom as she came out of the shower naked, reaching for a towel.

God, she's gorgeous, he thought, seeing Tina's full rawness as she was drying herself off. But that was the problem for him. There was too much of seeing and not enough feeling and touching. Being a man and twenty-five, he had never experienced what some men craved for every day: the softness and pleasures of feeling a woman from the inside—pussy.

There was not a doubt that Mathew felt lust. He was horny. He kept his eyes transfixed on Tina's miraculous figure—her long legs, her soft and supple breasts, and her curving shape.

She was going to be his wife soon—forever—even though sometimes it didn't seem right.

But trying to hold his hormones in, fearing that he might receive the same outcome every time he tried to get him some, hearing her telling him no, that they must wait 'til after the wedding, was driving him up a wall.

Mathew arose from the bed, approaching her quietly while she was drying herself off and staring into the bathroom mirror.

He came up behind her, placing his arms around her waist and softly kissed her on her neck. She had a large blue towel wrapped around her and was brushing her hair gently. She smiled as Mathew caressed her and continued to kiss her on her neck.

"Umm, somebody's feeling romantic tonight," Tina said, pausing from her actions with the brush and glancing at Mathew's reflection in the mirror.

"Romantic is not the word," Mathew responded.

"So, what are you feeling?" she curiously asked.

Mathew slowly slid his hand across her breast.

"Mathew," Tina uttered, breaking free from his grip, then turning and facing him. "What are you, out of your mind?"

"What did I do wrong, Tina?"

"You know what you did wrong. Do I have to keep explaining it to you?"

"But I thought—"

"You weren't thinking, that's the problem. I told you how I feel about having sex. I want to wait until I'm married. And then legally, we can fornicate."

Fornicate? Mathew thought. He sighed, shaking his head, feeling both horny and disgusted. *How long?* he thought. Yeah, he was a rich boy, but he had emotions, desires, and cravings too. There was nothing that meant more to him in the world than to be with his fiancée physically for one night. One night was all he wanted—one night, so he could decide if this really was for him.

Tina remained in the bathroom for a few more minutes, stroking her hair, then putting on her nightly bedtime attire. She joined Mathew in bed. He was almost asleep, but she cuddled against him, then gave him a quick peck on his cheek, and said, "I love you."

At that moment, he wondered if he really loved her or if he was just marrying her because everyone thought that it would be best for them—especially his mother, who thought it would be great for him and

Tina as a married couple to carry out the family name and continue to increase the family fortune and inheritance.

The next morning Mathew awoke to find Tina dressed and ready to head out somewhere.

"I'm having a breakfast meeting at Lashes'. I shall be back sometime around evening. Call my driver and let him know to have the limo parked out front."

Mathew looked at the time to see that it was eight-fifteen. At this point, he didn't care where she was headed or how late she would be out. The previous night was a major disappointment to him. He plopped back down against the soft pillows, closed his eyes, and didn't open them 'til she was gone.

By ten, he heard the buzzer being sounded. He dragged his behind out of bed to go answer it.

"Sir Mathew, it's Ms. Toni here to see you again," the doorman informed.

"You may let her up," he said, then clicked off.

He smiled. Toni made him laugh, even sometimes when she was being sarcastic toward him. The place wasn't a mess, just one unmade bed, and probably one of the bathrooms needed to be done, but other than that, Toni had left his place looking shipshape.

Mathew covered himself in his silk red robe and walked toward the door to let Toni in. She came through smiling and greeting him with, "Good morning."

"Good morning," Mathew greeted back.

Toni strutted in, carrying another bag of groceries, ready to cook and prepare breakfast.

"You seem to be in a good mood this morning," Mathew said.

"Yeah, I'm cool," she said back.

Toni was excited about seeing her brother the following week and being able to put three hundred dollars into his commissary—looking out for him. And she really liked her job working for Mathew. Also, she couldn't help but catch feelings for him. She admired him, walking around in his red silk robe, looking too cute. But then she had to snap herself out of it. He was engaged, and besides, her life and his, they wouldn't be compatible, her being from the streets and him being upper class and all—rich, with a well-educated background.

It just wouldn't work out, she thought.

"What's on today's agenda for me?" Toni asked.

"There's nothing much to do, except for the bedroom and my bathroom," Mathew said.

"You hungry?"

"A little."

"Good. I plan to cook up some scrambled eggs, French toast, bacon . . . you do eat pork?"

"I'm not Muslim."

"Nah, you're too rich to be," she joked.

"You and these rich jokes. What if I started telling some poor jokes," Mathew said, trying to think up a few.

"Do you know any?"

"No."

"Too bad. I would love to hear a few."

"I promise next time that I'll have some for you."

"And they better be funny."

Mathew fixed himself a cup of coffee, then walked into the bedroom tittering to himself. He looked back at Toni and thought that she was just too much.

Toni started to prepare breakfast, scrambling eggs, and frying up some bacon as she danced around to the kitchen radio playing some 101.9, singing along to the Sade jam, "Smooth Operator."

Mathew peeped her singing her little tunes as he stood from out of her view. She had a somewhat good voice. She wasn't a Whitney Houston, but she had a cute little singing voice. He watched her dance around his kitchen cooking and looking happy. Just watching her was making him happy.

Toni cooked up the perfect breakfast: scrambled eggs, bacon, French toast, home fries, and some biscuits. Then she placed the dirty pots and pans in the sink, planning to wash them out later, and she fixed her and Mathew decent-sized plates.

She went into his bedroom to tell him that breakfast was ready. She heard him in the bathroom.

"Mathew," she called out, but he didn't answer.

She saw him in the bathroom as he was dripping wet and naked, coming out of the shower and drying himself off. She wanted to turn her head, but she couldn't make herself do so as she gazed at every part of him, feeling herself getting a bit excited.

He had thin arms and a flat stomach. His hair was wet and curly. She focused on his butt, then his back as she stared on, smiling. Every part of him was too cute, too tempting. He looked so innocent.

She took a deep breath, and said to herself, *This ain't right,* then she slowly stepped out of view and went back into the kitchen. A few minutes later, Mathew came to the kitchen wearing a blue silk robe.

"I already fixed you a plate," she told him, passing it to him.

"Thank you," he said, taking it.

She was starting to feel a little coy as she had secretly seen him in the buff, and she was feeling herself getting turned on.

"Umm, this is good. Once again, I give my gratitude to the chef," Mathew said after taking a bite of her eggs and French toast.

Toni smiled and did a little curtsy.

"This is a really good meal," he once again complimented.

"Okay, okay, you can stop being so polite. I know my eggs and biscuits are good. Just sit your butt down somewhere and enjoy."

Mathew took a seat at the kitchen counter, still digging into his meal. Toni also took a seat at the kitchen counter sitting opposite him.

"So, no power lunches? No dinner meetings? No exotic trips across the Atlantic in your Lear jet to dine at some fancy Paris restaurant?" Toni asked.

"No, my schedule is completely free for today," he replied.

"I'm surprised. I thought rich folks usually always had something to do or somewhere to go, something on their agenda."

"No. Can we not relax and enjoy being home some days too?"

"But you gotta keep that money flowing, though, right?"

"We have enough."

"Shit, give me a hundred thousand, and I'll be cool. I would buy myself a nice little house, a nice car, take me a trip to one of the Caribbean islands, and chill on the beach under the sun all day, not worrying about a damn thing. But you probably done been there and done that."

"No, actually, I've never been to the Caribbean," Mathew answered.

"You mean, you're sitting on all this cash, and you've never been to any of the islands, like Barbados, Jamaica, the Bahamas, or Bermuda?"

"Never had the time."

Toni sighed, not believing him, thinking he must be crazy.

"You speak as if you've been there already," Mathew said.

"No, I never in my life left New York. I've heard stories. My friend, Vinita, traveled to Bermuda once. She said she loved it there, and that it was the most beautiful country she'd ever been to. Me, I've only dreamed about going."

"So why don't you?"

Toni shot him an ignorant look. "Do I look like I have that kind of cash? Money is real tight right now. I ain't got any Swiss bank account like you, or any stocks and bonds. And besides, before I travel anywhere, bills and other expenses have to be taken care of first."

"I see."

"See. Y'all rich folks kill me with y'all silly antics, drinking tea, having brunch, being driven around in a stretch limo, traveling the world when you want. You think it's that easy for everyone else? I know you heard that money doesn't grow on trees. A girl like me, I have to fight to survive out there, trying to make that dollar and support myself. I ain't got no rich uncles or relatives to leave me a million dollars when they die. My life don't work that way."

"But you have talent, Toni. I mean, just your cooking . . . you're a great cook. That can take you somewhere far someday."

"Please. Ain't no one trying to make me famous for cooking."

"Don't limit yourself."

"Sometimes I feel that the world limits me. You want another piece of French toast?" she asked, seeing that he was on his last bite.

"Yes, please."

She got up out of her seat, getting him another two pieces. "I'm curious," she blurted.

"About what?" he asked.

She placed his second helping in front of him, then sitting back down in her seat, she asked, "How much are you, or shall I say is your father, worth? What seventy, eighty, maybe ninety million?"

Mathew let out a slight chuckle, gazing over at her. Then he said, "Seven hundred million."

Toni, taking a sip of her orange juice, nearly gagged when she heard seven hundred million dollars.

"Seven hundred million . . . seven hundred million . . . I didn't think a man could have so much money," she proclaimed.

"You didn't? Look at Bill Gates," Mathew said.

"Who?"

"Never mind."

"What do you do with so much money?"

"You let your money work for you. Investments, companies, buying and selling shares, IPO's, you know, all that boring stuff that they don't teach you in elementary school."

"Oh, that's cold, that's like hitting below the belt," Toni protested.

"Funny though, right?"

"Yeah, ayyite, I'll give you that one," she told him, cracking a smile. "So, where's your fiancée?"

"I guess she's out shopping with her girlfriends."

"Yeah, running up your credit buying Gucci, Armani, and Donna Karan, huh?"

"Don't forget Versace," he added.

Toni and Mathew were funny and looked great together. They admired each other. They both had a lot to say, and they both were enjoying each other's company. They were also curious about each other's lifestyles.

As they were talking, laughing, and enjoying breakfast together, their eyes met, saying, "I find you attractive, charming, and want to be with you"—that "let's have sex" stare. They both kept quiet, peering at each other. Toni's heart was racing as she thought about him coming out of the shower. And Mathew shuddered, thinking about what it would feel like to be with her—physically. He tried to deny it, but he couldn't. He was starting to catch strong feelings toward her, feelings he knew he should only be having for his fiancée.

"Um, are you done?" Toni asked, breaking that little love moment between the two as she got up to collect his plate.

"Yes," Mathew replied.

Toni collected his plate, along with hers and placed them into the sink, running hot water over them. Mathew retreated to the living room, trying to get his mind off Toni, but it wasn't working.

Toni walked into the living room while Mathew sat on one of his couches, gazing at television.

"Toni, I need to tell you something," he said.

"Yes."

"It may be bad news," he added.

Toni took in a deep breath. She was used to hearing bad news. It wouldn't be anything new to her. She'd probably be more shocked if Mathew told her that it was good news.

"My regular, Miranda, is coming back to work in a few more days," he said, "and there's no need for me to be having two housekeepers around."

"I understand," Toni said.

But Toni would have continued to work for him for free, loving what she was doing and where she was working—journeying out of the hood twice, sometimes three times a week. She loved the different environment, loved working and staying in his apartment, and couldn't help but like Mathew and his company just a little too much.

She stood in front of him, holding a wet rag in her hand. She didn't want to leave or relinquish her temporary position, but it wasn't her choice to make. Her little fantasyland had lasted too long. *It was fun while it lasted,* she thought.

"But, I don't want you to leave," he blurted, surprising her.

"Excuse me?" she inquired.

"Toni, you're a remarkable young woman. I've never met anyone like you. You make me laugh. You're witty, smart, and talented. You're the one person I've met who actually treated and talked to me like an adult who listens to me."

Toni was thinking the same thing of him. He treated her with respect, kindness, and trust. It was unnatural to her.

"So, what are you trying to say?" she asked.

"Maybe we can work something out," he said as he got up off the couch.

"Like what?"

He slowly walked up to her. His heart was racing. Toni stood there, peering at him as he came toward her. Their eyes met again, showing that love connection. The room was quiet. Everything was still.

Toni's heart also started to race as she thought about a million things at once. Mathew came up to her, barely touching her. He was nervous, very nervous. His heart beat rapidly, trembling just a little. He had caught strong feelings for Toni during the past weeks. And the same went for Toni.

Nothing was said as Mathew gently pressed his lips against hers, kissing her passionately. Toni accepted him, opening her mouth so their tongues could entwine. He pulled her into his arms, embracing her.

It'd been a while since Toni kissed a man like that, feeling passionate and loving. Her boyfriend, Tec, didn't have a romantic or loving bone in his body. To him, it was basically a fuck and claim thing, like she was a piece of property. But Toni, being a young woman, nearly melted as she kissed Mathew. They gripped each other tightly, forgetting about their separate lives. For that split moment, they both shared the same world.

Then suddenly Mathew broke away from her. "I'm sorry," he apologized, breathing heavily.

"Sorry about what?" she asked.

"I shouldn't have . . . I shouldn't have taken advantage of you like that. I apologize."

"There's no need to apologize, Mathew. I feel the same way too," she proclaimed.

"Yes, but . . . but," but he couldn't mention her.

"It's your fiancée. I understand," Toni said to him.

"No. I think I love her," he said.

"You think?"

They got quiet again, both lost for words. Mathew, being new to all this and still a virgin, didn't know the right approach. Just the touch of her made him so aroused and horny that he didn't know how to control himself and how to come across to her.

"I should go," she said, heading toward the kitchen.

She grabbed her belongings, then looked over at him. "It was nice working for you, Mathew. You're a sweet guy. And what you did for me, I will never forget this. Thank you, thank you so much, Mathew." She didn't want to leave. Her steps were slow. She loved it there. "Your fiancée is such a lucky woman." She stared at him.

Something she said woke him up out of whatever trance he had been in. It was when Toni said that Tina was a lucky woman to have him, yet, she didn't act like it, always criticizing him, mocking him, and sometimes speaking to him like he was some kind of young child.

Toni headed for the door. *It's better this way,* she thought. She couldn't bring him into her lifestyle, her world—the drugs, the killings, the ghetto, and her crazy boyfriend. He didn't need the drama. He lived in his own world, sheltered from the streets of Brooklyn. She thought that was best for him. He didn't need to know or find out what she was about and how she earned a buck. So she thought that this was the best option for both of them. This day was always coming soon, she knew. But it was hard to accept it.

"Toni, wait," Mathew said. She was a foot away from the door.

Toni paused, hearing him tell her to stop. She turned around, and there he was, right up on her. He grabbed her in his arms, and once again they began locking jaws with each other.

It felt so good to her as Mathew's warm lips were pressed against hers. She wrapped her arms around him. He had her pinned against the door. They both felt their hearts thudding against their chests, as this intense moment was about to get even stronger.

Mathew carried her off into the bedroom where he gently set her on the bed. Then sitting beside her, they locked lips again. Toni gently placed her hand on his thigh, feeling her way up to his crotch, then up to his chest. Mathew placed his hand on her thigh, on her stomach, then stopped there.

"What's wrong?" she asked. "You can touch me."

He looked at her. "Toni, I must admit something to you."

Toni glanced at him, curious as to what he was about to say. She already knew that he was engaged, so what else was there to tell?

"Um, um . . . I'm . . . I'm," he stammered.

"You're still a virgin?" she finished his sentence for him.

Looking ashamed about it, he nodded yes. She was surprised. *Tina isn't giving him any? That's a damn shame,* she thought. *How can you be engaged to a fine man like Mathew and not be having sex with him?* And it was weird to her, because if this happened, then she would become his first. He had never experienced a woman sexually—touching her from the inside.

The question was, was this right? Knowing that he was a virgin and still going ahead and having sex with him—this privilege or the honor, should belong to his fiancée. And for her to take that away from Tina, well it was totally wrong.

"Well, are you comfortable?" she asked.

"I'm just nervous," he told her.

"What about your fiancée? Don't you think you should save yourself for her, maybe on y'all wedding night?" she asked.

"That's the problem. I'm not too sure about her. But I'm sure about this. I want this, Toni, but I don't know how to come across about it," he said, being honest, and not knowing how to start it off.

Toni smiled, placing her hand against his face. Then she slowly kissed him, and said, "I'll help walk you through it."

She then lay down on her back as Mathew still sat on the edge of the bed. He glanced down at her as she unbuckled her jeans and pulled them off. She lay on the bed in a pair of blue-and-white panties, socks, and her T-shirt pulled up to her breasts.

Mathew slowly hunched down toward her, gliding his hand along her smooth thigh. He was definitely turned on. He couldn't hide his hard-on as it showed from underneath his robe. They both wanted every part of this. Mathew was so excited, so aroused, and not thinking about Tina at all.

"Where do we go from here?" he asked.

Toni then pulled off her panties, exposing her rawness to him. Seeing her nicely trimmed pubic hair, he gazed on wide-eyed. Being the mamma's boy that he was, he had never seen anything quite like what he was seeing.

"Take off your robe," she told him.

He rose off the bed, untying his blue silk robe and looking bashful and reluctant, but he eventually dropped the robe to the floor. He stood in a pair of blue casual-looking silk boxers.

Toni chuckled as she gazed on at him, standing in his expensive underwear with what appeared to be a mighty hard-on.

"You can lose those, too, if you feel comfortable enough," she said.

He smiled, looking at Toni as she seemed very comfortable, while he was totally the opposite. No woman—only his mother when he was young—had ever seen him naked before. Tina refused to see her man in the buff. When he showered, she told him to close the door. When she showered, she sometimes closed the bathroom door, but sometimes she'd be nice and let Mathew catch a glimpse of her, giving him a little treat.

He took a deep breath, and slowly pulled down his boxers, exposing his manhood and showing Toni how hard he was. As for penis size, he was well equipped—about eight inches, maybe more.

Toni gazed on, surprised that Mathew was packing

such a lethal thing. He wanted to cover himself, but didn't. He was a man feeling like a little boy—how wrong was that?

Toni rose off the bed, approaching Mathew while he stood there, looking lost or maybe scared. She knew that he had it in him. She just had to give him that initiative. She went up to him, gripping his erect hard-on and started to massage him gently down below. Mathew closed his eyes, feeling the pleasure of Toni's hand grasped around his thick, long penis. It felt so good to him. She pulled him toward her as she backed up toward the bed, plopping down, bringing him down on top of her. She began kissing him on his neck, touching him all over as he stayed against her.

"Condom," she blurted out.

"Huh?"

"I have a few condoms in my purse," she told him.

She went to go retrieve one, coming back into the room to see Mathew standing on his feet again.

"Relax, Mathew. Are you sure that you're up to this?" she asked him one more time.

"Yes," he answered.

She strapped a roughrider on to his erect penis, then pulled him back down onto her. Her back was pressed against his soft, king-size mattress, with him lying on top.

She slowly led his erection into her, panting as she felt his size penetrating her and opening her up. She straddled her legs around him, while his hands laid flat against the mattress, thrusting himself into her.

"Oh, Mathew," she faintly called out as she felt him. It'd been a long time since Toni felt this passionate about another man. For once she was not getting paid to fuck and not having Keith just have his way with her, with that same ol' wham, bam, thank you ma'am routine. But she felt a little guilty, him being with no one else and her being with so many. But it felt good, so good, that she didn't want him to stop.

Mathew continued to thrust himself into her. It felt so good, Toni feeling so warm from the inside and so moist. He couldn't control it anymore. It felt too good. So good, that he had to let it out. His penis pulsated inside of her as he felt like he was about to burst.

"Oh, Mathew," Toni faintly called out again as she felt his hardness inside of her, feeling him about to explode in her.

Mathew clutched the sheets tightly, his butt cheeks tightening as he came inside of Toni. Toni gripped his back while Mathew shook, having had his first orgasm inside a woman. He couldn't believe it. He had just had sex. He lost his virginity, and at the same time, cheated on his fiancée.

Still suspended over her, he stared down at her as she looked up at him, still lying on her back with her legs spread. She had loved every minute of it. It wasn't that cheesy and rough sex she was used to having with tricks and Keith. Nah, this was something special to her. She wanted to savor every moment of it, even though it was quick—only about four minutes.

"Did I do OK?" Mathew asked as he collapsed beside her, down on his back.

"You did more than OK, Mathew. You did more than OK," she said to him, feeling emotional.

"You OK, Toni?" he asked.

"Yeah, Mathew, it's just . . . I have to be honest," she said, wanting to tell him the truth about her, what she did for a living, but she didn't want to bring him into that world. *He's better off not knowing,* she thought.

"What is it?" he asked.

She held her tongue for a minute, not so sure that it

was wise to tell him all about herself. She didn't want to ruin this lovely moment between the two of them.

"Can you please hold me, Mathew?" she said in a civil tone.

Mathew didn't even hesitate as he placed his arms around Toni and brought her closer to him, cuddling like they were a true couple. No one ever cuddled with her after sex. Keith, please, after he finished fucking her, he would then act like he was allergic to her or something. He would either fall asleep or bounce right up after he got his. And her tricks, there was no love there. They paid her, she pleased them, and that was it. It was just a need type of thing—they needed pussy, and she needed cash.

Mathew continued to hold Toni in his arms throughout the afternoon as they lay naked under satin sheets and talked. And not once was Mathew thinking about Tina. All his thoughts were on Toni and how good the sex was, even though this was his first time.

Toni lay next to him, enjoying his company and feeling like a woman as Mathew embraced her. They cuddled, and she loved every second of it. For the first time in a long while, after sex she didn't feel dirty or feel like scrubbing herself after some nasty niggah had ejaculated all over her after a quick blowjob, or giving them a hand-job. Nah, she felt right loving his scent on her. But then she started thinking. It wasn't stressing her, but in her head, she kept asking herself, *Where do we go from here?*

-Sixteen-

Toni's alarm went off at 3:35 A.M., disturbing her from a good night's sleep. It was Thursday, and she was excited because she was going to see her incarcerated brother. She'd planned to arrive early, around eleven, maybe twelve the latest. That's why she had set her alarm for so early in the morning.

She stepped out of bed, stretched, and began preparing herself for one long day. She showered, dressed, and retrieved the three hundred dollars she had hidden from her mother, to put into his commissary.

By 4:40, she was out of her apartment door, and ready to catch the six o'clock Greyhound that made frequent trips to upstate prisons. She darted down the building steps, unfortunately catching a vulgar act being committed in the dimly lit staircase. A young hustler was getting his shit knobbed by some young female base head who was probably sucking him off for a hit. She quickly hurried past them as the base head glanced up at her, then continued with her business.

She arrived at the prison at 10:45 that morning, once again filing into a single line as visitors checked in one by one. Dressed in a pastel, printed wrap skirt; ankle-high leather boots; and a white one-shoulder top, she caught the attention of some correction officers and a few other visitors as they gawked at her for a few seconds. She was looking cute, and they couldn't deny her that.

As usual, she was asked who she was there to see, went through about three metal detectors, and placed all her contraband and other valuables into a small locker. Then she was escorted into the visitor's room where she was seated and waited for her brother's arrival.

She waited for about twelve minutes before she saw him coming out. He walked single file with about four other inmates, and as usual, he was draped in a blue prison jumpsuit, his hair unbraided and frizzled out.

"What up, sis?" he called out, embracing her in a deep and loving hug.

"Hey, Thomas," she greeted him back.

They both took their seats. Thomas was smiling, happy to see his one and only loving sister again.

"So, what's been going on?" he asked.

"Damn, you ain't braiding that shit?" she asked, staring up at his wild-looking hair, looking like an uncontrollable Afro.

"Nah, you know, ain't no bitches up in here, just niggahs. And the ones that do braid, you know, they faggot niggahs. They can't do as good a job like how you used to do it, sis," he mentioned, running his hand across his scalp.

"So why don't you just cut that shit?" she asked.

"Please, I ain't tryin' to cut my shit."

"I wish I had a comb. I would take care of that mess right now," she said.

"It's cool. Don't be stressing my hair, Toni."

"I got your letter," she informed.

"Word. So you took care of that for me?" he asked, curious to see if she put money into his account.

"Yeah, you know I had to look out for you."

"How much did you bless me wit', sis?"

"I'm not telling you," she said to him, smiling and tittering.

"C'mon. Yo, it better not be no lousy five or ten dollars. You know a niggah can't live off that up in here. Shit, I gotta eat too."

"Thomas, don't worry about it. I looked out for you. You're set," she happily informed him.

"Ayyite, ayyite, I know you did. So how's Ma doing?"

Toni sighed, wishing that he hadn't bought up that question. She hated coming to see him alone and then having him ask about their mother. The trips she made would be better if their mother came along to accompany her and she got to see Thomas too.

"It's the same. Ain't nuthin' change wit' that woman, Thomas."

"Word," he sadly said.

"It's hard, Thomas."

"Toni, hang in there. I can't do nuthin' for her up in here, but you, you're out there. Take care of her. All she needs is help, Toni. Don't give up on her," he said, pausing. "You know, I still love that woman, even through all the shit she done put us through."

"She don't even be home like that anymore. All she does is go out and get herself fucked up, then, the other day, I saw her having some young boy in her bedroom."

Thomas' expression sunk. He didn't need to be a rocket scientist to know what that was about—his mother, trickin' for hits. He couldn't even picture his mother doing what she was doing. And if he was out of prison, he knew for a fact that certain shit that was happening now, wouldn't be.

If he would have caught that young niggah in his mother's bedroom with his pants down, you best believe he would've probably put that niggah to rest, or put him in a serious coma.

Thomas still had the respect he earned out there on the Brooklyn streets, even though he was gonna be caged for the remainder of his natural life. Niggahs in C.I. and in other parts of Brooklyn still spoke his name, still respected him. And now with his boy, Tec, trying to carry out and continue what he had started, it was probably gonna be wildfire out there.

Thomas asked about around the way, curious about his boy Tec, Little Boy Ronny, and so on. He was up on certain things, like the beef that was escalating between Tec and Chills. He knew about Wallace's death, and the twenty-five-thousand-dollar contract on his boy's head. But he wanted to know about his sister's relationship with Tec. After he got locked up, he found out that they'd become a couple. That shit didn't sit well with him at first, his baby sister fuckin' his number one boy. But what was he to do? When she first came to see him, when he was still in Rikers, he warned her. But you know, she didn't care. Tec was doing his thing, taking care of her, watching out for her, something that her big brother used to do before he got himself locked up. It was known around the hood that Tec and Toni were fuckin', that was Tec's bitch, and you best not be disrespecting her or he was gonna carry out that 187.

"So, what's up wit' that club? You still stripping down there?" he asked.

"Yeah. Why you keep asking?"

"You know how I feel 'bout that, Toni."

"C'mon, Thomas, let's not go through that again. I need the damn money," she said with a scowl.

"So, get a real job," he spat back.

"Doing what, Thomas? You know I dropped out of high school. You know Ma's sick, so what the fuck else am I supposed to do?"

"What about your cooking?"

"What about it?" she countered.

"You can burn, sis. I know you can make money off that. Grandma taught you how to cook like you were a gourmet chef. Yo, you can start something."

She sighed, leaning back in her chair. She was getting tired of hearing this shit from him, and how she needed to do something different, how it wasn't right for her to be dancing up in some grungy club.

"Sis, I've been hearing things about you. Things that I shouldn't be hearing," Thomas continued.

"Like what?"

"Like you in that club doing more than dancing," he told her, leaning across the table with his hands clasped together.

"Thomas, please."

"You're my baby sister, Toni. What the fuck you doing out there spreading your legs like you some kinda ho?"

"Thomas, I ain't come up here to be lectured about my life," she angrily told him.

"What, you trickin' like Ma now?" he asked.

"Fuck you, Thomas," she barked, angrily rising from her seat and causing a bit of attention on herself as the C.O.'s looked on cautiously.

"Look, sis, sit down. I'm sorry. I ain't mean that," he calmly said.

Toni slowly took her seat, sitting upright and peering at Thomas.

"It's just that I care about you, Toni. You is the only sister, the only family that I have out there, and without you, I have nothing. I can't even look out for you, protect you while I'm wasting away up in this bitch. If anything would ever happen to you, I don't know what I'd do wit' myself."

"Thomas, I can take care of myself," she assured him.

"Yeah, everyone says that, 'til they end up dead," he said.

Toni kept quiet. They remained silent. Thomas scratched the side of his face and glanced around the room at other inmates and their visitors. He gave another inmate a nod, one of his boys, whose girl came to visit him. She was looking right.

After that little bitter incident between the two, they got back on track. Toni was laughing and joking with her brother again. Thomas told her that a few niggahs up in there were checking her out, and they still were eyeing Toni from the corner of their eyes as they sat with family, friends, and girlfriends.

It was going on three, and visitor hours would soon come to an end. Thomas told her about Muhammad and how he was continuing to stay out of trouble and trying to be with Allah—trying to. He broke away from some of his homies that were from the streets and caught a few new friends with some Muslim brothers.

Toni was so happy for her older brother, seeing this new transformation in him. He hadn't been violent in a while. He told her that he was trying to stop doing drugs and smoking weed, and that he might marry his long-time girlfriend and sweetheart, Alicia. Besides Toni, Alicia had been coming to visit him frequently too. She lived in Flatbush and held down a job as a schoolteacher.

Thomas couldn't wait for those conjugal visits.

Toni hadn't seen Alicia since her brother's incarceration. They didn't keep in contact, and they'd never been that cool. Toni felt that Alicia was too uppity and shit, and she still didn't know how a female like her fell in love with her gangsta brother in the first place.

But she was still happy for him.

Visiting hours were over, and inmates and visitors slowly started to rise from their seats, giving their loved ones long-lasting and loving hugs. Toni clutched onto her brother tightly. She hated these moments, telling him good-bye, and not knowing when she would next be able to come and see him again. Her brother was the world to her, and every day she asked herself why he had to spend his life in a place like this. She wanted him home, where he belonged. But just like so many other black inmates, home was a place he wouldn't see in a very long, long time. These men had to accept the fact that being behind bars, in prison, was where their home was, where the warden was their mother and the C.O.'s were their daddies.

And it was fucked up for them, not being able to see or roam the streets, waking up in a ten-by-ten cell and looking at the same fate every day of their lives. They worried about loved ones, were curious about changes, and became teary-eyed over their children, who they would not be able to raise, shelter, love, or advise as they sat withering away in a jail cell.

Toni became teary-eyed as she watched her brother being escorted back into the jail, led by the C.O.'s. She tried to dry away her tears, but more soon followed after she wiped away the first ones.

Back on the Greyhound, Toni sat back in her seat, threw her headphones over her ears, pressed play on her CD player, and prepared herself for the long ride back to New York City.

-Seventeen-

Mathew stood next to the kitchen counter with a glass of white wine clutched in his hands. He was chatting with Paul, a friend he'd known for a few years. The ladies were in the great room flipping through bridal magazines and discussing wedding dates.

Tina was still unsure if she wanted a winter wedding in December or a spring wedding in early June. However, she was very sure that this wedding was going to be the most beautiful and artistic ever.

"I'm thinking about having my wedding in the Bahamas," Tina boasted to her friends as they sat around, smiling and giggling.

"You are such a lucky woman, Tina," one of her friends said.

"Yes, that Mathew, he is definitely a catch," another one mentioned.

"Yes, ladies, I know. My Mathew, he's my pride and joy," Tina said.

"Handsome too," another lady complimented.

"Yes, he is," Tina said, "and it doesn't hurt that seven hundred million dollars comes along with that handsome face."

They all chuckled.

Mathew, who remained in the kitchen with Paul keeping him company, was thinking his own thoughts about Toni. It had been a week since his sexual encounter with her—and a week too long since he had heard from her. She hadn't called him, and she didn't answer her phone when he called her apartment to check and see if everything was OK with her. He heard the females chitchatting away in the next room, but he paid them no mind.

"So, Mathew, how does it feel to be marrying such a stunning and beautiful woman?" Paul asked, interrupting his thoughts.

Mathew shrugged, not knowing how to answer.

"Are you nervous?" Paul asked.

Nervous wasn't even the word—unsure was more like it. He heard Tina boasting about the wedding and her girlfriends laughing and wishing her the best and congratulating her.

"Boy, I tell you, Mathew, you're a lucky man. That Tina, she's a catch, if you know what I mean," Paul said to him, then took a sip from his wine.

"You think so?" Mathew finally said.

"Yes, I think so. So, tell me a secret," Paul suddenly whispered. "How good is she in the sack?"

"Excuse me?"

"Is the sex with her fantastic or what?" Paul wanted to know.

"I wouldn't know," he admitted honestly.

"What do you mean, Mathew?"

"I mean, we haven't had sex yet."

Paul looked at him as if he had to be kidding.

"You mean to tell me that she's holding out on you, buddy?"

"I'm afraid so."

"Ah, how sad. Did you at least try?"

"Too many times," Mathew said, setting his glass of wine on the counter.

"It should be a crime for a beautiful woman like that to hold out on her fiancé. Every man should at least know how the bedroom action is with his woman before he goes and marries her. Are you OK, though?"

"Yeah, I'm holding out."

"Well, don't stress it, buddy. Just think about your wedding night—when the day finally comes—and you'll be able to make love to your beautiful wife all night long, until morning. But until that day comes, take this card." Paul passed him a green-and-white card with the name Dreams written across it.

"What's this?" Mathew asked, taking the card from his hand.

"It's a private escort service. They have some of the most beautiful women at that place. All you have to do is call up that number, tell them your sexual preference—if you want them black, white, big, or small—and they'll send someone. It's expensive, but they'll come and serve you real well. A man of your status doesn't need to be worrying about how much the girls are going to cost, right, pal?"

Mathew flashed a light smile as he glanced at the card Paul had given him.

"What about Nadine, your wife?" Mathew asked curiously.

"What about her, buddy? I love my wife, but she's too uptight sometimes. She can't perform some of the things that these ladies at this escort service do. I ask my wife for a simple blowjob, and she tells me no, like I'm a stranger to her."

Nadine was one of the girls sitting in the great room with Tina, discussing marriage and bridal gowns with the other girls.

"Mathew, I know how you feel, but believe me, that number is worth giving a call."

Mathew looked at the card, then placed it in his pocket. Tina walked into the kitchen to refill her glass. She gave Mathew a quick kiss on his cheek while Paul watched and smiled.

"How is everything?" Paul asked.

"Just fine, Paul," Tina responded, taking the bottle of wine from off the kitchen countertop and heading back to the great room with her lady friends. Paul gazed at Tina's rear end for a few seconds, fantasizing about things he shouldn't be fantasizing about with his friend's fiancée.

It was a Friday evening, and Mathew sat at home alone wondering about Toni. Giving up on her, he retrieved the card that Paul had given him and glanced at it. He was actually thinking about calling this escort service Paul had mentioned to him just a few days ago.

Tina, as usual, was out with her upscale friends, socializing at the Oakdale Country Club. *Does she ever get tired of the place?* Mathew asked himself as he sat in front of the television watching the headline news.

He glanced at the card a few more times, contemplating if he should give it a try. That experience with Toni made him want to explore his sexual horizons even more, give himself more practice. It was his first experience, and he loved every minute of it. He even started to think more about how it would feel to be with

Tina physically, but was it worth marrying her just to find out?

Not being able to hold out any longer, and not wanting to stress Toni, already thinking that she was gone from his life for good, he picked up the phone and dialed the number on the card.

Around ten-fifteen, she showed up. Her name was Julie, and the night doorman did not have a problem letting her up to Mathew's luxury apartment. Mathew came to answer the door in a pair of burgundy silk pajamas. He opened the door and was stunned by how beautiful and exquisite Julie turned out to be. Paul wasn't lying.

"Can I come in?" she asked, gazing at him and smiling. She was dressed in a long, lean, luxurious silk dress. Her hair was long and dyed light brown with blond highlights, and her figure was to die for. She stood there, clutching her purse in her hand and smiling at Mathew as he stood in the doorway.

"Yes, I'm sorry," he apologized for keeping her standing in the hallway for so long. He moved to the side, allowing her to step into his place.

He was nervous, having second thoughts for following Paul's advice. But she was so beautiful, and her services were expensive. She charged fifteen hundred dollars for the night.

Julie, overwhelmed by the opulence of his apartment, peered around the place before she took a seat on the plush leather couch.

"Can I get you a drink?" he asked.

"Yes. Do you have any rum?"

"Um, I don't think so, but I do have some white wine," he told her.

"Fine, that will do."

He went into the kitchen to prepare her drink. Julie gazed at him, admiring everything about him. *He's cute,* she said to herself. *And he's rich.* She knew that tonight would be worth her time.

Mathew came back into the room with a nicely filled glass of white wine. She accepted it, taking a few quick sips, then setting the glass down on a coaster he had placed on his glass table.

They'd spoken over the phone, and she had already informed him of her price. Mathew had the cash. He had a little over twenty thousand dollars stashed away safely in his apartment.

Julie remained seated on the leather couch while Mathew remained standing. The room was quiet. There was not a word being said by either one. Julie sat there with her legs crossed, hands resting on her lap, waiting. Mathew, nervous and still unsure, tried to bring himself to do the deed. He needed this. His body ached for it. Having had his first taste of sex, he regretted that he'd been missing out on it for the past twenty-five years.

"So, are you OK with this?" Julie asked.

He let out a soft sigh, then said, "I think so."

In his silk pajamas, Mathew took a seat across from her. Once again, his heart pounded rapidly. *Damn, why do I have to go through this? Why can't Tina be like any other female and have sex with her fiancé?* But she wanted to remain pure 'til her wedding day. Not that it was a crime, but it was hurting him deeply. He needed to feel the softness of a woman, the comfort and joy of sex.

Julie stood and straightened out her dress while Mathew went into the bedroom to get her fee. She was ready for him. He was handsome, charming, and wealthy—the three qualities she loved about a man. She charged fifteen hundred dollars and was worth every cent. She gave one hundred percent to her date, not holding back on a damn thing.

Mathew came out of the bedroom with a white envelope that was filled with cash. She counted it and stuffed it into her purse. For some strange reason, Mathew began to think about his friend Paul, wondering if he dated her, too, but he was interrupted from his weird thought when Julie pushed up on him, grasping his penis through his silk pajamas. He became hard within seconds.

"Relax, Mathew," she seductively whispered in his ear as she fondled and groped him.

His eyes widened. He was too excited. She took his hand and slowly placed it over her breasts, allowing him to squeeze and massage them. She tenderly kissed him around his neck, up to his ears, then lightly on his mouth. She backed away from him about two feet, and she started to undress herself, taking off her dress and standing there in a pair of exotic underwear—a purple thong and a lace bra. Her stomach was flat with definition; her breasts, perky, just the right handful; her bottom, firm and tender. She looked like the perfect specimen of how a woman should be built. Julie, Tina, Toni, they all had wonderful bodies, and they were all beautiful women, but tonight, he was going to experience sex with Julie. He was a man—a horny man—and he had waited too long in his life, he felt, only to be having sex now. There was a lot of catching up he had to do.

Julie came toward him as Mathew slowly placed his hands on her hips. He leaned over and gave her a kiss on her lips. Her breath smelled like winterfresh gum, and her perfume awakened his nostrils with a foreign and pleasant fragrance. She placed her arms around him, bonding them intimately together as they passionately kissed each other. She felt his erection peeking out from his silk pajamas, so she decided to remove them, having Mathew come out of his clothing and see what kind of package he was working with.

She was astounded by the magnitude of his erection. He gave her a bashful smile as he stood naked in front of Julie. He wanted to cover himself, but Julie wouldn't allow it.

"Don't be modest. You carry a wonderful size," she told him. She grasped his penis in her fist, stroking him gently.

Then she also stripped, removing her thong and unsnapping her bra. She stood there nude and allowed Mathew to fondle and feel on whatever body part he wanted. It was his money, and he was able to do whatever he wanted to do with her for the night, as long as it didn't involve her getting herself killed or injured. But she didn't have to worry about any harm coming from him. He looked like a meek fellow anyway.

The foreplay went on for about ten minutes. They both stood naked in the living room, excited. Julie caused Mathew to act like he was having convulsions because she was stroking him down below so good and so gently, her small fist containing his hard erection.

"You ready for me, Mathew?" she softly asked.

He nodded. And like before, he did not once think about his fiancée, Tina. And that was neither a good thing nor a bad thing, for him or for her.

In the bedroom, Mathew stroked her submissively as he lay between Julie's parted legs, clutching his satin sheets tightly and thrusting himself into her. His mouth was wide open as he moaned, feeling every bit of Julie's insides—her moisture. She straddled him, gripping his back, as she felt the fullness of his erection buried deep inside her. Mathew continued to moan while he stroked. He couldn't control it anymore. He let out a loud roar as he felt himself coming, and caused Julie to also pant as she felt him deep inside her. He then collapsed on his back, staring up at the ceiling.

For twenty-five years, this was what he had been missing out on. He never imagined that it could feel so good, to climax inside a female, to make love to her. He wondered how he was able to maintain his virginity for so long. Were his parents—or should he say, his mother and his fiancée—that possessive over his youthful life that he never got to experience what being young and spirited was all about? He was missing out on a lot. He was the son of a multi-millionaire and he had advantages to many things. But during the past twenty-five years, it felt like he'd been limited from many things, even having sex.

He looked over at Julie while she laid beside him, tickling his chest, and he gave her the warmest and deepest smile, wanting to tell her thank you—to her and Toni. They'd helped him experience something that he'd been missing from Tina and throughout his entire life.

He also wanted to thank Paul for opening his eyes. He'd been stuck on Tina for far too long. Now he felt that it was time to live his life—as Toni would say, it was time for him to do him.

-Eighteen-

Gangstas—some people loved them, and some people despised them. Some females flocked to that gangsta, thug, and roughneck image/lifestyle like many fans praise Elvis. What was it about that thug and roughneck image that ladies admired so much? Why did some ladies risk their lives, put themselves in danger so that they could hang around and fuck a thug? What kind of qualities did women see in that type of character? Was it the money, the danger, that street rep, or that respect they received out there on the streets every day, hustling, dodging police, and constantly watching their backs from the haters, competition, and the stick-up kids? It was a life where Hollywood profited big from hood movies and gangster films that were based on the streets. They knew many fans would run to the theaters to go see that new hood flick with the latest rap star playing that hoodlum, or go cop that bestselling book depicting how rough and hard street life was.

It was entertainment for some, but it was also reality for others.

Out there, in the streets, image was everything. That street name could carry a thug a long way, holding down that credibility. Sometimes when people heard a certain name, they knew what to expect from that person, knew what he or she was about. And it was intriguing to some who were unaware of the streets. The game, to some, was a joke—nothing but amusement to them. They might watch and read about it, but for many, that was all they knew.

Tec stayed in Karen's bed throughout the morning. He'd been doing nothing but fuckin' her all night. Tec rarely spent the night at the same place twice in a row. He would sleep in his apartment maybe once or twice a week. But he would mostly shack up with local bitches around the way or chill with his boys throughout the night. He was not a predictable muthafucka, making spontaneous moves most of the time. He knew that his lifestyle would cause certain muthafuckas to come searching for him, ready to gun him down whenever they could catch up to him. So he made it difficult for them, not resting his head too long in the same place, always carrying a gat, and not informing everyone of his moves or his whereabouts.

When someone was in dirt as much as he was, he had to be cautious, constantly glancing over his shoulder and ready to cap anyone, anywhere, at anytime.

Karen, some big booty ho he knew for a minute now, rolled out of bed ass naked, leaving Tec still asleep, with the .45 not too far from his reach in case some stupid shit went down.

Karen walked back into the bare, hardwood-floor bedroom, furnished with only a bed, a television set placed on the floor, a full-length mirror against the tattered, stained white wall, and sheets emulating shades over the windows. She had a bowl of cereal in her hands. She turned on the old black-and-white TV, sat down next to Tec, and began to eat her bowl of Apple Jacks.

Hearing her munching, Tec woke up, cursed her, and told her to be quieter with that shit. But he couldn't sleep anymore. She had already woke his ass up with her loud-ass smacking.

He strolled into her bathroom, taking a long piss, then came back into the bedroom to join her in bed.

"Bitch, you ain't fixed me a bowl?" he cursed.

"You were sleep, niggah," she chided back at him.

"Whatever."

He then got up, peered out the window down the street, and saw nothing but the usual. Coney Island around eleven in the morning, ain't shit going on. It was still too fuckin' early.

He jumped back in bed with Karen, who was finishing up her bowl of cereal by slurping the remaining milk from the bowl. All three of her kids were down the block at her mother's, and as far as she was concerned, they could stay their bad asses down at Grandma's for the entire day. Karen was rested up on some dick, and she planned to get some more dick action right after she finished her next bowl.

A little after one, Tec left from her crib after digging into Karen's stuff for the last time that day. He left her passed out on the bed, and he didn't plan on coming to check her again anytime soon.

He stopped by Toni's place, catching her preparing breakfast, telling her to fix him a plate too. And she did, preparing him an omelet and some toast.

"You still working that other job?" Tec asked.

"No," she answered, taking a seat at the table.

"Good. I was gonna tell you to quit that shit anyway," he said, then dug into his omelet.

She sighed, glaring over at Tec, feeling like she wanted to smack him across his silly face. *How dare he?* she thought, trying to tell her what she could and could not do. He was very disrespectful. She had quit working for Mathew because she had her reasons. It was guilt, mixed along with a little compassion. Mathew was too sweet of a guy for her to have him get involved with her complex lifestyle. She also felt embarrassed that she would have to tell him what she did for a buck, and she didn't want to take it that far. Besides, he was engaged.

But that one moment she spent with him, she thought about it every day—how special he made her feel, how good it felt to have a man love her, make love to her, and then not passing her a buck afterward and leaving her to clean up herself.

Tec continued to dig into his plate while Toni sat at the table, lost in her own thoughts.

"You dancing down at the club tonight, right?" Tec asked, finishing up his omelet.

"Yeah . . . why?"

"No reason," he said.

It got quiet again, then suddenly Tec's pager went off. Removing himself from the seat, he went to go make the call back, using the phone in the kitchen. He spent about three minutes on the phone, and as usual, afterward he left the place without informing Toni about shit. He had a full belly and got his fuck on earlier with Karen, so he was straight for the day.

"Shots fired, shots fired, shots fired," a patrol officer yelled through his radio as six shots were fired into two unknown hoodlums. The assailant retreated south, down 33rd Street, having the foot officer give chase with his gun drawn, and screaming into his handheld police radio.

A man, wearing a white tank top, baggy blue jeans, and a fitted baseball cap pulled down over his eyes, scampered down the block, then got into a red Buick that screeched off, passing the foot cop and a fleet of bystanders and witnesses.

A half an hour later, law enforcement was all over the crime scene. Yellow police tape bordered the perimeter, and the two bodies were sprawled out in front of a dingy bodega, while many local folks looked on. There was even a helicopter in search up above, looking for the red Buick that sped off. But the search was a bust, and the bandits got away.

People were scared to talk. Many saw, as usual, but no one would say a word to anyone wearing a badge, a gun, or a uniform. Folks knew the deal. They knew that there was a drug war going on and that dangerous people were involved, cold-hearted killers with quick trigger fingers and no conscience in their hearts. When police or detectives started asking questions, they ignored them and walked away, fearful of getting involved.

Night was about to fall, and word traveled quickly around the hood. Almost all of Coney Island heard about the shooting and the two dead men. They were well known around the projects, and many felt what went around came around. The two dead men had definitely played their hands in many dirty activities, even murder. Now they'd finally played the part of being on the other end of a smoking barrel, dying by the sword.

It wasn't long 'til Tec heard the news about his two fallen comrades, Lamont and Pinch-Back, and he was beyond upset. He felt that a violent vendetta must begin. They got at him, then he would get at them—the urban law, eye for an eye—because rarely would a gangsta turn the other cheek.

Tec rounded up a few of his homies, including Little Boy Ronny. They piled into two cars and hunted after those fools—Chills and his niggahs. They headed out to Brownsville, where Chills also held down operations in the Van Dyke houses, Tilden houses, and Unity houses—quite the entrepreneur he was. They searched all night, but found no one, not even one of his close associates. Tec wanted to shoot someone between the eyes and give him that message, "We're out for you and we're close."

After about an hour and a half of searching, they headed back to Coney Island. Tec was ready to kill anyone, even one of Chills' two-bit, unknown dealers.

He circled the blocks over by Brighton Beach and Neptune, and one of the guys in the crew pointed out two known dealers working for Chills. *They'll do for now,* Tec said to himself. They rolled around the block one last time, then the cars pulled up to the curb, where two small-time hustlers took notice. They peered at both cars pulling up toward them. A nervous and cautious look surfaced in both men's eyes. They were young, but not that young, about nineteen or twenty.

The window in the first vehicle was rolled down, and Tec glared out at them as an Uzi rested on his lap. Hard glares were exchanged as one tried to intimidate the other, but Tec was winning the stare-down. He didn't blink or move. He was 'bout ready to put those little niggahs to sleep. He could smell the fear in both men, no matter how hard and threatening they tried to look or play the part. He knew they were scared. He saw it in their eyes. They had to be scared when there were two unknown cars parked in front of them, a crew of niggahs strapped, and no one was smiling. They would be fools if they didn't know that it was about to go down.

After a few quick seconds of hard stare-downs, doors abruptly flew open, and with an Uzi gripped in his hand, Tec started firing, hitting them both as they tried to flee for safety. The others raced out of their seats, firing along with Tec and riddling both men with gunfire, tearing them open, spinning them violently around, and having them fall dead to the ground. The gunfire could be heard blocks away, echoing throughout the streets, startling some and warning others. Tec and his crew hastily retreated into their cars and sped off—an eye for an eye.

Tec and his boys lay low for a while, trying not to bring too much attention on themselves. With that twenty-five-thousand-dollar contract lingering over Tec's head, and his boys Pinch-Back and Lamont dead, Tec knew that he definitely had to be cautious and alert.

They mostly stayed out in Gravesend housing, gambling, smoking, and hanging out on the benches. Everyone was armed, and everyone was alert to any strange activity going down. But they refused to let this little drug war and this deadly beef divert them from living their lifestyles—doing them. Nah, with that gangsta blood in them, they had to play the part. If shit went down, and they died while in the process, then so be it. At least they went out like true hood niggahs—down for themselves and their crew—and that's what separated the real niggahs, the gangsters, from the wannabes and the pussy niggahs.

It was going on midnight, and the projects were jumping. Everyone was outside. There was the young and old chilling in the streets, radios playing, cars cruising by, niggahs kickin' game, marijuana being smoked, and dice being rolled.

Tec and the rest of his crew mourned the loss of Pinch-Back and Lamont. They were his niggahs. But what was done was done. They would be buried, and life would move on. Death and murder were common to most folks out there. Some saw it every day, especially the hustlers in the game. It was like a clause in their contract.

As the night progressed, some folks retreated indoors, wary about hanging out too late on the streets, especially with this drug war going on. Tec, Little Boy Ronny, and a few others continued their little dice game, blowing smoke out their mouths from the cigarettes and the blunt being passed around. Seven hundred dollars was up for grabs, and there had been a few arguments, but nothing physical—at least not yet. Two .45s were placed down on the bench as the owners of the guns were tired of concealing them and were more worried about rolling the dice and snatching up the loot.

A green 328i BMW convertible came driving around the way. The top was down, the system playing, and the driver was in search of Tec. The car parked on Bay View, across the street from the park, and the driver stepped out, glancing everywhere then heading into Gravesend, seeing a group of fellows in a circle, loud and looking rough.

"Yo, Tec, who this bitch?" one of the fellows asked.

Tec stopped what he was doing, with the dice in his hand, and glanced up at shortie as she came his way.

"Oh, shit, that's that bitch, Lana," Little Boy Ronny mentioned.

"You mean Chills' bitch?" Nate, another close and deadly friend of Tec's uttered.

"Yeah, dog."

A .45 was cocked back, and Nate said, "Yo, Tec, let's kidnap this bitch, hold her for ransom."

"Nah, niggah, hold it down," Tec said, dropping the dice and walking her way.

Nate glared at her. He wanted so bad to either rape and kidnap this bitch, or put a bullet in her head for being Chills' bitch and being so stupid coming out there alone—sweet vengeance for his niggahs Pinch-Back and Lamont.

"What's up?" Tec greeted, not smiling at her.

"I'm sayin' tho', Tec, it's been days since we hooked up. I was starting to think that you weren't interested in me no more."

"Shit is getting hectic and thick out here . . . "

"Too hectic for you to throw a fuck in me?" Lana said, up close and personal against Tec, her breath mixed with his, her eyes fixated on him. She saw the coldness in his eyes, his expressionless grill, and it was turning her the fuck on.

Lana was hooked on the dick, and she was playing a dangerous game between two dangerous men. She knew it too. These past days, she and Tec had been fuckin' like they were trying to make babies and shit—doing it in motels, under the Verrazano Bridge, late at night in the park, and occasionally, back at his place.

The pussy was good. Tec couldn't deny that. The bitch was a nasty freak, and he'd been fuckin' her like her pussy was about to fall off. But also being cautious, Tec was wary that this could also be a setup for him—Chills sending his bitch out to do his dirty work for him. That's why when he was with her, he didn't stray too far from home, and he made sure he was packin' more than one gat. This bitch could be two-faced.

Wearing a tight little leather skirt, a halter top, and some stilettos, Lana was looking too tempting, too sexy, too pleasing. Her hair was in two long, sexy pigtails.

"I ain't got no panties on right now," she seductively informed Tec. She took his hand and placed it between her legs, moving his hand up her thigh and onto her moistness. "I'm horny, Tec."

"Lana, what game you playing?" Tec barked.

"What you mean, baby?" Lana asked.

"First off, bitch, I ain't your man. Second off, why should I keep from blowing your muthafuckin' head off? You might be setting me up for that niggah Chills to get at me."

"Tec, it ain't even like that. I just wanna fuck. Chills can't do me like how you be doing me, Tec. You be working my shit."

He glared at her, then said, "Lana, if I find out you setting me up, I swear, I'll ram the barrel of a long and cold .357 magnum down your neck and shoot your pussy out from the inside."

"Tec, why you gotta be like that? I'm telling you, Chills don't know nuthin' 'bout me and you. If he did, then I wouldn't be standing here right now."

He stared at her for a moment, and not being able to resist, he took her by her hand and led her into one of the buildings.

"Yo, niggah, where you going? You ain't gonna finish rolling?" one of the niggahs rolling in the circle shouted out.

"Niggah, I'll be back," was all Tec said.

They went into one of the building lobbies, then into the poorly lit, pissy-smelling staircase, where Tec forced Lana down on her knees, and she began to suck him off. He told her to stay down on her knees, and the stupid bitch did as she was told, blowing Tec for a full twenty minutes. Then he forced her against the wall, hiking up her skirt, and he stuffed himself into her, raw and all, hittin' it doggy style with Lana loudly panting and scratching the wall.

About forty-five minutes later, Tec came out the building lobby, zipping up his pants, and leaving Lana walking back to her car with a gap—dick did her justice.

Fucking, using, and taking advantage of Chills' bitch was so sweet. Like Snoop would say, "Niggah, your bitch chose me." Tec had been disrespecting Lana in all kinds of ways, bustin' off in her mouth, cursing her out, and one time he even smacked her across her grill because she got loud over some stupid shit. But she kept coming back for more. She was a beautiful girl, but a dumb fuckin' ho.

-Nineteen-

Vinita sat cordially at her table, waiting for Myron to arrive. He was fifteen minutes late. They had reservations at the Brownstone Elite, an upscale restaurant located on the lower east side of Manhattan.

It was a special night for her. It was her twenty-third birthday, and Myron had planned a special night out. He called and told her that he would meet her at the restaurant. He had to take care of a little business. So Vinita called a cab and made her way to the place early, fifteen minutes before their reservation time. She was sitting at a table, drinking glasses of water and nibbling on rolls that the waiter kept bringing by for her. And she was dressed to kill. Men in the place eyed her sexiness while she sat in a black, sheer mesh camisole and a skirt with silver sequined trim and scalloped edging. Her hairdo was up in an exquisite French roll with two strands falling down to her eyes, giving her an enticing style and causing her to be the center of attention in the place.

"Excuse me," she said to the waiter, "have there been any calls for me?"

"No, ma'am, not any that I know about," the waiter said to her.

Vinita looked at her watch, and the time was 9:45. Myron still hadn't showed up yet. She was starting to doubt if he'd come. But this was her birthday. *He wouldn't stand me up on my birthday,* she thought. She glanced around the room and noticed a few men smiling, lusting for her. She paid them no attention while she waited for her boo to show up.

Ten-fifteen, and he was still a no-show. Frustrated, and about ready to leave, Vinita blew air out her mouth and raised up from her seat. She was soon greeted by a handsome young gentleman who introduced himself to her.

"Hello. Please, don't leave," he softly told her.

Vinita looked up at him, giving him only a cold stare.

"I'm waiting for someone," she informed him.

"Well, by the looks of things, it seems like that someone is not coming. It should be a sin for a man to keep a beautiful woman like yourself waiting for so long. Your date should be here in ample time."

She looked back, thinking that Myron would walk through the entrance at anytime. The young man was very handsome, with dark, thick eyebrows; slanted eyes; a nice mustache; smooth, brown skin; and he stood about six feet, one inch, dressed in Armani.

"May I buy you a drink?" he asked.

"I'm quite all right," she responded.

"Well, may I know your name?"

"May I know yours?" she countered.

"It's Aaron . . . Aaron Jackson."

"Well, Mr. Jackson, I'll give you ten minutes," she told him.

"Ten minutes of what?" he asked.

"If my date doesn't show up in ten more minutes, then I'll come have dinner with you."

"Promise?"

"Yes."

He gave her a warm smile, then retreated to his table, taking a seat and raising his glass filled with red wine toward her. It was a toast to her from across the room. He couldn't wait for her company.

Still frustrated, Vinita didn't want to tell him off because he looked wealthy and important. For some chicken-head reason, she thought about what kind of car he drove and what numbers he was holding down in his back account. She wasn't going to waste away her birthday waiting for Myron, and Mr. Jackson seemed just the right type of guy to fill the position if Myron didn't show up.

She glanced over at Aaron, and he raised his arm, tapping his watch, indicating that five minutes had already passed. She flashed him a smile, then glanced back at the door, only to see another couple strolling in.

About ready to keep Aaron company, she gathered her things and was just about to remove herself from out of her seat when Myron finally showed up.

"Vinita, I'm so sorry," he apologized.

"Where have you been?" she angrily asked. "I've been sitting here for more than an hour, on my birthday, and now you decide to show up."

He took a seat at the table, sweating, and out of breath. "I caught a flat on the way here, and I didn't have a spare, so I had to call AAA, and it took about thirty minutes just for them to reach me and another ten minutes for them to change the flat, and then there was traffic."

"Myron, it's my birthday. You promised me that tonight would be special."

"And it will be. I promise."

She glanced over at Aaron, who seemed not too thrilled about Myron's sudden presence. She shrugged as he sulked in his seat and tried to enjoy his dinner and wine alone.

Myron tried to clean himself up. He went to the men's bathroom, splashing cold water on his face and fixing his suit and tie. He popped a few breath mints into his mouth, then joined Vinita at the dinner table. They ordered, and he wished her a happy birthday. Vinita's sour mood slowly diminished as the night progressed.

After dessert and a hardy conversation with them holding hands across the table, peering at each other and smiling, Myron took in a deep breath.

"I want to ask you something," he said.

"What is it?"

He smiled, reached into his suit jacket pocket and pulled out a small black box. Vinita's eyes widened as she started to breathe heavily.

"I'm in love with you, Vinita," he said, getting down on one knee for all to see and gently grasping Vinita's hand, holding hers in his. "We've only known each other for a little over two months, but those two months have made me realize that I want to spend the rest of my life in love with you. So, will you marry me?"

The whole restaurant—staff, patrons, and even Aaron Jackson with envy in his eyes—looked on. To Vinita, this was like a fairy tale. She couldn't believe that Myron had proposed to her on her birthday. How romantic he was.

Her hand covered her mouth as she felt a few tears

welling in her eyes. She wanted a big wedding, a romantic wedding. Her heart raced. This was really happening. A million things roamed through her mind. Now she finally felt that it was time to leave the projects, the crack heads, and the drug dealers. They could keep all that. She didn't belong there in the first place. Now she felt that she could live the life that she always wanted and always dreamed of—a big house, a fine husband, and money in the bank. She couldn't wait to go home and boast to people about Myron's proposal. She wanted to tell everyone—let all them know that she was getting married and leaving Coney Island. She was going to spend the rest of her life how she had imagined it—anywhere but there.

"So, will you marry me?" Myron repeated, still on one knee, still waiting for her answer.

"Yes," Vinita happily blurted out. "Yes, I'll marry you." She reached down and gave him a long and loving hug. She clutched him tight, telling him, thank you, thank you. It was like a prince coming to rescue his bride out of slum village and taking her back to live in the castle. She felt that no one in Brooklyn could have a finer husband or make a finer couple than her and Myron.

Her mother was thrilled as she clasped Vinita's hand tightly, staring at the engagement ring Myron had given to her. It was an emerald-cut diamond with a wide platinum band, 1.01 carats—price, eight thousand dollars. She was showing it off so much that her hand was getting tired.

Vinita's mother was so excited, people would have thought that she was the one getting married—again. She had never owned or seen anything as expensive as this ring, shimmering like it was the hot sun itself. The ring Vinita had on was too rich for both her parents' blood. Only her fiancé, Myron, could afford such a thing, and she doubted that anyone in C.I. had such an expensive piece of jewelry to sport—except maybe the big-time pimps and hustlers.

She got on the phone and immediately dialed up her sister to boast about the proposal, how romantic it was, and of course, the engagement ring. When Vinita told her sister the price and the quality of it, she could hear her sister gagging over the phone. Vinita felt on top of the world.

She had to go down to Toni's apartment and brag about her new engagement and her new diamond ring. She knocked on the door about three times 'til Toni answered.

"What's up, Toni?" Vinita greeted, smiling like she just won Lotto or something.

It'd been a while since they had last seen each other, and it was a shock to Toni to have Vinita coming to visit her. The last time she came by just for a visit . . . shit, Toni couldn't remember. They still were friends. In fact, Toni was really the only friend Vinita had in the building, and in C.I. Vinita didn't get along with too many other females. They either envied her, or Vinita thought that they were beneath her, not living up to her standards. The only reason Toni and Vinita got along and became cool friends was because Toni's mother and Vinita's mother both used to hang tight, playing bingo, bringing their kids by, and Angela and her kids would have dinner with Vinita's family sometimes. But now, those days were long gone, probably forgotten, as both ladies traveled down different paths—one of them for the worse.

Vinita stepped into the apartment, taking a seat on

the couch. Toni, about ready to head for work, took a seat next to Vinita.

"So, what brings you by?" Toni asked.

"I can't check up on a friend?"

"Oh my God. Is that what I think it is?" Toni inquired, staring down at Vinita's engagement ring as it shone brightly on her finger.

"Yes, Toni. Myron proposed to me on my birthday."

"Are you serious?"

"Yes," Vinita said, sounding like a happy little girl.

"Congratulations," Toni said, taking Vinita's hand and staring at her ring.

"It's happening, Toni. My dreams are really happening. I'm getting married and finally leaving Coney Island."

And Toni was happy for her. She always wished the best for her friend Vinita, even though Vinita never wished the best for her. Even though they were friends, Vinita always saw Toni as her underling. She had to be better than her, better than all the bitches in C.I. and Brooklyn. Vinita was a high-quality girl who felt that she deserved the best. It was eating her up, still living in that cramped apartment with her parents and seeing her parents living paycheck to paycheck, and her sister—how pathetic, she would always tell herself.

"See, Toni, if you work hard enough and keep believing, then your dreams will come true. Look at me, girl. I'm a prime example."

"You are so lucky, girl. I have to meet him someday."

"You will, I promise. He is so fine, and soon he will be my husband."

Toni smiled. "So, when is the wedding?" she asked.

"We haven't set a date yet. But I'm pushing for next year, maybe June or July."

"I'm gonna be one of your bridesmaids?"

"Of course, girl. We must have you start looking decent before my wedding. Don't worry, Toni, someday maybe I'll become one of your bridesmaids, and we'll have a ghetto-fabulous wedding."

Cheap insult, Toni thought.

"Of course . . . right," Toni sarcastically replied back.

"Look, I have to go. I'm so happy and so lucky. You know Myron paid eight thousand dollars for my ring. That shows that he really loves me."

"Eight thousand dollars? Damn, it musta broke his pockets."

"No, my baby can afford it."

Closing the door after Vinita left, Toni shook her head. She couldn't believe that girl, and she was starting to wonder why or how they had stayed friends for so long. Toni wasn't ignorant or naïve. She knew Vinita came strictly down to her apartment to show off and brag about her wedding. But after all these years, Vinita's supercilious attitude never bothered her. Her grandmother always told her that some people liked to hype themselves up and look down on others because they were insecure about themselves.

That's why Toni always told herself, Vinita had her life, and she had hers. They were cool, and friends, but they were two different peas in a pod.

Toni stood in the dressing room at the Bottom Dollar, peering at herself in the mirror. She couldn't help but think about Mathew. It'd been two weeks since she had heard from him or seen him, and she'd been avoiding him. But she had her reasons. She was about ready to go out and perform and dance in front of a bunch of horny Brooklyn men waving dollar bills and wanting to get their gropes and probably their fuck on.

Wearing a skimpy white T-shirt, a mid-thigh leather

skirt, and a pair of stilettos, Toni walked toward the stage, having the men drool, gawk, and ache for her.

"Ayyite, my niggahs up in here, this sensational piece of pussy that's coming to the stage right now is my favorite bitch . . . Miss Toni. She be fuckin', so if y'all got her price right, then this is y'all night," the deejay announced.

Toni turned and glared at him, very unhappy as to how he was dogging her out when she was stepping to the stage—very rude and disrespectful. She flipped him the bird, and he just chuckled.

Toni stepped on stage, staring down at the mostly middle-aged men who were in the house that night. The young niggahs, she guessed, had to be somewhere more important than there. She swung herself around the pole a few times, then started touching and feeling herself up—having her hands reach under her skirt, cupping her breasts, then bending over to freely give her audience a sight to see.

"Yo, I be hearing her pussy's mad good, y'all," the deejay once again added insult to injury. "I would try to get up in her and fuck, but as y'all can see, I'm working tonight."

"Fuck you," Toni raged.

"She's feisty too. What niggah up in here got the balls to tame that?"

Toni stopped dancing, glaring at the deejay. She wanted to fuck him up, slap him across his rude and insulting mouth. *How dare he?* she thought. It was bad enough that she was doing what she was doing, but to have this derelict muthafucka advertise and announce it over the mic, that was straight-up tasteless.

"C'mon, Toni, after work, suck my dick tonight," he continued. "Yo, fellas, I heard she be sucking it down to the balls and the bones. Deep throatin' that shit like a white girl."

"Fuck you," Toni yelled, then stormed off the stage, hearing the dick-head deejay laughing. She was headed toward the ladies' bathroom 'til Malice grabbed her arm and asked where she thought she was going.

"Toni, you got customers to tend to. They came here to see some pussy, not to see your ass walk off."

"Fuck you. I'm sick of this shit," she yelled.

"What? Toni, get your ass back on that stage and work."

"No," Toni rebuked. "I'm taking the night off. Fuck you and this place." She jerked her arm free from his grip and stormed into the bathroom where she sat propped against the wall and cried for the next twenty minutes.

"You ayyite, girl?" Brandy, a brown-skinned female with a lot of ass, but no tits, asked.

"I'm sick of this shit," Toni angrily responded.

"Girl, don't be letting that niggah Anthony upset you like that. You know that niggah hating because bitches don't be giving his ugly ass no play. He gets off by being rude to girls on the mic. And you know he likes you."

"Fuck him," Toni blurted out.

"You going back on stage?" Brandy asked.

"Nah, I'm through for the night."

"Why don't you get that crazy-ass boyfriend of yours to fuck him up and teach his bitch ass a lesson?"

Toni always thought about it. If she told Keith, then he would have dragged Anthony out of the place onto the street and beat him vigorously—probably killing him. But she didn't want anyone's blood on her conscience because of her crazy-ass man. She knew Keith was uncontrollable, and when it came to disrespecting him, then his .45 did the talking. That's why she never told Keith about the night that dick-head asshole pulled out a gun on her and didn't give her her three hundred dollars.

Toni continued to sit in the ladies' bathroom/changing room, and she thought and thought and thought, 'til she said to herself, *Fuck it,* and just bounced, catching a cab to Manhattan.

Toni arrived at Mathew's building a little past midnight. She paid the driver and hurried out of the cab into the main lobby. She walked right past the night doorman, having him holler, "Excuse me, miss, you have to be announced. Excuse me, miss."

But his voice was mute to her. She hurried toward the elevator and had the doorman about ready to call for the police. When she reached Mathew's floor, she paused in her steps, thinking, *What if his fiancée's home or he hates me for not contacting him for two weeks?* She took a deep breath and proceeded forward.

Wearing a pair of old Levi's jeans, a Knicks jersey, and a pair of Reeboks with her braids pulled back into a ponytail, she raised her arm and began knocking on Mathew's apartment door. She stood there for about five minutes 'til she heard movement from the inside. She was nervous and anxious. Mathew was all she could think about at the moment.

"Who is it?" she heard someone ask from the other side of the door.

She paused, feeling like she was a mute, then she said, "Mathew, it's me . . . Toni."

She heard quick movement, the door being unlocked, and then just like that, the doorway to heaven had opened up for her. She saw Mathew standing in front of her, shirtless, and in a red silk robe, with some blue boxer shorts. She tried to smile, but instead a frown appeared.

"Toni, where have you been? I've tried calling you, but had no success in reaching you."

She peered at him for a few seconds. Her heart was racing, then she lunged toward him, wrapping her arms around him and pressing her lips against his. Mathew didn't resist. He embraced her and started exchanging fluid kisses.

She straddled him with her back against the wall. "Is your fiancée home?" she asked.

"No," Mathew said, taking a breather then continuing his actions, kissing her on her shoulder, neck, and mouth. Clothes started being pulled off, breasts fondled, and heated bodies rubbed together. Suddenly there was a disturbing knock at the door. It stopped and startled them both. They became curious as to who could be knocking on Mathew's door so late. Mathew put his robe back on and went to the door, only to be surprised to see two policemen standing there.

"Excuse me, sir. Sorry to have disturbed you, but we received a call from the doorman downstairs about a young woman trespassing on the premises. Is everything OK in there, sir?"

"Um, yes, officer. I'm just in here enjoying my money. You know a rich guy like me can't become too lonely tonight," Mathew joked.

Both officers looked at him baffled, as one tried to peek in his apartment while Toni stood hidden behind the door, smiling and quietly laughing with her hands cupped over her mouth.

"Well, we were just looking out for your safety, and once again, we're sorry to disturb you. You have a good night."

"You have a good night, too, officers," Mathew said, then quickly closed the door. Toni burst into laughter, staring over at Mathew.

"Why didn't you tell 'em that it was me who walked past the doorman so rudely?" she asked.

"I just wanted to mess with them." He gazed at her. "God, you're beautiful," he proclaimed.

Toni shyly turned her head, smiling and tittering. And to think, just a few hours ago, she was feeling like shit and really upset because of some asshole deejay. It was a miracle how Mathew could change her whole mood. He made her feel like a woman who deserved to be loved, embraced, and cared for.

"I'm in love with you, Toni," Mathew warmly proclaimed to her.

Toni just stood there. No man had ever made her feel so wanted without her feeling so used at the end. She started to undress herself, unbuttoning her jeans and removing them. Soon she stood raw in front of Mathew. He gazed delightfully at her as he slowly felt his manhood rising. He walked up to her, took her by the arms, and pulled her toward him, holding her nakedness. She then started to undress him, pulling down his boxers and removing his robe, so they both stood naked in the room holding each other—like a straight-up sexual romance novel.

Mathew picked her up and carried her off to the bedroom, feeling more comfortable and relaxed than his last intimate session with her when he lost his virginity. He dropped her down softly on the green satin sheets, then he rested himself on top of her, parting her thighs. This time he felt more confident in his sexuality.

"Wait, Mathew. Do you have any condoms?" Toni asked.

"No," he told her.

"I don't have any either," Toni regretfully stated.

"What are we supposed to do?"

Toni sighed heavily and gazed up at Mathew, wanting this to happen once again, wanting to be touched and sexed by him, wanting to feel his thick penis inside of her. She contemplated doing the unthinkable. Mathew began rubbing her thighs, and Toni uttered out, "Go ahead."

"Excuse me?" Mathew inquired.

"Go ahead, enter me. But promise when you feel yourself about to come, you're gonna pull out."

His heart once again started beating rapidly. He promised her, then slowly rested himself between her thighs. He penetrated to Toni's womb, gasping loudly and causing Toni to grip his back with her nails.

Twenty minutes later Toni was resting her head on Mathew's chest, feeling like the world was beneath her. As promised, when Mathew felt himself climaxing, he pulled out and shot his stuff all over her belly and thighs, then apologized and ran into the kitchen to get some paper towels and wipes so that he was able to clean it up. Toni laughed, not used to seeing a man react like that toward her.

An hour later she was fast asleep, resting between Mathew's sheets and arms, sleeping like a newborn infant. Mathew was still awake. He peered at Toni, and thought about the best of her. *Maybe this is fate,* he thought, *having her coming into my world like this.* He had never felt happier. He felt that it was time for a change—for the better. Being with Toni made him realize that he had to start living his life, do the things that he wanted to do, not what his mother or Tina always thought was best for him. He wanted to venture out into the city, go check out nightclubs, and go do things that urban folks did, like eat a hotdog from a street vendor, or go check out a movie in Times Square. He looked down at Toni and again said to her the unimaginable.

"I love you."

Saying and doing were two different things. That's why it was hard for Mathew to try and utter something to Tina that seemed to be the impossible. He thought about it over and over in his head, but the words just would not come out.

Mathew and Tina were on their way to the opera, to see *Madam Butterfly*, and Tina had tickets up on the balcony. They were very expensive to get. The show had been sold out for months.

Dressed in a flowing, long, expensive evening gown, her neck shimmering with jewels and her hair pinned upright, she looked as elegant as a princess in a fairytale. Tina was as stunning as a freshly cut diamond straight out of an African coalmine.

Strolling into the famous Lincoln Center arm in arm with Mathew, she smiled broadly. She couldn't wait to catch the beginning performance of the opera. Attending operas was something Tina adored so much, a culture she thrived on.

Taking their seats in the balcony, the lights were bright in the hall, and the rest of the crowd was still arriving. Mathew shifted around, uncomfortable.

"Tina, I have to tell you something," Mathew quietly said to her. But Tina's gaze was focused downward at the stage, with the curtains still closed.

"Mathew, my sweet, can it wait? It cannot be that important for you to tell me, now that the performance is about to begin. Now hush, and let's enjoy the show tonight."

"But, Tina—"

"Mathew, hush. I did not pay for these tickets to hear you yapping about nonsense all night."

The lights in the hall went dim, and the rest of the crowd continued to take their seats. It became quiet as men and women waited patiently for the curtains to open and the main performance to begin.

Act I took place in Nagasaki, Japan, around the 1900s, and Madam Butterfly was a Japanese girl who fell in love with an American naval officer. They ended up getting married, but the naval officer had to ship out, and the Japanese girl was left behind to give birth to his child.

Tina sat with her legs crossed, holding a pair of small binoculars and peering down at the stage. Mathew remained seated next to Tina, his hands clasped while he glanced around everywhere. He had always hated the opera. His mother used to drag him to see either the opera or a Broadway show when he was young, and he despised her for that. His father tagged along once in a blue moon, when he wasn't away on business. As a young boy, he always wished to be anywhere but there. Now here he was, a grown man, repeating the same process since he was young, but this time, instead of his mother dragging him, it was his fiancée.

About an hour into the performance, Mathew found himself dozing off, and Tina nudged him, telling him to wake up because he was embarrassing her.

"I have to use the bathroom," Mathew said.

"Now?" Tina angrily asked.

"Yes, Tina."

"You can't wait 'til the intermission?"

She glared over at Mathew, feeling that it was rude to walk out in the middle of a performance. That's why they had intermission. But Mathew didn't care. This was a drag to him, and he couldn't take being seated any longer. He needed a break now. So he got up and quickly but quietly left to go to the men's bathroom. He must have spent over twenty minutes there, thinking to himself. He was in the bathroom so long that when he came out, there was a group of men coming in. It was intermission. Men and women poured out of their seats into the ladies' or men's rooms or to have a cigarette and discuss what they did or did not enjoy about the show so far.

He wandered around in the crowd, wanting to go outside and relax in the limo. But Tina was in search for him, and she caught up with him by the exit.

"How dare you?" she angrily uttered out.

"Excuse me?" Mathew asked.

"Mathew, how dare you leave me seated alone for so long? I might as well have picked up a homeless man with no class from off the street, because that is how you are acting right now—like a man with no class at all."

Mathew looked at her. He couldn't believe that she'd just insulted him by telling him that he had no class.

"Tina, we really need to talk," he tried to say.

"There is nothing to say to me right now, Mathew. Now, I want you to hurry along to your seat before the next act begins."

"I'm not a child, Tina," Mathew stated.

"Excuse me?" Tina replied.

"I'm not five, ten, or twelve, Tina. I'm twenty-five—"

"Don't be silly, dear. I know how old you are," Tina interrupted.

"Really? Well sometimes you don't act like it, the way you treat and talk to me, like I'm your little brother or just a child in a man's body," Mathew loudly said to her.

"Really, Mathew, you're drawing attention to yourself. We can discuss your little problem later, when we're somewhere alone and private."

"No, Tina, I feel we need to address the problem now," he said, feeling like a man and finally standing up to his bossy woman.

"Please don't cause a scene, Mathew. You're embarrassing me," Tina quietly chided.

"That's the problem, Tina, am I nothing but a big embarrassment to you? You're always becoming embarrassed by stupid shit," Mathew cursed.

Tina gasped, shocked that he would use such language toward her. "Ooops, I said 'stupid shit.' Was that too much of an embarrassment to you, Tina?" he asked.

"Mathew . . . I'm appalled."

"Fuck you, Tina."

"Mathew!"

"Yes, I said 'fuck you, Tina,' " he repeated.

Clutching her chest with her hand and looking like she was about to have an asthma attack, Tina was speechless for a moment. In all her life, she had never been so humiliated in front of a large crowd, who was witnessing Mathew finally standing up to her.

"Mathew, your mother would have your hide if she heard you using such vulgar language," Tina warned.

"You know what, Tina, fuck my mother too," he said very clearly and very loudly. The people around them looked stunned, not believing what they were hearing.

"You're sick, Mathew. We can get you help," Tina tried to say.

"Sick? I'm sick of your bullshit, Tina. I'm sick of the way you treat and talk to people. I'm sick of the way you treat me, your fiancée. I'm sick of you not wanting to have sex with me," Mathew proclaimed.

"Well, I never," Tina uttered out.

"Tina, you'll never change. I can't marry you."

"Mathew, don't you dare. I've spent months planning this wedding."

"No, Tina, I need to do what's right in my life, and marrying you is not what's right. I'm starting to realize that I was about to make the biggest mistake of my life by marrying you just because you and my mother felt it was best for the family and me."

"What am I supposed to tell your mother, my friends, the guests we already invited?"

"That there will be no wedding. You can have the limo drop you off. I'll take a cab home."

"Mathew," Tina called out, but he just ignored her, heading for the exit. "Mathew," she called out for a second time. "Mathew, don't you dare do this to me," Tina exclaimed, with people still looking on. Although the next act was about to begin, they seemed to find this little drama much more interesting.

"Mathew!"

Mathew caught his first cab ride in New York. He was settled down in the backseat and on his way home. Not once did he feel guilty about cursing Tina out and leaving her alone at the opera in the Lincoln Center Theatre. That was something he really needed to get off his chest for a while, and now that he had, he felt like he had dropped a huge burden. He felt happy, finally feeling like a man. He loosened his tie, let out a deep breath, and said to himself that the first thing he was going to do when he entered his apartment was call up Toni and excitedly tell her that it was over between him and Tina, that he'd finally broken off the engagement.

The phone must have rung over a dozen times, as Mathew waited for someone to pick up, but no luck. She wasn't home. Unhappy because he really wanted to see Toni, he plopped down on his bed, closed his eyes, and suddenly fell asleep, not realizing how tired he was.

He slept with a smile on his face the entire night, feeling really good about what he'd done and thanking Toni because she'd been such an influence on him.

At eight in the morning, Mathew heard his phone ringing. Groggy, and still sleeping in his clothes, he reached for the phone only to hear his angry mother nagging him over the line.

"I did not raise my son to abuse and disrespect women," she chided.

"What are you talking about, Mother?" Mathew asked.

"Tina. She came by last night, hysterical, crying her eyes out. She told me that you canceled the wedding plans. Is this true, Mathew?"

"Yes, Mother."

"Mathew, you come to my home now and make right by her. Tina is a good woman. She's good to you and good to the family. I want you to apologize to her, and I want the two of you engaged again."

Mathew held the phone away from his ear, looking at the receiver, thinking, *Is she serious?*

"Mathew, I will not allow you to screw up your life by breaking an engagement with a beautiful, smart, and well-mannered woman. The two of you all are made for each other. Don't be a fool, Mathew. You come home and apologize to her now."

"But Mother—"

"Mathew, I know what is best for you, so don't you dare talk back to me. I've known Tina since she was young. I know her family. How dare you embarrass this family by acting a fool to your fiancée in front of hordes of people, at the opera, no less? Now, I'm sending the limo to your apartment, and I expect for you to be in it when it returns," his mother warned.

Mathew sighed. He heard his mother hanging up. *Will it ever stop?* he wondered. He wanted to pull out his hair. He couldn't believe that Tina actually went crying to his mother and had her call him up to apologize and make him renew their engagement. It hadn't even been twenty-four hours yet.

He thought so much of him becoming a man, but how could he, with his mother still combing his hair and changing his diapers?

-Twenty-

"Yo, fuck an automatic. Dem shits jam too quick, sneak up on a niggah on some cutthroat shit, slit his wrists, make it look like a suicide hit, bleed his grip, and if niggahs retaliate, try to hit back, then dem the niggahs we assassinate, shots to the frontal lobe—hear 'em scream, 'cause they wanna try to get bold. You better be ready to die when you creep through C.I. Even got the boys in blue weary eyed. Because I'm a hustler, don't give a fuck about ya, straight bust ya, look at me wrong, and I'll be quick to dust ya, latex gloves gripped around a chrome nine, evil was born in the year '79 . . ." Butta tried to rhyme.

"Niggah, shut the fuck up wit' that shit," Little Boy Ronny cursed as they rode around Brooklyn with Tec driving and Little Boy Ronny riding shotgun, listening to the new Notorious B.I.G. CD, *Life After Death.* "Niggah, you ain't no real gangsta."

"What? Niggah, I can get down wit' mine, niggah," Butta countered. He was a light-skinned kid, only seventeen, with baby-faced features.

"Yeah, whatever, niggah," Tec said.

"C'mon, Tec, why you trying to play a niggah?" Butta asked.

Butta looked up to Tec like he was some kind of role model to him, in the worst way. He loved the way Tec was respected and feared throughout the hood, and he wanted that same dignity. Since Butta was twelve, he had tried to become a thug, a gangsta, but not yet a killer. He heard many stories about the infamous duo—Sheek and Tec, and how they were notorious together around the hood. And he would do anything to gain Tec's respect—even kill a niggah.

They rode down Atlantic Avenue, smoking Ls and listening to B.I.G.'s hot album, feeling sorry about his tragic death. It was a hot July night around eleven, and these three didn't have shit to do but find trouble and get themselves into deeper shit with the law. And trouble is what they were about to find, when Little Boy Ronny spotted Cory-D's hunter-green '93 Cadillac Allante convertible parked out front of a small bar on Atlantic. Cory-D loved Cadillacs. He had about three, and he always kept them shits looking nice and polished, wiped and clean, and always easy to spot in traffic.

"Oh, shit," Tec uttered out, making a quick U-turn.

He had the .357 under the seat, and Little Boy Ronny had the .380. Butta was left clueless as he sat in the backseat.

"What's the deal?" Butta asked.

"Yo, you sure that's that niggah's whip?" Tec asked, staring at the car parked across the street.

"Yeah, dog, that's his shit," Little Boy Ronny confirmed.

"Ayyite then, we about to set this niggah shit on fire," Tec said, grinning.

Cory-D sat at the bar with his drink in hand, and as

always, he was accompanied by a beautiful young lady at his side. This was one of his local hangouts. He was cool with the manager and most of the employees. Chills and him had shop set up in the back.

"Yo, love, you want another drink?" Cory-D asked the young lady.

"You're still buying, right?" she asked.

"I wouldn't be asking."

"Then I'll take another cosmopolitan."

A fifty was placed on the counter, and Cory-D continued to be the baller he was, flashing wads of cash and wearing two diamond stud earrings in both ears and a diamond pinky ring, pimpin' a three-piece suit.

A nervous young man approached Cory-D, wishing he didn't have to tell him the bad news. The young employer knew about his rep and pulls in Brooklyn. But someone had to let him know. He stood behind Cory-D, saying, "Mr. D . . . excuse me, but . . . "

"What, niggah? Can't you see I'm busy here," Cory-D angrily told the nervous young man.

"But . . . "

"Mike, this shit better be important. I told you that I didn't wanna be bothered by no stupid shit tonight."

"But your car is on fire," he quickly blurted out.

"What?" Cory-D shouted.

"Your car is on fire," he repeated.

Cory-D rushed to the door, followed by half the people in the bar who were rushing out along with Cory-D to see what all the excitement was about. He hurried out the door and saw his convertible in a blaze of fire.

"Yo, what the fuck? Yo," he hysterically shouted, running around like a madman. "What the fuck?"

"You think we should call the fire department?" Mike stupidly asked.

Smack. Mike caught a quick, hard hand across the

face from Cory-D for being so stupid and asking a stupid muthafucking question.

"Yo, ain't nobody see shit?" Cory-D angrily asked. "Nobody saw shit, right? All y'all just sat around and let this shit happen," he said, glaring at everyone like they were all potential suspects.

Still parked across the street, Tec and his crew sat back, watching Cory-D run amuck. *Now is the perfect opportunity to catch this niggah,* Tec thought.

"Yo, Butta, you ready to earn your stripes?" Tec asked.

"You know me, Tec, I'm down for whatever," Butta replied.

"Ayyite, my little niggah, here's what I want you to do. Take this shit," Tec said, handing him the .357, "and pop three into Cory-D."

Butta gripped the .357 tightly, trying to hype himself up. He had never killed a man before, so his heart was pumping with adrenaline, trying to feel that same rage he knew Tec would be feeling when he gunned niggahs down.

"That little niggah scared," Little Boy Ronny proclaimed.

"Nah, niggah, I'm gonna do it," Butta assured.

"Then go ahead, niggah. We ain't got all night. Make it happen," Tec said, looking at him with much intensity.

Nervous as a muthafucka, Butta took in a deep breath, feeling that this was his chance to prove himself to Tec and the rest of his crew. He stepped out of the car, concealing the weapon in the waistband of his jeans and slowly started to walk across the street toward the burning car and Cory-D. Tec and Little Boy Ronny peered at him from the car, both of them thinking, *Do he really got the balls to pull this shit off?*

As Butta stepped closer, he reached for the .357, which was fully loaded. He had Cory-D in full sight. No one seemed to notice this young kid stepping toward the crowd holding a loaded gun down by his side. They were too distracted by the burning Cadillac. Not aware of the fire trucks roaring down the street with their flashing lights, Butta raised the gun, then without a second thought in his head, he fired at Cory-D, but missed. The abrupt sound of a gunshot startled the crowd and had many scattering for quick cover. A second shot was fired at Cory-D, but that shot also missed him, and Cory-D plunged to the concrete. Then he dashed behind a parked car, praying that this kid's bad aim kept up.

"What the fuck?" Cory-D mumbled to himself.

A third shot was fired, and then a fourth, but unfortunately for Butta, all shots missed their potential target. The fire department was already on the scene, along with the NYPD right behind them.

Guns were quickly pulled out as the boys in blue saw that Butta was armed and dangerous.

"Drop the gun, kid," one of the officers screamed with his weapon raised and pointed at the kid's chest. "I said, drop it," he repeated angrily.

Butta, all crazed out, scared, and nervous, didn't know what to do with himself. He still clutched the gun tightly. Now there were over a dozen officers on the scene. Each of them had their weapons out, being wary about the kid's next action.

"Don't be stupid, son. Drop the fucking gun," another officer shouted. With a car still burning heavily on the streets, the heat was becoming intense. And as the cops saw it, there was a lunatic on the scene with a loaded gun. This situation wasn't good.

Butta glared at the cops, knowing he had exceeded

past the level of giving up. With tears streaming down his cheeks and feeling he had something to prove, he raised the .357 toward the cop, but he didn't let off a single round. Cops quickly open fired at him, shooting him down. Butta collapsed to the ground, falling to his death. He died instantly.

Tec and Little Boy Ronny stared from their car still parked across the street. They were both stunned. "Damn, that little niggah really did have heart," Little Boy Ronny stated.

"Yo, Butta went out like a fuckin' soldier," Tec said, knowing that Butta went out like a true muthafuckin' gangsta, representing the hood fully.

News of Butta's shooting against Cory-D and the cops spread throughout the hood like wildfire. It even made the ten o'clock news. Some never knew that Butta had it in him. The attempt on Cory-D's life was about to stir up more shit in C.I. A few local drug dealers left town, fearing that the worst was about to happen, and they didn't wanna be around when the fire went from being on the stove to spreading throughout the kitchen.

The day after Butta's death, a few detectives went to see his grandmother at his home. They started asking questions and telling her that they were sorry about his death. When they left the building, bottles, garbage, and all kinds of shit were tossed and thrown at the police and detectives. The projects hated the NYPD for shooting Butta down.

"They ain't had to shoot that boy down like he was some fuckin' dog," one young neighbor yelled.

Two days later, they found two bodies in the park—two bodies that were affiliated to Tec. And then there was a drive-by done on Little Boy Ronny's grandma's crib. The shooters fired thirty-five shots into the home of his grandmother who wasn't there at the time. Fortunately for Little Boy Ronny, he didn't stay at his grandmother's anymore.

All this senseless violence that was being committed in C.I.—the killings, the beatings, and the shootings—was bringing more and more heat on the blocks. Homicide, the DEA, and the ATF started knocking and banging down doors in the projects and on the back blocks of Coney Island, arresting any young black male who they could lock up, hoping it would at least decrease some of the high volume of crime that was being committed every day. Police were pulling over any suspicious cars that were out on the streets, or stopping any young, black male to do unreasonable searches, hoping to seize them for some illegal substance or catch them with a burner or out on a warrant, or maybe violating their parole.

This was making Chills very unhappy. It was slowing up his business in C.I. a lot. And the fact that Tec tried to take out his right-hand man made him furious. Shit needed to be done. He knew the root of the problem was Tec, but Tec was a hard niggah to catch up with for his killing crew to be able to carry out that 187. A lot of Chills' dealers were being locked up, harassed, robbed, and even murdered. So Chills raised the ante on Tec's head, from twenty-five thousand dollars to fifty thousand dollars. Chills wanted that niggah Tec dead—yesterday.

-Twenty-one-

I'm getting married, Vinita thought as she was in the bathroom changing. She happily stared at herself in the bathroom mirror, then she came out, sporting a purple slip with slim adjustable straps and a spa wrap—short and sweet with a simple tie sash. Her fiancé was trying to wait patiently in the bedroom, sprawled out on the bed, ready for some action.

"Damn, you look beautiful," he praised, rising up in a pair of black silk boxers and shirtless.

"You like?" Vinita asked.

"Definitely."

Vinita casually strolled over to him and took a seat on his lap as Myron cupped his arms around her.

"I can't believe that I'm actually getting married," Vinita said.

"Believe it, baby. It's going to happen."

"I love you, Myron," she proclaimed, then passionately kissed him.

Myron lay back as Vinita pulled down his boxers, removed her nighttime wear, and slowly mounted Myron.

He groaned with pleasure, gripping on to Vinita's waist, while she gradually came down on him.

An hour later, they both lay sated. Vinita was hugged up in Myron's arms, smiling. She had just had a tremendous night out with Myron—dinner, dancing, and great sex.

"Vinita, when are you going to introduce me to your parents?" Myron asked.

"Why are you so anxious to meet them?"

"Because, I would like to meet the parents of the woman that I'm soon to marry—and before our wedding day," Myron explained.

"It's just—"

"It's just what, Vinita?" he interrupted. "Are you embarrassed of them or something?"

"My parents, they're different from your parents," Vinita tried to explain. She really meant that his folks basically had more class than her parents. His family was middle and high class, and sometimes she felt that her family had no class.

"I'm sure your folks are wonderful people. They're not serial killers, are they?" he joked.

"No, you'll meet them, Myron. I promise."

"I hope so. I would love to meet the folks that created such a wonderful and beautiful bride-to-be."

Vinita blushed, tittering. "You're so good to me, Myron," she said.

"Because I feel that you're the best thing to ever happen to me."

Damn, she thought, *why can't my life, my folks, my parents' home, be compatible with Myron's?* She hated everything about her family.

Spending the weekend at Myron's place did Vinita real good. She needed a break from her parents' place. It saddened her when she was brought back to reality as

Myron pulled up in front of her building, dropping her off. Her building was what she would call home until they were married—or until Myron asked her to move in with him.

It was Monday night, and Vinita and Myron gave each other one long hug and a passionate kiss. They remained in the car for a good thirty minutes 'til they parted ways. She stood outside, watching him drive off, then turned to go inside. Facing her building, she saw four local thugs in their baggy jeans, Timbs, backward caps, jewelry, and street attitudes staring at her. Not acknowledging them, and somewhat mocking them, she clutched her purse and hurried by them, hearing rude comments directed toward her as she entered the lobby. She just wanted to head upstairs and bury herself in her room all night.

When she walked around the corner toward the elevator, her heart nearly skipped a beat. She saw a certain young man lingering around, playing dice with two guys by the elevator doors.

"Damn, it's been a long time, Vinita. What, you moving up in the world now, bitch?" Little Boy Ronny asked her.

"Leave me alone, Ronny," she said, trying to walk by him. But he stood in front of her.

"Yo, let me talk to you for a minute," Little Boy Ronny said, up in her face, not giving her any breathing room.

"Please, Ronny, I'm tired and it's late," Vinita meekly said to him.

"I don't care if you're about to pass out, I wanna talk to you," he strongly repeated himself. He grabbed her by her forearm and pulled her into the building staircase.

Vinita felt intimidated by him, so she stopped even

though she really didn't want to. What was she to do? This was Little Boy Ronny, a notorious figure in the hood, and also her ex-boyfriend from about six or seven years ago.

"Damn, you lookin' good, Vinita," Little Boy Ronny complimented.

"Thank you," she faintly replied, sounding short with him.

"What you been up to?" Little Boy Ronny asked.

"School, work, you know, the usual . . . "

"I hear that."

He stood just a few feet from her, peering at her strongly. Vinita stood there. Her heart was racing, her mouth quiet. She didn't want to say the wrong thing to him, get him upset.

"I hear you got a new man now. Heard that niggah drives a BMW and shit," Little Boy Ronny mentioned.

"We're just talking. It ain't nothing serious," she lied.

"Word? He the one that gave you that phat ring on your finger? He be fuckin' you better than I used to?" Little Boy Ronny bluntly asked.

"Ronny, why you gotta go there?"

"I'm just asking you a question."

"C'mon, Ronny, that's personal," she softly said to him.

"Ayyite, I ain't trippin' over that niggah. That niggah's a fuckin' square anyway. I can't see how a beautiful bitch like you could end up with some lame muthafucka like that anyway. You remember how we used to get down, Vinita?"

Vinita did, and she tried so very hard to forget.

"What you doing for the rest of the night, anyway?" Little Boy Ronny asked as he took a few steps closer to her.

"I told you, I'm tired, and I'm going to bed."

"Even too tired to be with me again?" he asked. He was up on her, placing his hands on her waist and trying to kiss her, trying to become affectionate with her. "You know I fuckin' miss you, right?" He gripped her buttocks and tried parting her lips with his tongue.

"Ronny, stop," Vinita said. She quickly pushed him away from her.

"What's up wit' that, Vinita? You know I'm still in fuckin' love wit' you, right?"

"C'mon, Ronny, that was seven years ago. I've moved on."

"Moved on wit' who, that BMW-driving niggah? Tell that niggah to come around and check me. I'll show that niggah how a real man gets down," he barked.

"Why you gotta be like that, Ronny? I thought we were through. I went my way, and you went your way. I'm not with that anymore."

"Vinita, you still trippin' over that night? C'mon, that was seven years ago."

"And that's the reason we broke up. You disrespected me in the worst way any niggah could, Ronny," she said, getting emotional as a few tears trickled down her cheeks.

"C'mon, Vinita, I thought you done been forgot about that night. Niggahs were drunk and shit. Shit, bitch, I wanna be your fuckin' man again."

"I've changed, Ronny. I've moved on. And besides, like you already know, I'm seeing somebody right now."

"C'mon, Vinita, don't be fuckin' playing me like that. Fuck that other niggah. What, you think he got money, bitch? I got money too," he barked as he pulled out a bankroll filled with hundreds and fifties. "I'm trying to take you out."

"Ronny . . . "

"You saying no to me?"

"Why you gotta be like this?" Vinita asked, scared, wishing she was back over at Myron's.

"It's been seven years too long, and I fuckin' want you back. I've been fuckin' missing you for too long now. You know a niggah been in and out of prison for the longest."

"Ronny, can I go?" she asked.

"No, you can't fuckin' leave," he madly said, grabbing her by her arm.

"Ronny, please. Why are you acting like this? It's been seven years now. I thought this shit was over."

"Well, it ain't. I'm still fuckin' in love wit' you. I don't care if it's been ten years, you're still my woman, and ain't no niggah in a fancy BMW gonna come in between what the fuck you and I have I've been out fo' a minute now . . . ."

"Please, Ronny," Vinita timidly said to him.

"Look, I see it in your eyes. You know you're still in love wit' me. Why you frontin', Vinita?"

"Ronny, please, I need to go," she begged.

"So, I'm gonna talk to you, right?" he asked, still holding her forcefully by her arm as they stood in the dingy staircase.

With tears streaming down her cheeks, she nodded reluctantly, really not wanting to see this muthafucka any longer in her life. She thought that the past was the past, and she tried so hard to forget about what had happened in her past.

"So, I'm gonna holla at you, Vinita," Little Boy Ronny said as Vinita hurried up the stairs, teary-eyed and trying to get away from him. She rushed into the apartment, stormed into the bathroom and hovered with her head over the toilet bowl. She threw up. In her mind she thought about that horrible night with Little Boy Ronny seven years ago.

* * *

She met Little Boy Ronny when she was fourteen. With his boyish good looks and street attitude, Vinita couldn't help but fall in love. Back then that was her sexual preference. She was into the hustlers, drug dealers, the thugs. They had that certain je ne sais quoi about them that attracted her to them. But she was only fourteen. She and Little Boy Ronny used to hook up all the time, hanging out at the amusement park with Toni; her brother, Sheek; Tec; and Lamont, before they all became heavily involved in the drug game. They were all nickel-and-dime hustlers back then.

Vinita was always smart, into her books and school, and always wanted to go to college after high school. She was more down to earth when she was younger, before everyone started calling her a stuck-up, uppity, tight-ass bitch. She would smoke, drink, and bug out with the fellows—hanging out with her fine ass, and having everyone in the hood wanting to hook up with her. She and Toni, they were C.I.'s catches. But since they were tight with Tec, Sheek, and Little Boy Ronny, no one really messed with the two girls, knowing their status.

Vinita even lost her virginity to Little Boy Ronny one warm July night on the building rooftop. All Little Boy Ronny needed was a thick blanket, no rain, and for Vinita to spread her legs. It took about twenty minutes for him to talk her into it. They were only dating for one month when it happened.

Vinita was in love with Little Boy Ronny. She loved his spontaneous lifestyle and the way he and his boys used to get themselves into trouble, sometimes into serious danger. But all that changed for her one night while she was hanging out with niggahs she thought she was cool with.

Vinita, Tec, Sheek, Toni, Little Boy Ronny, Lamont, and two other niggahs were chilling up in Little Boy Ronny's grandmother's basement. They were doing the usual—smoking, drinking, cracking jokes, bugging out, and having a good time. It was going on one in the morning, and they all thought nothing of the time. Sheek decided to bounce. He got a page and left. Toni followed out the door with her older brother, leaving Vinita there as the only girl with five other niggahs. Vinita didn't think much of being left alone with a bunch of males she knew and was cool with.

They all were still smoking and drinking heavily. Little Boy Ronny, being her boyfriend, had his arm around Vinita and a cup of Alizé in his other hand. Soon niggahs started talking about sex and pussy, how they would love to be fuckin' some bitch at that moment, and they complimented Vinita on how fine she was, saying that Little Boy Ronny was a lucky muthafucka. One niggah asked to speak with Little Boy Ronny privately, taking him into the corner and whispering something into his ear. He smiled and peered over at Vinita. Little Boy Ronny went back over to Vinita, pulling her up by her arms, and trying to lead her into the back bedroom, wanting to get his fuck on. At first she felt reluctant, but with a little persuasion from Little Boy Ronny, she soon followed him into the room while the others continued to chill, smoke, and drink.

It took him less than a minute to have Vinita's young ass butt naked and sprawled across an old mattress. He fucked her for ten minutes, then got up off her, saying that he had to go and take a quick piss and that he'd be back.

The room was dark. Vinita could barely see the face of the person who soon entered the room. At first she thought it was Little Boy Ronny, but the guy coming toward her was taller and more built. He climbed onto the mattress, causing Vinita to become alert and wary.

"Vinita, it's only going to take me a few minutes," he said as he tried to spread her legs.

"Where's Ronny?" Vinita nervously asked, trying to back away from him. She knew his voice.

"Come here, Vinita. Why you trippin', bitch? You know me," he said. He grabbed her by her ankles and pulled her back onto the mattress. Vinita screamed as the guy strongly forced himself onto her. Pulling down his jeans, he inserted his erection into her, pressing his weight against her and pinning her to the mattress. She screamed out frantically.

The others who were standing outside the door heard her screams, heard her cries for help, but they stood around not caring at all. They all just waited for sloppy thirds, fourths, and fifths. Vinita was still pinned on her back, with her eyes red, her cheeks moist with tears, scared, and her heart crushed as this male continued to rape her in the dark room, downstairs in her supposed-to-be loving boyfriend's house. This rapist cared nothing about her emotions or that he knew and used to hang and chill out with her, and that this was his man's girl. The only thing that was on his mind at the time was pussy.

After pumping a few more strokes into her, he pulled out and ejaculated all over her breasts, stomach, and thighs.

"There bitch, I'm finished," he said, rising from off his knees and smiling. He fastened his jeans and went to the door, opening it and letting the next man step in.

"Damn, Lamont, what you do to the bitch?" Tyrone

asked as he was about to step in and continue where Lamont left off.

"Yo, she still tight," Lamont told him, giving niggahs dap, sweating, and plopping down on the couch.

Tyrone stepped into the room, not even bothering to close and lock the door. He unbuckled his jeans, got down on top of Vinita, and started fucking her vigorously while niggahs stepped into the room behind him, crowding around the mattress and watching as this niggah fucked and raped Vinita. They cheered and clapped him on. He started laughing and yelling at her to be still as he propped her legs in the air, thrusting himself into her. He didn't even bother to pull out after he was finished. He just let himself come inside her. And then after he was done, the next man stepped up, forcing his way down on top of her.

Vinita had no more tears to let out. While she was being raped and abused, she just lay there, lifeless like a Barbie doll, and let the niggahs that she trusted and thought she was cool with, fuck her like she was some strange ho that they just picked up from off the streets.

But what really hurt her the most was when she saw Little Boy Ronny standing there, cheering and shouting out sexual comments with the other fellows, like they weren't together. *How could he do me like this?* she thought over and over. The man she thought she loved had pimped her like she was some five-dollar trick.

After everyone was done with her, they left her in the room, naked, bleeding, and stripped of whatever dignity she had left. She couldn't bring herself to get up and run her ass home. Instead she just lay there. Her eyes were so red that she looked like she was about to cry with blood instead of tears. Her body was aching, and in between her legs was sore. Hours must have passed, and dawn was soon to rise. Vinita couldn't even bear to take herself home. She wanted to die. She felt betrayed, embarrassed, and violated.

Little Boy Ronny, who had passed out on the floor for hours, eventually came into the room where she still lay. He didn't even acknowledge her. He just changed clothes and headed out. It wasn't until ten that morning that Vinita removed herself from off the mattress, got dressed, and hurried home. When she arrived, both her parents were at work. They thought Vinita was spending the night at Toni's, and her older sister was tending to her newborn. Vinita locked herself in the bathroom for an hour, throwing up, crying, and feeling ashamed. She couldn't even bear to tell anyone what had just happened to her. It was too awful to tell.

For the three days that followed, she locked herself in her room, not communicating with anyone. When her parents asked her what was wrong, she wouldn't say. All she would tell them was that she wasn't feeling well, and that she needed some rest. When her friend Toni tried to come by and visit, she told her to leave and go away. She wasn't in the mood for any company. Nobody could figure out what was wrong with her, and why she was becoming distant from everyone, so everyone just let her be, feeling that she was dealing with personal issues that only she could handle.

And that's how Vinita bore the pain of being raped. She became distant from family, friends, and the neighborhood during the following years—concentrating on her books and studies, putting what had happened behind her and moving on. She despised Brooklyn, and she felt that she deserved better. She always felt that she was owed something. She became the smartest in her school and received numerous academic awards. She enrolled in a great college and majored in a prosperous field.

Two months after her rape, Little Boy Ronny was incarcerated. He was busted for selling drugs to an undercover cop. Pleading guilty, he received a two-year sentence. She hated him, hated who he hung out with, hated where she was raised, hated being poor, and hated not being able to leave the projects when she wanted to. She hated Coney Island so much that one of her main goals in life was to get herself established and leave her neighborhood, never to come back again. She'd been striving to accomplish that dream ever since she'd been raped.

-Twenty-two-

He couldn't believe that the wedding was on again. Mathew wondered how in the hell his mother persuaded him into marrying Tina again. He had to face it; his mother and his fiancée ran his life. His mother threatened to cut Mathew off the family's account if he did something stupid, like canceling the wedding. As far as Mrs. Peters was concerned, Tina was the perfect woman for him. She couldn't do him wrong.

So Mathew found himself on the verge of becoming unhappy and going crazy. All he could think about or say to himself, was why? He thought about Toni. He missed Toni, he wanted to be with Toni, but he found himself stuck in the twilight zone—not being able to escape, no matter how hard he tried.

He sat out by the pool, watching Tina sunbathe from the other end. His mother was having some tea and reading the *Times* over by the patio. He took in a deep breath, slumping down in his chair and sitting with incorrect posture. It was a seated position that his mother wouldn't approve of. Good thing she was facing the

other way. He peered over at Tina, eyeing her long, sexy legs and the two-piece bathing suit she was wearing. The way she was slightly sweating under the sizzling sun, he couldn't help but to catch a hard-on in his swimming trunks. Tina was gorgeous. There was no argument in that. But she was a bitch, and it pained him to think that he might have to spend the rest of his life married to her.

So what if Mother drops me from the family's account? Maybe it will be worth it, he thought. He'd been around money all his life. Maybe he needed a change to find out how it was to live out in the world, on his own like common folks. He wanted to see the city like he'd never seen it before—tour the clubs, roam around Times Square on foot, instead of driving through in his limo. He wanted to jog in Central Park, eat a hotdog from a street vendor, see a movie—shit, see Harlem.

Mathew stood abruptly, causing Tina and his mother to stare over at him.

"What's wrong, Mathew?" his mother asked.

"I have to go," he said.

"Go? Go where?" Tina asked.

"Nowhere," his mother interrupted. "Sit your butt down and enjoy this warm and glorious afternoon with your mother and fiancée."

"But Mother—"

"Mathew, I said have a seat," she chided.

And like he was seven years old, he took a seat, sulking in his chair—embarrassed and angry. He glanced over at Tina, who he could have sworn was smirking.

Later on that evening, he played chess with Tina. He won three games out of four, humiliating his fiancée, who always thought that she was so smart and great at everything she did. His father was away in Japan, on business as usual, and Mrs. Peters lingered around in the magnificent master bedroom, keeping to herself on the lovely and quiet evening.

"Mathew, after the wedding, I was thinking that maybe we should leave this dreadful city and move," Tina said.

"Move where, Tina?"

"Paris," she stated.

"Paris?"

"Yes, Paris, Mathew. It's so wonderful out there. The city, it's so dazzling, so breathtaking. It's a great place to live. Much better than this awful city we've called home for so long."

"But I like living in New York. There's so much we haven't seen or done yet," he tried to defend.

"What is there to do in this horrendous city? I feel like this city has no class, no art. It's nothing like Paris. Paris has history, culture, and art. Paris is a city of greatness and of great things."

"But thousands of tourists come to visit this city every year. How can you say that this city doesn't have any art? This city was built on history and art. And I don't want to leave here. This place is my home."

"Well, it's been home for you for too long. I feel that it's time for a change, something better. And I feel that moving to Paris is something better, something better for us. Besides, I've already made plans to move after our wedding," Tina bitchily informed him.

"What?"

"No arguments, Mathew. We're moving to Paris after the wedding."

"Does my mother know about this?" he asked.

"She will."

"When?"

"After we're married. It'll be a surprise."

He sighed, feeling the need to curse her out again,

just like the other night at Lincoln Center. *Damn, that felt good,* he remembered.

"You'll love Paris, Mathew. The city is for people like us—the high, the ones who set morals for themselves. Let the homeless, the panhandlers, the drug dealers, and the tourists have this place. I will not spend another year of my life calling this place home," Tina proclaimed. "I might even be inspired to have a baby if we lived in Paris—the place, the city, it's just so romantic," Tina added.

Paris, Paris, Paris, fuck Paris, Mathew shouted out in his head, adding, *Bitch, bitch, bitch.* He didn't want this, he didn't ask for this, so why was this happening? He couldn't see himself living in Paris. He loved New York. He couldn't see leaving the city. It'd been home to him for twenty-five years.

On the way home to his apartment in Manhattan, he thought about Toni while riding in the limo with Tina sitting next to him.

"Why are you so quiet?" she asked.

"No reason."

"Thinking about me, about Paris?" she asked.

He wanted to scream out, *Hell no,* but instead, he said to her that he was tired and just wanted to go to bed. He asked if Damien, the driver, should drop her off at her apartment, but Tina volunteered to spend the night over at his place, which displeased Mathew.

And as usual, he watched her get undressed in the bathroom. Once again he got aroused, being able to look, but not touch. She climbed into bed with him, wanting to cuddle, with absolutely no sex, which was really beginning to irritate Mathew. Feeling her touch, her warmth, but not being able to feel her pleasure box was torture.

To him, getting himself that first piece of ass was like

a junkie having his first hit. All he could think about was the next one, and the next one after that, until he officially became a full-blooded crack head. But in Mathew's case, his high wasn't just sex, it was Toni. He loved being with her, being around her, and he would do anything at that moment just to see or hear from her.

As Tina lay asleep next to Mathew, he couldn't sleep. His eyes were wide open, peering up at the ceiling, thinking. He wanted to get up and call Toni's place, but he was frightened, thinking that Tina may hear his conversation. He glanced at Tina, then back up at the ceiling. And then suddenly the buzzer rang. It echoed throughout the room. He jumped up, becoming startled and worrying that it might have awakened Tina. Someone was downstairs, and that someone was Toni. He was thrilled that she had come by, but then he became paranoid as he saw Tina sleeping in his bed. He informed the doorman to let her up, then scurried around the room quietly in his silk robe and slippers and went to go answer the door.

He opened the front door quietly, smiling as he saw her standing there, dressed in a lovely belted Lurex herringbone mini-skirt, white sneakers, and a white sleeveless shirt. She was looking so lovely and smiling radiantly.

As she stared at Mathew in his bedtime wear, she asked,

"Can I come in?"

"To be honest, no," he said.

"Why?"

"My fiancée is in the bedroom asleep," he informed her.

"Oh," she blurted out.

"But I don't want you to leave," he told her.

And she didn't want to either. She couldn't help but feel a little jealous of his fiancée being in his bedroom, but what was she to do? They were engaged. He stood in the doorway, thinking, *Why did Tina have to spend the night?* He shoulda been a man and told her to stay the night over at her own damn place. Then he and Toni could've become intimate together. He definitely yearned for her.

"Well, we can go somewhere," Toni stated, which was a wonderful idea. "She's a big girl. I'm sure she can manage being alone in your apartment for a few hours. I did it."

Mathew was thrilled. It gave him a chance to spend a night out on the town with Toni, something he was looking forward to doing. Toni waited patiently by the door while Mathew went to change. He came back out dressed in a suit. Toni chuckled.

"Where do you think you're going? To some kind of business meeting?" she joked.

"What? You think it's a little too much?" he asked, looking down at himself.

"Yes, I do. We're just hanging out in the city, not trading stocks. Do you have anything else to wear besides another fancy suit? You're gonna get us mugged."

"Um?"

"Any jeans, sneakers, a T-shirt, a baseball cap, maybe?"

"Um, not that I know of," he responded.

Toni sighed, shaking her head as she gawked at Mathew dressed sharply in a three-piece gray suit, slick shoes, and looking like he was Mr. Money Bags himself.

"Why don't you just try wearing some slacks and a collared shirt," Toni suggested. "You do have a pair of slacks, don't you?"

"Of course," he answered.

It took him another ten minutes to change, coming

back out dressed in a pair of black slacks and a white button-down shirt, still in the expensive shoes. "Well, it's better. We need to take you shopping," Toni suggested.

They both snuck out of the apartment like young teenagers, gently closing the door and giggling while Tina lay asleep.

They caught a cab to midtown Manhattan—Times Square—where it was a quarter to midnight on a warm summer night. The streets were filled with people, filled with activities and events. Yellow cabs were lined up and down 42nd Street, and people of all races and ethnicities toured Times Square, some tourists and some regular folks. The lights from dozens of advertisements illuminated the streets, large billboard ads lingered over the city streets, and hordes of people busied themselves with the pulsating activity that the city had to offer. It was the place to be.

Mathew and Toni stepped out of the cab. Mathew tipped thc cabdriver an extra twenty and stepped onto the city streets like he was a damn tourist himself, peering up at the bright signs and displays.

"So, where do you wanna go?" Toni asked.

He shrugged, thinking that there was so much to do, so much to see. They walked hand in hand, taking notice of a group of young males dressed in ol' skool blue windbreakers, trimmed with white stripes, wearing Nikes and breakdancing on the sidewalk to ol' skool hip-hop, making tips. It definitely caught the attention of Mathew. He'd seen it done on television many times, but he never had the pleasure of seeing it in person. He was content as he looked on wide-eyed, bouncing to the beat blasting from the small radio they danced to. Hordes of people crowded around the trio as they watched them move with precision, jumping up in the air, spinning around on their backs, and walking on their hands.

"These guys are good," Mathew commented.

They watched for about fifteen minutes, 'til Toni stated that there were other things to see and do, and that they should move on. So Mathew, being the kind-hearted gentleman he was, reached into his pocket and tipped all three gentlemen five hundred dollars. The young men were overwhelmed by that much money being handed to them. They didn't know what to say, but they stopped dancing, and their mouths hung open.

"Yo, good looking out," one of them finally managed to say.

Mathew smiled and moved along with Toni.

"Let me give you a little advice," Toni said. "Try not to be flashing your wad of cash so openly. You wanna get us robbed out here? This is New York City. There are a lot of crazy people out here."

"Oh, I'm sorry."

"And damn, Mathew, stop being so apologetic."

"Oh, I'm—"

Toni just looked at him before he could even finish his sentence. He smiled. They headed toward the arcade, and then after that, to the Marriott Marquis, where they had a few drinks at the bar. They both were having a good time, enjoying the city and each other. Next on the agenda Mathew took Toni on a forty-minute horse-and-carriage ride through the city, where she hugged and leaned on his shoulder during the whole ride. To her, it was the perfect night. She had never had so much fun with a man—innocent fun. She was in love with Mathew. She loved being with him.

It was going on 2:00 A.M., and they both felt that it was time to leave, so they summoned for a cab and headed back to his place. Pulling up in front of his building, they remained in the cab for about ten minutes. Mathew paid the driver an extra fifty for his time. They both hugged and kissed and talked for a minute. Mathew wished that he could bring her upstairs, but he was fully aware of his situation.

"So, when will I see you again?" he asked.

Toni smiled. "I had a wonderful time tonight," she told him.

"So did I," he stated.

It was a night that they both did not want to end, but it was getting late, and he had his fiancée in the penthouse. And Toni had to journey back to Brooklyn. They gave each other one long hug and kiss good night, then he stepped out of the cab, tipping the driver another one hundred dollars and telling Toni to have a safe ride home.

Back in the penthouse, he snuck into his place like it was way past his curfew. He eased the door shut, stripping off his clothes in the great room and eased his all-night ass back in between the sheets next to Tina, who was still asleep, not having a clue as to where he'd been for the past three hours.

Seeing and hanging out with Toni was the perfect cure from the stress and depression he was going through during the day. He couldn't wait to see her again.

-Twenty-three-

A brilliant-cut diamond and pear-shaped sapphire platinum necklace hung from around Toni's neck, a small gift to her from Mathew. It was his way of telling her "thank you" for their night out.

Toni was stunned when she saw the gift. She didn't want to accept it at first, but it was so dazzling that it was hard for her to turn down, as it would be for any lady for that matter. Mathew had the store deliver it to her personally. A small man, accompanied by an armed guard, delivered it to her at her apartment door at four in the afternoon. It was awkward, seeing a white man in a nice-looking suit wander through the pits of the ghetto, carrying a ten-thousand- dollar necklace with a six foot, two inch uniformed guard standing by his side. People gawked and looked, whispered among themselves, but none thought to ask the man and his tall friend what or who they were there to see.

Nervous, the man delivered the gift, announced whom it was from, said a little poem, then scurried outta the projects to his car, worrying that the locals might have already vandalized it.

Toni hesitated to try on the necklace. It was so beautiful, and she had never owned anything like it. She stood in front of the mirror and stared at it, admiring the cuts, the pear shape, the way the sapphire gleamed, that she just couldn't stop gazing at it. This was surely a wonderful gift. And when she touched it, she couldn't help but to think about Mathew, smiling uncontrollably with him on her mind.

But having such a gift meant keeping it well hidden, knowing better than to have it lying around the place, and for sure keeping it out the sight of her moms. If her mother knew about it, she would be rummaging through the whole apartment in search of it, so that she could pawn the expensive necklace for a measly few hundred dollars, just for a lousy high. The thought of her mother stealing her new necklace and selling it cheap for drugs made Toni cringe, and a few tears trickled down her cheeks. Her new necklace meant so much to her, the reason being that it was from Mathew, and she was truly in love with him. Whenever she thought about him, a smile would loom, and she would go into a daze.

Unfortunately, hearing the front door being unlocked snapped her out of whatever fantasy she was in and put her back into reality. She knew it was her mother, so she quickly removed the necklace from around her neck, clutching it tightly in her fist and scurried toward her bedroom.

She hid it safely inside one of her old shoes in the closet—shoes that she hadn't worn in years, and she thought that her mother would never think to look in them. She then walked back out of her room to see her mother's room door closed. Frightened, she knocked first, thinking the worst of what her mother was up to in her bedroom.

"Ma," Toni called out, knocking lightly on the bedroom door again.

"What, girl? I'm busy," her mother answered back.

It became too quiet in the bedroom, and Toni let out an irate sigh, knowing that her mother was either shooting up or fucking some hustler for a hit. Toni rolled her eyes and yelled from the other side of the door, "I'm going out." But she received no answer at all, just silence.

Toni was scheduled to be at the club around ten that night, but she didn't feel like going. She would rather be with Mathew doing whatever, doing something that she hadn't done in a very long time, and that was having fun. Her life was just too fuckin' stressful and hectic, dealing with her drug-addicted mother and worrying about her incarcerated brother, making sure he was being taken care of while he was behind bars. Then there was the struggle to earn a buck, pay the bills, and keep her home in order. The worst of it was her boyfriend, Tec, notorious for being a gangsta and a killer.

Toni wandered around Coney Island for a few hours, heading toward the amusement park and strolling along the boardwalk, peering out into the waters. The evening was warm and pleasant. Lots of folks were out enjoying the summer weather and having fun. The rides were packed with folks, and you could hear the screams of people riding the Cyclone.

Toni bought herself some cheese fries and took a seat on one of the benches that was bolted down sparsely along the boardwalk. She kept peering out into the sea, lost in her thoughts, enjoying her solitude, even though the boardwalk was filled with people. She thought about Thomas, then smiled, reminiscing on the good times she and her brother used to share back in the day when they both were young—before the gangs, before the drugs, before Derrick. How their grandmother used to bake for them every weekend, teaching Toni in the kitchen. How Toni and her brother used to ride the Cyclone 'til they became sick and bet on who would be the first to throw up after eating a ton of cheese fries and candy. How their mother was a mother and loved her children to death.

It was amazing how her life tragically changed, becoming fucked up. And what used to be a household filled with love was now filled with nothing but bitterness and pain. She missed those days, missed them so much that the more she sat and continued to reminiscence on them, a few tears began to flow from her eyes and trickle down her cheeks.

Toni wiped the tears away with the back of her hand and stood. She quickly walked off, leaving her cheese fries on the bench for the birds and rodents to enjoy.

"Oh, it's beautiful, Mathew," Tina cheered as she gazed down at the twenty-four-thousand-dollar necklace.

Mathew stood next to his fiancée in the high-quality jewelry store, the same jewelry store in Manhattan where he'd purchased a necklace for Toni just a week ago.

"You like it?" asked the manager who'd always given Mathew VIP treatment, knowing his status.

"Of course, Langston," Tina said, admiring the necklace in the mirror.

"So should it be safe to say that madam is going to wear the necklace out?" Langston asked, staring over at Mathew while Tina continued to admire the necklace.

"Yes, Langston," Mathew said. "Put it on my account."

Langston smiled. Mathew continually gave his store good business because for one, he had a very expensive fiancée, and, for two, she had very expensive taste. The necklace wasn't going to leave Tina's neck anytime soon. She loved it.

"Damn man, that's the second expensive necklace you bought this week. Pussy must be that good, huh?" a young hustler asked. He just so happened to be in the store the same day when Mathew bought Toni the sapphire necklace.

Mathew cut his eyes over at him and so did Langston. But the young hustler didn't know what was going on. He just happened to open up his big mouth around the wrong woman. The kid, who looked to be no older than nineteen, dressed in lavish jewelry and designer clothes, smiled, admiring Tina, then saying, "Damn, I know the bitch must be worth it, as fuckin' good as she looks."

"Excuse me," Mathew uttered at the young man.

Langston kept quiet even though the kid was being rude to one of his top clients, because, just like Mathew, this young hustler brought him good business, too, purchasing tons of shines with his illegal cash.

"What is he talking about, Mathew?" Tina inquired.

"Nothing, Tina. He doesn't know us," Mathew said.

"What necklace did you buy a week ago? I haven't received a necklace," Tina chided, her expression flaring up.

"Yo, you mean you ain't get that phat sapphire-and-diamond necklace that homeboy paid some serious cash for the other day?" the hustler blurted out.

"Yo, why don't you just mind your damn business?" Mathew angrily said.

"What, c'mon dog, you can't be serious?" the young boy chided, being from Brooklyn with a quick and deadly temper.

"Um, excuse me," Langston interrupted, acknowledging the young man.

"Yo, Langston, you better teach your customers some serious respect up in this muthafucka. Rich Boy don't know me."

But Langston did, knew the kid by name and all, even gave him dap when he walked into his store to buy jewelry. And Langston didn't want any conflicts between two of his top clientele.

"What necklace?" Tina angrily repeated.

"Tina," Mathew said.

"Mathew, what necklace?" she repeated.

The young hustler leaned against the glass counter, smirking, knowing that he had just probably ended a serious relationship.

Tina stormed outside toward the limo. Mathew followed right behind her. The necklace was already paid for, so Langston was cool. He'd already charged it to Mathew's account.

"Mathew, are you cheating on me?" Tina asked, glaring over at Mathew while the limo prepared to pull off.

Mathew was quiet. He thought about it.

"Mathew, I asked you a question," Tina reiterated.

Mathew thought about it some more. Shit, this could be his only chance to tell Tina the truth, tell her about Toni, and maybe, maybe, she would see the light, and there would be no wedding. He wasn't nervous. He just wished that maybe she had found out some other way than having some young thug leak out information.

"Tina," Mathew slowly said.

Tina continued to glare at him. She was upset, but she deserved the truth, and she would demand it from him no matter what. *Maybe this is just some big misunderstanding,* Tina thought. Maybe the necklace was meant to be a surprise for her, and that nasty drug dealer spoiled everything, and now Mathew was forced to reveal her surprise.

"Tina, I'm not in love with you," Mathew managed to say.

"Excuse me, but we're getting married in a few months, or did you forget?"

"No, I haven't."

"So what's the problem?" she asked.

"You, Tina. I'm not in love with you. I'm in love with another woman," he revealed.

"Mathew, if you're trying to make me jealous, then it's working," Tina angrily said to him.

"No, Tina, I'm not trying to make you jealous. I'm in love with another woman, and we've been seeing each other for a couple of weeks now, and the necklace, it was for her."

"I see," Tina said.

"I don't mean to hurt you . . . but—"

"But what, Mathew?" she chided. "What am I supposed to do? We're getting married. People expect us to be together. Hundreds of people are attending our wedding, and now you expect me to believe that you're in love with another woman? How idiotic is that? Your mother and I put so much into this ceremony, and now your feeble-minded self thinks that you're in love with another woman? Who is she?"

Mathew sighed. *Damn, how thickheaded can she get?* he asked himself.

"This is embarrassing, Mathew, not just toward me, but also to your family. How dare you . . . how dare you, Mathew?" she continued. "You're committing adultery before the both of us even say 'I do.' "

"Tina, please," Mathew irritably interrupted.

"This woman you think you're in love with, what is her name?" Tina demanded to know.

Mathew looked at her and then said, "You know what, Tina, you're a straight-up bitch."

Tina's mouth dropped open. She couldn't believe what she had just heard.

"Stop thinking that everything is always about you, because it's not. I'm not telling you this to hurt you, get you jealous, or however you may consider it, embarrass you," Mathew continued. "I'm telling you the straight-up truth. I'm not in love with you. I'm in love with someone else. Now how you take it is how you take it," Mathew said, sounding a little gully with her.

Tina sucked her teeth and crossed her arms. She was very upset. She couldn't believe what her ears were hearing. Her love, her fiancé, had just told her that he was in love with another woman. All she could think about was how this was gonna take a toll on her, what people would start to think of their so-called perfect fairytale relationship—Mathew and Tina, they were like the perfect couple. Everyone expected them to get married. But now, she felt that her life was taking a drastic turn. *How dare he?* was all Tina could think.

"So, you're willing to just throw everything away so easily, after what we've built together?"

"Tina, stop being so naïve. You and I both know that you never expected us to work out. The only reason you're pressing this wedding is probably because of my family's fortune."

Tina felt insulted. "Are you calling me some kind of gold digger?"

"If the shoe fits," he said.

"Driver, take me home," she snarled.

Damien was more than happy to. He was happy to get this stuck-up bitch out of the limo.

"I can't believe you, Mathew. I love you, and you . . . How can you do this to me?"

Tina was looking really sentimental. It was like what Mathew had just told her had hit a nerve. Like he had just cracked through a big force field, finding her heart.

"Mathew, can you please answer an honest question?" Tina asked.

"What is it, Tina?"

"Are you still a virgin?"

There was a long silence. Neither party saying a word as Tina looked over at Mathew and waited for an answer. But by his long silence, Tina already knew the answer. Mathew couldn't even look her in the eye, and that made it obvious.

"You've just answered my question," Tina said, turning her head and peering out the window.

"I'm sorry," Mathew apologized.

Surprisingly, Tina remained quiet throughout the entire ride home. That stunned both Mathew and Damien because it was usually Tina who had to have the last word. But she'd run out of bitchiness, and they weren't complaining. The thing that was on Mathew's mind was what she was gonna tell his mother this time, especially now that he'd just admitted that he was in love with another woman.

He sat back in his seat with his head resting against the leather and cherished this moment—with Tina being quiet or at a loss for words. He knew that his mother wasn't going to take him dumping Tina, calling off the wedding, and admitting that he was in love with another woman too lightly. She would loathe his actions and call it imprudent on his behalf, especially when she came to find out that Toni was from the ghetto streets of Brooklyn and would definitely not fit the criteria of how a Peters woman should be. Tina definitely fit that standard, and in his mother's eyes, Tina would always be the perfect woman for Mathew, no matter what he believed. That was why it was imperative that Mathew marry Tina. There was no other woman on this earth that Mrs. Peters felt would be able to fill her shoes when she was long gone, and somebody needed to take care of her baby—somebody.

-Twenty-four-

In order for one to be respected in the hood, one had to combine action with boldness. In other words, prove that he or she was 'bout it, 'bout it. Pussy muthafuckas got no kind of respect whatsoever, and so went the same for people who were nothing but talk and no action. Rep was everything in the hood, especially in Brooklyn, and once a man lost that, then he was vulnerable to the leeches, vultures, and others creatures who waited to prey on the weak and take control. Reputation was power, and without it, a man was nothing, and he would definitely be attacked by all of his enemies.

Being a weak and timid muthafucka would get a person nowhere, no respect. It might even get a niggah killed, especially if other niggahs knew that someone was too scared to bus' off his guns, even knowing that his enemies would not hesitate to come at him and seize what he possessed, even if it was his woman. But if a man was a hardcore niggah to the bone, done already proved too many times that he'd kill for his, that he was 'bout it, 'bout it, and bold as a muthafucka, then his enemies would wait and ponder, even relinquish the idea of trying to come at him, 'cause his actions spoke louder than words.

Two men sat across the street from the Gravesend housing projects in a dark blue Pathfinder—waiting. Word around the way was that Chills had put out a two-man hit-man crew for Tec and whoever, and they'd been lurking around the projects trying to hunt the niggah down and end the frivolous civil war in Coney Island. For a cash amount of fifty thousand dollars paid to both men, they were willing and ready to execute Tec in the worst possible way—even in public—to let everyone know that Chills was not to be fucked with. And let this hood niggah Tec's death prove a point that if someone was ignorant enough to fuck with Chills, his business, and his money, then this would be an example of the consequences.

The two men who were seated in the jeep would prefer it to be done that way, out in public, in front of a small crowd. They wanted to show the world, or better yet, the hood, that they were the ones who murdered and slaughtered their little ghetto icon. They waited in the jeep, both men concealing .45s. An AK-47 rested in the backseat. They waited and waited. They got information that Tec might be up in a certain building, chilling with his girl, but they were not sure of what apartment. So rather than going up in the place and knocking down every fuckin' door in search of him, they waited out front, like professionals, waiting for him to step out of the lobby. Then that's when they would attack, and the execution would take place. Money was being passed for information, and someone leaked information back to both men that he was currently up in the building that they were parked in front of.

Now when a niggah was looked up to and respected, like how Tec was around his peers, niggahs would come to his aid quickly, knowing about his murderous tendencies. Someone would probably warn him of the danger that was lingering outside.

It was evening out, and Tec was resting in Toni's apartment, sprawled out on her bed, butt naked. He was fondling between Toni's warm thighs. Toni wished it was her other man, Mathew. She just couldn't stop thinking about the damn man. Tec had no idea that two men were waiting outside to spill his blood as soon as he stepped foot out of the lobby.

"Stop," Tec barked. Toni had tried to get romantic and a little frisky, kissing and rubbing on Tec's chest.

"What's wrong, baby?" she asked, looking over at Tec. He was looking a little irate.

"You're bugging me now. Chill, Toni."

Toni sighed. Tec could molest and touch between her thighs without any consent from her, but when she tried to show him a little lovin', even when her heart was for another man, this muthafucka had the nerve to try and cop an attitude with her.

"Yo, can you do me a favor?" Tec asked.

"What, Keith?"

"I'm hungry. Go make me a quick sandwich."

"What?"

"I said, go and make me a sandwich," he repeated, glaring over at her.

Toni sighed, thinking that she should tell this muthafucka no. In fact, she should scream, *Hell no! Make your own damn sandwich.* But instead, she shot him a dirty fuckin' look, removed herself from the bed, and walked into the kitchen naked, doing what she was told.

Just as Toni was finishing making Tec a bologna-and-cheese sandwich with mayonnaise, lettuce, and tomatoes, she was alarmed by three quick knocks at her apartment door. Wary about being naked and answering her door, she rushed back to the bedroom, telling Tec that someone was at her door. She threw on a robe and went to see who it was. Tec didn't even thank her for the sandwich.

Toni voiced out a quick, "Who is it?"

"It's me," a young voice answered back from the other end of the door.

"Me? Who is me?" she suspiciously asked.

"Danny, yo, I'm looking for Tec. You his girl?"

"Hold on," she uttered out. She headed back toward the bedroom to tell Tec that someone, most likely a stranger, was asking about him at her door.

"Some young kid is at my door asking for you," she told him.

Tec peered up at her with a mouthful of cheese and lettuce, and said, "What? Who the fuck is it?"

"I don't know. Probably one of your young wannabe hustlers," she said.

"You told that niggah that I was in here?"

"I think he already knows. He said that his name was Danny."

Danny, Danny? Tec tried to recall the name, but couldn't place it. He started to think the worst, thinking that this Danny was more of a foe than a friend. He was thinking fast. He got up outta the bed, still nude, and walked up to Toni, glaring at her for being so stupid and already letting whoever it was at the door know that he was up in there. But he had to think. If it was one of Chills' goons ready to gun him down, then why didn't they just break down the front door and come in shooting? He reached for his gat, a .357, and approached the door very carefully—naked still, not givin' a fuck.

"Yo, who's asking for me?" he hollered with one hand on the doorknob and the other gripping the .357 tightly, ready for whatever.

"Tec, it's Danny. I got sumthin' to tell you," Danny shouted out from the hallway.

"Niggah, you can't tell me from out there? I don't know you."

"Yo, Tec, you got two men waiting outside the building for you. I think they trying to body you, son."

"What?" Tec asked.

"They sitting in a blue Pathfinder."

"How the fuck do you know this?"

"'Cause they been asking all around for you, and I never seen these niggahs before."

"Yo, I'm gonna open this door, and if you make one quick and stupid move, niggah, then I'm gonna smoke you."

"Ayyite, man, I'm cool, yo," young Danny assured.

Tec carefully turned the doorknob, unlocking it and cracking the apartment door slowly open, peeping out at young Danny, who was about five feet, six inches, and looked like he was twelve. He didn't look like a threat, standing in front of Tec in a pair of blue sweats, Reeboks, and a torn T-shirt. *Ugly-looking kid,* Tec thought.

"What the fuck did you say about niggahs outside looking for me?"

The gun in Tec's hand caught Danny's instant attention—and his nudity was shocking. Danny had never seen a real gun before, especially one so close up. His mother tried to keep him on tight watch, but that was hard since she worked all the time. He was new to the hood and had been living in C.I. for about a year now.

He was really trying hard to be down, trying to hang with the young locals. And now, having the chance to inform Tec of the so-called dangerous men downstairs that were out to kill him, he felt that this could be a step up for his reputation—probably Tec might take him under his wing, look out for the little niggah.

"Downstairs. Two men in a jeep, they've been asking about you and stuff like that," Danny informed.

"Show me, niggah," Tec said, pulling Danny quickly into the apartment. Tec dragged Danny by his shirt to Toni's bedroom. Toni was surprised by the sudden appearance of a young boy showing up in her bedroom. She quickly covered herself, already allowing Danny to get an eyeful of her goods.

"Tec, what the hell?" she blurted, becoming a little embarrassed.

But Tec didn't pay any attention to her as he walked to the bedroom window and peered outside with Danny standing by his side.

"Ayyite, li'l niggah, where they at?" he asked, still gripping the boy by his T-shirt. Danny peered outside the window, looking for the Pathfinder. "There," he shouted. Tec took a good look, trying to see if he could make out the faces of the occupants in the jeep.

"How long have they been waiting there?" Tec asked.

"I don't know. They just been asking around about you."

Tec looked at the boy, looking at him like he was angry with him or something. This could be a setup. They probably paid this little niggah. He didn't know this muthafucka, and now this little niggah comes to this apartment and was trying to warn him all of a sudden. He became wary.

"Niggah, you wait right here. Don't go any goddamn where," he told Danny.

Tec went to the kitchen, leaving Danny in the bedroom with Toni. Danny smiled, admiring Toni's beauty and her almost butt nakedness in front of his eyes, damn near a dream come true for the young lad, who was still a virgin.

Tec was making a few phone calls from the kitchen phone. Niggahs wanna come at him, then they better come at him correct, 'cause it was about to be murder. His first phone call was to his right-hand man, Little Boy Ronny. He informed him of the situation, and Little Boy Ronny was only a few blocks away. Best believe that he was on his way with some serious company.

It was around seven on this humid day, and C.I. was packed with folks, bearing the hot and humid weather that they'd been having lately. There was a little barbecue in Kaiser Park, filled with kids and adults. Locals lingered around the building steps and sidewalk, chatting the evening away. Despite the gangs and the drug war, people still tried to live their lives, doing everyday activities and going on with day-to-day living. The drugs, violence, and gangs that plagued their neighborhood didn't intimidate some. To these people, this was still home, and most folks had been living there for more than twenty years. They refused to be driven out of their neighborhood by dumb derelicts who robbed, murdered, sold drugs, and were killing themselves over poison that addicted their kids and imprisoned the youth.

The dark blue Pathfinder remained parked in front of Kaiser Park, across the street from the Gravesend housing projects. Both men were growing a little impatient. They'd been waiting for almost four hours for this niggah. The job was only going to take them less than a minute. People took sight of both men in the jeep, but no one paid them any real attention. They were not trying to look inconspicuous either, since they chose to be seen so out in the open.

Tec still peered at them from the bedroom window, with Danny still present. Fifteen minutes had passed since he'd been made aware of their presence. Toni was getting a little restless. She knew something was up, and having this young kid in her bedroom was not making her feel any more comfortable. She wished that she was somewhere else at the moment.

"Keith, is everything okay?" Toni asked, seated on the bed, staring at both males.

"Shut the fuck up right now, Toni," Tec barked. He still gripped the .357 tightly. Danny was becoming a little nervous. All he wanted to do at that point was go home. But Tec wouldn't allow him to leave, not until this little situation was taken care of.

Toni sighed, getting up from off the bed.

"Where the fuck you going?" Tec shouted.

"To the kitchen. I'm hungry," she proclaimed.

"Sit the fuck down."

"What?"

"I said, sit the fuck down," he repeated.

"Niggah, you're bugging. Listen, whatever bullshit you got yourself into out there, that shit don't involve me, Keith," she said, still proceeding to the kitchen.

"Toni, I said sit the fuck down," he angrily reiterated for the third time, but this time he pointed the gun at her.

Her heart stopped for a quick second. This was the second time in weeks someone had a gun pointed at her and by her boyfriend of all people. She stood there, frozen in horror, with her eyes wide open.

"Keith, are you crazy?" she managed to say, her voice a little jittery.

"Sit down, Toni," Tec warned.

She was sick of this shit. She couldn't take any more. How could she love a man who in return did nothing but treat her like shit—constantly disrespecting her all the time, talking down to her, treating her like she was nothing but some sex toy, and now this niggah had the nerve to point a loaded gun at her. *He must be fucking crazy,* Toni thought. If her brother, Sheek, ever found out, he'd probably have Tec bodied.

The phone rang, alarming Tec. He placed the gun back down at his side and walked outta the bedroom to go and answer the phone. It was Little Boy Ronny on the other end, calling from a payphone. He informed Tec that he was at the corner with a loaded black S&W concealed under his dark sweatshirt, and Nate was seated in a burgundy Ford, ready to pop off.

"Where the problem at?" Little Boy Ronny asked, eager to cause some trouble.

"Dark blue Pathfinder in front of my building," Tec quickly informed. "Take care of that."

Little Boy Ronny didn't say another word. He just quickly hung up and got back into the Ford with Nate driving. They slowly crept around the corner and down Bay View Avenue, cruising right past the Pathfinder. Then they made a quick U-turn and parked across the street from the jeep, just a few cars down.

"You ready, niggah?" Little Boy Ronny asked Nate, cocking back the S&W.

"What the fuck you think? Let's do this, niggah."

Nate and Little Boy Ronny stepped out of the Ford, creeping across the street. The hood was busy with people, but those two niggahs, just like the two hit men parked across the street, they didn't give a fuck about who was around. All they cared about was business and respect, and killing those who got in their way or posed a threat, no matter what the consequences. And if there were any witnesses, then there soon wouldn't be, 'cause many people who would see the day's actions would be too scared to tell, maintaining the code of silence and fearing the worst.

When they were only a few feet from the Pathfinder, Little Boy Ronny and Nate raised their guns, and without warning, both men in the jeep were suddenly stricken with a barrage of intense gunfire. The driver was quickly hit with multiple shots to his chest. He slumped over the wheel while the second man tried to take cover. That man reached for his gat and quickly opened the passenger door. Hearing the sound of abrupt gunfire, folks began running around trying to take cover behind trees, cars, and inside lobbies, dropping down to the ground like they were on fire. Everybody scampered around like roaches after the light comes on.

Gunfire was quickly returned from the rival party as he quickly let out a few rounds back at Nate and Little Boy Ronny. But both Nate and Little Boy Ronny continued to shoot with rage in their eyes.

"Fuck Chills. Fuck Chills," Little Boy Ronny shouted, squeezing multiple rounds into the jeep and at Chills' hit man. With success, three shots hit the man in his chest, and one round struck him in the neck, violently collapsing him to the ground. Then both men retreated to their parked Ford and drove off.

What must have felt like an eternity for some, being engulfed in a hail of gunfire so quickly and so dangerously, only lasted about forty seconds. What started out in the projects as a peaceful evening, quickly turned to death. Two men lay dead in the streets, quickly gunned down, instead of doing the gunning like they had planned.

Tec peered from the upper window of the apartment, watching everything. A smirk appeared on his face. He felt like he was one up on Chills and his goons. He was feeling invincible. He had eyes and ears everywhere in his neighborhood. That was why he felt he couldn't go down so easily. This was a drug war that he was winning. It was just gonna take a little time to cut the head off the chicken and watch it squirm and die.

Toni and Danny both heard the shots coming from outside. Toni flinched when she heard the first few shots. They had startled her. She had heard gunshots before, so they were nothing new to her, but the gunfire that came from downstairs rattled her nerves a little, because she knew that whatever took place, Keith definitely had something to do with it, and that really bothered her.

Danny had nothing to say. He feared Tec, and all he could think about was going home. Toni wanted Tec outta her apartment. In fact, she wanted him outta her life. She couldn't take the shit anymore, and it could only get worse.

The ten o'clock news was shocking and very disturbing as news reporters from all the different stations reported to viewers about the violent shootout that took place just a few short hours ago in Coney Island, Brooklyn.

But it wasn't the two men dead and the hail of gunfire that inundated this urban neighborhood just a short while ago or the ongoing drug war that was shocking. It was when the reporters informed the viewers that a six-year-old girl had been shot in her chest, having been hit by a stray bullet, and now she was in critical condition at Coney Island Hospital. This brought tears to many people's eyes.

"She was just playing," one man informed viewers. His voice was filled with sorrow and sadness while he was interviewed by a reporter. "Then the shots just happened so quickly. She didn't even have a warning."

"She's a sweet little girl," a woman told reporters, peering into the news camera as a few tears trickled down her cheeks. "Sad . . . it's sad when a six-year-old girl can't even play out on the street without worrying about some drug war."

"Animals, nothing but damn animals. They don't care about nothing, but the drugs that poison this neighborhood," a man raged, sounding very angry and furious. "We live here, imprisoned in our own homes."

Over three dozen cops, homicide detectives, and the crime scene unit flooded the area, knocking on apartment doors, dusting for prints, asking questions, and wanting to arrest and convict the savages who had committed such a senseless and meaningless shooting, sending an innocent little girl to the ICU. This time, a few witnesses spoke out, telling what they saw and knew. It was not fair for such a little girl's life to be almost cut short, falling victim to a senseless drug war.

Local police would do whatever they could to catch and indict the two suspects. One lady was already giving two homicide detectives a brief description of one of the shooters. Her name was Mary Lawrence, and she wasn't scared. She showed a tremendous amount of courage despite the risks. She was sixty-two years old and had been living in the neighborhood for about thirty-five years. She remembered her home back when the neighborhood was predominantly white, and the Coney Island boardwalk was fun and safe to stroll on at night with her husband.

She gave a description of Nate, the tall, slender shooter, who had on a black hooded sweatshirt, denim jeans, and a pair of boots. "Timberlands, I think they call 'em," she softly said to the detective as he took notes in his pad.

"What about the second shooter. Do you remember what he had on?" the next detective asked.

"He was smaller. I don't know, about five feet, five inches, maybe five feet six," she recalled.

"Any scars? Anything that stood out about him?"

"No, nothing, officer. They both were covered up pretty good in dark clothing. I didn't get a good look at their faces," she sadly informed him.

"Well, thanks again for your help, ma'am," the one jotting down the information on his pad told her. "We'll keep in touch."

What the cops had to go on was nothing much, except that the shooters were driving a burgundy Ford, which they would ditch and burn later; that one was taller than the other; and that they were both dressed in dark clothing.

It was sad. The shooting happened so fast that most folks were just trying to take cover and protect themselves from gunfire, rather than trying to witness and be able to describe both shooters thoroughly. That gave Nate and Little Boy Ronny some advantage.

Toni sat in front of her television with tears trickling down her cheeks. She had just finished watching the segment on the shooting and the little girl who was in critical condition at Coney Island Hospital. She knew the little girl. She lived a floor above her, and whenever she saw Toni, she would speak, saying "hello" or "hi." She was such a doll, a cutie.

Toni would say nothing about the shooting. She feared that if she informed the police and told them that her boyfriend, Keith, had something to do with it, then he would definitely come after her, and he'd probably kill her. Besides, she said to herself that they probably wouldn't have enough evidence to hold and convict him anyway, so why waste her breath and put her own life in danger? She already had enough shit to worry about in her life without the police harassing her, wanting to set up wiretaps and go after her drug-dealing boyfriend. Nah, she'd rather just let it be and get on with her own poverty-stricken life. No sense in throwing more fuel on the fire.

-Twenty-five-

"You okay, baby?" Myron asked, sitting across from Vinita at the dinner table, trying to have a nice, quiet romantic dinner with his lady. But she'd been quiet all night, not saying a word to him. In fact, she'd been acting strange all week, and Myron noticed. He wanted to know what was up with his love.

"You haven't touched your dinner yet," Myron said, getting up from his seat and walking over to her. He stood behind her while she sat still and gently placed his hands on her shoulders. He gave her a soothing massage. But that didn't ease Vinita's worries, with her mind still wedged on her confrontation with Little Boy Ronny, being unfortunate to run into him when she was able to avoid him for so many years—reason being, he'd been in and out of jail. Now it felt like her past was catching up to her. She never told a soul about that horrible night when she was abused and raped by the men she trusted. She kept that secret deep inside her, causing her to sometimes become bitter with others and not trust many.

Myron was different. She trusted him, and that was rare because she didn't trust many men. But she felt comfortable being around him, feeling that she could tell him anything, talk to him about whatever and he'd listen and be understanding. That's why she was feeling compelled to tell him the truth, confess to him about that horrible incident—it was eating her up inside, having that dreadful night buried so deeply inside. And with Little Boy Ronny threatening her, it didn't help matters much. She was horrified of the man. Running into him brought tears to her eyes and made her stomach turn. Seeing his face brought up terrible memories that she had tried so hard to forget.

Myron tried hard to have her speak up on what was bothering her, and she wanted to. The dark and awful secret sitting on the top of her tongue was ready to escape. She wanted to tell the man she loved what had happened to her seven years ago. She wanted to cry on his shoulder and have his masculine arms console her and assure her that everything would be OK, that there would be nothing for her to worry or fear for the rest of her life—he was going to take care of her and protect her.

"If you're not hungry, then that's OK. We can have dinner later," he said, still massaging her shoulders with his strong hands.

Vinita turned around and looked up at her prince while he was looking down at her, giving off a warm and gentle smile. Tears started to build up in her eyes, then slowly trickled down the sides of her face. "Myron," she called out, but then she remained silent after saying his name.

Myron sensed that something was wrong with her, and he knew she was willing to tell, so he gazed at his fiancée, then said to her, "Whatever you want to tell me, but feel that you're not ready to, it's okay, baby. I'm a patient man. Take all the time you need. I'll be here whenever you feel the time is right to confide in me about whatever is bothering you."

"Myron," Vinita spoke, "I love you." She stood, turned to him, and hugged him strongly, not wanting to let go of his love. Myron wrapped his lady up in his arms, with her head nestled against his chest, and Vinita just broke out in tears, leaving a wet blot on his T-shirt.

That night they lay in his bed, Vinita cuddled in his arms. They huddled together tightly like they were both protecting each other from the cold. Vinita felt that she was one step closer to sharing her secret with him. She loved this man and knew that she would be spending the rest of her life with him. But the only thing that truly scared her was if or when she admitted to him about being raped, and how she used to be back in the day, whether he would still love her the same. Would he still see that woman he fell in love with in the first place, instead of some first-rate abused slut?

It was a day that both Mathew and Toni kinda dreaded, but they knew it had to be done. This day was going to come, sooner or later. Toni was extremely nervous, pacing around her apartment, waiting for the limo to come pick her up. She was dressed like she was going to meet the Queen of England, and she wished that's who she was actually going meet. She probably would've been more at ease and relaxed, 'cause this evening Mathew was boldly taking Toni out to Long Island so that he could introduce her to his mother. May God be with them both.

Toni was dressed in a red, stretch matte jersey evening gown, her hair up in a French roll, and her new expensive necklace glimmering around her neck. She looked like she could be royalty herself. She stood in front of the living room mirror, gazing at herself. She loved the look. It made her feel sexy, and at the same time, sophisticated. But no matter how glamorous she appeared, it still couldn't take away the tension she was feeling, along with the million butterflies that were squirming around in her stomach.

Okay, Toni, this is only one night, she said to herself. *You'll be fine.*

She glanced over at the clock on the wall, and it read 7:25. Matthew said the limo would be around by 7:30 to come pick her up. She was already dressed and ready. It was a formal affair, and Mathew had bought her the gown a week ago. It was only dinner, but to her, it felt like it was much more. No man had ever gone through the trouble of introducing her to his mother, and this was really special to her. She didn't want to mess this up in any kind of way.

Toni heard the front door open and saw her mother walk in. Her eyes were red, and she had on this huge extra-extra-large T-shirt that was way too big for her, hanging down to her knees. She looked over at Toni, seeing her daughter dressed so elegantly. She spotted the necklace immediately, walking up to her, reaching out, and grabbing the necklace.

"Oooh, girl, this is nice," she said, clutching it tightly. "Where did you get this?"

Toni pulled back, causing Angela to let go of the necklace. "It was a gift," she spat back at her mother, staring at her with contempt in her eyes. She knew her mother was high—fucked up—and probably had just come from shooting up.

"Well, since you looking mighty fine, looking rich and shit, loan me fifty dollars," Angela said.

"I don't have it," Toni shot back.

"What you mean, you don't got it? It's not for drugs, if that's what you think. It's for something else."

"I don't have it," Toni sternly repeated.

"Shit, girl, you got this shit around your neck, and you can't loan your own damn mother fifty damn dollars? Didn't I raise you better?"

"I gotta go soon," Toni said, passing her mother and walking into the kitchen, peering out the window to see if the limo had pulled up in front of her building.

"Toni," her mother called out, "who you fucking? 'Cause you gotta be giving a niggah some pussy for him to buy you some shit like that."

Toni turned around and glared at her mother. "Leave me alone, Mom. I'm sick of your shit. Why you gotta be like this?"

"Like what?" her mother chided.

"Look at you, what you've become. You're a disgrace."

"I'm a disgrace? Fuck you, bitch. You think you better than me, huh? You think 'cause you're dressed nice in fancy clothing and got some niggah's jewelry around your neck that you're better than me? Get real, Toni."

"No, you get real," Toni shouted. "I'm sick of this, sick of you. I've been doing everything that I can for you, and you do nothing but shit on me. No more."

"So, I'm an embarrassment to you now, huh?" her mother angrily said, stepping toward her. "You think you better than me, Toni, huh? You think so. Well if so, then you can get the fuck outta my apartment."

"Your apartment," Toni said, returning her attention to her mother. "You're high, Mom."

"Fuck you, Toni. You think you're better than me? Well, you ain't, bitch." Toni knew her mother was definitely fucked up and probably drunk 'cause she was able to smell the liquor on her breath. She really didn't need this shit tonight. Mathew was about to pick her up soon, and she didn't need her mother aggravating her, putting her in a foul mood, especially during the night when she was gonna meet Mathew's mother. She tried to ignore her mother's foolishness by walking away and heading to her bedroom, but her crazy mother followed her, nagging her about silliness and stupid shit.

"Who you, Toni? I fucking took care of you, bitch. You're my daughter. You think some niggah out there really care about you, huh? No, all that muthafucka care about is pussy. And shit, don't think I don't know what you be doing up in that club, dancing. Nah, you ain't dancing, you fuckin' niggahs just like me. And you think you better than me? You ain't nuthin' but another project ho."

That hit a nerve for Toni. A few tears started to well up in her eyes. She turned to catch eyes with her moms. "You know the difference between me and you, from what we both do? I do it to survive, to pay the rent, take care of the bills, to try and fuckin' take care of us," she wailed out. "But you . . . you do it to support a habit. You don't give a fuck about nothing but yourself. You're not my mother. My mother died years ago."

"Welcome to reality, bitch," her mother spat back while coming closer to her. She stumbled, bumping against the hallway wall.

"Look at you. You're high, you're drunk," Toni said, taking a few steps back from her.

"I'm fine, bitch."

"Ma, you gonna stop calling me a bitch."

"Oh, what you gonna do? I'm still your gotdamn mother. You respect me. You respect me, Toni."

"Ma, just take your ass to bed, please."

"No."

Toni walked past her, heading toward the living room window and peering outside to see if her ride was there. She prayed that it was. She couldn't put up with her mother for too much longer. Unfortunately, her ride hadn't showed up yet. She checked herself in the mirror again and ignored her mother's foolishness.

"Survive," her mother said, chuckling. "Bitch, you're still a ho . . . a ho will always be a ho. Fuckin' ho."

"Whatever."

"I wanna meet this man that's taking you out. Where is he?"

Toni ignored her, reaching for her purse. She wiped away her tears and continued to get herself ready, making sure her makeup was still fine, that her hair was still done up nice, and that her nerves were still strong. Her mother tagged along behind her, still talking nonsense, trying to upset Toni even more, but Toni tried hard to ignore her, no matter how loud she got. She went to the window for the third time and smiled when she saw the cream Lincoln limo pulling up out front. She grabbed everything and rushed for the door, but stopped in her tracks when she heard the phone ring. She picked up, and it was Mathew, telling her that he was waiting downstairs.

"I'm still your mother, gotdamnit," Angela burst out.

"You haven't been a mother to me in years," Toni finally said, then proceeded to the door. Her mother grabbed her by the arm, nearly yanking her back, and causing Toni to turn around. Toni was met with a quick slap to her face from her mother, shocking her. Toni just glared at her, speechless, and didn't even react.

"I fuckin' hate what you've become," Toni said, sounding upset, backing away from her mother, then leaving. She rushed down the steps, eager to get away. Before she reached the front doors of the lobby, she stopped and dried her tears for the second time that night, straightened herself out, got herself together, and once again told herself to get her mind and her nerves together.

The dozen or so residents who were loitering around the building steps on the warm summer evening were all amazed by the limo that just pulled up in front of their eyes, each of them curious about who was inside. They gazed at the limo like they all had X-ray vision. Toni casually stepped outside, walking between everybody, dressed up, and feeling like she was headed to her senior prom. She felt everyone gawking at her.

"Damn girl," one lady voiced out, "you going to your prom?"

"She thinks she cute..."

Toni just walked right by everyone, giving no one any hellos or any formal greeting. She didn't even acknowledge anyone.

"That bitch thinks she Cinderella now," another lady said, stirring up a few laughs from her peers.

Everyone watched as they saw a tall, black, and very handsome young man step out of the limo, smiling, while he looked on at Toni heading his way. There was jealousy and hate among a few residents as they watched Mathew hold the door open for Toni like a true gentleman, escorting her inside. All eyes were on them, catching a full glimpse of what, in their eyes, looked like true ghetto heaven—richness. It felt like the whole neighborhood was watching them, all eyes on them, and some of the wrong eyes were also watching, something who could cause trouble in the future.

"You're beautiful," Mathew proclaimed.

"Thank you."

The ride to Long Island was mostly silent. Toni tried

not to look nervous and fidgety. Mathew was a little worried about his mother's expected reaction toward Toni. He hadn't heard from or seen Tina in days, and he didn't know why, but that bothered him. He spoke to his mother the other day, and she hadn't said a word to him about his breakup with Tina or the marriage being called off. He wondered if she knew, and if Tina called and informed his mother about it. He didn't have the courage to tell his mother that he was in love with Toni yet, so he figured that the best way would be to bring Toni to dinner and tell his mother the news while Toni was present.

"Are you nervous?" Mathew asked, reaching over and taking her hand in his.

"A little," Toni answered, which was a lie. She was extremely nervous—trying not to panic.

Mathew was looking sharp, dressed in a gray pinstripe three-piece suit. His smile eased her tension a little.

"You'll be fine," Mathew assured. At least he hoped so, fully knowing how his mother could be.

"I hope so."

They became quiet again. Toni stared out the limo window as it got on to the Belt Parkway, and Mathew's mind was in two different places.

When the limo reached the border of Long Island, Mathew instructed Damien to pull over at the nearest 7-Eleven. Toni looked at him, wondering why, and plus, she didn't want to be late for meeting his mother.

Damien did what he was told, pulling into a 7-Eleven parking lot, with the stretch limo taking up about five parking spaces.

"Do you want something from inside?" he asked.

"No. I'm fine."

Mathew got out and walked up to the entrance. When he got inside, the first thing that he did was pull out his cell phone and call his mother.

"Hello?" he heard one of the servants answer.

"Yes, this is Mathew. May I please speak to my mother."

"Hold on, young Mathew," the butler with an English accent said.

He waited a minute or two, looking at items on the shelves while he was on hold. He watched a pretty young girl who looked to be about seventeen shoplift a bag of potato chips and a few candy bars. He laughed to himself.

"Mathew, darling," his mother answered, sounding exultant.

"Hello, Mother."

"Your father and I thought that it would be best if we went out to dinner instead," his mother suggested.

"Oh, really."

"Yes, Mathew, give the help a little break, some time off."

"That's okay with me, Mother."

"Splendid. So when can I expect for you and Tina to arrive?"

"You haven't spoken to Tina recently?"

"No, dear. Is there a problem?" she asked.

"Um, no . . . um, that's what I'm calling about," Mathew said, feeling the sweat drip down from his forehead. She didn't know, and he was wondering why Tina hadn't called up his mother and informed her of the terrible news. This made him even more nervous.

"Mother, I have to tell you something."

"We can discuss it over dinner. I can't wait to go over some of the preparations with Tina for the wedding," his mother happily said over the phone, causing Mathew's heart to beat a little harder.

"Yes, Mother, well, Tina's not coming," he said.

"No? Is she OK?"

"Yes, I think so. But Mother, I'm not coming with Tina. I'm bringing another guest," he said.

"A guest?"

"Yes, Mother, another woman," he finally admitted, feeling like he'd just told his mother that the world was ending.

"Mathew, my son, what do you mean by you're bringing another woman to my home? Who is she? And what happened to Tina?"

"Mother, I can explain. We're on the Long Island Expressway right now."

His mother became quiet over the other end of the line, and that worried Mathew, had him thinking the worse.

"Mother?" he called out.

"Mathew, I want you home as soon as possible," she demanded.

"I'm on my way."

"You have some serious explaining to do to your father and me," she said to him in a very harsh tone.

"Yes, Mother." He heard silence, and he knew she had hung up on him.

He took in a deep breath, feeling a bit relieved that he had at least let that part out of the bag. Now all he had to do was live through the introduction and then through the night.

He walked back to the exit and saw the same pretty, young girl arguing with the store clerk. The Hindu man was accusing her of stealing, and he was threatening to call the police on her. The young lady looked scared, so

Mathew reached into his pocket, pulled out a fifty, and gave it to her. He told her to get whatever she wanted out of the store and to keep the change. The Hindu man looked at him like he was crazy.

"Is everything OK?" Toni asked as soon as Mathew stepped back into the limo.

"Yeah, everything's fine. Let's roll," he said to Damien.

Toni's eyes widened when they pulled up to his parents' 11.4-acre estate. "Oh my God. Your parents have a beautiful place," she commented, gazing from the limo window.

"Wait 'til you see inside," Mathew said, grabbing her hand. He was nervous, but he tried not to look it.

The Lincoln pulled up in front of the stylish, grand home. It would soon be dusk out, causing the temperature to become a bit cooler. Damien came to a complete stop.

"Well, we're here," Mathew said.

"I see."

Mathew looked over at Toni. *She's beautiful,* he said to himself, eyeing her like this was the first time that he'd ever seen her. *If my mother doesn't like her, then she's crazy. She's a wonderful and remarkable woman.*

"OK, ain't this the part when we're supposed to get out of the car?" Toni asked because they'd been sitting there for about a minute with no one attempting to move.

"Oh," Mathew uttered.

"Is everything OK with you?"

"Yes. Oh, Toni, you're beautiful. No one can ever tell you different," he said.

Toni started to blush a little, smiling. "You're crazy," she said, laughing.

"Oh, I am, huh?"

"Yes."

"I'll show you how crazy I am," he said, then started tickling her in the limo. Toni jumped, laughing, trying to avoid being grabbed by his tickling hands. She pushed him away, smiling and laughing.

"Stop it, Mathew. I can't go inside there to meet your mother with you tickling me, messing up my hair. I wanna look my best."

"But you look wonderful."

"Whatever."

Toni checked herself in a handheld mirror, fixing the strands on her hair, applying a little bit of lipstick, and checking her earrings. She let out a quick sigh, then said, "OK, I'm ready. Let's do this."

"Before we go in," Mathew said, "there's a little something you should know about my mother. She can be a little, um, how can I say this . . . bitchy."

"Oh, yeah, Mathew, that's great to hear," Toni said. Hearing this wasn't good news to her. Just when she was starting to become calm, he told her this shit, making her nerves jump again.

"Don't worry. I'll hold your hand," Mathew joked.

Damien came around and opened the limo door. Mathew got out first, then reached down, taking Toni by the hand and helping her out of the car. Toni looked up, becoming bowled over by the beauty and the structure of the place. Now this wasn't the projects. She was in a whole new world, a world she'd never visited before, and she didn't know what to expect when she walked inside.

They walked up to the front door. Mathew rang the bell. Within seconds, a middle-aged gentleman, wearing a black-and-white tux, came to answer the door.

"Hello, young Mathew," he greeted.

"Hello, Jacob. My parents?" Mathew asked.

"They're both in the great room waiting for your arrival," he informed.

"Jacob, this is Toni. Toni, this is Jacob," he introduced. Jacob reached out and gave Toni a warm handshake. "Nice to meet you, ma'am."

"He's been with the family for years now," Mathew added.

Mathew proceeded to the great room where his parents waited for his arrival, curious to see this new woman Mathew was bringing into their home. Toni was only a few steps behind him. Her eyes were fixated on so many great things that his parents had in their home.

"Hello, Mother," Mathew said, seeing both his parents seated opposite each other on their new imported Italian furniture.

"Hello, Mathew," his father greeted first, getting up and welcoming his son home with a hug and quick kiss to his son's cheek.

"Mother," Mathew spoke.

Toni stepped into the room just a few short seconds after Mathew, and immediately attracted both of his parents' attention. His mother instantly shot her a quick glare, scowling at this new guest, this woman that her son had brought home.

"I would like for y'all to meet Toni," he introduced.

"Nice to meet you, Toni," his father greeted, making her feel welcomed.

"Mother," Mathew voiced.

Mrs. Pamela Peters remained seated, still glaring over at Toni, making it clear to everyone in the room that she didn't approve of this lady's arrival to her home.

"Mother," Mathew called out again.

Toni just stood there. She glanced at Mathew, then looked over at Mrs. Peters. The room was quiet for a few short seconds. It was like Mrs. Peters was the center of attention, and everyone was waiting on her reaction to Toni.

Mrs. Peters slowly rose out of her chair, heading toward everyone. She came up to Mathew, and uttered, "I want to talk to you." She shot a fierce look over at Toni, then added, "Privately."

Toni was shocked, not at her sudden harshness and rudeness, but how beautiful Mrs. Peters was . . . gorgeous—stunning. Mrs. Peters had on a two-piece purple suit; her long, flowing black hair fell to her shoulders; diamond earrings adorned her earlobes; her skin was moist and flawless; and she wore a hundred-thousand-dollar diamond necklace around her neck. Toni thought, *How can such a beautiful woman be such the bitch that Mathew says she is?* Toni just couldn't help but gaze at this beautiful woman who was in her late forties, but looked to be in her mid-thirties.

Mathew followed his mother into another room, leaving Toni alone with his father.

"Would you like a drink?" Perry asked.

"Yes, please," she said.

Perry Peters was a handsome man, dressed in Armani, with his peanut butter complexion; six-foot, one-inch slim frame; and short, black curly hair. She smiled every time he turned to look at her. She couldn't help but notice how attractive he was, and she said to herself, *This is where Mathew got his handsome looks from.* Both his mother and his father were definitely very attractive people.

Perry went over to his mini, well-equipped bar and fixed Toni a nice drink. They hit it off well. Toni was comfortable around his father. He was polite and charming, complimenting Toni on how beautiful she was, and now she saw where Mathew also got his charm. His father was good with words, but he had to be. He was a lawyer, a businessman, and an entrepreneur. He ran a seven-hundred-million-dollar operation.

Toni took a seat on one of the many plush, imported furniture pieces that decorated the room, crossing her legs. She chatted with Mathew's father. He was good to talk to, funny, intelligent, and also great to look at. He made the best of her company.

"Who is this woman you brought into my home, and what happened to Tina?" his mother barked, her hands placed on her hips, staring angrily at her son.

"Mother, her name is Toni, and she's really a nice girl," Mathew tried to persuade. "She's smart, funny, intelligent, and fun to be with."

"Mathew, where is Tina?" she demanded to know.

Mathew took a seat in one of the chairs in the room. "Tina and I are no longer together," Mathew said to her in a soft voice. "I called off the wedding and broke off our engagement."

"You did what?" she yelled.

"Mother, please, your voice."

"My son is a lunatic. The devil must be in you. How dare you?"

"Mother, it's my life."

"And it's obvious that you don't know what to do with it. Are you insane?"

"Tina wasn't right for me."

"And this tramp is?"

"Mother, I will not let you disrespect her like that," Mathew defended.

"I need to speak to Tina. Mathew, I will not let you embarrass this family," she barked, pacing around the room with her hands still strongly on her hips. "You know how much this marriage means to your father and me. We care about you so much."

"If you do, then you will let me go on with my life, Mother, and not try to run it."

"You're still a boy, Mathew."

"Mother, I'm twenty-five."

"Only a boy would make such a stupid decision in his life. We know what's best for you, Mathew," she said.

"Mother—"

"No, Mathew, you listen. Where did you meet this tramp? We don't know anything about her. Where is she from? Her background? Her family? What school does she attend? No Mathew, I will not allow such a foolish relationship to take place in my home," she ordered.

"I love this woman," Mathew spat back.

His mother placed her hand against her chest, looking in complete shock at the words that had just come out of her son's mouth. "Foolish Mathew, you love Tina," she returned.

Mathew shook his head. His mother was so bullheaded, just like Tina. No wonder she liked her so much.

"This is my life, Mother, and I'm in love with that beautiful woman who's standing out there."

"I see," she said in a low voice.

They both just stared at each other. There was bitterness throughout the room. His mother was holding her ground.

"You already got this preconceived notion in your head that Toni is bad for me and out to do me wrong. You don't even take the chance to know someone before you judge 'em. You know nothing about her, Mother, and already you're patronizing her."

"Imprudent. Mathew, I'm older, I'm wiser, and I know what's best for my son. Now, I'm not going to continue this conversation any further. You have two options, either you call Tina and apologize to her today, tell her you're sorry, and the wedding is back on, or, Mathew, I will cut you off from this family for good, forever, if you continue to see that girl."

"I see," Mathew said, rising from his chair.

"I know my son will do the right thing."

Perry and Toni chatted and got to know each other really well. He liked her. They both made each other laugh, and he saw why his son was so attracted to her. She was wonderful, had a good sense of humor, and a great personality.

Their little moment together was interrupted when Mathew came back into the room, looking upset. His mother came in right behind him.

"Toni," Mathew said, looking like he'd just lost his best friend.

Pamela came into the room. She looked over at her husband, then Mathew, then over at Toni.

"I'm sorry to say, but dinner has been called off," she said to everyone.

Her husband looked at her stunned. "Why?" he asked.

"We're leaving, Toni," Mathew said, taking her by the hand and having her rise out of her chair.

His mother walked up to the both of them as they stood side by side. She stared Toni in her face, and with no smile, no sign of emotion, she said, "It was nice for you to come, but you are no longer welcome here in my home. Mathew is engaged."

Toni stared into her face, trying hard not to flip out in front of everyone.

"Mother, how dare you," Mathew chided.

"I'm sorry, son, but she needs to know the truth," his mother spat back.

Her husband just stared at her, saying no words, just looking lost. He didn't know what was going on. He liked both women, Toni and Tina, but he kept out of his son's love life and affairs. He didn't even know that his son had lost his virginity recently. He was always out of town on business, leaving his wife behind to run or ruin his son's sex life.

Toni zipped out of the room. Mathew glared at his mother, shaking his head, then chased after Toni. Mrs. Pamela Peters stood her ground with a sinister grin across her face and her arms folded across her chest. She didn't want to know anything about the damn girl. She didn't care. She already had this preconceived notion in her head that Toni was not the type of girl for her baby boy. Toni didn't belong in this family. Only one woman did, and Pamela was determined to give Tina a call and get to the bottom of this silly nonsense that her son created. Shit, it was a good thing that Mathew didn't mention that Toni was from Brooklyn, let alone the projects.

"Well, it looks like our son made his choice," she blurted, then turned and looked over at her husband as he was standing there holding a glass of wine.

Mathew tried to apologize to Toni for his mother's terrible actions. They were in the limo on the Long Island Expressway, and Toni was a bit upset. Her eyes were wet with tears as she peered out onto the expressway.

"My mother can be such a damn bitch," he angrily said.

"Well, it's obvious that she doesn't like me," Toni said, turning to face Mathew.

"Who cares what she likes, Toni? I'm in love with you, and that's all that matters right now."

Toni was well aware that Mathew had broken off his engagement to Tina so he could be with her, and she was thrilled, she thought.

"Do you still love her?" she asked.

"I was never really in love with her," he answered.

"You sure? I mean, she is really beautiful."

"Yeah, and so are you," he softly said, then slowly hunched toward her, taking her chin into his hand and placing his mouth against hers. They kissed so hard that it almost seemed as if they were trying to swallow each other up.

"Who cares what my mother thinks? Fuck her," he sputtered. "Yeah, fuck her. All that matters is you and me. I love you, Toni—never met a woman like you before."

Toni smiled, drying her tears, and she finally said to him, "I love you too."

Mathew consoled her, embracing her tight. He loved holding her, with her petite and sexy figure. He loved the way she conducted herself, and he loved the way she made him feel when he was around her. He felt so wanted, so loved. And he loved how Toni saw him as a man and not a boy.

Toni had something that hundreds, maybe thousands, of women would envy and hate her for. She had a rich and loving man who was willing to take care of her. He was sexy, handsome, charming, caring, and not to mention, well endowed, so many things that females crave, and she had him in love with her—pussy whipped. He even was probably ready for marriage.

Yeah, Toni should have felt like she was on top of the

world right then, but instead, she was feeling so bad, like shit, out of place, feeling fucked up. Sometimes it felt like it was a dream to her, a dream she thought would later turn into a horrible nightmare. This fairy-tale life wasn't for her, couldn't be for her. She was a lie, a curse, and she felt that Mathew needed to know the truth, but she always hesitated in telling him. He knew nothing about her junkie mother or her incarcerated brother or her *sales* job down at the Bottom Dollar. And she wondered if he knew all this, if he would still be in love with her. How long would she let this go on? It felt good, for once, to be treated like a lady—the romantic dinners, the gifts, the sex, everything. *But everything must come to an end,* she thought, *no matter how good it was.*

The man had dumped his fiancée and had already introduced her to his mother, even though that didn't go quite well, but the pussy must have been good for a man to do that.

Mathew smiled, holding Toni in his arms, kissing her and loving her. Toni did the same.

"Are you taking me home?" Toni asked.

"No. Damien, back to my place," he announced, then he looked over at Toni and added, "I'm not going to let my mother ruin this night for us."

-Twenty-six-

"Fuck me, Tec. Fuck me," Lana shouted out. Tec had her positioned doggy style, her hands gripping the headboard while Tec pounded his eight-inch erection into her vigorously, loving every piece of the pussy she was giving him.

This was like the umpteenth sexual encounter between the two. This time Tec decided to meet up at a motel at around one in the morning. He didn't trust her. He only brought her back to his place one time, and that one time was enough. No telling who this bitch done told in Chills' crew. He'd been thinking sometimes that she was trying to set him up, so the niggah didn't give her the benefit of the doubt. He never met her at the same place twice. This made it difficult for them, but luckily it was summer, and they got the chance to fuck outdoors too.

Lana rolled over on her back, spreading her legs, massaging her pussy, and waiting for Tec to continue. His .45 was close within his reach. Tec pressed down between her legs, feeling her wetness, and thrust himself deeply into her, causing Lana to pant out and dig her nails into his back. He felt himself coming, and without giving it a second thought, he bus'ed off another nut in her, not bothering to pull the fuck out.

Tec then rolled over on his back and got to his feet, looking down at her as she lay naked on her side, peering up at her lover. He wiped the sweat from his face using a T-shirt, then started to get dressed.

Lana lay there, blowing air out of her mouth, then she uttered out, "You know he fears you."

"What? What the fuck you talking about?" Tec asked.

"Chills."

"Word? The niggah needs to fear me." Tec chuckled.

"You're unpredictable to him, and that worries him the most."

"Keep talking, bitch," Tec said, fastening his pants and loving what he was hearing from Lana.

"That li'l stunt you pulled with his hit men the other day, he wasn't expecting that to happen," Lana continued.

"'Cause that niggah doesn't know who he's fuckin' wit'."

"He's worried. I can tell."

"Yeah, well, that niggah got the right to be. I'm taking over shop, Lana. That niggah's nuthin' but yesterday's news. I'm the niggah taking over. What, he thought that he could just come up in the hood, set up shop, run niggahs out, and it was gonna be that easy? Fuck him. We at war, Lana, and I advise you to choose sides. You rollin' wit' me or you rollin' wit a niggah soon to be six feet under?" he asked.

Lana smiled, getting up from the bed and approaching Tec. She cupped her hand around his penis and seductively said, "I'm rollin' wit' you, big boy. You know you got my pussy on lock."

"That's right, luv," he said. "You know I'm feeling you, right, luv?" he lied.

"I know, baby. I love you too," she said.

Tec smirked at her. He didn't say anything about love. He was just feeling the bitch. He was just fucking the bitch, more like using the bitch, and lying to the bitch.

"Look, baby," he said, snuggling up to her, "you want this war to be over between us?"

"Yeah, baby. I don't want you to get hurt out there."

"Really? You got my back, right?" he said, kissing her on the lips.

"What is it, baby?"

"Let's end this war and help me set this niggah up, take him out permanently, give this fat country niggah a dirt nap," Tec said.

Lana looked up at Tec, and she couldn't help but to be a little scared. This was definitely a dangerous game she was playing. Chills would fuckin' put a bullet between her eyes if he ever found out what was going on, who she was with, what she was thinking.

"You know a li'l about this niggah, right?" Tec asked.

"He doesn't tell me much," she returned.

"Come on, Lana, you must know some personal shit about that fat, greasy fuck. He ain't just fuckin' you, right?"

"He keeps his business his business mostly."

"Look, Lana, I wanna end this fuckin' shit, and I need your help, baby. I can't do this without you. You and me, Lana, to the end, baby," he softly tried to persuade.

Lana was quiet, contemplating the idea. She saw something in Tec, something she loved. He was unlike Chills. She was in love with the dick, in love with his thuggish ways.

"You love me, right?" he added.

"Yes, baby."

Tec picked her naked ass up in his arms, having her legs straddle around him, her bare pussy rubbing against his crotch.

"We gotta do this, baby, so that we can live. With that niggah trying to run everything, he ain't gonna try to let other niggahs eat. He's a selfish fuck. I need you, Lana. I need you a lot."

Lana liked hearing Tec say that he needed her, needed her a lot.

She took in a deep breath, then said, "Yes, baby, let's do this. I'll do it. I'll help you take him out."

"That's my girl," he proclaimed. He walked her back to the bed, lying her down on her back, parting her legs, and getting ready for round two with her. Tec softly came down on top of her, removed his jeans, then quickly penetrated her again.

"We take out that fat fuck, then we gonna live, baby. You'll see. I'm gonna run this fuckin' town, with you by my side, ayyite?"

"Ayyite, baby," she said, panting while Tec pushed himself deeply into her. "I'll do it, baby. I promise," she screamed while enjoying the dick.

She had only known this niggah for a few short weeks, but she had heard about his reputation for months. And now she was doing the unthinkable, betraying the man who had given her everything, and all he had asked for in return was her trust, her loving, and some pussy here and there. And now she was ready to stab the niggah Chills in the back, betraying his trust—her love now belonging to his deadly rival.

It could make a man think sometimes, *What the fuck these women be thinking about?*

* * *

It was a world where disputes were mostly solved through death and violence, where betrayal was nothing but part of the game—trusting your man, not knowing he was plotting to take you down and stab you in the back—thirsting for that power, craving for that respect. If a dealer kept coming up short, then there was only one option—a swift bullet to the head, relinquishing the dealer of his/her position permanently in the drug game. And if dealers wanted out, then they better leave fucking town during the night, and never bring their asses back. Sometimes, in a world so dangerous, there was no out, the past would sometimes come back to these dealers, catching up with them, haunting them. It was a game where their enemies were everywhere, sometimes even standing close and strong by their sides. They didn't know who was who, or who was out to get who. It was a world where jealousy and grudges never ended, and the women, the ladies, they lusted after the men who held control, desiring a bit of the lavish lifestyle and getting attached to these men so that they could deepen their pockets and live like queens. It was a world where so many became prey.

Lana soothed herself in her home, taking a long, hot shower in her marble bathroom. Her apartment, which was paid for by her lover, Chills, was located on the Lower East side of Manhattan. It cost $2.6 million.

The water surged out of the shower stall, slapping against her bare breasts while she washed her hair. She'd been living there for about a year. Everything was in her name, her bills were always paid on time, and more than three million dollars worth of gifts, jewelry, and clothes were in the place. Her home was fit to please a king and queen.

Lana didn't hear him come in. She was still in the shower, soaping herself down, listening to a little of Sade on the small handheld radio that was placed above the toilet. She'd been in the shower for about ten minutes, and her mind was on Tec, thinking about what he'd said to her the day before. Was she really willing to give up all this? Chills gave her a lot, and yet, Tec was still a street hustler, working his way up, killing and maiming those who got in his way. Chills was a kingpin, bringing in ten, fifteen million dollars a year. He could afford her. Tec, he had cash, but he was nowhere yet banking what her lover was banking a year. And still, Lana was in love with this man, Tec. She was trying to work out the situation.

The door to the bathroom opened, and Chills walked in, drawing back the glass door to the shower. He stared at his naked honey looking all good and fine, wet and soaped up from head to toe.

"Shit, baby, you fuckin' scared me," Lana said, being a little startled by his sudden presence.

"Hurry up and come out of there. I need to talk to you," he said. His voice was deep and demanding, showing a powerful presence.

"OK, baby, give me one more minute."

"Now, Lana," he strongly demanded.

Lana, looking worried, washed the soap off her and stepped out of the shower, reaching for her bathrobe. She knew not to keep her man, her lover, waiting. He hated it, so she rushed to dry herself off, then scurried into the next room, still dripping wet.

Chills was standing in the center of her living room with his main bodyguard standing tall by the apartment door. Jacob, Chills' personal bodyguard and assassin for the past three years, kept quiet, wearing a blue-and-white Polo sweat suit with his .45 holstered under his left arm. Dark shades covered his eyes, and a toothpick rested in the corner of his mouth. He didn't say much, but he was a man of action.

Lana came into the living room tying her bathrobe together. Her eyes were fixated on Chills as he stood in front of her, wearing a gray Armani suit, a Rolex, and sunglasses, with his hands in his pockets.

He stood tall in front of her. He was a very big man who looked really threatening—menacing. Chills had a small scar over his right eye and a thick beard, which was trimmed and lined up. His eyes were slanted, dark, and black, and his shaved head was glistening.

"What is it, baby?" Lana asked, coming up to him and wrapping her arms around his huge frame, trying to hug him. But Chills was unaffected by this. He glared down at her and pushed her back.

"Yesterday, where were you?" he asked.

"I went shopping yesterday, baby. You know how I like to shop," she said to him in her softest and sweetest voice. "And plus, I got you a li'l something."

"Lana, don't fuckin' play games with me," Chills bluntly interrupted, backing away from her.

"What's wrong, baby? Why you looking so upset?" Lana asked, looking worried.

"You ain't been in this apartment all fuckin' day. And don't fuckin' lie to me about shopping. Now listen, bitch," Chills angrily spat, grabbing her powerfully by her bathrobe and causing Lana to feel weak in his grip, "I want to know where the fuck you were all fuckin' day. I had one of my men constantly coming by to run a check on you, and you weren't here."

"Chills, I swear to you, I went out shopping, and

that's it," Lana lied, tears trickling down her cheeks. "Baby, I wouldn't lie to you."

Pow! Lana caught a hard right hand across her eye from Chills' fist. She cupped her eye immediately, crying hysterically while Chills still had her in his grip. Jacob stood back and watched the whole thing, knowing not to interrupt his boss when he was handling something—business or personal.

"Bitch, where were you yesterday?" he strongly repeated. He slammed her against the living room wall. The pain in her back made Lana just want to collapse down to the floor. But Chills continued to hold her up, demanding an answer.

"Chills, I love you, baby. Please don't do this to me, baby, please."

This time Chills hit her with another hard right across her face, causing her nose to bleed and her eye to swell. She was terrified.

"Bitch, I'm gonna kill you in this fucking apartment if you don't answer me correctly," he told her through clenched teeth.

"Baby, please. I don't know."

"What the fuck you mean you don't know, bitch? Do I look stupid, bitch . . . Do I?" Chills shouted, glaring at her.

Lana was silent. Her eyes were glued to the floor, and she felt weak and shaken.

"Fucking answer me, bitch," Chills yelled, causing Lana to flinch. "And don't tell me you went shopping, 'cause I swear I'll blow your muthafuckin' brains out against this wall," he said, reaching for his gun and shoving it into Lana's mouth, telling her to open wide.

Lana was so shaken, so horrified, that she began to pee on herself. A stream of piss trickled down her legs on to the expensive imported carpet. Chills glanced down and said to her, "Bitch, you better not get any of that on me."

A smile came across Jacob's face while he still stood next to the door, his tongue playing with the toothpick in his mouth. His hands were placed over each other near his crotch, and he stood tall, keeping a watchful eye out like a true professional.

"Lana, I swear, if I have to ask you again, you gonna hate me, bitch," Chills threatened.

The gun was out of her mouth, but still close against her cheek. Her eyes were wet, red, and full of tears. Her nose and upper lip were crusted with blood, and her eye was puffy, swollen, and black and blue. She couldn't move. Chills was too strong for her to even attempt to escape his hold.

She averted her eyes from him and managed to mumble out, "Brooklyn."

"Bitch, did you just fuckin' tell me Brooklyn?"

Lana nodded, affirming her answer. She was scared of what he was gonna do to her next.

"Coney Island, Brooklyn, you dumb, stupid bitch?" Chills asked.

"Chills, I was just in Brooklyn. I didn't do anything wrong, baby, I swear to you. I love you too much," she said between sobs.

"Shut the fuck up," he yelled, knocking her across her head with the butt of the gun, causing Lana to collapse to the floor and become unconscious. Chills stood over her, still in a rage, with the gun gripped in his hand.

Jacob walked over. "You want me to handle this bitch?" he asked.

"You don't fuckin' touch her. I'll deal with this stupid bitch," he said to him.

Chills wanted to kill this bitch, but he didn't, he couldn't. He already knew that Lana was out in Coney Island, Brooklyn. One of his dealers put him on to it, about her being out there—probably fuckin' wit' some niggah. But he didn't know who.

Chills didn't like his crew—his dealers, his men, and especially his women—to be gone for an extended amount of time. If one of his dealers or men went missing for a few days, he wanted to know everything. He wanted to know their family, friends, where they rested at, where they be at. He kept track of everything, no matter how small or big. If people left town, they better come back with a good excuse, or they shouldn't come back at all. And if they didn't come back, then when he tracked them down and found them, then he'd deal with those people—and they'd be gone for good, sleep forever.

And if a niggah got pinched, got arrested, that was a strike against him. No telling what niggah done turned informant or ratted out information to the cops, Feds, DEA, or whoever. They ain't gonna be the same in the crew, probably would get demoted if he liked the guy, or else he would just get to take that dirt nap.

Chills was very wary of everything and everyone. He'd been in the game for a long time. He was running shop, and he was determined to end this war between him and Tec—that bitch-ass niggah in C.I. He'd become a real pain, and Tec was a hard niggah to get at, but Chills knew that Tec would eventually get got. Shit just gonna take time, that was all.

Chills stared down at Lana for several moments, thinking the worst, because if what he thought turned out to be true, then she'd be a dead bitch soon. But right then, it was just that gut feeling talking, and he loved Lana. But disrespecting him in that kind of way, oh, the bitch must go—respect, power, and money before pussy, always.

Chills dragged Lana to the bedroom, placed her on the bed with her body still bloody and bruised, then he headed for the exit. He'd deal with the bitch later. He had more important issues to handle.

He met Jacob out in the hallway. He lit a cigarette, then turned, facing Jacob, who stood behind him.

"I hear our little problem got a brother incarcerated upstate," Chills said to Jacob.

"Yeah, Lonny. We used to hang back in the day," Jacob told him.

Chills took a drag from his cigarette, pondering, then he faced Jacob again and uttered out, "Make it happen."

"I'll get my peoples right on it," Jacob quickly responded.

Chills nodded.

"You wanna make it personal, muthafucka, then we gonna make it personal," Chills mumbled to himself. He then took another drag from his cigarette while they headed for the exit.

-Twenty-seven-

Vinita's head lay against the soft white pillows on Myron's bed. She rested on her back with her legs spread widely apart, trying to forget her worries while her man licked between her parted thighs.

Her legs were thrown over his shoulders, and she panted out in ecstasy, forgetting her troubles and enjoying the pleasure. Myron's tongue was moving rapidly up and down her moist pussy and circling her clit. She clutched the sheets, squirming, with her eyes flickering and her body in heat.

Myron paused, raising his head from between her thighs. He looked up at her and said, "I'm gonna help you forget everything tonight. No worries, baby. Enjoy me, Vinita."

"Oh, Myron," she faintly replied with her head plopping back down against the pillow.

Myron continued to eat the love of his life for the next fifteen minutes. Vinita had been looking stressed at first, but these past few days, she'd been cool. Myron was determined to have her come out of the little slump she was in. So during the past four days, he'd been pleasing her sexually and mentally comforting her, taking care of her, loving her, assuring her that everything was going to be fine, that he was going to take care of her for the rest of her life.

She had practically moved in with her man. Vinita hadn't been home in almost two weeks. He took her shopping, buying her clothes and gifts, and he drove her to school and work. This was the life that she wanted, and being with him was what she needed. She forgot all about her run-in with Little Boy Ronny. They both talked about the wedding constantly. Myron wanted to take Vinita to Barbados for their honeymoon.

Myron got up from between his woman's thighs, hovering over her, resting on his hands. Her peered down at her while she stared up at him. He smiled, admiring her beauty, her smile, then he leaned down and gave her a sweet kiss on her lips. "I love you, baby," he proclaimed.

"I love you, too, baby."

Vinita reached up and brought him down to her, gesturing that she wanted him to enter her, make love to her. Myron did, penetrating her softly, moaning as he did so, feeling his woman's love.

She straddled her legs around his back, and she felt Myron's erection thrusting hard into her. She panted out, digging her nails into her lover's back, enjoying their moment of sex and love with each other.

After their sexual encounter, Vinita laid her head against Myron's chest while he rested on his back, peering up at the ceiling.

"I'm curious, Vinita," Myron said, playing in her hair with his hand while she nestled against his chest.

"Yes."

"Are you hiding or running from someone?"

"What makes you say that?"

"It's not that I'm complaining, but you've been spending a lot of time over here with me. You haven't seen or heard from your parents in days."

"They know that I'm OK," she said.

"Baby, you know that if you have a problem that you can come to me, right? Don't be scared to tell me the truth. If someone's messing with you, I feel I have the right to know."

Vinita was quiet. Myron had it on point. It was like he was reading her mind, probing her brain.

"It's nothing serious," she lied. "Just a few girls hating on me from my buildings."

"Well, try not to let it stress you so much. And besides, they got the right to hate. Look how beautiful you are, and you got all this," Myron said, referring to himself.

Vinita smiled, letting out a laugh, and freed herself from his grip, looking over at him. "All what?" she joked.

"All this, baby," Myron told her again, this time pulling back the covers and exposing his hard-on.

She smiled. "Didn't you get enough of it?"

"From you? Never."

Vinita took his erection in her hand and started stroking it gently, causing Myron to lay on his back with his hands folded behind his head while his lady took care of business. Vinita slowly moved her way down to his penis, then gently took his erection into her mouth. She blessed him with a blowjob while he just sat back and enjoyed.

After the second time, Myron was out of it. She did him well, and he couldn't ask for anything more out of a woman than what he had. He loved her, and he couldn't wait till their wedding day. He was just as excited as she was.

He let out a quick breath as Vinita put it on him the second time, mounting him, and riding him like she was trying to win a horse race.

"You're too much for me, baby," he proclaimed when they were finished.

"I know. That's why you better marry me."

"Shit, you think I'm just gonna let all of this go?" he said, peeking at her from under the covers.

"You're not stupid."

"So, baby, when am I gonna meet the folks?" Myron pressed again.

Vinita sighed. She really didn't feel like discussing that. He was going to meet her folks, but she didn't want to bring him into the projects.

"I mean, it ain't right. We've been dating for a few months now, and we're engaged, baby. I got to meet your parents. What, are you ashamed of your family?" he asked.

"No," she murmured. But that wasn't completely true.

"Look, I tell you what. If you don't want me to come to their home, then why don't you invite them over here, to my—no, our—place, to have dinner?" he suggested.

Vinita looked over at him. "Our place?" she questioned.

Myron got out of the bed, butt naked and all, and went over to the pinewood dresser, where he opened it, reached in, and came back to the bed with a silver key in his hand. Vinita looked up at him.

"Here, baby. It's a key to our place. I want you to move in with me. Since you're practically over here with me all the time, you might as well move in with your soon-to-be husband."

Vinita couldn't contain herself. She jumped up, hugging Myron strongly. "Oh, baby," she cried out. "I can't believe this, oh my God . . . Oh, my God."

Myron's smile was massive.

"So, how soon can you get your stuff and move in to our place?" he asked.

She broke away from his arms, smiling. "Consider it already done," she answered, then hugged him tightly once more.

Her dreams were finally becoming reality. She was out of the projects, that awful place she'd called home for too many years, and now it was her time to shine, live comfortably, and soon enjoy being a bride and a wife.

"So, when can we invite your parents over?" he asked.

"I'll get on it right away, baby," she said, giving him a quick kiss on the lips.

Vinita continued to hug her man, and Myron being a horny man, asked his ecstatic fiancée, "So, you think that we can go for round three?"

She smiled. *Shit, we can go the whole twelve rounds,* she thought, smiling uncontrollably. Myron pushed her back down on the bed and was about to start something that he knew he could finish.

Vinita felt shaken as she stepped out of Myron's BMW. She was about to head up to her parents' apartment. She felt shook, but she couldn't wait to tell her family the news that she was moving out and would be living with her man, her baby, her fiancé.

She glanced worriedly around the place at first. It

was late, soon to be midnight, and there were still a few folks outside enjoying the warm August night. But there was only one face that she was concerned about, and so far he wasn't in her sights, nowhere to be found. She glanced back at Myron, who was seated in the driver's seat listening to the radio. He looked up at her, gave her a reassuring smile and nodded.

She walked up to the lobby where there were a few young boys loitering around by the entrance, as always in Coney Island housing. They paid her no mind, thinking she was cute, and just kept going on about their business.

Seeing Vinita walk into the lobby, Myron pulled off, already missing his woman. But he would be back around the next night to pick her up, and whatever things she needed help with.

Vinita made it safely up to her apartment without any run-ins or incidents with Little Boy Ronny. She had her keys already out, making it quicker for her to enter her apartment. Inside, the kids were already asleep. She didn't even know that they were spending the night.

Marvin and Danielle were sprawled out on the living room floor, on a blue-and-yellow comforter with the TV still on, displaying some black-and-white late-night movie, which probably came on after they fell asleep.

They're cute, she thought, as she passed by them, walking quietly across the living room floor and heading for her bedroom. The living room window was cracked just a little, bringing in some late-night wind from outside, along with the sound of a few boys rolling dice. The apartment was mainly dark, except for the TV illuminating the small living room and just a bit of the hallway. She made it to her bedroom. She figured that li'l Terrance was asleep with her parents, and that her sister left her kids there, probably to go out and party all night, and get pregnant again by the next man she hooked up with.

As she reached for the doorknob, she was surprised it was open. She never left her bedroom door open. Curious, Vinita slowly opened her bedroom door, only to see her older sister, Nancy, sleeping in her bed with li'l Terrance clutched in her arms.

"Oh no, see," she uttered, walking toward her bed.

Nancy was sound asleep, all cozy and cuddled up in Vinita's bed. Her room was a mess. Her stuffed bears were spread out everywhere, her closet door was open, and she noticed a few of her skirts and blouses lay on her bed. Her shoes were out of order, and there was leftover food on top of her dresser and on the floor.

Vinita was furious. She was gone two weeks, and this bitch had come over and violated her room.

"Nancy, get up," Vinita loudly barked, shaking her sister and li'l Terrance. "Nancy, I said get up."

Nancy turned, looked up, and saw her baby sister scowling down at her.

"Oh, Vinita, you're home," she uttered, squinting up at her.

"Why you in my bed? In fact, why are you here, in my room, up in this place? Don't you have a place of your own?" Vinita chided.

Nancy looked tired. She placed Terrance down on the bed and got up, standing in front of her sister. She had on worn-out gray sweats, and a white tank top with a multicolored scarf tied around her head.

"We got kicked out," Nancy informed her.

"Kicked out? What the hell you mean kicked out?" Vinita inquired while picking up a few of her clothes that shouldn't have been out of her closet in the first place.

"Last week our landlord evicted us."

"Ain't you on Section 8? Don't the government pay your rent? How in the hell you get evicted?"

"I don't know. Shit, it just happened, so we came here 'cause we needed a place to stay, and you know Mama don't care."

"Nah, Nancy . . . what happened to that job that you were applying for?"

"I didn't get it."

Vinita sucked her teeth, disappointed with her sister—more like disgusted.

"Look at this place," Vinita fussed.

"I'm sorry, Vinita, but Mama said that we could share your bedroom, and besides, you ain't been home in two weeks . . . "

"So what?" she shouted. "This is still my room, and you got it looking like y'all already been up in here more that two weeks."

Nancy took a seat back down on the bed, scratching at her breast.

"You wearing my clothes too. Damn, Nancy."

"Vinita, damn, why you trippin'? It ain't like I don't be looking out for you."

"I don't need for you to look out for me. I just want you out of my room. Look at this," Vinita said, pointing down to some old crusted, fungus-looking meal, food, whatever on a white plate that looked like it had been there a few days too long.

"You can't clean up? Damn, y'all some nasty people," Vinita chided.

"Y'all?" Nancy said, getting up.

"Yeah, y'all," Vinita dragged out. "Y'all do know that dishes go in the sink to be washed, not left out on my gotdamn floor. Shit, you feeding all the damn roaches and rats in the whole building."

"Whatever, Vinita. It's late, and I don't need to hear your shit at this time of the night."

"No, you gonna listen. I want all my stuff picked up."

"Why you trippin' for?"

"You want to know why I'm trippin', huh? Look at this," Vinita hollered, picking up her expensive six-hundred-dollar Gucci shoes that someone had spilled Kool-Aid on. "And look at this," she continued, picking up her Donna Karan skirt that looked like it had been worn by her sister all week. "This is my stuff, but you don't give a fuck with your ghetto ass."

"Oh, fuck you, Vinita. You think you better than us? You think that you're better than everybody? Bitch, you ain't," Nancy countered.

"Please, at least I got a damn job. You and your three kids, and no baby daddy around," Vinita insulted.

"Whatever. You know what? I don't need this shit. Fuck you," Nancy hollered, scooping Terrance up outta bed, disturbing his sleep and holding him in her arms. "You ain't shit, Vinita . . . I swear."

Vinita paid her sister no attention. She was just trying to put her room back in order, cleaning up after her sister.

Nancy stormed outta the bedroom with li'l Terrance's head resting against her shoulder and headed to the living room to share a comforter with her kids.

"I swear," Vinita mumbled, "can't wait to get the hell out of here." Vinita slammed her bedroom door shut.

It took her almost the whole night to clean and arrange her room the way she had it before her sister moved in. She cursed Nancy, hating the way her sister lived.

* * *

The next morning Vinita didn't get out of bed 'til ten. The only reason she awoke was due to the loud noise from her niece and nephew running up and down the hallway like they were at some damn playground. And then there was li'l Terrance banging on Auntie's door, like he had absolutely no home training.

Vinita stepped out of her bedroom wearing her Nautica bathrobe, a gift from Myron. She walked into the kitchen to see her mother and Nancy at the table having breakfast—scrambled eggs, toast, grits, and bacon.

Nancy scowled at Vinita, and Vinita returned the look. Nancy was still perturbed about the previous night.

"Good morning, Ma," Vinita greeted.

"Good morning, baby," her mother said while frying more bacon.

Nancy sighed, turning her head away from her sister with her legs propped up on a neighboring chair.

"Hey, Auntie Vinita," Marvin said, strolling into the kitchen with his sister following him.

"Hello, Marvin."

"You kids ready to have breakfast?" Nancy asked.

Marvin and Danielle both ran to the bathroom, leaving li'l Terrance behind. You could feel the animosity between the two sisters, and their mother took notice.

"What's wrong with you two girls this morning?" their mother asked while stirring the grits.

"Nuthin', Ma, she just being a bitch," Nancy chided.

"At least I'm not the one who got kicked out of her apartment. How that happen, huh, Nancy . . . drugs?"

"Fuck you, Vinita."

"Nancy, hush your mouth," their mother proclaimed.

"And Ma, why did you let her sleep in my room in the first place?" Vinita asked.

"You ain't been home in two weeks. I thought you'd shacked up with your fiancé. And Nancy needed somewhere to sleep."

"How did y'all get in my room in the first place?"

"I picked that stupid lock," Nancy said, smirking over at her.

"See what I mean? She ain't got any kind of respect, not for me or for her kids, 'cause if she did, then those kids wouldn't be having different daddies."

"You know what, Vinita . . . " Nancy said, rising out of her seat.

"Y'all two behave y'all selves," their mother chimed in. "Danielle, Marvin, y'all get in here and come have breakfast."

"You walk around this place like you better than somebody, like your shit don't stink," Nancy said.

"You know what, Nancy, at least I got my life together. Look at you—homeless, unemployed, with three bad-ass kids. Please, you supposed to be my older sister, and look at you. When you gonna get it together, instead of living off everyone else?" Vinita harshly asked.

"You ain't nuthin' but a stuck-up bitch," Nancy proclaimed.

"I'll be a bitch."

"Y'all two hush all that language around them kids. I don't want 'em talking that filth."

"You need to be talking to Nancy about her dirty mouth. And anyway, how did you get kicked out of your apartment? Did she explain that to you Ma, huh? I mean, she was living off the damn government for how long, and now she ain't got a pot to piss in. Yeah, I ain't that gullible like Ma, Nancy."

"You know what, I'll be back," Nancy said, glaring over at Vinita.

"See, look at you, shit start heating up in the kitchen, and all you do is run, like you've been doing."

"Vinita, leave your sister alone," her mother chimed in.

"Nah, she needs to hear this, because it's obvious you ain't telling it to her."

"See, look at that, and she's trying to say that I'm disrespectful," Nancy said, stepping outta the kitchen and heading toward the door.

"You know what, I have an announcement to make," Vinita announced. "I'm moving out tonight. I'm going to live with my baby, Myron."

Nancy turned, glaring back over at her baby sister. "What?" she stated. "You're moving out, and you're beefing 'cause I slept in your room? You selfish, dumb bitch."

"Nancy," her mother shouted.

"I'm sorry, Ma, but she acting real stupid right now over some silly shit, and this bitch is moving out tonight? Bye then, bitch."

"You know what, I'm sick of the name calling between y'all two, and in front of these kids. Now y'all cut out that damn bickering between the two of y'all right now."

"Already done, Ma. I ain't got nuthin' more to say to her. I'll be back," Nancy repeated, this time cutting her eyes over at her sister.

"I don't know how you put up with her, Ma," Vinita stated, taking a seat at the kitchen table with Danielle, Terrance, and Marvin.

"Because, she's my daughter, Vinita," she explained.

"But I mean, look at her. What does she got going for herself?"

Not wanting to discuss her daughter in front of the

children, Vinita's mother motioned that they have this discussion in the next room.

"Let me tell you something, Vinita. Nancy might not have her shit together like yourself, but she's still my daughter, your sister, family. She made a few mistakes in her life, and it's up to us to help her out with these kids, not criticize her."

"But I'm just tired of her constantly making mistakes and using people. She needs to learn, Ma."

"And she will."

"When? When it's too late?"

"Vinita, we're family, and I'll be damned if any one of us will turn our backs on family. Thank God that you're blessed and don't have to travel down that same road she went down. You're smart, Vinita, in fact, the both of y'all are smart, and you just took advantage of your gifts. Now, Nancy, I admit, she did make some mistakes in her life, some really bad ones, but let's not penalize her for them. Instead, let's help and support her. Right now she doesn't need a judge and jury in her life. She needs a strong family by her side."

"Yeah, but Ma . . . "

"Vinita, I know sometimes you may look at her and see hopelessness, but when I look at my daughters, I still see young, scared little girls, and those same scared little girls still need guidance in their lives, no matter how old they get."

"I'm not a scared little girl, Ma. I'm a grown woman," Vinita stated.

"I know you are, baby, but I still see it in your eyes, the worries . . . like you're hiding something . . . fear . . . and like Nancy, you're running from something. That's why you always pushed yourself in school, getting an education, and I'm proud of you, baby. But you also must learn to trust, help, and confide in others. Vinita, if you're in trouble, let us know."

Vinita became quiet, confused. Did her mother know something? Did she know about Little Boy Ronny? Nah, she kept that a hidden secret in her life for so damn long. But her mother was right about one thing. She was running, hiding from something—someone—and after so many years of keeping it within herself, it was eating away at her.

"Ma, I'm OK," she said.

"I believe you, but I also want you to know that I'm always here if you need someone to talk to. I know that you now have your own life, your fiancé, and your career, and you may not admit it to us personally, but we can be an embarrassment to you sometimes, but I understand—"

"Ma," Vinita uttered, "I never said that."

"You didn't, but I can see it in your actions and in your eyes, the way you stray away from us . . . "

"Y'all are not an embarrassment to me," Vinita uttered.

"Oh, really? Then why haven't you brought your fiancé by so that we can meet him?"

Vinita was utterly speechless.

"Vinita, it's been weeks now since your engagement, and we have not yet met this man, the wonderful Myron. You know, Vinita, I know that your father and I don't have lots of money and that we don't live in a big, fancy house and drive nice cars, but the one thing that this home is rich with is love. We love you no matter what, Vinita, and for you to feel that it's an embarrassment to bring Myron into our home, well that kinda hurt your father and me."

Vinita had no words to say to her mother. What she was saying was partially the truth, and at that very moment, she felt like confiding in her mother about everything—her rape, her reason, and why she was running and hiding. A few tears welled up in her eyes while they were having their little mother-and-daughter moment together. They hadn't had one of those moments in years, and it was funny that it took sibling rivalry to bring the two to talk.

Vinita took a seat on the couch, looking worried. Her mother came and sat right next to her, placing her hand on her daughter's legs, peering into her daughter's beautiful face.

"Vinita, I know when there's something wrong with my children. Call it a mother's intuition. I'm here to listen, not judge. You're keeping something in, and it's not good to conceal your worries."

Vinita slouched over with her face buried in her hands, and with tears streaming down her cheeks, she found herself sobbing in front of her mother. She was trying to be strong, but she was weak on the inside. She thought about Myron, then this horrible image of Little Boy Ronny strong-arming her in the staircase popped into her head. Truth of her rape had to escape. It had been concealed in her for far too long. Someone needed to know, someone—someone. She slowly turned to face her mother, and she confronted her with the truth, saying the words aloud that she'd kept hidden for far too long. She said to her mother, "Mom, I was raped . . ."

-Twenty-eight-

Mathew woke up in the middle of the night, rolled over, and noticed that Toni was not in bed. Her space was empty. He quickly got up, hoping that she hadn't left to go home. He threw on his robe, tying it together as he walked out into the next room.

"Toni," he quietly called out.

He walked into the great room and saw the terrace doors ajar, and Toni standing outside gazing over the city skyline, with her hands clutching the railing, still in her panties and bra.

She didn't turn around when Mathew stepped out onto the terrace to join her. Mathew wrapped his arms around her, squeezing her tightly.

"You OK?" he asked.

Toni nodded.

"Why you out here?"

"Just enjoying the night," she said to him, still peering out at the city. From his penthouse apartment, the city seemed so quiet up on the twenty-third floor. The night felt so tranquil and looked so picturesque. It almost felt like they weren't in New York at all. The warm wind brushed against their semi-nude bodies, and Toni felt so close to the stars, since there were no clouds in the sky.

Mathew continued to clutch Toni in his arms. He had seen this view dozens of times. It was nothing new to him, but he never got tired of it.

"I never get tired of coming out here," he said to her. With his chin nestled against her shoulder, he gently rocked her from side to side in his arms.

"I can see why," she said. "It's so beautiful out here. I've been standing out here for the past half hour just admiring the view."

They both became quiet for a moment while they gazed ahead. Toni had spent the past three days over at Mathew's apartment. They'd gone shopping in Manhattan, where Mathew spent over ten thousand dollars on her clothes alone, enabling Toni to stay with him so she wouldn't have to troop back to Brooklyn. He loved her company, and she loved his.

"I've been thinking," Mathew suddenly said.

Toni remained quiet, feeling comfortable just being held in his arms.

"I'm in love with you, Toni, and I want you to come and live with me," he continued.

Toni slowly turned around, looking into his face. He was serious.

"You mean move in?"

"Yes."

"But you hardly know me," she said.

"I know that, but I'm in love with you, and you're a wonderful person to be with. You make me happy. I mean, I've never had so much fun in all my life. When I look at you . . . I see this woman that I want to become my wife."

Toni gasped, "What?"

Mathew got down on one knee, peering up at her, holding her hand in his, then he slipped his hand into his robe, pulling out a small, velvet square box. He opened it, and in it was a twenty-four-thousand-dollar oval-cut diamond ring, set in eighteen-karat yellow-and-white gold.

Toni's hand immediately cupped over her mouth as she became really emotional. "Mathew," she said.

"Toni, I never met a woman who seemed so right for me," he mentioned, rising from off his knee, the ring in his hand.

"What about Tina?"

"I'm not in love with Tina. That's a sure thing, believe me. And besides, I haven't heard from her in days."

"But your mother? I know she doesn't like me."

"My mother doesn't like anybody. That's her excuse. If you weren't born with money, don't come from money, or didn't inherit money, then she feels you're no use to her. But she can come with her threats. She's not running my life anymore. You helped me realize that there's a whole different world out there that I haven't experienced yet. I've been a rich kid all my life."

"Mathew—"

"Please don't say no, Toni. I know what I want, and it's to be with you," he said softly, he placed his hands on her hips while he peered into her lovely eyes.

"Mathew—"

"Toni, I promise that nothing will go wrong. I definitely want you to become my wife."

"How would you know?"

"I'll take care of us. I have money in trust funds, investments . . . my father, I know he likes you. He'll look out for us, despite my mother's disapproval."

Toni turned her head, averting her eyes from his and looking down at the floor. This was definitely too sudden for her. Shit, two months ago she was worried about her next dollar, paying bills, and niggahs ripping her off. Now she had Prince Charming proposing to her in the middle of the night, in the middle of Manhattan, on the twenty-third floor out on the terrace of a penthouse apartment. As Black Rob once said, "Whoa."

"If you need time to think, I understand," Mathew said.

"It's just . . . it's just that this is too sudden . . . Mathew, you really don't know me, or my life, my family."

"I can get to know your family."

"Mathew, it's not that simple."

"Why not?"

"It's just not."

"But I feel that I know so much about you already," he said, once again clutching her in his arms.

She couldn't keep on living this lie. She wanted to tell him, but what would his reaction be to her? She turned herself back around, facing out toward the city again. She took in a deep breath and thought about her life—how it had led to this point, what went right or what went wrong? She felt the kisses from his lips wetting her shoulder blades, then her back.

"Become my wife, Toni. Please don't make me beg," he whispered in her ear, then began kissing the back of her neck.

Toni shuddered lightly, clutching the railing tightly, feeling Mathew's sweet lips pressed against her skin. She had taken his virginity, and now he was giving her his heart. Was she cursed or blessed? In the hood at that moment, she would be the envy of all women. This would be like heaven to all of the women in the ghetto.

Mathew wrapped his arms around Toni's waist. His lips and kisses soon made their way to her ear and back down to her shoulders. Her eyes were closed, and her chin was up. She was caught up in the moment with him as the gentle night wind swept by them on the warm and humid August night.

"C'mon inside with me," Mathew suggested.

Toni turned around again, looking into his beautiful eyes. God, he was handsome, and it was hard to resist what he was proposing. If she said yes, then her life would probably change dramatically. She'd be living like a queen. But if she told him no and blabbed the truth, who knew what road she would be traveling down next?

Mathew kindly pulled her by her arms back into the penthouse where he wanted to make love to her one more time before the night ended. And he was going to, because Toni didn't seem to be resisting. She loved the way he touched her, stroked her, talked to her. He made her feel more like a woman every day.

She pondered his proposal while they headed for the bedroom. Could she really do it? Just marry the man and tell him nothing, and leave behind her ill-fated, drug-addicted, crazy mother and live a life with him? And what about her brother? What would his reaction be? Maybe with Mathew's help and his money, Thomas could appeal his case, this time getting high-priced lawyers to defend him and probably overturn his conviction. She felt that he was robbed from having a fair trial in the first place because those court-appointed lawyers ain't shit. The first thing they told a black man when they received a case was, "Take a plea bargain.

You'll probably get less time." They didn't care if he was guilty or innocent, even though Thomas was guilty. But what choices did he have? The muthafucka he killed was beating and abusing his mother every night. How long could one man allow for that to happen, especially in his home?

And what about her boyfriend Keith? Shit, she didn't even want to go there, knowing that his reaction wouldn't be a good one, probably a hurtful and deadly one if he found out that she was leaving him and engaged to another man.

The unsnapping of her bra brought her back to reality, and the touch of Mathew's soft hands exploring her body made Toni exhale sumthin' lovely. She found herself lying on her back, her lover over her, with her nipples happy to have his mouth fastened on them.

Think about it, Toni, she thought. *This is something that most women would jump at, if they were put in this position.*

Mathew removed her panties and his silk boxers, and he positioned himself between her thighs, inserting his erection deeply into her, causing Toni to gasp.

Don't be stupid, Toni. Just think about it, she repeated to herself while Mathew made love to her. *This is something that happens to like what, one out of every million women?*

It was her move, her choice, which could either be good or bad.

It was ten after nine the next time Mathew awoke, and just like the six short hours before, he'd once again awakened to find Toni gone, not by his side in the bed. He got up, stretched, and glanced around the bedroom. He threw on his robe and his house slippers and headed into the next room. He looked and saw that she wasn't out on the terrace or anywhere in the apartment.

He figured that she had gone home and needed time to think about getting married to him.

He'd definitely had a wonderful night. In fact, these past three days had been great for him. Spending time with Toni was like having a long, much-needed vacation, and he wanted to stay on that vacation as long as possible.

Mathew fixed himself a cup of tea, turned on the TV, and flipped to BET. He began watching music videos, dancing around his place like he was Tom Cruise in the movie *Risky Business.* He was happy, really happy.

Toni got into her Brooklyn apartment around nine that morning, leaving Mathew's place around seven. When she stepped into the place, she saw her mother sitting at the kitchen table. She hadn't heard from or spoken to her mother since their argument days ago.

Angela was sitting down at the kitchen table, staring at the wall, holding a cigarette in her hand. She glanced up at her daughter, watching her enter the kitchen. Angela looked somewhat sober. That rage she had in her the other day seemed like it had seeped outta her, because she was looking much calmer. But her eyes looked heavy, like there was so much to tell.

"Hey," she said to her daughter.

At first, Toni had no words for her, but then she turned to her and asked, "You OK?"

Angela took a drag from her cigarette then said to her daughter, "I could be better. Listen, I'm sorry about the other day."

Toni didn't respond. Instead, she just went into the fridge, poured herself a glass of orange juice, and peered over at her mother.

Angela scratched her chest. She was wearing a bright

red T-shirt and a pair of Levi's jeans. She looked like she'd seen better days.

"I'll be in my room," was the last thing Toni said to her. Angela pulled another drag from her cigarette, remaining seated with her legs crossed, and exhaling smoke from her jaw. She heard the door to her daughter's room shut, and she let off a smirk.

Toni had no friends to call. She had no one she could talk to and tell them of her situation. The only person she would talk to was Vinita, and she hadn't seen or heard from her in days. These past years, they had somewhat drifted apart, Vinita doing her own thang and going through her own problems, and Toni doing the same. Once in a while, they would speak to each other, get the rundown, but that was about it. The only time they really got to hang out was at that banquet at the Plaza two months ago, and Vinita had dissed Toni there.

Them hos down at the club, Toni didn't get along with most of them. A few of them were jealous because she attracted so much attention from niggahs, and some were wary of her man, Tec, knowing his status. But a few were bold enough to test her, and Toni had a few fights, winning almost all of them, only having lost one, and that was because a few bitches jumped on her after work trying to fuck up her looks. But she got one of them hos really good and struck one bitch across her face with a brick, breaking her nose and disfiguring her a little.

Toni dropped down across her bed and peered up at the ceiling. She had a wonderful night last night, no complaints at all, but Mathew's marriage proposal, now that was a trip for her. She thought, *Can I go through with it? Just leave Brooklyn and begin a whole new and better life for myself?* Her girl, Vinita, would trip if Toni told her that she had some rich kid ready to put a ring on her finger and take care of her forever. But Vinita was also in the same boat. In fact, she'd said yes and was getting married in a few months, and Toni couldn't be anything but happier for her girl. She deserved it, even though they were two different people, being that most of the people in the projects called Vinita a stuck-up bitch.

It was still early in the day, and Toni thought about going down to the club to hustle up some money. It was getting to the point where she was about to say "fuck it" and move on. But she hated mooching off muthafuckas, even though Mathew had asked her to marry him. She was an independent woman, and until the day came—if the day did come—that she and Mathew tied that knot, she was still gonna do her, and doing her was getting paid by selling sex. Bitches might call her stupid. They'd probably tell her to take whatever that niggah's giving her and bounce from the Bottom Dollar, but Toni wasn't raised like that. She wasn't raised to depend on no man to do her bidding for her. What she could do for herself she did, no matter how degrading her job was. At least she was still earning for herself.

Toni knew that Malice was gonna be pissed since he hadn't seen her in like three or four days, *but fuck him,* she thought. That niggah didn't own her, and neither did her soon-to-be ex-man, Keith. In a way, things were definitely starting to look up for Toni. Meeting Mathew was probably the best thing that had ever happened to her.

-Twenty-nine-

Lana heard her cell phone go off for the fifth time, but she didn't bother to answer it. She sat up in her apartment, healing from the injuries and wounds that Chills bestowed on her just a few short days ago.

She hadn't left her apartment since then, frightened to leave, knowing that Chills probably put out a man to watch her twenty-four, seven. She was in a pair of beige cargo shorts, a white T-shirt, and some sandals. She rested in her bed all day, crying and nurturing her wounds. She refused to see a doctor, worrying that he'd be all up in her business, asking the wrong questions about the wrong damn man.

But this beating from Chills wasn't her first, nor would it be her last. She thought about Tec and about his proposal to bring Chills down—set up the beast and kill the bastard, her lover, her provider. But if it failed, so would her life, and she knew that was a definite thing.

Her cell phone began going off for the sixth time that day, and it made her aggravated because she didn't want to be bothered by a soul. But then she thought, it might be one of her two men, and if it was Chills ringing for her, and she refused to pick up and answer her celly, then it was a sure thing that she would have another beating heading her way.

She picked herself up from off the bed, dragging herself to the cell phone, which was resting on the floor by the bathroom door. She pressed the send key on her phone while raising it to her ear.

"Hello," she dryly answered.

"Lana, what the fuck happened to you?"

She knew the voice right away and was somewhat thrilled that it was Tec on the other end.

"Baby, I'm sorry," she meekly apologized.

This was the third time that Tec had ever called her phone, and he only called if he needed something from her, or something done. By the tone of his voice, Tec sounded furious.

"That fat niggah gotta fuckin' go, you hear me, Lana? I want that muthafucka dead. Toe tag that fat muthafucka," he yelled with much contempt and hatred in his voice.

"Baby, calm down. Why is you yelling?" Lana asked, sounding concerned.

"You give me sumthin' on that muthafucka right now," he demanded.

"Like what, baby?"

"Lana, any fuckin' thang, anything. Where the fuck he be resting at?"

"But, baby, I don't know."

"Nah, bullshit. Bitch, you can't be stupid. Give me sumthin' on that muthafucka. Where he be at?"

"But baby—"

"Lana, I'm so fuckin' serious. I'm gonna kill that niggah, and if you ain't down, then I'm gonna kill you, too, bitch," he exclaimed.

"Baby, why you acting like this?" Lana asked, sounding frightened.

"Bitch, give me sumthin' on that fat muthafucka. I'm ending it now." Tec sounded crazy, possessed, like he'd lost his mind. He was making Lana worried.

"If I hang up, bitch, you're dead, literally, 'cause I'm gonna catch you and that fat muthafucka creeping, and believe me, y'all ain't gonna see it coming."

"Tec, I think he suspects something about us," she told him.

"I don't give a fuck what he knows."

"Tec, don't hang up, please."

"Bitch, start running your fuckin' mouth."

By now Lana was in tears, with her knees pressed to the carpet and the phone clutched in her hand away from her ear, contemplating what she should do. She breathed heavily, keeping her discreet lover waiting for some kind of answer. She knew one personal thing about Chills, an event he loved so much. And she came across it by accident. She heard him discussing it to Jacob in her living room one morning while he thought she was in the shower. If Chills had heard her eavesdropping, then that woulda been more trouble for her, but luckily he hadn't.

She put the celly back to her ear and softly uttered, "Dogfights."

"What?" he asked.

"Chills loves to attend dogfights. He bets large sums of money on them. Once I heard him bring up Brownsville. I think that's where he goes."

"Ayyite," he mumbled.

"You gotta kill him, Tec. Promise me you will," Lana

said, while touching the side of her jaw, as it still ached from the bruises Chills put on her.

"This shit ends now," Tec said. "He definitely don't know who he fuckin' with."

"Tec, he hurt me, baby. He beat me," Lana mentioned to him.

But Tec didn't give a fuck about her. He had the little bit of information he needed from her, something he was undeniably gonna put to use. As far as what Lana was to him, that bitch was yesterday's pussy. The bitch was confused anyway. She had tried to play both sides, and so she would end up getting burned.

Lana heard her cell go dead. She looked down at the screen and it read, CALL ENDED. The niggah had clicked off without saying good-bye or nuthin'. She was furious. She tossed the phone across the room, cursing everyone, including herself. Then she just collapsed on her carpet, lying in the fetal position and crying her eyes out. Tec had to succeed, because if he didn't, then she knew that she was definitely a dead bitch.

Armed with two chromed Berettas, Tec meant business, and business to him meant that there was trouble to come. He got the lowdown on underground dogfights from his number one niggah, Little Boy Ronny.

Little Boy Ronny was the type of niggah who knew where everything went down—from where the hos were at to where there was money being made. He knew Brooklyn. The muthafucka lived, ate, and shitted Brooklyn. And he definitely knew the underworld, who the key players were, what kinda shit went down, and where. That's why Tec loved the little niggah so much. He kept him up to date on every fuckin' thang, and Little Boy Ronny had been down with him since day one of the game.

Some said that without Little Boy Ronny and Sheek, Tec woulda been just another dead or jailed niggah. But what gave Tec his rep was his boldness and craziness. He ain't give a fuck about nuthin', that's why most niggahs didn't doubt his words or test him on nuthin'. He done lived hell, been shot six times before, incarcerated twice in his juvenile years, and practically raised himself, because he pretty much didn't have a mother or a father. He done seen his mother smoke and shoot up crack and heroin in front of his young eyes, and he never had a spot to call home. He made running the streets his muthafuckin' home.

But some questioned his leadership—not personally to his face, but behind his back. He didn't have that same quality that Sheek had when he was out and running the streets. Some said that Tec was too crazy to become a kingpin in the game. It took boldness to step up in the game, but it also took smarts and being quick on your feet, and Tec was the type of niggah with a quick and deadly temper, where he'd react before thinking. So if someone pissed him off, disrespected him, or tried to move in on his turf, then there was only one way he knew best, and that was to blow that person's fuckin' head off. All he knew was violence on top of violence. Death was easy for him. It came natural to him—like taking a shit.

The first time Tec ever murdered someone, he was fourteen. He'd been having this rivalry with this one dude since grade school. The guy was three years older than him, but he kept testing Tec, trying to bully him whenever he saw Tec around, playing him in front of bitches and acting like he couldn't get got. Tec didn't have caring parents to run to and tell them what was happening, and his older brother was locked up at the time. So he had to fend for himself. He got his father's .38 special and brought it outside with him, concealing it in the waistband of his jeans. He'd fired off a gun before, but he'd never shot anybody. Tec knew for sure, though, that if homeboy came stepping to him and tried to beef with him again, then he had it in him, and that would be the last time the niggah would ever touch or disrespect him again. He was gonna kill that muthafucka.

Tec carried the .38 for four days straight, and he didn't run into the niggah, Larry. He thought that maybe someone tipped the niggah off about him being strapped, and maybe Larry just left town for a while. But nah, it didn't happen like that.

Tec met up with Larry late one night while he was on the boardwalk with a few friends of his. And there was Larry, with a few friends of his too. Their eyes met, and Larry had no clue that Tec was packin' heat.

"Look at this cornball-ass niggah here," Larry snubbed, smirking over at Tec.

"Fuck you," Tec countered.

"What, niggah?" Larry replied, stepping closer to Tec.

"Fuck you," Tec reiterated, this time even louder.

"This li'l niggah thinks he ill," Larry said, grabbing Tec by the collar and jerking him around a little.

"Yo, get off me," Tec tried to warn, his eyes flaring up.

"What da fuck you gonna do? Pussy-ass niggah."

"Get off me," Tec yelled.

Tec's boys stood aside and watched while this six-foot, one-inch, 185-pound, seventeen-year-old niggah harassed their friend. But what could they do? They were only fourteen and thirteen at the time, and plus, Larry had two of his boys with him, too, so they couldn't jump in.

The boardwalk was empty, being that it was eleven in the evening on a breezy fall night in October. But some of the locals, or the young hoodlums of the neighborhood, had gone out to the boardwalk to chill and smoke, bug out, hang out with girls, and so on. And that's exactly what Larry and his niggahs were doing, smoking, until Tec showed up with two of his little homies.

Tec tried to fight off Larry, but he was too strong, and a hard right caught Tec off guard, knocking him in his grill. That pushed his limit. Reaction—reaction, reaching for the .38, and springing it out on Larry, catching everyone off guard and causing niggahs to run, even Larry. But it was too late. Before Larry even took three steps, Tec had already popped off three shots into his back, dropping him suddenly.

It was his first kill, and it damn sure wouldn't be his last. He got used to firing a gun and putting shells into many niggahs who tested him or disrespected him. Shit, he learned by watching his older brother whenever he was out of prison.

But tonight Tec rode with his niggahs in a stolen green Cherokee. It was gonna be a special night, a night that would go down in history throughout all of Brooklyn. 'Cause that night, Tec was gonna fuckin' gun down one of the most notorious kingpins in Brooklyn. Chills was gonna get murked, bringing an end to this war, and allowing Tec to step up unhindered in the drug game—giving him the throne that he had deserved for so long. And his niggahs knew that he was crazy enough to go through with it—reaction, it was all about reaction, baby.

The hit on Chills would be more personal than business. The recent news of Tec' s brother being murdered in prison had brought him over the edge—caused a rage in him that made him just not truly give a fuck. Chills had had Tec's brother murdered in the worst fuckin' possible way. He put out a hit on him while he was doing his time. Tec's brother, Lonny, got stabbed forty-nine times in his chest, heart, neck, face, dick, and jaw, and then they cut out his eyes. Word got out, because Chills wanted word to spread, and when Tec got word, the niggah flipped out. His brother was the only family he had, even though he didn't give a fuck about family, but it was the disrespect involving his older brother in a war he had nothing to do with—yeah it was personal now, it was definitely personal.

Little Boy Ronny put Tec on about a top underground dogfight that was happening in an inconspicuous location in Brooklyn. Little Boy Ronny knew the peeps to enter, and with their street credibility, no one would question the men as they entered the dingy, grayish, concrete basement of a Brooklyn building, ready to see two vicious pit bulls tear at each other for substantial amounts of cash.

It was a little after ten in the evening; the basement was filled with mostly men and the owners of two ferocious Nigerino pit bulls. The owners were preparing their dogs for another gruesome match, with the stakes being as high as fifteen thousand dollars. The fight was set to start around eleven, and it was an event in which one needed a strong stomach to watch, as two powerful dogs with ferocious jaws and teeth tried to tear into each other's flesh and bones. Each dog would try to disable the other in a ring that was sixteen by sixteen, and the carpet as high as three feet. Before the match, the dogs were washed down with milk and alcohol. It was a precautionary measure for the dogs and the owners. The matches could go on for thirty to forty minutes, sometimes even two, three, or even four hours.

Tec, Little Boy Ronny, Nate, and Willow were all mixed together in the crowd keeping a watchful eye out for the main man. No one paid any attention to them, thinking that like everyone else, they were there to watch the dogfight.

Tec kept an incisive eye out for Chills. He tried to be inconspicuous in the crowd, with his Berretta concealed under his Lakers jersey and his Yankees cap cocked to the side. Little Boy Ronny stood next to Tec with the other Berretta, just as eager to take down Chills as Tec was.

Willow and Nate circled the basement, armed with two Rugers, the P95 and P97. Willow was the tallest, standing six feet, three inches. They'd been calling him Willow ever since he was young. It was a nickname given to him by his mother, because when he was born, the doctor and the nurses told his mother that he was the smallest thing, weighing only five pounds and fragile, so she nicknamed him Willow. Later he grew up to be a tall man, but the name stayed the same.

Nate was just another neighborhood crazy, more of a follower. He'd do anything or anyone, especially if you paid him the right price. He was the oldest, a few years shy from his thirtieth birthday, still lived at home with his great-aunt, and he was not too keen on fashion. Tonight he was dressed in a tattered blue Georgetown sweatshirt, torn jeans, and a pair of hand-me-down Timberlands. Everyone said he was not too right in the head because when he was young, he was abused and mistreated by foster parents, and possibly even dropped on his head when he was an infant.

Everything was set and ready to go. Now all they needed was for the man of the hour to show up.

"Yo, this my number one bitch right here," a tall, lean guy hollered, hyping up his pit bull, smacking the dog across the face. "She ain't no joke."

There was money exchanged, and bets were made. Overall, there had to be about fifty eager muthafuckas in the basement ready to see a vicious dogfight happen. Chatter filled the concrete basement, and even though most of the crowd happened to be young, there were a few old heads mixing in with the bunch.

But the main event wouldn't start 'til the main niggah showed up, and that was Chills. This was his event, his dogs, and he'd be the one to profit from such a highly anticipated match.

Both dogs were undefeated, having three wins under their jaws, and as they said in boxing, somebody's zero had to go. These dogs were ready to mangle each other for a fourth win—that championship. Little Boy Ronny had been to many of these dogfights, winning bets, and he'd even breeded a dog of his own—a Chinaman pit bull, which sold for $750 on the streets.

The time was 10:45, and in another fifteen minutes, the fight would begin.

"There he is, baby," Little Boy Ronny pointed out to Tec.

And no doubt, there was the man himself, Chills, stepping into the room with his entourage of men backing him to the fullest. They all looked intimidating, dangerous, and by the way they all entered the room, everyone knew that these were men who were not to be fucked with—even if someone didn't already know their reputations.

There was Chills, accompanied by his number one killer, Jacob, and his right-hand man, Cory-D, along with two other unknown men.

Seeing three of the most important men on a niggah's hit list enter the place at once put a grin across Tec's face. He reached for his gat, 'bout ready to make history in this bitch. He watched as Chills greeted certain muthafuckas, looking like he was the Don of all Dons, dressed lavishly in Versace, a cigar clutched between his fingers, a Rolex around his wrist, and dangerous men standing steadily by his side. The muthafucka was looking like a niggah couldn't get touched.

Chills went over to one of the dogs and its owner, peering down at the pit while he placed the cigar between his lips and took a drag. He said nothing, just fixated his eyes on the pup, then nodded.

Jacob was the one with the keen eyes. He didn't seem too interested in the event as he analyzed the place, searching for unfamiliar faces and possible enemies that could be lurking around. He was dressed in his usual sweat suit, packin' the usual .45, with the infamous toothpick dangling from his lips. His gaze darted past Tec and Little Boy Ronny. Tec had his head held low, his Yankees cap down low over his eyes, and Little Boy Ronny was trying to be incognito, trying to hide behind these two chubby muthafuckas as he noticed Jacob scanning the room.

This was the first time that both men had ever been in a room together.

Cory-D, looking like and being the pretty boy that he was, was dressed down like he was attending the Grammy awards.

Ten-fifty and the match was soon to begin.

Chills was having a one-on-one with Cory-D, with the cigar still in hand, and Jacob stood behind him. Five minutes had already gone by since the menacing trio had entered the room. For Tec, that was five minutes too damn long. Now was the chance. He thought about his brother and about that disrespect, and knew these murders had to be done—for the thrill, that kill, the turf, that money, and the power. He wanted to pull the trigger and blow Chills' brains out his damn self—Cory-D and Jacob, they belonged to his niggahs to handle.

Tec lifted the Beretta from under his jersey, with Little Boy Ronny doing the same, and he watched every move Chills and his men made.

Both dogs were now in the ring, still leashed, and ready to be let loose as they jumped at each other from their hind legs, with the chains jerking them back into position. The owners weren't ready to let them go yet.

Tec made his way toward Chills through the dense crowd, with Little Boy Ronny right behind him. Their guns were gripped firmly in their hands, index fingers lightly pressed against the triggers. Nate and Willow were over by the exit.

Tec had to smile 'cause he knew that Chills wouldn't even see it coming, nor would his crew, and that gave him the advantage. He could feel the taste of a kill in his mouth. He was so used to this shit, that the shit just came easy. He wouldn't be hesitant—never that. When he was right up on Chills, he would fire off a quick headshot and splatter his brains all over the concrete. He wouldn't think twice about it. He'd lost his conscience a long time ago.

Just then the dogs were let loose, and they rapidly tore at each other, fangs tearing into fur and flesh. Hearing the fierce growling by the pups, the crowd began to yell and scream, with all eyes fanatically fixated on the ring at the two clashing pits.

Suddenly, a loud shot was fired, causing panic throughout the dense room. Then another shot was fired. Tec, thinking, *What the fuck?* glanced around, gat still gripped in his hand, and saw Jacob with the smoking gun in his hand putting two into his niggah Willow.

Jacob, being on the job, and keeping that keen eye out, saw Tec and Little Boy Ronny, and let off numerous shots at both men, but instead he hit innocent bystanders. Intense gunfire was exchanged, causing Chills and Cory-D to run for cover while their troops did what they were paid to do.

Tec didn't even run, duck, or hide. He just stood there, licking off shots, aiming for whoever, causing chaos throughout the place as Little Boy Ronny did the same. Nate had been hit twice, and Willow's body was twitching against the cold, hard concrete. He also had been shot twice, one slug penetrating the belly and the other going through his chest.

Chills managed to quickly exit the basement, followed by Cory-D.

Thanks to his number one killer, Jacob, Chills got to see another day.

The basement was swept out quick, everyone fleeing for safety, not knowing what the fuck had happened. All they cared about was not getting shot or caught up in the crossfire.

Jacob hurried and escorted Chills into the back of a black SUV, like he was the president and the vehicle sped off, leaving behind an angry and very frustrated Tec, with only the wounded and the dead to keep him company.

-Thirty-

Mathew was cooling off in his air-conditioned limo, relaxing in the back, while temperatures outside soared nearly to a hundred, with the humidity making it feel like it was reaching two hundred degrees on this August night.

He'd just come from having a private dinner with his father at an exclusive Long Island restaurant. And now, he wanted nothing more than to just reach home and take a nice, long, hot, soothing bath in his Jacuzzi. That was the only thing he was focused on at the moment.

He listened to the soul sounds of some classic Marvin Gaye play throughout the speakers, while his eyes were shut, with his head resting against the soft plush leather, and his feet stretched out in front of him.

He thought that he understood his father, but after having dinner with him, he'd found out that his father held some of the same views as his mother, only he was more discreet with his.

They both sat, waiting for their meal to be served—

both dressed casually. Perry Peters wore a teal blue sports coat and solid gray slacks, and Mathew wore a burgundy sports coat and black slacks. Mr. Peters sipped on a Martini while Mathew nitpicked at the rolls.

"You still in love with her, son?" Perry asked, placing his drink down on the table.

Mathew looked up at his father, his father's handsome features peering at him, while he waited for an answer. He was always out of town, so this was the first time in a while that these two had been alone together, having a heart-to-heart conversation.

"You mean Tina?"

"Yes."

"I never was," he said.

"She's a good woman, Mathew."

"I never said she wasn't, but what about Toni? She's a good woman, too, Father."

"But you hardly know her, son. Tina has been family to us for years; her father's a good man. Don't get me wrong, son. Toni's a beautiful woman, and I understand that you want to go out there and experiment with the ladies, sow your royal oats until it's time for you to settle down with the right woman," he said with a slight titter. Taking another sip from his Martini, he continued with, "I've had my share of many beautiful women, too, in my lifetime, even with a few of my receptionists. But you want a woman that's compatible to you, grew up around the same surroundings, and understands where you're coming from."

"But we are compatible, Father," Mathew proudly mentioned.

"How? The both of y'all are from two different worlds. What can she do for you, Mathew, besides spend our money?"

The look Mathew gave his father clearly expressed his thoughts. *I don't like what you're saying. You're ignorant just like Mother. Toni's not like that.*

"She's talented, smart, funny, and she treats me like I'm a man," Mathew said in her defense.

"Listen, son, I understand that the pussy has you whipped," his father said, "but I have to agree with your mother. Tina's the right woman for you. Believe me, I've been there when I was your age. The first woman that makes you find your penis is the one that you think you're in love with."

Mathew just stared at his father. This was the very first time he'd ever heard his father utter the word *pussy*.

"You already had sex with her, Mathew?"

"Yes."

"And was she your first?"

"Are you assuming that I was still a virgin before I met her?"

"It's not shameful to lose your virginity at such a late age. I understand Tina probably had you backed up for a while now, and you needed to let loose, and now you've done that. As your father, I feel it's time for you to move on."

"But Father—"

"Listen, Mathew, I'm forty-seven years old, and believe it or not, I know about women like Toni. They know how to give a man some sex in order to get what they want—an equal exchange. I never mentioned this to your mother, but I grew up around women like her."

"Women like what?"

"Of the streets, Mathew. Listen, I met your mother when I was a junior in Harvard, living off a full academic scholarship. But I never once told her about my past, the life that I used to live before I met her. I grew up in Brownsville, Brooklyn. And I never told your mother, because I was scared to. She was so beautiful, and that woman still is, but she was also a stuck-up bitch that I fell in love with. And she thought that I came from money, so I lied to her, telling her that my parents had passed away and left me their inheritance, and that was how I was paying my way through school.

"Your mother, she expected so much from me," Mathew's father continued. "She always wanted the best, so I worked my ass off, always giving her the best, always trying to hide the truth from her. Her father—your grandfather—he was some hotshot surgeon from California. I met the man once, and we didn't quite get along. I guess he saw the truth in me. He remarried and moved out to the Bahamas, where he lived out his life 'til his dying day.

"A year after I met your mother, you were born," Mr. Peters said, "and I did the right thing that any man would do back in those days. I married your mother and helped raise you."

"You're really from Brooklyn, Father?"

"Yes. And let me tell you something, I said to myself each and every night that it was not a place where I was going to raise my children. I was with many women before I met your mother, and I know what they're about."

"But Father, Toni's not like the women that you're talking about. I know she loves me, and I love her."

"Have you ever been to her home?"

"No. But I know where she lives."

"Did you ever meet her parents?"

"No."

"Does she talk about her family?"

"No," Mathew sadly uttered out for the third time.

"Then pardon my French, but son, you don't know shit about this woman."

"I know enough."

"Mathew, give Tina a call, tell her you're sorry, do what's right."

"And what's that, being unhappy?" Mathew spat.

"Son, I've come a long way. I know a lot about life, and I know that you think that you're in love with this woman, but believe me, son, it's just another good piece of ass. She's got you wet behind the ears."

Mathew was quiet for a few short moments, gazing everywhere except into his father's eyes. He had his arms folded across his chest. He was hurt. He thought that his father would understand—especially now, knowing that his father was from the rough streets of Brooklyn. *They won't even give her a chance,* he thought. Toni really was a good person, trustworthy, reliable, and responsible.

Mathew turned to look at his father, then said, "I've asked her to marry me."

"You did what?"

"I want her to become my wife."

"Mathew, you're making a huge mistake."

"Am I, Father? You sit here and contradict yourself. You're nothing but a lie. When you met my mother, you were different from her, and you couldn't even admit the truth to her. Instead, you've been living a lie to her for the past twenty-six years now, fabricating something that you never were in the first place—a rich boy like me. Now you sit here and you tell me how to live my life. At least I know what she's about—ambitious, funny, and talented, honest too. So what if she wasn't born around wealth. From what I've just heard from you, you weren't either, and look how you turned out. You've made millions for yourself."

"Mathew—"

"No, Father. I thought out of everyone, at least you

would be the one to understand, but obviously, you're just like everyone else—naïve. Tina has nothing in common with Toni, but I guess you see my mother in Tina, and I guess that's all you're going to see. I'm happy with Toni. Tina never made me feel that way."

The silence that suddenly fell between them made it look like it was two strangers having dinner.

Perry picked up his Martini and Mathew caught the gaze of the young waitress heading to their table with their meals.

"Is everything OK?" she asked, smiling.

"Excuse me, Father," Mathew said, rising from his seat. "I'm not hungry. I just lost my appetite."

The young female waitress still set his meal in front of him, then Perry's.

"Mathew."

But Mathew wasn't hearing it. He just nonchalantly strolled out of the restaurant and into his ride.

Mathew's driver, Damien, crossed the Triboro Bridge coming off Grand Central Parkway, and they were now heading into Harlem, uptown, where Damien was going to take the FDR downtown to bring Mathew home.

Mathew opened his eyes, peering out the window and seeing that they'd reached Manhattan. His Marvin Gaye CD was coming to an end, so he switched it, placing in good ol' Curtis Mayfield and skipping to one of his favorite tracks.

He closed his eyes once again, falling into a trance while listening to Curtis' lyrics. Curtis and Marvin were his favorite singers. He could listen to their CDs all day, every day, and not once get tired of them.

He hadn't spoken to Toni in two days, and he was thinking that was two days too long. He wanted her to say yes. Everyone was resenting his proposal it seemed, but what did they know?

Damien pulled up in front of his building around ten that night. He quickly stepped out, unlocking Mathew's door and letting him step out after a long drive from Long Island.

"Are you gonna be good for the night?" Damien asked.

"Yes, Damien, I'll be fine," Mathew said, stepping toward the entrance to his building.

Mathew entered the lobby, saying his usual hello to the night doorman, and headed for the elevators. He was tired. It had been a long day for him, and all he could think about was dipping in the Jacuzzi and relaxing all of his bones and muscles, and just forgetting about his father, his mother, and everyone else. He wanted to fantasize about the woman he was in love with—wishing she was upstairs at that moment, with the water ready, the temperature set right, a little bubbly in her hand, and her petite figure decorated in some sexy lace lingerie.

He stepped off on his floor with his keys already out and in his hand. He walked quickly to his penthouse door.

He entered his place. It was dark and quiet. He flipped on the lights, unbuttoned his shirt, and placed his keys on the kitchen counter. He was definitely ready for that Jacuzzi.

He stepped into his bedroom with his shirt open, flipped on his bedroom lights, and surprisingly saw Tina stepping out of his bathroom, nearly giving him a heart attack. She came to him in a netted robe. Underneath, she had on purple-and-black panties with side ties. Her breasts were exposed, and she wore a pair of imported leather evening sandals.

"Tina," he surprisingly uttered out.

Tina approached him, looking so damn fine and sexy, strutting up to him and running her hands softly down his chest, down to his stomach. Then she cupped his chin, bringing his lips closer and tenderly kissed him. At first Mathew didn't resist, feeling himself getting a bit aroused, never having seen Tina look quite so exotic and tempting all at once. But then he pulled back and asked, "What are you doing here? How did you get in?"

"You forgot, silly. I have a key," she seductively responded.

"But what are you doing here?"

"I came back for you, Mathew. I came back for my husband. I missed you."

"Tina . . . look," he stammered, not able to take his eyes away from that beautiful figure of hers.

"No, Mathew, you listen. I want you back. I love you, baby." She took hold of his hand, pulling him gently toward the bathroom. He followed without much resistance. They came into the bathroom where Tina had white candles lit all around the Jacuzzi. The water was already warm and bubbling, the lights dimmed, and rose petals were spread out on the marble floor. A bottle of Dom Perignon lay by the Jacuzzi.

She held his hands while he observed his surroundings, then he refocused his attention on her.

"This is all for you, baby," Tina said to him, peering into his eyes.

"Tina," Mathew weakly uttered.

"Mathew, I know that I was wrong for the way I've been treating you, but I promise that tonight, I'll make it up to you."

She slid his shirt off his shoulders, letting it fall down to his arms. She kissed him tenderly on his shoulders then on his chest. Mathew stood still, feeling his manhood awakening more. He started to breathe heavily, feeling Tina's soft lips connecting with his skin. He wanted to say something, but damn, this was something that he had wanted from her for a very long time—sex.

He closed his eyes, feeling Tina's hands run across his skin while she continued to kiss on him, enticing him. She reached her mouth and tongue up to his neck, and she pressed her tongue against his skin. Then she began to play with the stubble on his chin with her tongue.

"Ohmygod," Mathew quietly mumbled.

"I understand now, Mathew, that it's my job to keep my man—my husband—happy, and I've been depriving you of it for too long now. I'm willing to have premarital sex before the wedding," she said to him proudly and sexily.

She removed his shirt completely, dropping it to the floor, then began to unbuckle his slacks, reaching into his pants and caressing something that she'd been ignoring for years—his dick.

To Mathew, it felt funny having Tina fondle his penis, gripping it. But he had to admit, it damn sure felt good. He let out a soft moan as Tina's hand grasped his manhood, stroking it gently. Mathew looked at her, and to his surprise, she seemed comfortable doing it.

She dropped his slacks to the floor, along with his boxers. Even though Tina had caught a glimpse of his penis a few times when they were together, it amazed her to see that Mathew was so well-endowed, especially seeing him so hard. Her eyes widened a little, amazed, feeling the need to step out of her sophisticated ways and scream, *"Dayuum!"*

Mathew stood in his bathroom, butt naked. Tina backed up a few steps and slowly removed her netted robe, letting it fall off her shoulders and down to her feet. It looked like a small puddle around her ankles. Her breasts were so firm and tempting. Her skin looked so warm and flawless, and her sensuous long, black hair was falling off her shoulders.

Mathew gulped a mouthful of saliva. *Oh, God,* he thought. He was horny, really horny, and it was shocking how Tina had made him so aroused, so eager. He always found her very attractive, and she had always turned him on, but tonight—damn, it was like there was a whole new and different woman standing in front of him, and he couldn't believe it.

"Tina, what's gotten into you?" Mathew asked.

"Shhhh," Tina hushed, pressing her index finger against his lips. She removed her panties and took Mathew by his hands once again, leading him into the Jacuzzi.

Toni, Toni, Toni, Mathew thought. He was in love with Toni. He couldn't allow this to happen, no matter how enticing Tina looked—and damn, she was hot, with her long legs stretched out in the leather evening sandals.

Tina pulled him into the steaming water, their skins absorbing the soothing bubbly wetness, relaxing all of their body parts.

Toni, Toni, Toni, Mathew kept thinking. But damn, he had waited to have Tina for so long and tried so hard. Now that she was giving it to him, was it worth it? he wondered. *Was it fair?*

But to him, it was ironic. First he had his dinner meeting with his father, who informed Mathew of his past, then told him to go back to Tina. And now he found Tina in his place, nearly butt naked and seducing him in the most excellent way he could ever think of. What was going on?

Mathew's back was against the marble tub, with Tina resting on his lap, nibbling his ear.

"What's gotten into you, Tina?" he asked once again.

"Mathew, I'm not letting you go," she said to him, breaking away from his ear and staring into his handsome face.

"But I told you, I cheated on you and that I'm in love with another woman," he proclaimed.

"Mathew, no you're not. I understand now. This is what you want, and now I'm offering it to you."

"But why now, after I've tried so hard before?"

"Mathew, let's not get into this. What . . . you don't want it now? Is that it?" she indignantly voiced out at him.

"I can't do this," he said, removing her from his lap and stepping out of the Jacuzzi.

"What?" she chided.

"I can't do this, Tina. It's not happening. I love Toni too much for me to be having sex with you."

"Mathew, did you go crazy? You desired me for so long, and now that I'm giving it to you, you're going to turn me down?" she asked, stepping out of the tub, too, and reaching for her bathrobe.

"I can't pretend, Tina, I was never in love with you in the first place. I was just listening to people who always told me what was best for me, that getting married to you would be right, would be the best thing for me. But now, I'm tired of listening to other people telling me how I should live and run my life. Now, I'm listening to myself, and myself is telling me right now, that I can't do this with you."

"Mathew, you're a goddamn fool. That's what you are . . . a damn fool," she belligerently said to him.

Now this is the old Tina, Mathew thought, pulling up

his boxers. She was probably up to something, and that was not good.

"Who in the hell do you think you are, Mathew? Rejecting me . . . you gonna leave me for some ho?"

"Watch your mouth about her, Tina. You don't even know this woman for you to be belittling her like that."

"From what I understand, neither do you," she countered. "Mathew, you're just so naïve and so damn gullible. You would choose to date a ho—a prostitute—rather than be with your fiancée?"

"We're not engaged anymore, Tina. Do I have to keep reminding you about that? And you know nothing about her to be calling her names," he chided.

"Oh, I don't, huh? I know enough about her, my sweet," she said to him sarcastically, "a little more than you know about her."

"And what's that supposed to mean?"

"Your little girlfriend, the one that you think you're in love with . . . is nothing but a downright tramp, one of those nasty hos from Brooklyn."

Mathew glared at her, thinking that she was just speaking out of jealousy, lying through her damn teeth.

"Tina, if you think that making up stories about her is going to bring me and you back together, then you're wrong."

"Oh, Mathew, I'm not making up any stories here. You see, after our little encounter in the limousine the other evening, I hired a private investigator, a very damn good one—expensive too. Had the both of y'all followed."

"You were following me?" he blurted out, folding his arms across his chest.

"Yes. I love you, Mathew, and I didn't want to see you get hurt out there, so I hired somebody to investigate her, do a background check, and I've found out some interesting things about her. Things that you should know."

"Like what?"

"For starters, did she ever talk about her occupation?" Tina asked.

Mathew thought about it. Not once did Toni really explain to him what she did for a living.

"What about her family?"

He thought again. She'd mentioned her deceased grandmother once, the one who taught her how to cook.

Tina shook her head. "I love to be the bearer of bad news about your little girlfriend—this Toni, this slut—she's nothing but a cheap hooker who works down at some indecorous club in Coney Island, Brooklyn, called the Bottom Dollar. Her mother is a drug addict, and her brother, he's doing life for murdering her mother's boyfriend. These filthy people are nothing but barbarians, Mathew."

Mathew just stood there, soaking in what Tina had just said to him. It was hard to believe. Toni—nah, it couldn't be. She didn't seem like the type. He thought Tina had to be making all of this up. She had to be lying because she was jealous. There was no other reason. She was just jealous.

"Like I said, Mathew, I did a perfectly thorough background check on her, and it's all true. You can check for yourself. Even better, ask her and see if she admits to this."

Mathew walked by her, back into the bedroom, taking a seat on the bed. He thought, *What if all this is true? Why would she lie to me? Why hide?* Tina walked in, smirking, feeling first-class about herself by busting a bubble filled with secrets. She took a seat on Mathew's lap, then had the nerve to say, "Listen, Mathew, the first thing that I want you to do is go and take an HIV test. Lord only knows how many diseases that tramp carries."

Mathew didn't even respond to her. He didn't even acknowledge her sitting on his lap. The only thing worrying him was Toni. If everything was true, then how many more secrets was she hiding from him?

Maybe his family was right. Maybe he didn't know a damn thing about her. He thought that maybe his father, even his mother, did know what was best. Like his father told him earlier, he should be with someone he was compatible with, grew up around, someone with the same surroundings as him. Right about now, Tina fit that profile. At least he knew from straight up that she was a snobbish, stuck-up bitch, just like his mother could be.

He hated himself right then.

-Thirty-one-

It was late, and Lana rode the elevator up to her sixteenth-floor apartment. Her arms were filled with bags from Saks Fifth Avenue and Victoria's Secret. She wanted to look ravishing in her new leather pants, even with her face still bruised a little from last week's beating. She applied as much makeup as possible, covering what she could. At least the swelling had gone down.

She stepped off on her floor, fumbling for her keys while she tried to carry the bags. A passing neighbor heading for the elevator gave her a quick hello and admired her package from behind as he passed by.

She entered her apartment, dropping the bags near the door and running her hand across the wall in search of the light switch.

As soon as she clicked on her kitchen and living room lights, her heart jumped. Letting out a quick gasp, she became startled by the presence of five men sitting in her living room, staring over at her.

"What the fuck?" she uttered.

"Yo, chill shortie," one of them said, rising up from the couch, walking toward her.

"How the fuck did y'all get in here? Get the fuck out of my home," she shrieked.

"Nah, luv, that ain't happening. We here on business," the same man informed, leaning near her against the kitchen counter, his voice snarling, sounding straight hood, while his other homeboys stood, glaring over at Lana.

"Do y'all know who the fuck I am? My man, Chills, will have y'all fuckin' heads if he catches y'all up in my crib like this," she bellowed.

"Nah, luv, he the one who sent us."

Lana's face became swathed with fear and terror—thinking the worst. She watched as homeboy who did the talking picked up his phone and made a call.

"Yeah," he spoke in the phone. "She here . . . Ayyite . . . Cool . . . In a minute." He clicked off, placing his cell back on his hip. He looked over at Lana and said, "Have a fuckin' seat, bitch."

Lana didn't know what to think. She glanced at all five men surrounding her in her apartment, frowning at her like they wanted to hurt her sumthin' lovely.

She waited thirty-five minutes, seated on her couch like a quiet child, encircled by the presence of straight thugs and killers. Two of 'em were smoking, and the others were engulfed in their own thoughts, slouching all over her couch while they waited for the main man to show up. They raided her home and went through her belongings—even her personal shit, sniffing through her underwear, raiding her fridge, and drinking her liquor.

"Bitch, you know you sexy, right?" another hoodlum said, staring at Lana like she was prey.

Lana ignored him. Her heart was beating rapidly, her nerves shaking. She didn't know what to do with herself, or what the fuck was going on. They just had her sitting—waiting, for God knows what.

"You wanna fuck me, huh, Lana? 'Cause you know I like you. Shit, I wanna fuck you," the same niggah who called her sexy said, causing shivers to scamper down her spine. He had an eerie voice, raspy and shit.

Suddenly there were a few quick knocks at the door, grabbing everyone's attention. The hood who made the call got up to go and answer the door. He opened it, stepping to the side, and in walked Chills, followed by Jacob.

Lana's eyes widened when she saw Chills enter the room, looking menacing. His face was in a scowl, cigar clenched between his fingers, and he was dressed opulently in his usual attire.

Lana sprung outta her seat, heading toward Chills, saying to him, "Chills, baby, can you please tell these goons to leave my home, baby, so . . . "

Chills clutched her face tightly, jerking her head back with his fingers pressed firmly against her cheek, shutting the bitch up. Lana looked up at him, her eyes filled with fear.

"You think you can just set me up, bitch?" he barked at her, his fingers squeezing harder against her cheeks, feeling like her face was cracking and about to explode like he was only holding a piece of fruit.

She was shaken. Tears flowed from her eyes as she tried to speak, but with his powerful grip clutching her face strongly, all her lips could do was quiver. He pushed her, causing her to fall off her feet and into the glass table, shattering it as she plummeted down on it. She suffered minor cuts on her forehead and hands.

Chills stood over her and swooped her off her feet

again, causing Lana to cry out, "Chills no, baby . . . no . . . please."

He threw her against the wall while everyone in the room watched. This time, his hand was clenched around her neck as he choked the living shit outta her.

"You fuckin' that niggah, right?" he wailed at her, applying pressure to her neck and causing Lana's eyes to bulge. But he wasn't going to kill her—not yet.

She grabbed at his wrist, but his grip was too tight, and the muthafucka was just too huge. The look in his eyes said it all. She was a dead bitch.

"Lana, you disrespect me . . . you dare to fuckin' disrespect me, huh?" Suddenly he let go, and Lana reached for her neck, dropping to the floor and gasping for air.

Breathing heavily and between breaths, Lana spoke, crying out to him, "Baby, I'm sorry . . . it just happened . . . I didn't mean it . . . it was an accident, please, baby, I'll never do it again." Her eyes overflowed with tears, and she trembled with fear.

"Come here, you stupid bitch," Chills yelled, grabbing her by her feet and dragging her across the room. "I give you all of this, and you tried to have me killed. You tried to have me fuckin' killed?" He tore open her top, exposing to the fellows her firm breasts that were decorated in a lace bra. The fellows looked on, drooling, thinking to themselves, *Damn, what a fuckin' waste of a beautiful bitch like her,* 'cause they knew that Chills was gonna kill the bitch, no doubt about that shit.

Chills pounded on her sumthin' serious, striking her multiple times with his huge, heavy fists, causing Lana to cry out so loud that the bitch sounded like some kinda wounded animal and shit.

"You know what? Fuck this shit," he said, huffing, standing over Lana's abused and battered body. She was still conscious, looking up at him, crying, and shaking. "Yo, y'all niggahs make sure that door is locked and them windows is closed tight. This bitch is getting fuckin' tortured tonight."

Everyone did what he said, securing the apartment. Chills then picked Lana up and tossed her on the couch. Jacob's phone ringing was what paused his actions for a minute. Chills glanced up at Jacob answering his cell. It was a quick conversation. Jacob clicked off, looked over at Chills, and said to him, "Yo, that was the connect . . . an hour from now. He said you know where," Jacob informed him.

"Ayyite," he responded. He then looked over at Lana and her pitiful, abused ass. He looked over at his five-man crew and said to them, "Y'all niggahs have fun with her. The bitch is y'all's. Fuck that cunt-ass bitch."

He headed for the door—Jacob opened it for him—but before he exited, he said to them, "After y'all done finished raping and torturing that bitch, 187 her ass."

"Ayyite, Chills," one of the men said, smiling and nodding, very happy to comply with his boss' orders.

Chills walked out, and the five thugs carried Lana off into her bedroom, shutting the door tight, getting ready to have themselves a wonderful night on Chills' expense. Some of them had been waiting and wanting to fuck this bitch for a minute now, and now they were about to get their chance. They quickly stripped her naked, muting her pleas and cries, and raped and beat her the entire night—'til fuckin' dawn. When all five were done having their way with her, they did what Chills told them to do, and they 187'd the bitch by smothering her with a pillow.

* * *

It could have been a number of niggahs who set Chills up, even the niggahs that he had up in Lana's crib. But he knew for sure that it was Lana, and he was positive that bitch was fuckin' Tec. The bitch had even fuckin' confessed. Shit, he had many other beautiful bitches willing to take her place. The bitch was special, but not that special.

Before stepping into his ride, Chills peered up at Lana's apartment one last time, placing his cigar in his mouth and smirking, and thinking about what his crew was doing to the bitch. He knew for a minute that niggahs had wanted to get up in them panties, so he gave her to them, as a treat from him. *Let that bitch suffer,* he thought. She disrespected and betrayed him, and then she fucked the niggah he was at war with. She had to die. Ain't no other way. If he would've let her live, then niggahs woulda been thinking that he was becoming soft, and that's sumthin' he couldn't be having niggahs thinking in his line of business.

"Fuck that cunt bitch," he uttered one last time before stepping into his ride with Jacob as his chauffeur.

Now it was crunch time for Chills. Tec almost succeeded in taking him out. If it hadn't been for his number one player, Jacob, he woulda been toe tagged and put on ice.

But shit was heating up around the way for everyone. Since that little girl got shot and was in intensive care, law enforcement was all over the place. There was even talk that the Feds and DEA were stepping up to bat in Coney Island. There had been too many dead bodies over the past months, and that definitely wasn't good for his business. When the Feds got involved, it was a whole new ballgame. They had paid informants, major high-tech wire taps, maximum mandatory sentences, conspiracy charges, and raids. Shit was getting bad for everyone.

But Chills' number one concern at the moment was Tec. Now he had a hard-on for the niggah. He was fuckin' up his business, and that niggah was fuckin' his woman—for a minute now too. And the muthafucka brainwashed his bitch to set his ass up. The niggah was becoming like a virus, spreading everywhere, and Chills needed to nip that in the bud—permanently.

-Thirty-two-

Mr. Brunson, Vinita's father, wanted so badly to take his old 1890 Remington, single-action handgun and hunt down the bastards—no, those animals, those monster—out there who had raped and attacked his daughter.

But his wife wouldn't allow any such thing. She understood his anger and frustration, but she also knew that if her husband went out searching for Little Boy Ronny and others with a gun, he might not make it back home alive.

The truth was out, and her parents tried their best to console and comfort their daughter, both of them being a little upset that she had kept this from them for so damn long, keeping it in, bottled up like old wine. They wanted justice, but since it had happened seven or eight years ago, they didn't know how to go about it. But what angered Mr. Brunson the most was when Vinita mentioned to them about her little run-in with Little Boy Ronny recently and how he'd threatened her in the building staircase.

Even her sister apologized and promised to be there for her, and that made Vinita feel a little better.

They talked about taking their daughter to counseling, maybe going down to the local church, and they even talked about involving the police. But since it had happened so many years ago, Mr. Brunson told his wife that it probably wouldn't do any good. They might just write it up and do a lazy, half-assed investigation.

But his wife was more concerned for Vinita's feelings, and how she had handled such a thing by keeping it so deep within her. She hugged her daughter, consoled her, and tried being there for her. Now that it was out in the open, her mother wanted to be there for her, to help her cope with it and have her move on with her life. Her only regret was that her daughter didn't come to her when it first happened, instead of being ashamed about something that wasn't her fault. Maybe then these horrible young men would have been prosecuted and sent to jail for a very, very long time.

They talked for hours, with Mrs. Brunson trying to give her daughter the best comfort and advice that she could, especially when Vinita asked her mother if she should tell her fiancé, Myron, about the incident. Her mother's response was yes. She told her daughter that she should be honest with him, that keeping it from him would hurt and disturb her even more.

Vinita's mother even suggested that she bring Myron to their place, if she didn't want to tell him alone, and she wanted family to be around. Vinita thought that was a cool idea, and it would give them a chance to finally meet Myron, the famous fiancé who had Vinita head over heels lately, even though they would be meeting him under fucked-up circumstances.

Now that her secret was out, Vinita was still hurting,

but Myron was finally going to meet her parents, and she thought that maybe she could finally get on with her life a lot easier and with less stress. She made the call to Myron, and he was quick to tell her yes to dinner. Vinita even mentioned to him that she needed to tell him something really important.

Myron came around the very next evening after Vinita had called, inviting him over for dinner with her family. He was very eager to meet her parents, his future in-laws, and he wanted to impress them, so he brought over a bottle of champagne for Mr. Brunson and some flowers for the misses.

He parked his BMW out front, getting lucky and finding a parking space right in front of her building. He stepped out, looking like new money, and that caught the eyes of some of the locals who were forever loitering out front.

"Damn, girl, who that is? With his fine ass," a resident said, peering at Myron like he was some star.

"I don't know, girl, but damn, that muthafucka better be bringing flowers for me," her friend added, fanning herself from the liquid hot sun.

Myron walked up the steps, dressed down in some navy blue slacks and a white T-shirt.

"Hello, ladies," he politely greeted.

"Um, um, um . . . " they muttered, gazing at his assets from behind as he passed both females, walking into the lobby.

"I could just squeeze that butt like it was fruit."

Myron, being very unfamiliar with the projects, glanced around the grungy, graffiti-scrawled lobby of his fiancée's building and took a deep breath. He was a bit nervous, not about being in the projects for the first time, but about meeting Vinita's parents. He went up to the elevator door and pressed the button.

He took a step back from the thick black elevator door while he waited and glanced around the lobby one more time. Up above his head was a flickering light that definitely needed to be fixed, and the exit stairway door had cracked glass and was missing its handle.

Finally the elevator door opened. Stepping out was a young man scowling up in his face as he sized up Myron from head to toe while he quickly passed him by. Myron hesitated for a minute, then dashed into the elevator and pressed the button for his destination. He noticed a foul smell and looked down by his feet. He was standing near urine. *Disgusting,* he thought.

When he reached his floor, he heard someone screaming and yelling in the hallway. Stepping off, he caught the surprise of his life. There standing in the hallway was this stout, big-boned female yelling and shouting her head off, which was probably common there, except for one thing—she was standing there butt-ass naked.

"Fuck you, muthafucka . . . You gonna kick me out? You gonna try and fuckin' kick my ass out . . . you weak-dick muthafucka . . . fuck you . . . fuck you." She banged and kicked on the door, and continued with, "Niggah, you better let me the fuck in . . . niggah, I ain't playing. I'm gonna fuck your ass up . . . Jimmy . . . I ain't fuckin' playing wit' you."

She turned around and noticed Myron gawking over at her, holding a bottle of champagne in one hand and flowers in the other.

"What da fuck you looking at?" she shouted at him. "You ain't ever seen pussy before? Huh?" Her big breasts were flapping all over the place, along with a few other things, as she flung her hands angrily in the air at him and rolled her eyes.

Myron was just shocked. He had never seen anything quite like that before, and she didn't have any shame being butt-ass naked and shit. She just diverted her attention back to the apartment door, yelling, insulting, and screaming her head off.

Damn, that's a lot of ass, Myron thought.

He looked for Vinita's apartment door, spotting it down the hall. He walked up to it and knocked twice. He stood there, holding the flowers and champagne down by his side.

He heard the locks, then the door came open. Standing there was Vinita, looking so fine, dressed in a brown skirt and a beige top. He smiled at her radiant beauty lighting up the hallway.

Vinita heard the yells, glanced down the hall, and uttered out, "Ohmygod," seeing her butt-naked, stout neighbor embarrassing herself.

"Yeah," Myron responded, smiling. "We've met."

"Come inside, come inside," she gestured, taking one last look down the hall and shaking her head.

Myron stepped in, stopping in the tiny foyer/hallway while Vinita locked the door. She let out a quick breath then gave him a quick kiss. She took Myron by his hand and led him into the living room where her parents were sitting and waiting for the fine young man.

Mr. and Mrs. Brunson both looked up, seeing Vinita enter the room with Myron, and they both got up out of their seats. Mrs. Brunson walked over to Myron and instead of greeting him with a formal handshake, she embraced him with a deep hug.

"Oh, it is so good to meet you, finally," she said to him. "Vinita wasn't lying. You're such a handsome young man," she complimented.

"Thank you," he replied. "Oh, these are for you." He handed her the flowers, and she smiled.

"Why, thank you, they're beautiful," Mrs. Brunson said, taking a sniff at them.

"Oh, and sir, this is for you," he said, passing Mr. Brunson the bottle of champagne.

"Champagne . . . nice," Mr. Brunson said, inspecting it like it was priceless.

"Oh, have a seat, make yourself comfortable," Mrs. Brunson instructed.

He took a seat, and Vinita sat next to him, placing her hand on his lap while her parents sat across from them.

"So, the two of y'all are getting married," her mother said, smiling.

"Yes, ma'am. I'm in love with your daughter. She's a wonderful person," he told her.

"Oh, would you like a snack, something to drink?" she asked.

"No, ma'am, I can wait 'til dinner's ready."

"Oh, speaking of dinner," she uttered, springing out of her seat and rushing into the kitchen to check up on her roast beef.

"So, I hear that you're a businessman," her father said.

"Actually, not yet. My father, he owns a chain of stores. I'm still in school for business," Myron informed him.

"That's wonderful."

Her father was already thrilled about the young man. He seemed to be the right man for his daughter. And if Vinita was happy, then he was happy. He knew it took a lot to please his daughter, and this young man who was sitting in front of him seemed to have all the right qualities. He had just the right credentials. He was handsome, charming, and polite too.

Vinita was nervous. She clutched Myron's hand while he chatted with her father. She didn't know how to tell him her secret. She was having second thoughts, thinking, *Is it worth risking everything?* She was truly happy, and once they were married, then she could move on with her life.

"Vinita, can you come help me in the kitchen for a minute?" her mother requested.

"Sure."

She got up, leaving her fiancé and her father to talk about whatever. She walked into the kitchen, seeing her mother removing the roast beef from the oven.

"So?" Vinita inquired.

"He's definitely wonderful. I've known the man for only a few short minutes, and I'm in love with him already."

Vinita smiled, then her expression suddenly changed into a frown. "I'm so scared to tell him, Mom. What is he gonna think of me?"

"Vinita, he looks like he can be really understanding. What happened to you was not your fault, though I wish that the animals who did this to you would burn in hell."

Vinita sighed while helping her mother prepare dinner in the kitchen. She removed the drinking glasses from the cabinet, placing them on the kitchen table.

"Daddy likes him."

"I know."

"They're talking now."

Her mother got out their best dishes. They weren't exactly fine china, but they looked like the real thing, replicas of the famous, expensive dishes. She set the roast beef on the table with the string beans and macaroni, and then set out the silverware.

"Do you want to wait until after dinner or do it now?" her mother asked.

Vinita, seated in the kitchen chair, looking like she had a million and one stressful things on her mind, had her eyes fixated on the floor. She then looked up at her mother and said to her, "I want to tell him now."

Her mother came over, squatting down eye level to her, and embraced her. "It's going to be all right, Vinita. I know it. God is with you. It's going to be all right," her mother assured her.

Vinita couldn't help but tear up, thinking about the worst, reminiscing about the evil done to her. "I love him, Mom. I do, and I can't think about life without him. He's my heart."

"You're not going to lose him. I know . . . I know," she said, hugging her daughter deeply again.

Vinita wiped away the tears from her eyes, not wanting Myron to see her like that. She then stood and walked back into the living room where Myron and her father were deep into a conversation. She took her seat right back next to Myron.

Her mother walked in a few short moments later and said, "Sorry boys, dinner's not quite ready yet." She helped Vinita by giving her some more time.

She took a seat next to her husband, peering over at Vinita and Myron. Everyone was quiet.

"You have a nice home," Myron said.

"Thank you. But I'm sure our home is nothing like yours," Mrs. Brunson said.

"A home is what you make of it," Myron responded with words of wisdom.

Mrs. Brunson smiled, liking what he'd just said. *A home is what you make of it.* She couldn't agree more.

Vinita gently grasped Myron's hand, nestling against him, her heart throbbing rapidly. She squeezed Myron's hand tightly, turning to look over at him. She felt herself getting choked up—emotional.

"Myron," she softly uttered, then she paused.

This was an intense moment for her, for the family. She could have kept it a secret for much longer, but it was eating her up inside, and her fiancé needed to know the truth. Vinita felt like she was about to tell Myron that she was a ho and was HIV positive.

Both parents looked over at the two young adults, praying and waiting. *He seems to be a very understanding young man,* Mrs. Brunson thought once again. She grasped her husband's hand, waiting for her daughter's words.

"Oh God, Myron," Vinita said as a few tears began to well up in her eyes.

"Vinita, is everything OK?" Myron asked, now looking worried. He glanced over at her parents, then back at Vinita.

"Myron . . . something happened to me a long time ago, and I feel that it's only right for you to know."

She paused again, glancing over at her parents. They looked at her, giving her the courage and strength to go on.

"I was with this guy. I was young. And we were going out for a while. I was young and stupid. I trusted him." She stopped, looking away from his eyes. "They raped me, Myron, him and his friends. They raped me."

Myron was quiet, peering at Vinita. By now Vinita was fully crying, clutching her fiancé's hand as if she were holding on for dear life.

"I was scared to tell you because I thought you might look at me differently, see me as some ho. I love you, and I don't wanna lose you."

Her mother came over, sitting next to her and started consoling her daughter. Myron didn't know what to say. *She was raped,* he thought—*damn.*

He took Vinita by her hand, and finally he spoke, saying, "It's going to be all right. It's going to be all right. What happened, that's in the past. What's important now is that we move on. I know it wasn't your fault, Vinita. I still love you."

Vinita clutched her baby tightly, holding on to him with her arms wrapped around his neck. "I love you, too, Myron. I love you too."

It was a Kodak moment.

"We'll get through this, baby. I promise," he said. That was all she needed to hear. That's why she loved him so much and wanted to marry him and have his kids. He was a handsome man of responsibility, loyalty, understanding, forgiveness, and honesty. Vinita felt so much better now that she had told him. It was like a ton of shit had just fallen off her shoulders, and she could move on with her life with ease and a clear heart.

Dinner was served, and the Brunsons had their first wonderful dinner with their soon-to-be son-in-law. They couldn't have been any happier. Vinita and Myron looked like, and probably were, the perfect couple. It was a warm family affair. Everyone talked about the wedding and even a honeymoon in Barbados that Myron was planning. Mrs. Brunson was more excited than her daughter. Vinita was going to spend her honeymoon in Barbados, something she had never gotten to do, which was have a honeymoon, much less in Barbados. But everyone was happy for everyone else, and Vinita wished that this night didn't have to end, but it did, 'cause it was getting late, and Nancy and the kids were going to be home soon. She didn't want Myron to be hanging in the hood too late, knowing how bad things were around there.

Around 10:15, he got ready to leave. He had a full belly and a wonderful time. They'd welcomed him into their home with hospitality and open arms, and they couldn't wait 'til the wedding day. He was family already.

Vinita had never felt so close to her parents, especially her mother. They were having real mother-and-daughter conversations, and the following week Vinita was going out with her mom to shop for a wedding dress. She was just so thrilled and exultant about life. It was like she was a totally different woman. That darkness she was concealing was no more. She was happy and finally proud that she'd introduced Myron to her parents. Everything had gone so well, and there was no embarrassment like she'd always thought there would be.

Vinita was planning to walk Myron downstairs and say good night to her baby in a better way than just a simple hug and kiss on the lips in front of her parents. Nah, she wanted to chill in his car for a moment and entwine tongues with her lover, caress him, touch him, and show him how much she truly loved him. Shit, she would rather go home with him and show him how much she really loved him, in a more open way, but that could wait 'til next time.

Myron said good-bye to everyone and walked out the door with Vinita right behind him.

"You have a really nice family," Myron said while they waited for the elevator.

"Thank you so much. Thank you for everything," Vinita said, hugging her boo then slipping her tongue into his mouth. They tongued each other and held each other until the elevator came to their floor. Even then, they hesitated for a moment until the door was about to close again. They rushed in, with the door hitting Myron on his shoulder.

They laughed, then locked lips again.

The heat outside was ridiculous—make a niggah mad kinda heat, especially during the night and in the projects. Myron and Vinita walked outta the lobby, smiling and laughing, with the young girls outside looking on in envy and asking themselves, *Damn, what that bitch so happy for?*

"You ready to leave right now?" Vinita asked, wanting to hang around with her man for a few more minutes and chill up in his car.

"Why? You going to miss me so soon?"

"C'mon," she said, pulling him by his hand to his car. And like a gentleman, he opened the passenger door for Vinita, having her slide into the front seat. Then he went around to the driver's seat.

The leather in his car was a little hot, so they rolled down the windows and hovered their buttocks over the seats for a few moments until the leather cooled down. Laughing and giggling, they kissed, hugged, and whispered romantic things to each other, not giving a fuck who was watching them from outside. As far as Vinita was concerned, those stank bitches in front of her building could kiss her happy black ass.

"I had a wonderful time tonight," Myron mentioned.

"I'm glad you did. So did I. Shoot, you better marry me. You know how hard it was for me to tell you."

"Don't worry, baby. I will. I ain't crazy enough to let something so fine slip out of my hands, especially as fine as you are, um, um . . . I love you, girl," he said as he slipped her his tongue.

With both their eyes closed and hands locked, they

paid no attention to a damn thing outside of that car. Both of them felt like they were in heaven with each other. Love was definitely in the air.

But the cocking of a gun near the driver's side window caused Vinita to become alert and open her eyes. She was shocked to see the barrel of a chrome nine-millimeter pointed at her man's chest, causing her to jump back. Bam-Bam-Bam-Bam— four shots were fired into Myron, causing him to sag and slump in his seat.

Vinita wailed so loudly that her parents heard her cries from their apartment window. She rushed out of the car, running around and opening the driver's door, where Myron's body dropped out, falling onto the street. She clutched him in her arms, blood staining her hands. Myron wasn't moving, and he wasn't breathing.

"Myron baby, get up . . . get up," she cried out as she held him in her arms. "Baby, please, get up, please . . . get up."

He was sprawled out on Bay View Avenue in front of her building, and Vinita saw no signs of the culprit or culprits who had shot her fiancé. Myron's shirt was soaked with blood, and he was showing no signs of life. Folks ran, gathering around, some in shock as they started to tear up, trying to help her, and calling 911. Even the ladies who hated on her from earlier were feeling bad for her.

Mrs. Brunson came storming out of the building, praying that the woman's screams weren't her daughter's. She prayed, she prayed, and she prayed. But when she ran into the street and saw Vinita clutching Myron's lifeless body with his blood spilling out onto the street and in her arms, she covered her mouth. Her heart pounded vigorously as she tried to keep her own screams mute.

She ran to her daughter, dropping down to her knees and grabbing her, saying to her, "Let him go, baby. Let him go." Her eyes watered up as tears began to trickle down her cheeks.

"They shot him, Mama . . . they fuckin' shot him," Vinita screamed, not wanting to let go.

Mr. Brunson had followed Mrs. Brunson outside, and he couldn't believe the horror he was witnessing. He saw his wife and his daughter, then he peered down at Myron. He shook his head in disbelief, saying to himself, *This ain't happening.*

Five-O and the emergency units were soon on the scene, and EMS stated that Myron was already DOA—dead on arrival. Witnesses told police that they saw someone run up to the car and quickly fire upon the occupants. They said that the culprit was wearing a black hoodie and jeans.

They had to pry Vinita away from Myron. She went crazy, slipping into a state of shock when they covered him and waited to place him in the coroner's van. To hear a woman wail so loudly over a loved one, it was an eerie, eerie thing. People thought that she was going to lose it—go insane. Even her parents couldn't control her.

Vinita continually shouted, "I hate this fuckin' place! I hate this fuckin' place!"

The cops had to end up carrying Vinita off for care and observation. Her mother rode with her. She couldn't believe it, not tonight, not to him, not to them. *What is this neighborhood coming to?* she asked herself. Vinita had just met the man, and now he was dead, caught up in violence that he had no part in.

When will it end? Mrs. Brunson wondered. *When will this senseless killing between young black men end?* It was becoming too much. She held her daughter's hand in the ambulance on their way to Coney Island Hospital. Mrs. Brunson had no words. She was just bitterly shocked and knew that her daughter would never, ever be the same.

On their way to the hospital, Mrs. Brunson said a calm prayer.

Oh Lord, we're fighting, Lord, the killing of our youths, the burial of our children, too many, Lord . . . oh help us, Lord . . . the innocent falling prey to this senseless gunplay. Show our youth the way, please Lord . . . show 'em a different way . . . please, Lord . . . strengthen our journey . . . skill these children with better vision . . . manifest their way . . . if there's trouble, show 'em a better way, that life is too precious to waste . . . oh Lord, give these killers and sinners faith . . . having faith brings a better change in this world today. Bring us faith, Lord, and have us create a better way for our younger generation someday. Oh, Lord, please stop my people from envying and hating each other, say to them Lord, that You are their way . . . Oh, Lord...show 'em love and forgiveness . . . teach 'em that prayer is the only way. Oh please, Lord, those that are lost, show them the way . . . Oh, Lord . . . forgive my children for being lost . . . Oh, Lord, I pray . . . please help this generation before it's too late. In Jesus' name . . . Amen.

-Thirty-three-

"Damn, sis, you looking great," Sheek told his sister. And she was feeling great, sitting in the visitor's room clad in some tight Guess jeans and a denim jacket, and able to drop another three hundred into her brother's commissary.

"How you holding up?" Toni asked him.

"I'm good, sis. You know what's up."

She smiled. She had wonderful news to tell her brother, knowing that it would be something that he'd love to hear from her. She felt so radiant that day that it felt like nothing could go wrong.

"Guess what, Thomas?" she uttered.

"What you got to tell me?"

"I'm getting married," she blurted out, having decided to accept Mathew's proposal.

"What? You crazy? Not to Tec?"

"Oh, hell no. Remember I wrote you and said that I met someone new? Well, he proposed to me the other night, and I've decided to tell him yes."

"What? You serious?"

"Yeah, Thomas, and he's a wonderful person. You'll like him."

"That's good, Toni, as long as he knows how to treat my baby sister right and respect her, then I'm cool with the dude. What's his name again, Marvin . . . Mat?"

"Mathew," she reminded him.

"Oh, OK."

"And he's rich, and I thought that maybe he could help you appeal your case, get you the right lawyers this time."

Thomas laughed. "C'mon Toni, you know I'm in this muthafucka for life. Ain't no appealing my case. Them crackers ain't trying to hear me, let alone let my black ass go free."

"Why you gotta be so pessimistic about it? He can help you, believe me, Thomas."

"Nah, sis. You're happy and that's what matters. You live your life—do you. If you feel that this Mathew guy is the one for you, then go for it, baby sis. Don't stress yourself worrying about me," he suggested.

"I want you to meet him," she said.

"Whenever, yo. You know I ain't going nowhere," he joked.

"And I'm thinking about quitting my job at the Bottom Dollar and taking up cooking courses in college," she happily informed him.

"You serious?"

She nodded.

"When?" he asked.

"Tomorrow night is my last night."

"That's my sis. Do you, Toni . . . do you," he proudly said to her.

"I knew you'd be happy."

"What . . . I'm fuckin' ecstatic right now."

Toni laughed. Sheek leaned forward and gave his

baby sister a warm, deep, and loving hug. She needed to move on with her life and stop being tied down to the past. Sheek knew that his sister could make something of herself out in the world. She was smart, gifted in the kitchen, and she needed to use her talents elsewhere and make that money the honest way. That was the only family he had left, and he'd be damned if anything ever happened to his baby sister.

He sat back down in his chair and then asked the question he knew that he would regret asking. But he had to ask, even though he already knew the answer.

"How's Ma?"

"You know, same ol', same ol'. Ain't shit changed with that woman," Toni let him know. "We got into it the other day. That woman is becoming harder to deal with every day."

"You'll be ayyite, Toni. Just keep doing you," Sheek advised.

"I'm trying."

"So what's the situation with the hood?" Sheek asked, really meaning what the fuck was going down with Tec.

"Chaos. Thomas, you know that little girl that lives in our building, Ms. Janice's little girl? She got shot in her chest, hit by a stray," Toni told him.

"Yeah, I heard about that. She gonna be all right?"

"I think so. I'm scared, Thomas. I think Keith had something to do with that shooting and that little girl getting shot."

"Toni, you stay the fuck away from Tec. That niggah's a fuckin' lunatic."

Sheek definitely knew Tec had something to do with that shoot-out. He still had his ties to the streets, his eyes and his ears. If he really wanted to, he could put out a hit on anybody because he still had his connects.

"Toni, listen, and listen carefully, the shit is gonna get even worse. Too many things going down all at once. Get the fuck outta Coney Island now. Get the fuck outta Brooklyn period. Go move in wit' homeboy. You don't need to be around when shit really starts hitting the fan."

"What about Ma?"

"Don't worry about her, Toni. As much as this pains me to say it, you gotta leave and go and live your life. I love Ma, too, but she's only gonna bring you down. And you're never gonna be truly happy if you keep worrying and looking out for her. Move on. Let me worry about her."

"How?"

"Toni, just do what I say. Believe me. Everything is gonna be all right. I'm happy for you."

"Damn, Thomas, why does it gotta be like this? Why so much drama and death? When are y'all niggahs gonna quit? I'm tired of this shit." She bowed her head, thinking about how crazy the summer had been. Then she looked up at her brother and said, "You heard what happened to Vinita? To her man and all?"

Sheck sighed. He had heard. It was definitely fucked up. His heart went out to her. She was always cool with him, and he was always cool with her. At one point, they kinda liked each other, but that's when they were real young—things changed.

"Yeah. She gonna be ayyite?"

"I ain't seen her since they killed her boyfriend."

"They know who did it?"

"Nope. But word spreads."

"If you see her again, give her my condolences."

"I will."

By mid-afternoon it was almost time for the inmates to leave behind family and friends. Toni felt reluctant to leave. It'd been weeks since she had seen her brother, and visiting and talking to him was the one thing that she always looked forward to. But the guards made it clear that visiting hours were almost over, which meant muthafuckas better get in their last words, last hugs, last kisses, and last emotions before inmates were escorted back into lockup.

"I'm gonna miss you, Thomas," Toni said. They both raised outta their seats and embraced each other with a long hug.

"I'm gonna miss you too, sis," Sheek said, his arms wrapped around his sister. "You be careful out there. Shit is crazy right now."

"I will. I promise. I will."

"Let's go, Benjamin," a husky C.O. shouted.

"I'm coming, yo," Sheek hollered back.

Toni made her way to the exit while watching her brother walk back into prison. He was the last inmate inside. Toni hated these damn moments. It never failed that every time she was about to leave, she would feel herself getting all choked up and emotional, and then she would start to tear up, praying for the best, but forever living the worst.

It was going to be another long ride home for her, and being that this time she'd forgotten her fuckin' Walkman, it was gonna be even longer.

Before Sheek made his way back to his cell, he checked the phone, dialing a number in Brooklyn. The first call he made was to his man from way back. A niggah he knew he could trust with whatever he needed done.

"Yo, Hoarse . . . Yeah, it's me . . . Ayyite, ayyite . . . Yeah, I need a favor from you . . . I need something done . . . Yeah . . . that thing . . . yeah, gotta make that happen . . . too long, yo, too long . . . Ayyite . . . Good looking out on that, dog . . . peace."

That phone call pained him so much that he needed to squat down and wipe tears from his eyes. But truth be told, he knew it was coming soon, and that he had to put that hit through. There was no other way for him. It took him about ten minutes to get his full composure back, then he made the second phone call. This one was to the Sixtieth Precinct in Coney Island.

"Yeah, let me speak to Detective Glico." He waited for a few, and when the detective came on the line, Sheek said to him, "Detective Glico?"

"Speaking."

"Yeah, let me pull your coat to sumthin'. That shooting that happened a few weeks back with that little girl getting shot, well I may have some info on that."

"Talk to me," he said.

"Check out a Keith Patrick and Ronny Cooper on that. They be over on Bay View Avenue most of the time, and go by the name of Tec and Little Boy Ronny."

"You sure about this?"

"I know enough, detective."

And just like that, Sheek sang like a bird, telling Detective Glico everything he knew—where they were at, what was going down, and how it went down. Detective Glico jotted down every bit of information that this unknown informant was suddenly giving him.

There was one reason, and one reason only for Sheek's snitching, and that was to protect his baby sister. Tec was becoming a wild boy, a fuckin' lunatic. He and Little Boy Ronny were running the streets and shooting everything up, fighting a drug war that was probably too big for them to handle. Tec wasn't fuckin' thinking, and his actions were becoming too vulgar, mindless, and ruthless. And recently, Sheek had been having bad dreams. He'd been having fuckin' nightmares about his sister getting caught up in some serious shit because of Tec and his careless actions. And he loved his sister so much that he would rather snitch out his man and put a stop to this war than see his sister get caught up in some deadly shit.

She was happy, and he wanted her to remain happy. Sheek hadn't seen his sister smiling so much and looking so radiant in such a long time, and he wanted her to stay that way. That's why he did what he did.

He put his sister's future and happiness first, more than his loyalty and code of silence to the streets, knowing that it may even cost him his own life.

Toni couldn't believe that it would probably be her last night down at the club—the ruthless Bottom Dollar. Her life was changing, for the better. She had finally decided to take up Mathew's proposal and marry the man, move on with her life. But then she thought about her mother. Could she really just up and leave the woman just like that? During the past years, it had been nothing but pain and misery with that woman—nothing but her fuckin' drugs and wild ways. She wasn't the same woman she had been. There was a demon in her home, a demon that was hard to cast away.

Toni sighed and peered at herself in the bedroom mirror, thinking this was it, no turning back. She had to do what she had to do. Maybe with the help of Mathew, they could place her mom in a good and solid rehab center, or probably send her off somewhere far away from Coney Island and the streets of Brooklyn, New York.

Toni headed for the door, but before she left, she decided to give Mathew a call. No one answered, so she thought she'd just reach him the next day and tell him the good news. She headed out, but she decided not to wait for the elevator, taking the stairs instead. When she reached the first floor, she caught an eyeful, the surprise of her life—her moms, down on her knees, sucking a dealer off with her shirt open and nipples and breasts exposed. The young niggah was having the time of his life, with his head cocked back against the wall, moaning, while he gripped the back of Toni's mom's head, with his dick stuffed into her face. The impression of his dick head was pressed up against her mom's right cheek as it bulged in and out of her mouth.

Toni stopped and peered at them for a moment, looking disgusted. They didn't notice her for a minute, 'til homeboy looked over and smiled, then Toni's moms turned around, staring at her daughter's irritated expression. No one had a word to say. Then suddenly, Toni uttered out, "I'm fuckin' done wit' you."

"Toni," her moms called out.

"Leave me the fuck alone," she yelled as she scurried by them. "You're fuckin' dead to me."

"Fuck that bitch," the young dealer blurted out. "Get back to work, bitch, if you want this fuckin' hit."

And just like that, Angela Benjamin put her lips back onto his hard dick and continued where she'd left off, sucking him off for a high, ignoring her daughter's cries and only caring about pleasing her selfish ways.

Toni hauled her ass into the cab that was waiting for her downstairs, feeling that it was too fuckin' hot to walk down to any niggah's club. She couldn't get the image of her mother outta her fuckin' head. She was mad. That was her mom, and the niggah she was sucking off was as young as her, probably fuckin' younger. She would always see the niggah around hustling. It was some fucked-up shit to see. There was no changing her mother, and Toni had already accepted that her moms was going to be a junkie forever. *Once a crack head, always a crack head,* she thought. *Ain't no changing that.*

When she got down to the club, she paid the cabdriver his small fare and sighed real hard. She walked up to the entrance and glanced at her watch. It read 10:25. *My last night,* she thought. Malice could kiss her ass. No more of this shit—niggahs feeling her up, cupping her breasts, and trying to stick their fingers into her pussy, even though she sometimes allowed that to extract more money from the muthafuckas. No more VIP, sucking off niggahs' small, dirty dicks, jerking them off, and giving these niggahs some pussy when she knew that if she saw these same characters out in the streets, she wouldn't even give them the time of day. And no more abuse from perverted horny men, telling her to shake that and shake this, and let them touch that. She was through with all that shit—no fuckin' more.

She walked into the Bottom Dollar wearing her beige cargo shorts and a little white T-shirt, and she caught the eyes of many men.

"Home girl, let me buy you a drink," a small man said, staring her down from head to toe. She ignored him and kept it moving.

"Yo, slow down, luv. Let a niggah holler before you shake that pussy up on stage," another perverted asshole shouted. But Toni still kept it moving.

Toni wanted to make at least five hundred dollars that night, so she could go and buy Mathew something. He treated her so well, and loved her so much that she needed to get him something really nice, something that wasn't too cheap. She wanted to show her love in return. She'd seen this watch the other day up on

Broadway in Manhattan. The price was $425, and she thought that shit would fit him so nice. So she wanted to cop it for him, with her own dough, not his, and that was one of the reasons why she was dancing that night.

She stepped into the changing room and quickly began to change, removing her shorts and T-shirt, and putting together her outfit. Besides her, there were two other females in the room, but they paid her no mind as they talked and dissed about this one niggah in the club and about how cheap some niggah was with his ugly self.

It took Toni about forty minutes to change. She was looking so fine, so cute, going out with a fuckin' bang on her last night. She stepped out into the scene with her body decorated in a pink thong, a sheer robe falling off her shoulders down to her shins, some glass stilettos, and a tight, sexy pink T-shirt that stopped just below her breasts. Her tiny braids were tied into two long pigtails. Her skin looked flawless and sleek. She made niggahs wanna come just by the sight of her.

"Damn! I said . . . Gotdamn. You is one sexy-ass bitch," a niggah hollered as soon as she stepped outta the room. He automatically tipped her a twenty.

Almost all eyes were on her. She walked to the bar and ordered herself a drink.

"Yo, what's your name, luv?" a stranger asked, standing next to her gawking at her with this big Kool-Aid smile plastered across his face.

"Toni," she answered.

"I'm sayin' tho'. What's up wit' that for the night? You lookin' all good and shit."

Toni smiled. "What's up wit' you?" she countered.

"I'm sayin' tho'. You gotta niggah wanting to get wit' that real quick. You do VIP?"

Toni nodded.

"How much, luv?"

"A hundred," Toni answered as she took a quick sip from her drink.

"Word. That's cool."

Toni didn't really want to, but what the fuck? This was her last night, and besides, he was kinda cute.

"Yo, c'mon, I want that. That pussy looks too good for a niggah like me to pass up," he said.

Toni set down her drink and followed money to the VIP room where she was going to allow homeboy to get his fuck on with her. Homeboy turned around and saw Toni strutting in them stilettos, with them legs stretched out in them, and the niggah had to mumble out, "Umm, umm, umm . . . Damn, I can't wait."

It was a quarter to twelve when the cream Lincoln limo pulled up out front of the Bottom Dollar. Mathew sat back, nervous, thinking the worst. He was there to see if what Tina had mentioned to him was true. He was uneasy. What would he do if he saw the woman that he was in love with doing things that were immoral?

"Mathew, do you want me to come inside with you?" Damien asked.

"No. I'll be all right."

"You sure?"

"Yes, Damien," Mathew said.

Damien also felt uneasy. He knew this type of neighborhood. He knew how shit got down around there. He was from East New York, grew up around the hoods, the thugs, and the hustlers. And he was worried about his boss, knowing that this was definitely not the type of environment for Mathew to be in. He would rather go inside with his boss than wait in the car, but he had his orders.

Mathew stepped out onto the concrete, his posh Italian shoes stepping onto the cracked Brooklyn streets of Mermaid Avenue. He was dressed nicely in Armani, already looking out of place—looking like a rich boy from Long Island or way out west somewhere. He looked around. He saw a few winos standing on the corner and across the street, there were a few shorties waiting for a cab, dressed up, probably going to a club.

He looked ahead, reading the address that Tina had given him. It didn't advertise itself as the Bottom Dollar, like regular clubs such as Goldfingers and Diamonds did. In fact, people would hardly even know that it was there, unless someone told them. There was a thick black door, no windows, and the place even looked deserted—dilapidated. Trying not to be intimidated by the looks of the place, Mathew proceeded forward, knocking on the thick heavy door. He stepped back and waited for someone to come. Damien looked on from the driver's side window, praying that his boss would be OK.

A few seconds later, Mathew heard the unlocking of some locks, then the door came open. Standing in front of him was this burly black man wearing a black tank top and some denim jeans, sporting a thick black beard. His arms were swollen with a mixture of fat and muscle. He sized Mathew up, saying, "What the fuck you want?"

"I'm here for Toni," he said.

"What? Who?"

Mathew changed his statement, this time saying, "I wanna come inside."

The man laughed. "Yo, you outta place, homeboy. This ain't your thang. Try hitting up one of them other clubs, like Runway 69 over in Queens. You'll like it better there," he warned, about ready to close the door on Mathew.

"Wait," Mathew blurted, grabbing the door then reaching into his suit pocket and pulling out a wad of bills. "I got money, lots of it," he announced.

The man stared at him.

"How much?" Mathew asked.

"For you . . . shit, three hundred dollars to come in."

Mathew peeled off three hundred from his stack of cash and handed it to the man. The man took the money and stuffed it into his jeans. Mathew started to walk in when the man at the door grabbed him by his arms, stopping him in his tracks.

"Yo, dog, you need to get searched. You just can't be walking up in here like that. I don't give a fuck how sharp you dressed." He quickly patted Mathew down, checking for weapons, guns mostly.

"Ayyite, you cool, go on."

Mathew headed in. The thunderous bass from the speakers hit him instantly, with the lyrics and sounds of some Nas playing in the room. He walked slowly, in search of Toni.

"Umm, look at you. What are you, Donald Trump or sumthin'?" a half-naked female uttered toward him while she passed by.

He caught an eyeful on that one, with a thong up the crack of her ass and her bra open, exposing erect nipples on diminutive breasts. He was truly an outcast—the only one dressed in an expensive suit.

He walked toward the back, then stopped, peering at one of the naked ladies up on stage doing things that he'd never seen before. Shortie had her legs spread wide open, doing herself with a Heineken bottle as she moaned from it. He watched niggahs toss money at her, and some were grabbing her by her legs, fondling her. Shit, he even witnessed one man stuff a ten-dollar bill in her pussy, and then stood and watched this same man eat the girl out just like that—raw.

A few niggahs and bitches turned to look at him, wondering who the fuck was this lame muthafucka up in the club, looking like he'd never seen pussy before, with all these naked hos walking around the place.

Once again, he couldn't believe that Toni could work in a place like this. Seeing what these females were doing, Mathew knew Tina had to be wrong. Toni didn't get down like that. He knew her. At least he thought he did.

"Yo, you want a drink?" the man behind the bar asked him.

"Me?"

"Nah, the other cornball in the suit next to you," the guy sarcastically responded.

"Oh, um, um . . . I don't know what I want," Mathew said.

The bartender sighed, shaking his head and chuckling. "Yo, you look like you need some alcohol in your system, get you to loosen up a little." He passed Mathew a Corona.

"Thank you."

Mathew took a few quick sips and glanced around the area, seeing all the hos and strippers that filled the room.

"Yo, potnah, that's five."

"Oh," he uttered. He reached into his suit, pulling out the wad, not being discreet at all, and passed the man a twenty.

"Damn," this one ho uttered, noticing his stack.

Mathew couldn't help but feel a bit uncomfortable.

He stood around drinking his Corona, while the ladies passed him, some even coming up to him and expecting a tip—huge fuckin' tips.

"I'll be back," Mathew said, to whom, he didn't know. He just set his drink at the bar and went to the bathroom.

In the bathroom he stood around, about ready to leave. "She ain't here. Tina just messing with you," he said to himself. He looked at himself in the mirror, then decided to leave.

He came out of the bathroom and was about ready to head for the exit, when he saw a new girl up on the stage, and that new girl just happened to be Toni, strutting all her goodies in front of eager and horny men. He didn't know what to do. He just stood there and watched as Toni had men fondle her and help her remove the little bit of clothing she had on.

Toni continued to dance ass naked and standing tall in some stilettos, bouncing everything she had—cupping and fingering herself in front of strangers trying to make that money. So far, she'd already made her five hundred dollars, fucking two niggahs in VIP, and the rest in tips and dancing. And in another hour, she would be ready to leave and never return.

She danced to some R. Kelly. She moved her body provocatively, gliding across that stage. She was going out for her last night, making niggahs fantasize and visualize about her sumthin' lovely. She wanted her wonderful body entrenched into niggahs' memories, because after that night, they were never going to see that pussy or her ever again.

But when she turned to her right, clutching the pole on stage, she saw Mathew standing in the background, peering up at her and looking shocked. She just froze, and her mouth dropped.

Oh shit, she thought.

They both didn't move. Toni didn't know what to do with herself. Should she cover up? Or should she go over and confront him?

"Yo, why you stop dancing, luv?" someone asked her.

She paid the question no mind. She saw Mathew head for the door, so she reacted quickly, grabbing her things and quickly trying to throw them on as she scurried toward the door after the one man who truly loved her.

When she reached the outside, she barely had her thong on, with her top in her hand. Mathew was already in the limo. She ran toward the car, banging on the glass, begging for Mathew to let her in so she would be able to explain herself.

"Mathew, please. I can explain," she hollered.

She prayed that he didn't pull off, and fortunately for her, he didn't. The back door opened, and she quickly stepped in.

He couldn't even face her. Toni pulled up her thong and threw on her top, followed by the robe.

"Mathew, I wanted to tell you, but I didn't know how," she tried to explain, peering over at him, about ready to shed tears.

"What is this, Toni?" Mathew asked, his voice filled with resentment. "You lied to me."

"Lied?"

"Yes. I thought you were something else. I loved you. And then I find out that this is what you do. Why couldn't you be honest with me in the first place?"

"I tried," she said, "but do you know how hard it is for me to tell you something like that?"

"Toni, I stuck up for you, told my parents that you were a nice girl . . . different. I tried to defend you."

"But I'm still that nice girl you met from before. You gonna let this stop us?"

"You should have been honest with me from the beginning. Now I look like the fool. I guess my parents were right," Mathew said, sounding upset.

"You know what . . . fuck you, Mathew," Toni bellowed out. "You're the one who came into my life. You're the one who invited me to your place and tried to help me out. You're the one who introduced me to your parents. You're the one who called off your engagement. And you're the one who asked me to marry you, and now you sit here and try to patronize and judge my life. I thought you would be more understanding, but I guess you're just like the rest of your family, nothing but a bunch of stuck-up assholes. I thought you were different, but I guess I was so fuckin' wrong about you. I thought you were cool."

"Toni!"

"No, fuck you. You don't know shit. You don't know what the fuck I go through every day, or shit about my life. I wasn't born with a silver spoon in my mouth like you. My mother's a fuckin' junkie, and my brother's doing life in the state pen. And I have a crazy boyfriend who probably killed so many people in his life that I'd lose count if I tried to count them all." She let it all be known to him as tears of hurt and pain trickled down her cheeks. "And then you fuckin' come into my life, and I couldn't help but to fall in love with you. You gave me hope that there was something better out there than this shit here and my damn neighborhood. You opened my eyes to so many different things, and I love you for that. But I guess that this was nothing but a damn mistake. It seemed like heaven to me for a minute, but who was I fooling? It's still hell."

Mathew was quiet. He didn't know what to think. He didn't know what to do. Shit, his heart was still for her, but damn, what would his parents think now, finding out what he'd just found out?

"You got nothing to say?" she asked.

"Not right now," he countered. "I need time to think."

"I was gonna tell you, Mathew, but I just didn't know how to. You came into my life so quick, and then you proposed. And then—"

"Look. I can't do this right now," Mathew said, sounding sorrowful.

"You want me to leave?"

Mathew slowly turned to her, then said to her, "Yes."

Toni didn't know what to do or say. Why was this happening? At first she looked to her left, then to her right. She was becoming an emotional wreck. She had never loved a man like Mathew before, and now she couldn't bear the fact that she might lose him.

She reached for the door handle, but before she exited, she looked back at Mathew and said to him, "Yes."

"Excuse me?"

"I said yes to your proposal."

Mathew watched her leave, then slumped back down in his seat, sighing heavily. *Why?* he asked himself.

Toni just wanted to reach home and forget about the night. She was worried that Mathew might be out of her life forever. She regretted not telling him sooner, but he didn't live her life. He didn't know the trials and tribulations that she was going through. Having Mathew around had helped her a lot.

When she reached her floor, she was surprised to see

Keith standing by her apartment door, leaning against it, with some next niggah by his side, someone she hadn't seen before.

"What you want, Keith?" she dragged out, not in the mood for this niggah to be trying to get him some pussy.

"Just hurry up and open the fuckin' door," he barked at her.

She sighed, not even looking over at him and inserted her key, opening up the door. Keith and the stranger followed her in. He didn't even give her a minute inside 'til he yoked Toni up, slamming her up against the wall and scaring the shit outta her.

"What?" she blurted.

"What's up, Toni?" he barked, pinning her tightly against the wall.

"Keith, what the fuck is the matter wit' you?"

"A lot of things, bitch. What's up wit' you and Richie Rich? You in love wit' that niggah now, huh?"

"Keith . . . "

"You snitching on niggahs now, too, Toni? Huh, bitch?"

"What?"

"Don't play stupid with me, Toni. I will hurt you up in this bitch. The police raided my crib this morning looking for a niggah. What you know about that?"

"I don't know anything about that. I swear, Keith. I didn't snitch you out," she said, even though she had thought about it.

"C'mon, just tell me the fuckin' truth," he shouted, with his hand gripped around her neck.

"Fuck you, Keith," she barked, not giving a fuck anymore, feeling that her life was a waste. The way she saw it, she could never truly be happy, so why not die in this lunatic's hands and end this shit now? End all the bullshit that she'd been going though these past years.

"What? Fuck you, bitch," Keith snarled back. "Yo, Shot, keep an eye out in the hallway. I'm about to handle mines."

He dragged Toni into her back bedroom, where he was definitely planning on handling his business by raping and beating on her. He wanted to get this stupid bitch pregnant by him before the night was over and leave behind his seed in case something happened to him. The niggah Tec was losing his fuckin' mind.

No other niggah was taking what belonged to him, and he was about to leave his mark up in Toni that night. Toni had never seen Keith with so much rage and hatred in him. His eyes were black, like he was possessed. She tried to fight him off, but his strength was too much. He tore off her clothes and forced himself into her. When he felt himself about to come, he didn't bother to pull out. He did this over and over, bus'ing off in Toni multiple times, hoping to impregnate her with his mark, his seed.

He left Toni lying on the bed, crying, while she was balled up in the fetal position.

"You wanna fuck around and snitch, then snitch on your baby's father, bitch. I'll let you carry my fuckin' seed, and if you think about getting an abortion, then I'm gonna kill you, you dumb bitch." He zipped up his jeans and left Toni in her bedroom.

Enough was enough. Toni thought about taking her own life, wishing that Keith had done her that favor. She couldn't deal with the drama anymore. It was feeling like she was living in hell on earth.

She clutched her stomach, as it was hurting her. She felt like she needed to throw up. How could so many things go so wrong for her in one damn night? Just a few short hours ago, it felt like she was living in heaven on cloud nine. Now her shit got checked back into reality—back into her world—a world that she now felt she could never escape.

Little Boy Ronny gave dap to a few niggahs who were standing on the corner of Bay View and Neptune. It was late afternoon, the summer heat was still intense, and the hood was still hot. A couple of the fellas had a dice game going down, and Little Boy Ronny wanted in. He carried four grand in his pockets and was ready to start hustling.

Almost everyone on that corner feared Little Boy Ronny. Even though they were cool with him, they knew their boundaries with the man—knowing that he would cap off any one of them in a heartbeat if they ever tried to disrespect him. They also knew that he was forever strapped. He was carrying a .38 on him, the gat tucked in his jeans.

Little Boy Ronny already knew that cops had raided Tec's crib, and he heard that five-O was out looking for him, but he wasn't stressing it. Some bitch-ass niggah was snitching, and when they found out who, then it was shots to his head.

The fellows easily let Little Boy Ronny into the game without any quarrels or questions. And on his first roll, the dice all came up on six—Tripps 6. He'd already collected a hundred from niggahs.

"Yo, what's up with Tec? He ayyite?" one niggah asked Little Boy Ronny.

"Yo, don't worry about that niggah. He cool," Little Boy Ronny responded.

"I'm just asking."

"Don't ask," Little Boy Ronny barked, glaring over at homeboy.

Being intimidated by the young hustler, duke just shut his fuckin' mouth and concentrated more on the game.

By late evening, the hood seemed peaceful, but in the hood, you never knew what could suddenly happen, who was plotting what, or who was suddenly after who. The locals thought that this drug war was going to come to an end. That was because they'd found out that Tec's crib had been raided the other day. Everyone knew that Tec was a major player in the drug war, and in this game that too many niggahs were involved in, they also knew that Tec had a lot to do with the sudden rise of the body count over the summer. The locals in the hood just couldn't wait 'til the government locked his ass up.

It was true that the Feds were cracking down, and with the sudden phone calls to Detective Glico that began a few days ago, it gave law enforcement the opportunity and ammunition it needed to make its move and crack down on certain individuals and establishments.

During the past six days, the DEA raided more than a dozen homes and businesses, including such places owned by the notorious kingpin, Chills. They made more than two dozen arrests all throughout Brooklyn, and had more than one hundred cases pending, which included racketeering charges, extortion, drug trafficking, prostitution, conspiracy, and murder.

By the end of August and early September, so many niggahs were snitching on one another that you would've thought the shit was in style. There were a lot of niggahs in the game who were cooperating with the government and trying to minimize their sentences. Informants were popping up out of everywhere, testifying and ratting on certain major players in the game.

Certain unsolved crimes were suddenly being solved, like homicides that happened months ago, and all it took was for one muthafucka in prison to cause this domino effect in the game. It took Sheek's snitching, and that shit caught on like wildfire.

Little Boy Ronny knew that shit was getting hot out there, but with his attitude, he didn't give a fuck. The little niggah still thought that he was invincible. He continued to roam the streets, hustling and making his money, with or without his number one niggah, Tec, who kept himself on the down low for a few days.

He was up four hundred in the dice game, boasting his cash and not paying attention to his surroundings. If he had been, then he woulda noticed the blue Impala parked across the street with two undercover officers keeping a keen eye on him and the six other niggahs standing on Neptune and Bay View.

Before it got dark out, several unmarked cars and several police squad cars rapidly swooped up on all seven men on the corner. Then suddenly hordes of law officials draped in blue flight vests and uniformed officers jumped out of their vehicles with their guns drawn, quickly approaching the young black men and shouting, "DEA, everyone get the fuck down."

Six out of the seven complied, but Little Boy Ronny took sudden flight, dropping cash and all, and sprinted down Bay View Avenue with cops dead on his heels. He sprinted into the projects, then quickly darted into a building lobby, where he reached for his .38 and fired on the three officers who were closing in on him. He struck one officer in the shoulder while the other two quickly returned fire. They missed Little Boy Ronny as hey wailed into their police radio, "Shots fired, shots ired! Officer down, officer down!"

Little Boy Ronny took flight up the staircases, run- ing up the stairs two and three at a time 'til he reached he fourth floor. He ran down the hall, banging on a pecific door.

"Yo, Chica, let me the fuck in," he huffed, being out of breath, while he banged on his ex-girlfriend's apart- nent door. He turned around and had the .38 pointed at the stairway entrance, ready to shoot off at any more cops coming through that door.

"Chica," he shouted again. He heard the cops com- ng up the stairway, and he was ready to blast at them nuthafuckas again. But suddenly, Chica heard his cries and quickly let Little Boy Ronny into her apartment, where he ran and hid in her back bedroom.

DEA, and the local police swarmed the whole area in search of Little Boy Ronny. They were on all the floors, banging on all the doors and asking neighbors loads of questions. It was dark out, and they had the helicopter hovering above Gravesend projects with the illumi- nated blue light casting down on people's homes in search of their perpetrator. But they had no luck.

They didn't know if Little Boy Ronny was still in the building. They had a warrant out for his arrest and warned everyone that he was armed and dangerous. The search continued for hours, even well after mid- night. They brought an emergency service unit out and even the dogs, but they still didn't have any luck finding him.

After one in the morning, they began to give up the massive manhunt for their target. They still left behind a few officers on the scene. They couldn't raid every home in the building, and they had other options.

Detectives began questioning the other six men who were on the scene with Little Boy Ronny when five-O had pulled up. Luckily for the officers, one of the six men detained had been caught concealing an illegal firearm, and he was on parole. Another had in his possession fifteen grams of crack cocaine, which could lead to a federal mandatory sentence of ten years.

But the DA was ready to cop a deal with the two offenders, ready to cut them some slack on the charges, if one or the other gave up any information that they had on Little Boy Ronny—his whereabouts, his ex-girlfriends' homes, or places he might be hiding out. They wanted Little Boy Ronny, not them. And they sung like birds.

The very next morning, swarms of officers were at Chica's apartment door, ready to knock the fuckin' door down and capture this scum who almost killed an officer while on duty the previous evening.

They raided her crib in full force, making it readily known that they were DEA and NYPD, and that they had an official warrant for Ronny Cooper, aka Little Boy Ronny.

Chica cursed and raved, and nearly attacked the officers while shouting, "Y'all need to get the fuck outta my house. Get the fuck out. He ain't here."

It was early morning, around eight, and all she had on was a pair of pink panties, her bra, and some white tube socks. But she didn't give a fuck about her appearance, as she acted ghetto wild on the officers and agents.

Some of them couldn't believe how such a nice-looking young girl could act so ugly. But these officers saw it every day, beautiful young ladies protecting the likes of Little Boy Ronny. And they wondered why. What did these men have to offer these women except drama and legal troubles?

"Fuck y'all. Ronny ain't here," she angrily repeated

herself. "And I don't know where the fuck he's at, and if I did, I wouldn't tell y'all fuckin' pigs a damn thing anyway."

"Miss, please calm down," one of the agents said to her.

"Fuck you."

"Miss."

This time, Chica spat in his face, catching the agent in the eye, and that pissed him off. He turned to the officer standing next to him, wiping the spit from his eye, and ordered, "Cuff her."

"Get the fuck off me," she yelled, struggling and resisting arrest while they tried to contain her. She kicked, hissed, spit, and even tried to bite one officer while he tried to slap the cuffs around her wrists.

"We'll deal with her down at the station."

They searched the place, and Little Boy Ronny was nowhere to be found. They wondered how the fuck the little muthafucka had slipped through their fingers. Where the fuck did he go? They had the entire area on lockdown, and there was still no sign of him.

They carried Chica off in cuffs, making her walk out into the streets in her underwear and all, having her curse up a storm at the officers, while bystanders, especially young males being up and out so early in the morning, caught an eyeful of Chica and said to themselves, "Damn, yo."

Many felt that the drugs and the war around their neighborhood were crumbling because so many young men who were involved in that dangerous drug world were getting arrested and locked up. A lot of the tenants felt relieved seeing so many officers, detectives, and agents finally on the scene doing what their tax dollars were paying them to do—fight this war on drugs—and getting these thugs, drug dealers, killers, and kingpins off their city streets. They were helping to create an environment where there wouldn't be any more incidents like six-year-old Latish Jenkins, who got hit by that stray bullet, shot in her chest while she was playing in the park a month ago.

They were doing sweeps and pickups everywhere, locking up brothas and catching them with cases. Tenants were rallying and praying that their neighborhood was changing—they wanted better. Some were so tired of being cooped up in their apartments, scared to go out 'cause of the drugs and the crime, that they even thought about moving south, in hopes that they'd find something better out there.

-Thirty-four-

Toni rode the F train from Brooklyn into Manhattan, on her way to pay Mathew a visit at his Manhattan apartment. It had been a week since they had that little quarrel in front of the Bottom Dollar, and no matter how much she tried hating him, she couldn't help but miss him.

She tried to forget about Tec, his rape of her the other night, and his attempt to get her pregnant for whatever his reasons were. If she was in fact pregnant by him, then the first thing she was going to do was get an abortion. There was no way in hell that she was having that bastard's baby.

She sat quietly in the last car of the F train. It was the seventh day of September, so outside was nice and cool—temperatures in the mid-seventies. Toni looked like she was in her own world, wondering what she was going to say to Mathew once she arrived. What was she going to do? She definitely wanted Mathew back in her life, and she was willing to say, do, or give up whatever.

She reached his building around noon, standing out front of the main lobby and contemplating if she should confront him. She was nervous.

She headed inside, but as usual, she was stopped by the main doorman on duty.

"Can I help you?" he asked.

"I'm here to see Mathew Peters," she said to him, smiling.

"Is he expecting you?"

"No. It's a surprise visit . . . if you know what I mean," she said while flirting with the doorman as she flaunted her commodities in a pair of tight blue Levi's jeans that accentuated her curves and a plain white T-shirt that was tied in a small knot just below her breasts.

She batted her eyes at him, and he definitely found her to be very attractive, but trying to do his job, he said to her, "I'm sorry, but all visitors must be announced before heading up. That's the rules."

"You can't forget about the rules just this once? I promise that I won't tell."

"I'm sorry, miss."

"Here, maybe this can make up for it," Toni said, handing him a hundred dollar bill.

"But miss—"

"Here, take another one." She handed him another hundred. "Just this once, I promise."

The doorman hesitated, staring at her then sighing. "OK, just this once."

"Thank you."

When she reached Mathew's floor, she took in a deep breath, hoping that he was home, and praying that he was able to forgive her. She loved him, and there was no hiding that.

She knocked lightly on his door and waited for him to answer. When he opened his door, she just wanted to jump in his arms and kiss him, straddle him, and make love to him all day and all night.

She heard the door being unlocked, and when his penthouse door opened, Toni caught the surprise of her life. Standing in front of her was Tina, smirking at her, while dressed in pink-and-black silk, sheer baby doll lingerie, holding a glass of wine.

At first Toni didn't know what to say. She just stared into the cold eyes of Tina, who had a lot to say.

"You must be Toni, the bitch who tried to take my husband away from me. Dumb bitch, I remember you from the Plaza," she chided, gazing at Toni from head to toe, already expressing her disapproval.

"Excuse me?"

"You heard me. You need to remove your ghetto-fabulous ass from in front of this door. You are not wanted here."

"Where's Mathew?" Toni asked, trying to look past her and into the penthouse.

Seeing this, Tina stepped into the hallway and slightly closed the door, obstructing her view.

"I'm going to call the cops if you don't leave me and Mathew alone. It's bad enough that I had to get him checked out for any diseases that you might have given him, but now I'm not going to let you ruin our lives."

"I just want to see Mathew. Bitch, you ain't my business," Toni rebuked.

"Excuse me?" Tina responded.

"Bitch, you heard me."

"People like you, y'all ghetto nasty bitches, always trying . . . "

"Bitch, what the fuck you call me?" Toni scolded, her face flaring up.

"I don't want any trouble from you. Please just leave," Tina begged.

Toni was 'bout ready to bring it to the snobby bitch. She wanted to show Tina how she got down. Toni remembered her from their last encounter and how rude she was to her. But today, shit, today was a new day for her. Toni tried to be nice, but if Tina came out of her mouth with something else smart to say, then it was going to be on up in there.

"Mathew's in the shower, and he doesn't want to see you ever again. We're engaged, so just leave us alone."

Toni was already hurt seeing Tina answer his door, looking all exotic in sexy lingerie and being as beautiful as she was. She tried to compose herself, thinking all kinds of crazy shit. And then she started thinking that maybe this was for the better. She and Mathew were from two different worlds, and maybe she was never really meant to be happy.

She backed away from Tina, 'bout ready to head for the elevator until she heard Tina say, "I don't even know what he saw in your kind of people. You'll probably end up being a junkie just like your crack head mother."

Toni didn't even come back with words. She just came back with action, and quickly punched that bitch across her jaw, causing Tina to spill her glass of wine onto her breasts and outfit.

Tina gasped, looking at Toni in shock, clutching her bleeding mouth.

"Fuck you, you dumb bitch! Don't you ever talk about my mother like that! You don't know her and you definitely don't know me," she shouted.

"Oh my God, you just attacked me," Tina raved, with her hand clutching the left side of her jaw. It was beet red from the hit she'd just received.

Toni left, fed the fuck up.

Tina scurried into the apartment, raving mad, and called out for Mathew to call the police.

Mathew came out of the bathroom, clutching the towel that was wrapped around him, and asked, "What happened to you?"

"That tramp just attacked me. Call the police. I want her arrested."

"Tramp? Who?"

"That bitch . . . "

"You mean Toni? She was just here?"

"Yes, Mathew, and she just attacked me. Oh Lord, please call the cops on her, Mathew. She needs to be in jail."

Mathew ignored Tina's cries and hurried by her toward the door. He ran out into the hallway, still in his towel, and a little wet from just coming out of the shower.

"Mathew, where are you going?" Tina called out. "Mathew."

He quickly scurried for the elevators, catching one going down instantly. He chased after Toni so fast that he nearly fell on his ass a few times.

When he hit the lobby floor, he ran toward the doorman, huffing and wheezing, and asked, "Did a young lady just come by here?"

"Excuse me?" the doorman replied, looking over at Mathew while he clutched his towel, standing in front of him with his sweat mixing with the water from his shower.

Mathew took another breath, then asked again, "A beautiful young lady with braids . . . Did she just walk by you?"

The doorman shook his head. "No, sir."

He turned and looked toward the elevator, waiting to see if Toni was soon to step out. He wiped his forehead.

He was thinking that he had made a big mistake. He wanted Toni back. He loved that woman.

He suddenly heard the sound of the next elevator approaching the lobby and got excited when he saw Toni stepping out. She peered over at Mathew, looking at him like he was crazy.

"Toni," Mathew uttered, coming toward her.

"Fuck you," she angrily replied as she rushed by him, pushing him away.

"Toni," he called out again.

"Leave me alone, Mathew. I see you've forgotten about me real quick, with that bitch upstairs in your apartment."

"Toni, please don't leave . . . I love you."

Toni was about to exit the building, but she paused in her steps. She wanted to leave, but she couldn't. She turned around and looked over at Mathew.

"I love you," he repeated. "And I'm sorry about the other night. I'm sorry about how I came off. I was just so upset, I didn't know what to say or do. But I do know that I still want you in my life, no matter what happens."

Toni was quiet. She didn't know what to do or say. Mathew started to come to her, and as soon as he was inches from her, he grabbed Toni and said to her, "Be my wife. Marry me."

"What about Tina?" she asked.

"Fuck her . . . She's gone."

Toni smiled, feeling like she was in some kind of Terry McMillan novel, like *Waiting to Exhale.* It felt good being held in the arms of the man she was in love with. They peered at each other for a moment, then their lips and tongues entwined, and they showed their love right there in the lobby, and in front of the doorman, who was smiling and thinking, *damn.*

-Thirty-five-

It was early morning, and three serious-looking men followed Angela Benjamin into her home. They'd been waiting for her, waiting for her to come, so that they could get it over with.

They rushed her into her apartment, grabbing her, and shoving her into her bedroom. Angela tried to put up a fight, but with her frail self, and the drugs eating away at her body and soul, it was like a light summer wind fighting back.

Two young men forced her down onto the bed, where they placed thick, gray duct tape around her mouth, keeping her quiet, then they tied her arms to the bedpost. She squirmed and twisted, but it didn't do her any good.

The third man came into the room carrying a small pouch, and Angela peered up at him, fear drenched in her eyes, and a few tears slipping down her cheeks.

"Don't worry, luv, this shit ain't gonna take too long. Believe me," he said, crouching down by the bed and reaching into the pouch. He pulled out a hypodermic needle, something that she was all too familiar with.

The dark man then stood, grabbing for Angela's arm, and he stuck the needle into her. It was filled with poison. At first she resisted and jerked as the poison flowed through her veins, mixing with her blood.

"He said to make it quiet and peaceful," said the man who seemed to be the leader out of the three. All of them stood around the bed watching Angela take in her last breaths.

They watched her die slowly and peacefully, the way Sheek, aka Thomas Benjamin, had wanted it for her. His mother had been through so much pain, and he felt that this was the only way for her to escape, the only way for her to finally find peace.

His sister had already found happiness in her life, and he wished for his mother to find the same. But he would rather see her dead than to see her continuing to lurk these streets with her innocence drained from her every day as she shot up and got high.

Enough was enough. May his mother rest in peace—God bless her soul.

It'd been a week since Little Boy Ronny eluded capture by the police. He'd been hiding out here and there, having his true niggahs look out for him and telling him what was going down. He heard about Chica getting bagged and dragged downtown, but he didn't care. He had to look out for himself.

He hadn't heard about Tec. He hadn't seen the niggah in two weeks, and he was wondering if Tec had left town because shit was getting too hot. Or had niggahs got to him, killed him, and dumped his body into the river somewhere. If so, Little Boy Ronny would never know. That was how the game got down. A niggah could just up and disappear, and his closest boys wouldn't know if he had left town just like that or if niggahs had put him to rest.

But Little Boy Ronny couldn't stress it. He had to worry about himself. They had a warrant out for his arrest. The muthafuckin' whole police force was out looking for him. And when, or if, they found him, he knew it would be that ass-whooping first, getting hit with nightsticks and other shit, then it would be the charges—if he survived the beating.

He was out, but kept on the low, gambling in the building lobby with his niggahs. He still was doing him, but now on a more low profile. He couldn't be seen out in the streets like that. That niggah was marked, not just by five-O, but by Chills and other niggahs he had done wrong. Word was out. Tec and Little Boy Ronny's reign was over.

It was eleven at night, and Little Boy Ronny, encircled by a few young men, continued to roll until night ceased and morning came. They could be heard by all, as they were very loud and very vulgar. Little Boy Ronny had the dice in his hands. He had already lost five hundred dollars and was trying to make that shit up.

Little Boy Ronny, 'bout ready to roll, looked up and then uttered out, "Look at this bitch here."

Then bang!

Little Boy Ronny suddenly caught an instant slug to the center of his chest, causing him to drop the dice. He stared over at his shooter in shock. He looked at Vinita while she was clutching her father's handgun, the barrel still hot while she glared at him with tears streaming down her face.

"Oh shit . . . " Little Boy Ronny mumbled, grabbing at his chest, those being his last words. Then Vinita fired another round into his head—killing him instantly. She watched him drop.

Niggahs who were standing around suddenly scattered after the first shot, fleeing up the stairs and flying by her.

Vinita wanted Little Boy Ronny dead. She definitely knew he had something to do with Myron's death. He had caused her so much pain that she just didn't give a fuck anymore. If she suffered, then he would have to suffer. She hated him with every breath that she took, and she couldn't stand seeing him still living while her fiancé wasted away in some grave.

She felt that she was doing the neighborhood a favor in avenging Myron's death and getting justice for herself.

When cops found Little Boy Ronny's body sprawled out on the lobby floor, they smirked and uttered to themselves, "That's one less hood niggah for us to worry about."

Epilogue

Toni was very excited about seeing her brother again so soon. This time she was bringing Mathew along as they rode upstate in style, cruising along in his limo. She'd been through a lot, and she just wanted to introduce Mathew to her brother and tell him the good news. She was leaving town—leaving to be with her fiancé and live a better life, a life better than her old one, a life where she knew that she was going to be happy, a life far away from Tec, her mother, and the mean streets of Coney Island.

Mathew gave up everything for her. He didn't care—screw everybody. He still had funds, but as far as his family was concerned, they considered him dead. Tina, she was still young and beautiful. She would find some other rich man to marry.

They held hands while riding in the limo. Toni was beaming with joy, excited about telling Thomas the good news.

They got to the prison around noon that day. He wasn't expecting her.

"He's going to like you," she said to Mathew. "I know it."

They both walked into the prison, telling the guard who they were there to see. The guard looked at her, saying, "You here for Thomas Benjamin?"

"Yes."

"OK, you need to sit tight." The way he was acting was making Toni worried. He kept peering at her, then he picked up the phone and made a call.

Toni and Mathew sat for what seemed to be an eternity, waiting for someone or some news.

She got up and asked the guard at the desk, "What's the problem?"

She had never waited this long to visit her brother.

"There was a problem last night," the guard informed her.

"Problem? What problem? Is my brother all right?" she wanted to know, becoming worried.

Soon after, the warden, accompanied by a few guards, came to her.

"Are you his sister?" he asked.

"Yes. What's going on?"

The warden glanced at his two C.O.s standing next to him, then refocused his attention on Toni.

"I'm sorry to inform you of this, but your brother was killed last night during a prison fight."

The news hit Toni like steel and concrete. "What?" she stammered. "No."

"I'm sorry. We'll gather his things for you."

"No! No! No!" Toni was becoming hysterical. "Thomas . . ." she called out. Mathew came to her aid, clutching her in his arms. She collapsed to the floor with tears running down her face as she cried over the sudden death of her beloved brother.

"Thomas. Thomas. Thomas," she mumbled.

"Toni, I'm sorry," Mathew apologized. He didn't know the man, and he couldn't understand her pain, her loss. But he knew one thing was for sure. He was going to be there for her, no matter what.

He had entered her life and saw her pain and her hurt, and he knew that she'd been through a lot. She'd been through hell and back. He had seen a world that his rich life had kept him sheltered from for so long. He had seen a world that far too many die in every day, a world that he would never understand—the streets, the deaths, and the pain that the violence caused so many. He was more than happy to rescue Toni from such a harsh and malicious world. He was determined to make her once ghetto life completely different. He was gonna make her feel like she was in heaven. His heart went out to her. He just couldn't understand.

And he never really would.

None of us ever would.

About the Author

Erick S. Gray, author of the urban sexomedy *BOOTYCALL*, has been writing well thought out plots to keep the reader interested with every turn of the page.

This entrepreneur is also the owner/founder of Triple G publishing and is making moves in other markets as well.

Born and raised in the south side of Jamaica, Queens, this 28 year-old young, gifted author has brought himself out on a high note with his first endeavor. He continues bringing you good stories as he shows in his collaboration with Mark Anthony and Anthony Whyte, *Streets of New York* and his novels *Ghetto Heaven*, *Nasty Girls*, and Money, Power, Respect.

Erick S. Gray is showing that young African-American males don't all fall into the same categories of drug dealer/thief/statistic. His future is filled with the promise of more intriguing and diverse stories for the masses to digest.

"Don't judge the book by its cover!"

PREVIEW
CHAOS IN THE CAPITAL CITY
By D. Mitchell

Coming soon from Q-Boro Books

Chapter Two
Operation Safe Streets

I walked defiantly down the small, one-way street named Quebec Place, strolling with a jay of marijuana in my hand. Under the cloudy skies which represented the mood on our side of the city most days, I made my way for the playground, hoping to run into the fellas and see what we were getting into.

The Raymond Recreation Center consisted of a large field, basketball and tennis courts, the rec building and a children's play area. Raymond Elementary School was just on the other side of a grassy hill. Most times the fellas and I lounged on the jungle gym in the children's play area. Other times we would huddle behind the rec and gamble.

Our little crew, known as the QBC mob, consisted of about twenty to twenty-five people at any given time, though it never seemed to stay steady for more than a couple of months. At some point or another everyone did a little time. Once in a while someone was retired by way of violence. DC was hectic like that. I'm sure many of the residents wondered how life in the nation's capital could be so tough.

I ventured up the playground and found Vil and Shorty doing exactly what I expected—laughing, joking, and smoking. We had little cliques within our crew that hung together a little tighter than others in the gang. Our clique consisted of Vil, Shorty, Slim, Jake, and me.

Vil was the senior member and accepted leader of our crew. Vil, who resembled me in physical appearance, was very streetwise and devious. Shorty was small and tough. He was like Joe Pesci's character on the movie *Goodfellas*, always hype and ready for whatever. Jake was born here in America, but his people were from Jamaica. He was even darker than me and talked with a slight accent. Jake had all types of connections in the world of illegal activity. Slim, nicknamed for his tall and slender frame, was the quiet killer of the bunch. They called me D, taken from the first letter in my name. I was the neutral one with book smarts who got caught up in the wrong crowd. I did some pretty mean things with my friends and basically did them because of my friends and poor judgment.

"What's up wit' you?" Vil greeted me.

"D," Shorty acknowledged.

"Fellas. I see y'all got a nice rotation goin' over here," I said.

"Yeah. It's goin' be nicer when you put your jay in it," Shorty responded.

"Oh, it ain't nothin' goin' on. This here is a head jay."

"Whatever. You better pass that shit," Vil said. I took about five long pulls and passed the jay to Shorty. Vil passed me the jay he had.

"Vil, you hollered at your man yet?" I asked.

"Who is that? My man with the cracks or my man with the weed?"

"The cracks."

"No doubt. I got an ounce up off him early this mornin'. What you need?" The jays rotated between us again.

"I need a quack," I said, using the slang for a quarter of an ounce.

"Oh naw, I don't got that," he said, snickering. "I can decent you up wit a ho-ho," slang for wholesale, "or I'll give you his number and you can page him your damn self."

"Are you goin' give me seventy joints for my two fifty?" Shorty and Vil looked at each other with astonishment. Then they looked at me.

"Stop playing' wit' me, son," Vil said with a slight grin on his face.

Shorty added his two cents. "You shouldn't even give his bitch-ass the number." I got up from the sitting position and walked over to Shorty.

"Don't come over here playin' and . . ." His words were interrupted by the body shot I delivered. He sighed. "You goin' make me go get my joint."

"I'll give you fifty-five for your two fifty," Vil said.

"It's a bet," I agreed.

DC was a unique city for many reasons. It was the capital of the world's most powerful country. It hosted the political, judicial, law enforcement and military infrastructure for the entire nation. The city was predominantly black. The crime rates per capita in DC were some of the highest for all cities nationwide. The most unique aspect about the city was that in spite of the heavy presence of the government, it was our show. Many laws were made in DC and most of them were broken in DC.

The White House and FBI Headquarters were less than three miles away and I, like most of my friends, had never been or wanted to visit either. Their proximity to our location meant absolutely nothing. On any given day we had plenty of crack, weed, heroin and boat (also known as PCP) to go. Handguns were explicitly illegal in the city unless you were an officer of some sort, yet almost all of us had at least one.

When crack was first introduced to DC, the bad aspects of the city quickly became ugly. Young black men began making thousands of dollars a week and some in a day, easily exceeding the salaries of professionals with advanced degrees. Gang-related violence increased tenfold and the murder rate skyrocketed. Guns became very accessible. The younger generation, which I was a member of when the epidemic hit, saw the fast life and that was all that many of us ever aspired to be a part of. The "I want to be a doctor or lawyer" stuff went out the door when crack came in. The money, the women, and other material things seduced most of us to try our hand in "the game."

"You in da club tonight, son?" Vil asked me.

"I don't know. I gotta get my money together first."

"I'll do that for you after we finish hitting these jays," he said, concerning the drug deal. I nodded.

After we finished the jays, we got up and headed for Vil's house. When we got to the corner of Tenth and Quebec, the roar of car engines caught us by surprise. Figuring that it may very well be the police, we prepared to make a hasty exit as Vil and Shorty began tossing contraband. Before we could start running good, two unmarked police cars sped down the street and came to a screeching halt right in front of us. We turned to see that two more squad cars and another detective's car sped up Tenth Street and cut off our escape route. All twelve of the officers hopped out with their guns drawn. They forcefully hauled us over to one of the cars and began a thorough search.

"Damn, it smells like we just missed the party. Y'all done smoked all the weed up?" a white, plainclothes police officer asked. His question went unanswered. I noticed something very different about the officers. They all wore the cheap looking police jackets that usually had MPD for Metropolitan Police Department written on them, but their jackets were different.

"Well, since we can't take y'all in at this particular moment, I'll fill y'all in on what's goin' on," the white officer continued. "There's an initiative in effect called Operation Safe Streets." He turned so that we could read the yellow lettering on the back of his jacket. "To make it short and simple fellas, it's like the zero tolerance policy we ran last summer, except it isn't citywide. It only applies to triflin'-ass neighborhoods like this.

"We know that y'all have been puttin' in a lot of work on these streets the last couple of years, so some pretty important people decided to hook y'all up with some vacation time. It's our job to make sure y'all get there." The other officers laughed at their partner's jokes. My friends and I were not amused.

"From this point on, this is our neighborhood. We'll be here around the clock tryin' to get y'all up out of here. We're givin' this neighborhood the works. We're gonna set up roadblocks, sting operations, foot patrols, bikes—the works.

"If you get caught with a joint of marijuana, you're goin' to jail. You get caught drinkin'," he paused mid-sentence, "hell, I don't even think y'all are old enough. If y'all get caught with alcohol, you're goin' to jail. If we catch you with crack, you're not comin' back. If we catch you with a gun . . ."

"You might catch a hot one," one of the other officers chimed in. They thought that was funny too.

"Effective immediately," the white officer continued, "this is a 100 percent drug-free community. Anyone who violates that 100 percent is goin' away for a long time. This is our 'hood now, fellas. Y'all better give your boys the heads up, 'cause it's not gonna be pretty."

They all left as quickly as they came. After they were out of sight, my friends began to retrieve their drugs. We continued up the street.

"The only reason his white-ass told us all that is because he knew that we was gonna hip the fellas anyway," Shorty said.

"It's some bullshit. All they goin' do is harass us all the time and try slow down our money," Vil said.

"They just wanna show the media and politicians they're bein' tough on crime by comin' down and puttin' the press on us. They just put a name on it this time." We took his warning lightly.

Later that evening, the whole crew was up on the jungle gym. There were fifteen of us smoking large amounts of marijuana and drinking everything from forty-ounce beers to Remy and Hennessy VSOP. Everyone was high, drunk and ready to party.

The Go-Go, one of the rowdiest and raunchiest ghetto parties around, featured live bands doing improvisations of popular hip-hop songs and a few songs of their own. The show usually started about ten or eleven. We never entered before twelve.

Almost every gang or crew in the city did the same thing that we were doing before they entered the club.

Just about everyone who entered was smacked. There were a lot different 'hoods from all over the city in a not-so-large room. Go-Go's caused a lot of fights and most of the altercations that led to one neighborhood beefing with another. A few of them have made national headlines.

We were just preparing to mount up when Shorty noticed two cars driving through the alley. "Who in the hell is that in the alley? Somebody 'bout to get punished," he said as he pulled a gun from his waistband.

Everyone stared down the vehicles trying to make out who they were. They drove slowly through the alley, just on the other side of the field.

"It might be them niggas from up Second Street," Shorty said. After he said that, about eight of us instantly pulled guns from our waistbands or pockets.

Finally the cars passed underneath a lamp in the alley and their identities were revealed.

"It's the Jumps!" Vil said as everyone scattered instantly. The unmarked police cars quickly accelerated over to the steps that led to the play area where we had stood a few seconds before. On the basketball court about thirty yards away from the play area we heard car doors slam, which meant they begun the foot pursuit and the drivers would try to cut us off with their cars. That's what usually happened, but they never saw me again that night. We took the police a little more seriously after that incident.

Attention Writers:

Writers looking to get their books published can view our submission guidelines by visiting our website at: *www.QBOROBOOKS.com*

What we're looking for: Contemporary fiction in the tradition of Darrien Lee, Carl Weber, Anna J., Zane, Mary B. Morrison, Noire, Lolita Files, etc; groundbreaking mainstream contemporary fiction.

We prefer email submission to: candace@qborobooks.com in MS Word, PDF, or rtf format only. However, if you wish to send the submission via snail mail, you can send it to:

Q-BORO BOOKS Acquisitions Department
165-41A Baisley Blvd., Suite 4. Mall #1
Jamaica, New York 11434

*****By submitting your work to Q-Boro Books, you agree to hold Q-Boro books harmless and not liable for publishing similar works as yours that we may already be considering in the future.*****

1. Submission will not be returned.
2. **Do not contact us for status updates.** If we are interested in receiving your full manuscript, we will contact you via email or telephone.
3. Do no submit if the entire manuscript is not complete.

Due to heavy volume of submissions, if these requirements are not followed, we will not be able to process your submission.